ASTON NORTH
AND THE WINDOW
TO THE SOUL

ANTHONY GREEN

SIDE PUBLISHERS

5 Burt Street, Fremantle, WA 6160

Version. 1.0

ISBN: 978-0-9953945-2-0

ISBN-13: 978-0-9953945-2-0

CHAPTER ONE

"The blast of the cannons is deafening, a continual volley of sound above the cries of battle and the roar of the ocean, the swell of the sea is pulling me fore and aft trying to throw me off balance. The air is thick with the smell of gunpowder, mixed with sweat, salt and the stench of blood. Amidships in the lower gunnery section of his majesty's ship Belleisle, I'm looking out at the battle that is raging through the gaping hole where we've just taken a barrage to the central bank of cannons. The deck is awash with blood and bone where a second ago twelve-gun crew fought with powder and shot getting set for another barrage of our own. Timing in a sea battle is everything and maintaining our strike ratio of one shot every ninety-seconds was drummed into each gunnery officer, and my crew knew this. The remaining able-bodied crew heaved the 3-ton cannonade back in position or, at least, a position from which we could fire through. The ships mast has snapped and the sales are blinding the gun batteries so we are using the hole blown in our port side. I'm desperately trying to restore order; half the gunner crew is staring at me waiting for orders, but the remainder is busy reloading with the help of a fellow officer. He's covered in blood and has a look of a wild-man, in-sensed he is shouting orders at the crew, and now I'm arguing with him."

"What are you arguing about?"

Aston North, in his second year studying at Oxford University, sits wide-eyed and transfixed, staring out into the crowd at the University student union club. The audience, consumed with a night's alcohol intake, is half absorbed in the story and half entertained by the hypnotist who is doing his best to add a comedic commentary to Aston's intricate recall of a past life experience at the Battle of Trafalgar in 1805.

His past life regression is the final act in what has been a typically raucous mixture of hypnotism and pranks. Aston hadn't been impressed up to now, the guys on all fours barking like dogs was a little predictable and the girls acting like cute kittens was even worse, apart from when they started chasing balls of wool at the click of the hypnotists' fingers. He did laugh along with everyone else at the teaching assistant, persuaded to believe that his glasses had X-ray powers and then told that he was the only one who was naked in the bar. The poor guy still had not returned from the toilets.

Aston had refused his friends goading to take part in the hypnotist games at first. Although the chance of taking part in a past life regression did peak Aston's interest, it was something he'd always been skeptical. He believed the power of the mind was not something to be trivialised, due mainly to his early childhood exposure to Buddhist teachings. He'd volunteered more to put an end to his best friend Harrison's endless sniping than to satisfy his own curiosity. Betting him that he wouldn't be put under was a way of making it more of a challenge.

At first, he had resisted the deepener techniques as the hypnotist began his regression, walking through a dark forest, who does this guy think I am? He continued to put up resistance and concentrated his mind on the meditation techniques he'd been taught as a child.

"Concentrate on your breathing, hear only this, focus your mind" the words of his childhood nanny flowed through his mind. The clarity of his meditation did something to trigger his subconscious, it was becoming accustomed to the soft, subtle tones of the French accent, and the hypnosis technique began to take effect. He led Aston down a staircase in his mind, and as the intensity of the suggestions arose, the visions of his past life overtook his conscious state.

The hypnotist coached his subjects' regression expertly and with a passion he had kept hidden until now, enjoying the depths to which he has taken this engaging student. He continued to draw out the vivid tale of the battle as Aston recalled his former souls adventure much to the pleasure of his friends and the entire audience whose mutterings seem to match the rise and fall like the swell pitching the warships locked in battle.

"Describe what's happening now?" The hypnotist continued his questions while playing to the crowd.

"The confusion on board is compounded by the ceaseless barrage of gunfire from both sides. The argument I'm having with a fellow officer is becoming more intense."

"What is the issue?"

"The lieutenant just will not concede. He's driven by the ferocity of battle, buoyed by the battle cry from Nelson beforehand 'England expects that every man will do his duty.' He is too keen to reload the cannonade that the crew have manoeuvred back in place and resume firing."

"How are ..."

Aston interrupted "I'm not going to lose any more men. Stand away and let me inspect the tackle and breeches — we need the barrel checked too, there may be damage man." He wasn't just responding to the questions he was now acting out the events without prompting.

"How is the battle? Can you tell us more about your surroundings?" The hypnotist tried to regain control.

"We are locked in a broadside duel and can see our enemy face to face. The gun crews around us are firing in unison, everyone wants a hand in defeating Johnny Crapaud, as we like to call the French, and my crew are no different, but I know we need to follow procedure. 'Victory or death' the lieutenant rages and starts to load the barrel himself. 'Fire with all arms was the Captains order — victory or death' he's not listening to reason. Stand down! Do not fire that damn cannon you hear me. That's an order! The ship takes another hit to the stern blowing out another three guns."

"What next? How will this be resolved?"

"I jump onto the floor to check the cannonade. My hand feels under the belly of the barrel, there's something wrong. 'Victory or death,' again he cries and pulls the friction primer into place. I feel a crack with my hand, and there's powder spilling out. James for gods' sake do not fire this bloody cannon." Aston yelled out to the audience.

"He's lighting the bloody fuse we'll all be blown to hell..."

Aston fell back from his chair with a sudden jolt, his body's reflex to his mind recoiling from the blast. He crashed to the floor in a heap. The student union audience erupted, some cheering, others clapping and a number aghast at the shows apparent finale and the story the hypnotist had drawn from Aston's subconscious.

Aston woke from the hypnosis, sprawled on the floor of the student union bar, disoriented by the noise, blinded by the lights, his heartbeat racing and his face burning with embarrassment. It took him a moment to get back his senses. The hypnotist's beautiful assistant helped him sit. Her eyes gave away her Chinese heritage, her smile warm and welcoming she asked if he was okay. He meekly looked around, and the hypnotist was basking in the reaction from the crowd.

"Oh my God," he said under his breath. "I'm okay I think — what happened?"

The hypnotist, noticing Aston getting up, made his way over and helped him to his feet.

"That was outstanding, a very deep regression, we need to talk more, and I need to bring you out of the hypnosis correctly." His tone had changed and sounded excited as he raised Aston's arm to acknowledge the crowd.

Aston's mind was racing, first he was caught with embarrassment, before going under he'd bragged to the crowd that his will was too strong and would not be susceptible to hypnosis. They might be applauding the hypnotist, but for him, this was sure to be a catalyst for a semester worth of peer piss taking that would make his university life a nightmare. He could just imagine the ceaseless procession of comments about Nelson, Trafalgar, cannonballs and the like, not to mention his best friend being insufferable. Aston wished he hadn't bet him twenty pounds that he wouldn't succumb. He was looking directly at him now, and Harrison was laughing back at him and pulling faces. For a supposedly technical genius, there are times when he can be so childish.

The embarrassment he could live with but his mind was running through the incident he had just witnessed. It wasn't just a past life event he was recounting, it felt something more than that, something ethereal, like traveling back in time, he felt he was there on the ship experiencing the events first hand. He turned to the hypnotist, who was now giving high fives, shaking hands with and drinking in the audience appreciation.

"Can we talk?"

"Come backstage once it's died down in here."

You mean once your ego has eaten it's fill of adoration more like he thought. Aston walked off the stage and headed for the bar. Harrison was waiting for him.

"Don't say a word" Aston warned.

"Aye captain" Harrison's pirate impression was the least he expected.

"I need a drink."

"Rum?"

"Maybe a Napoleon brandy?" They both burst out laughing, Harrison threw his arm around his best friend and ordered.

Aston swirled the brandy in the glass then downed it in one.

"I've got to go and speak to the hypnotist about the whole experience. You know what was weird? It felt like I was actually there in person!"

"Okay dude, just remember your Jedi mind trick this time!" He smiled "I'll see if I can find Ellie and meet you after."

"Was she here?"

"I think so. She said she would try and make it."

Aston hadn't realised his other best friend was back on campus, as he made his way to the dressing room backstage he smiled, Ellie could be very helpful if what he had in mind came to fruition.

The dressing room was, in reality, a converted store room next to the club managers' office, only used when they had a headline act which felt the need to feel special. He knocked and the assistant, who'd helped him, opened the door and smiled.

The hypnotist had his hand on the head of the girl who he'd made meow and chase balls of wool around the floor. He turned to see Aston, smiling at him he said to the girl she would be entirely free from the hypnosis and then clicked his fingers twice. She hugged him, kissed him on the cheek then went to take a selfie with her phone. Abruptly he blocked her off almost knocking the phone out of her hands "No pictures" he sounded aggressive which shook the girl, her smile dropped, and she scurried out of the room.

"Bonjour Mon Ami" the suave, charming French persona returned immediately "sit down, how do you feel? That was quite a regression" he clicked his fingers above his head "hmm interesting it seems you are totally free from the hypnosis. I would normally have to walk you back out of such a regression. You seemed very deep, and the recollections were very detailed." There was a puzzled expression on his face but also Aston picked up on a glint in his eyes. "Are you on any medication?"

"No."

"Recreational drugs? It's okay I won't judge you, you are at Uni' after all!"

Aston laughed.

"No way. Look I wanted to mention this earlier, it didn't feel like I was under, it felt like I was actually there! It felt like I was part of that guys' feelings, his emotions, thinking his thoughts, I can't explain, but I feel we were connected."

The hypnotist smiled wryly and looked across at his assistant.

"I was raised in Hong Kong," Aston continued "my nanny was a devout Buddhist, and she used to get us to meditate daily. When you were trying to put me under I was using an accelerated breathing technique, she taught me to attempt to stay awake and not submit. Could it have been the two things messing with my subconscious that triggered it?"

"There are many things that medicine has yet to discover about the subconscious state and the human soul. The Buddhists have a greater grasp on the human conscious than most but I think you may have uncovered a gift, and I would like to help you explore it further."

"You mean now!" Aston was a taken aback a little by his eagerness. He wanted to learn more about what he'd just experienced, but there was something about the hypnotist that held him back. "I think I've been hypnotised enough for one night."

The ring from a mobile interrupted them, the assistant answered.

"It's Elliot, he says it's important, do you want to talk to him?" She handed him the gold-plated phone. Very fancy, very showman Aston thought, maybe hypnotism pays well.

"Oui" answered the hypnotist, then listened intently for a while "hold on one-second" the hypnotist turned to Aston. "We will have to continue this another time I'm afraid" he offered his hand, and they shook. "My assistant will see you out and give you my details to get in touch." He returned to his call and in a raised tone gave instructions in French. At the door, his assistant bowed and handed him a business card, two-handed. For a Chinese girl, she was rather tall, he bowed back and accepted the card two handed, just as he'd seen as a child.

"Thank you" the girls' eyes reminded him of his nanny although not as kind, maybe it was western heritage.

He pocketed the card and walked back to the bar to find his friends. Aston thought back to his childhood growing up in Hong Kong. Raised in an expat lifestyle, his father was a prominent accountant working for a large stock broker firm who spent far too much time away from his family. His mother an actress in her younger days engaged a nanny to look after Aston and his sister while she enjoyed the trappings of being an expat spouse. The two children were both profoundly influenced by Grace, a devout Buddhist she taught them yoga and meditation from an early age. Introducing them to the mysteries of the Orient as well as educating them in Eastern philosophy and the history of the Chinese people. When his father disappeared under a cloud of mystery, leaving them with nothing, his mother took him and his sister back to London. They never saw Grace again, but Aston still practiced yoga and meditation almost every day.

Grace had often spoken about her belief that a soul was eternal, how lives were connected. What if he had uncovered something? What if "this gift" as the hypnotist seemed to think it was, could unlock his soul and allow him to see his past lives. Aston knew one thing for certain; he was going to find out more and had a good idea who he could get to help.

Aston couldn't find Harrison in the bar after he left the dressing room, his head was buzzing with ideas and possibilities that he was bursting to tell his best friend. After suffering one too many comments about keeping things ship shape or renditions of Rule Britannia, he quickly made an exit and headed back through Oxfords' cobbled streets to the flat they shared. They had opted out of the accommodation supplied by the University and secured a two-bedroom loft style apartment just off Magdalen Bridge in the heart of Oxford. The place was solely down to Harrison's dad, who was a very successful technical liaison between China and the UK in the late eighties, and now sat on the board of a major electronics firm. He was happy to cover the cost of the rent, as his son had qualified for Oxford and was excelling in Computer Science. At first, Aston was a little bit jealous of his friends' fathers' attention but, in reality, realised soon enough that they both shared parent issues, Harrison's just came with fringe benefits. His friend was in his room on the top floor, sat hunched over his computer, typing furiously. Lines of code streaming across the centre display, a paused game of Call of Duty on the main display and a Skype video conference on the left hand.

"Hey man, what's up" Harrison didn't raise his head from the screen.

"Wassup Aston" the guys in the video conference welcomed him too. "Welcome aboard Captain."

"Not you as well, news travels fast — thanks mate" he clipped Harrison around the head.

"Hey, not me they heard it on Twitter. I think you're trending."

"Fuck off" he swiped him again and pressed mute on the Skype call. "I want you to help me do it again."

"What? Hang on I'm trying to hack into the main Oxford servers. These guys are racing me, but I reckon I'm there." Harrison clicked the mute button the smashed down on the keyboard " done — beat you guys, I do believe that's fifty quid fellas!"

"We didn't shake on it H."

"I've got this wired up to record brothers so put up or shut up — you can pay me in bitcoins if you wish!" Harrison laughed ended the Skype call and swung around to face Aston. "That plus the twenty quid you owe me from earlier Mr North, this is turning out to be a good night."

Aston took a twenty out of his pocket and handed it to Harrison. Who tapped the crisp note on its edge.

"Magnificent — so did you just say you want to do it again! I'm a computer genius dude, not a hypnotist. What exactly happened to you tonight?"

"That was no regression, my friend. It felt like I was there, the smells, the sound, I swear I can still taste the salt, it felt like I could reach out and touch that cannon myself. It was ethereal Harrison like I was part of that guys' soul. I reckon that actually happened just as I saw it and reckon we could do it again. You were there and you know what he did and said, a man of your talents, should be easy right?"

"I know I can reboot your hard drive, Aston. I'm not sure I'm qualified to reboot your soul. That's some weird shit, and I don't think we should mess, you know!"

"C'mon' humour me, your mom was a Buddhist right she taught you about..."

Harrison cut him off. "Don't start down that religious path, I'm not drunk enough to go there bro' you know how I feel."

Aston knew Harrison was an atheist or, at least, had no belief or faith, if pushed for his religious beliefs he would put down Jedi. Not long after they met, he had told Aston about his mother which led to a very lengthy and drunken debated about faith, religion and the rights and wrongs of the world. As a confirmed computer nerd Harrison believed in naughts and ones when the power fails he would argue, the light goes out.

"Hang on, there's an easy way to check this out" Harrison was back at his keyboard "let's Google it."

He pulled up the website of national archives and scrolled through the details of 21 October 1805, they read through the details of Lord Admiral Nelson's historic triumph over the combined Franco-Spanish fleet off the coast of Cadiz.

" I never knew Trafalgar was somewhere in Spain."

"No, nor I, but history and geography were never my best subjects" replied Aston. His mind was racing again as they searched through the detail of the battle.

"Can you remember what ship were you on?"

"Belleisle,"

Harrison searched the articles on the ships from the battle, and the Belleisle certainly did have a the most killed in action of all the 27 English ships.

"Whoa," he turned to Aston after finding a firsthand report from the ship. He was already reading the account from the gunners' mate about the cannon explosion on the Belleisle that almost crippled the ship, the explosion killing two officers and half the gunnery squad. They both looked at each other. The account has been taken from a diary entry and described the scene pretty much as Aston had recalled on stage.

"Okay, now you got my attention — what do you want me to do?

"I'm really not sure H, but if we can do this it could make quite a stir at the University, I reckon that we could get a research paper published, though."

"I was thinking of doubling in psychology."

"Psychotherapy more like!"

"Hey, speaking of therapy we should get Ellie involved, a bit of medical know-how could be handy."

"Not a bad call but I'm not sure she'd approve."

"I reckon you could talk her round, and if not we could just hypnotise her." Harrison looked at Aston cross-eyed his head tilted to one side.

"Seriously though I want to do this, and I'd rather do it without the help of Monsieur la hypnotist! He kind of freaked me after the show."

"Anyone who takes pleasure in making people bark like a dog has to have a few gig' missing from his hard drive!" The cross-eyes returned, and Aston tried to regain focus.

"Not a good look H, honest. Can you remember what he did to put me under? Do you want to have a go now?"

"To be honest, I'm not sure I can remember, but I know my friend could help us." Harrison tapped the Power Mac base unit, and he was always adamant he could find a tech solution to any problem. Aston thought he probably could, given the chance.

They started at Google and went from there. The search led them to a

YouTube video of a regression by another hypnotist, which they thought was very similar and also with a few backdoor tricks Harrison accessed a training manual that was only available to registered members of a hypnotist's chapter.

It was getting on for three am when they decided to call it quits. They had made some progress; Aston had mastered the accelerated breathing technique. This meditation allowing his subconscious to accept some of Harrison's suggestions from the script, but either a mixture of tiredness, or technique meant they couldn't replicate the regression.

Aston knew they were both getting somewhere, but they were also getting frustrated, Harrison's typing volume was amping up, each keystroke thudded with some menace. Aston himself had started stretching exercises which he knew was a telltale sign he was getting tetchy.

"Tomorrow we'll get it H, maybe I will speak to Ellie, she may have some take on the show that we haven't figured out."

CHAPTER TWO

Aston could normally get away with around six hours of sleep, but today he woke at seven totally refreshed, only fours hours and I feel great he thought. He went through his daily regime, ten reps of dynamic stretching, these included jumping jacks, arm circles, lunges, high knees, and squats. Followed by thirty mins of Yoga, using poses he was taught early in life. To vary the workout and muscle groups used he liked to interchange the ten poses, this helped improve his strength and flexibility and also kept the workout from getting to regimented. He always finished off with ten-minute meditation which not only helped focus his mind but also gave the muscles time to relax.

Before he jumped in the shower, he sent Ellie a text message to see if she had any tutes or classes today. He wanted to be straight up and ask about last night but thought it better to start the conversation off before addressing the real question. When he'd finished, she'd text back to say she had a tutorial she couldn't avoid at 10.30am and asked how he was.

His reply read "all good :0) do you fancy coffee need to pick your brains!"

Ellie responded, "nice - as long as you buy my brain breakfast - Bean @ 9.00?"

By Bean, he knew she meant the coffee house Bean around the World, which was a favourite haunt of theirs. They had gone there following their first meeting during their senior year at Magdelena school. He had been gifted a flying lesson as a result of winning the headmasters merit awards, and Ellie had also chosen the same prize after winning the girls school equivalent. They met on the tarmac after his flight. He was heading back to the flight school office, high on the adrenalin from the experience in the seemingly very small two-seater Cessna. He remembered being taken by her smile, it lit up her whole face, her green eyes sparkled, accentuated by long lashes. She'd asked him how it went, and he remembered stumbling for words and ended up saying

"I - I - I, really enjoyed it thanks" he thought he'd saved himself by turning and shouting back "it's awesome, you'll have a fantastic time, the landing is extreme!"

He'd watched her all the way to the plane hoping she just might turn her head and acknowledge him. When she didn't, he figured he'd blown his chance of making a good first impression. He waited on the runway tarmac to watch her take off and ever so briefly caught a glimpse of that stunning smile and was sure he got a little wave from her as the Cessna picked up speed down the runway.

He had hung around in the flight school deliberately to speak to her, when she came back he knew she had enjoyed the experience, she was laughing and joking with the middle aged pilot who was paying her compliments and being a little too attentive. He was about to leave when she called after him in her broad country accent "you were right about the landing, absolutely awesome, I nearly wet myself." That was the catalyst of their friendship. They continued talking with the flight school pilots and hit it off when they discovered a mutual affiliation to off from centre sports, fencing, mountain biking, and rock climbing. They shared a taxi back to Oxford, which is where they first went for coffee at Bean.

He was sat in the same window seat now, the smell of coffee and fresh baked bread fuelling his hunger waiting for her to get there so he could tell his tale and finally order breakfast.

"I didn't see the whole show!" Aston almost spat out the scrambled eggs he'd just taken a mouthful of when she told him.

"What?" He recovered after swallowing. "I thought you were there?"

"I left just after the guys barking like dogs, which was pretty lame. I had to be somewhere."

"Can't believe you didn't see it, officially miffed." Aston felt snubbed that she didn't stay to see him, and the fact that now she wouldn't be able to give her take on what the hypnotist said.

"I did see a clip of the show on YouTube, though, and it did look rather intense." Aston perked up.

" I can't believe he would do that in front of an audience, very unethical, we've covered this in med school, and it shouldn't be taken lightly, the brain I mean."

"It's on YouTube?"

"I was so worried when you fell off the chair, you could have had a severe head trauma, that guy should get banned! Yes, apparently you've got over 4,000 views."

"What?"

"Somebody posted it this morning, oh you've got 4,755 now, look!"

Ellie handed Aston her phone and continued to eat her Bircher muesli.

"This is great, this will really help, we can work out what he did and said."

Ellie looked bemused "I'm sorry Aston I'm not sure I understand."

Aston proceeded to tell Ellie about the lifelike experience the regression had been, and his plan to try and go back and attempt it again with Harrison's and hopefully her help.

"Are you mad, you're seriously not thinking of trying a hypnotic regression without the aid of a specialist!"

"That's why we need you, Ellie. You can be our specialist you've got the medical training."

"I'm only in the second year of my degree you fool." Ellie playfully swiped at him. "It will be four years before I start residency. If I make it that is."

"You're gonna make it, and I've got to give this a go Ellie. Can you imagine what this could lead to? You have to help, think of it as early practical experience" she swiped at him again.

"Look I'll help but only to make sure you don't zombie out or something, especially with Harrison involved he's probably got an app written for it already!"

Aston laughed "He reckons if we do pull it off he's going to write a thesis on it and major in psychology. But seriously if we do this and prove I've found a window to the soul ... just think if the ramifications."

"Sounds deep Aston but what are you going to do? Alter the course of his history! You've been watching too many late night movies." Aston could sense her indifference.

"If given the chance I would, but first I need to see if it was just a one-off or if I can do it again." His attention returned to the YouTube video which had now nudged past 5,000 "and this will really help!"

"Okay, as long as you're doing this for positive reasons, not just some ego trip I'll help, but I don't see how it was anything to do with this hypnotist guy. It may not be him, and if you had the ethereal past life event or whatever you call it, it's probably more to do with your state of consciousness, sorry, twisted state of mind more like!"

Ellie's phone sprang to life as a call came through, he handed it back to her and mouthed "new boyfriend?" She awkwardly took the phone and walked outside with it to her ear. Aston watched as she paced up and down outside for a few minutes she looked troubled as she headed for the door. The bell pinged above the door as she entered

"Are you okay?"

"Look I have to go. Sorry, I'll call you later."

"You're still good to help right?"

"Of course, I'll call you. Thanks for breakfast."

Aston watched her head away into the grey morning, he wondered what the call was about, made a mental note to find out later and then remembered the YouTube video. He grabbed his phone checked the time, "9.45, good he'll still be in bed." He ordered a double espresso to go, settled the bill and headed back to tell Harrison.

"Oh my god it's got over 6,000 views, that's sick!" Harrison was more concerned by the fact the video had gone viral, so he didn't get Aston's point.

"It's not the reason we're watching this."

When he got back, Aston had to beat down his roommate's door. He knew Harrison was a heavy sleeper, but he'd fallen asleep wearing his noise-cancelling headphones. The espresso had done the trick, and they were sitting at Harrison's workstation, he didn't like to call it a desk, watching the YouTube video sensation that Aston, his regression and fall from the stage had become.

"Check out the comments!"

Aston rolled his eyes and put his hand to his forehead "Oh no."

"Whose sharing this? Probably everyone from the show last night right?" His habit of answering his own questions straight away reminded Aston of how they had become friends.

They had met during a quiz night a few years back. They were in competing teams heading into a soul and jazz music round, and only Aston and Harrison seemed to be the ones with the right answers. They clashed on the final question of the round, Aston remembered it well. "What was the first track on Miles Davis' Kind of Blue?"

Harrison had jumped up out of his seat and shouted " Freddy Freeloader, no, no it was Blue in Green, no, no. What was the first track on Kind of Blue, I'm pretty sure it was Freddy Freeloader, yes Freddy Freeloader" his teammates were as confused as the quiz master.

Aston was impressed that someone else his age had an interest in Miles Davis. He called out his team name as per the rules and waited as the quiz master informed Harrison he certainly had two tracks from the album correct, but neither were the first track. He then asked Aston, who stood up, looked over at Harrison answered correctly. "So What!"

Aston went over once the quiz had finished to introduce himself. "Good to meet a fellow Davis fan, you maybe should have used your playlist like me." He held up his own phone which was showing the Kind of Blue tracks in order.

Harrison smiled shook his head. "Tech solutions work every time. Should've done the same but I got ahead of myself, it's a nerves thing."

"Yeah I think everyone noticed."

They had sat and discussed Miles Davis, Duke Ellington and other jazz greats for the rest of the night and been friends ever since.

"Just go back to the beginning of the video." Aston pointed at the screen, "We can hear what he says. This can help us."

"Right!"

"So now we can copy it exactly."

They watched the video again, and Harrison managed to integrate closed captioning on to the file so they could see and capture what was being said. It didn't appear to be too far from what they had tried the night before.

"I reckon it has more to do with me attempting to block his advances. Ellie said something similar this morning."

"Ellie was here?" Harrison looked shocked "she didn't say hi?"

"No, I met her at Bean while you were still in your comatose state, that's where I got your coffee. She said it might have been more my sensory control and seeing this again I think she might be right."

"So what did you do? Some Buddhist technique no doubt."

"You do know you're not supposed to answer your own question." Aston rolled his eyes. " Well, it was actually! I was spotlighting my attention, focussing on a particular area or part of my body. And yes it is an old Buddhist technique that Grace taught me. She said it went back longer than time and can help healing in some people."

"Check this out." Harrison had run a Google search on Spotlighting Attention Meditation techniques and pulled up a recent study by Brown University in the US. They had found that a form of mindfulness meditation known as MBSR acts as a "volume knob" for attention, changing brain wave patterns.

They read through the article and then looked at each other and Aston said: "that could be it, let's give it a go now!"

Harrison looked at the time. "Maybe, but not now - I've got a tute, and so do you. Can't miss another one so soon in the semester, and we've got 15 minutes to get there."

Aston managed to make it in time but might as well have missed the tutorial as he was not there in mind, his focus was far away, a different era and a distant place. He could hear Grace's voice once again telling him to breathe and concentrate, focus all your thoughts on a particular point. She had told him this technique had been utilised over two millennia by Buddhists in China and Tibet to reduce the distress and chronic pain from aching joints or specific parts of the body. Some had found it helped improve cognitive functions and stave off the effects of old age.

Aston lived in Hong Kong from the age of three until he was twelve, his father had been tempted by the lifestyle and financial rewards of being an expat, especially for an accountant at one of the largest banks in the region. Throughout the whole time, Grace went from being his nanny to his guardian and teacher, and on to be his best childhood friend. Grace Li taught him everything any child could want to know about Asia, the traditions, the culture, the history, the religions, everything. She was raised in a Buddhist temple so she was deeply entrenched in her faith, although she was also intrigued by the ways and motives of the West. His mother would say she was Grace by name grace by nature, she was kind and gentle, humbly bowing whenever she greeted people, courteous and respectful. Aston also remembered the firm and swift response if boundaries were crossed, and Aston often tried to cross them, typically receiving a rapier-like tap or slap which seemed to come out of nowhere.

He recalled one lesson regarding spotlight attention, and Grace was trying to get him to imagine his father backing the car out of the drive. A simple task but to reach the street safely, he must hold the destination in mind while steering and ignoring distractions from elsewhere: you children playing in the back seat, the news on the radio, the glare of the sun in his eyes. Aston didn't understand and was being distracted by a passing bee until Grace brought his focus back, she had knelt, spun and swung her leg around in a perfect semicircle, stopping just behind Aston, who was following the bees trajectory in the air until he tripped over the obstacle he hadn't seen. She spun around again to catch him just before he hit the floor. "See Aston, many people, filter out these distractions using their subconscious — but should irrelevant stimuli or bees distract you, backing out a car or even walking along can become an ordeal. Spotlight of attention can improve focus and have an impact on the alpha brain waves that help filter and organize sensory inputs, improving your attentional control."

Once again Aston was brought back to the real world by the sound of laughter and cheering although this time it was his tute class. The professor was staring straight through him, the glare intensified by his bifocals, "North, North!" He was getting louder and Aston opened his eyes "North! Finally, you're with us. Care to elaborate on where you've been for the last ten minutes; I 'm pretty sure no one has hypnotised you this morning." The class burst into laughter, and Aston's face burst into a deep shade of scarlet.

Ellie had called Aston as arranged, and he managed to confirm the time to meet in between babbling on about his embarrassment during a tutorial session with Professor Ferris. She had told him not to worry as he should be more concerned about what he was getting into. It was now eight o'clock, and she had serious doubts about letting one of her best friends dabble in regression hypnosis and god knows what else and paused outside his apartment before knocking the door.

They had been friends for almost two years now, the meeting on the airfield was the first time she'd ever really looked at a guy her age, she remembered his green eyes, he was attractive if a little nerdy, good hair, dark and a little curly. She liked the cute way he bit his lip as she passed him on the runway, obviously trying to think of something clever to say. She had purposely not looked back but did steal a look from the plane as they took off. She also remembered the flight instructor who, although a little older than most of her boyfriends, was quite dashing. She was glad Aston had offered her a lift as a way out of there because she may have been tempted. Older boys were always more mature when she was in her early teens, and that progressed as she matured herself. Her mom said it was a father figure thing, but her sister reckoned it was really the fact they could drive and had better jobs. Aston had intrigued her, his interest in unconventional sports matched her own, and they seemed to share a lot in common. She had agreed when he invited her to go to mountain climbing lessons a few days later. That was followed by fencing lessons although Aston never really asked her out on a date as such. Being good friends was where they managed to end up but she still harboured hopes it might develop although Ellie was adamant she wasn't going to instigate anything.

As she knocked on the door, she couldn't help thinking he was getting into something way more extreme than sports. Harrison answered "Hey Ellie" they hugged.

"Hey you, built any more killer apps lately?" She liked to wind him up about his tech obsession.

"No, but check this out" he showed off his iPhone that he'd switched out the Apple logo on the back to light up like a MacBook."

"Pretty cool, can you do mine?"

"For sure, if only you'd ditch that Android crap!"

"Hey no fair, we can't all have a father who buys us whatever we want."

Ellie was a little bit jealous of Harrison's father; she 'd grown up in relative poverty living on a farm in the West Country and always looked on with envy at the richer kids in school. Her dad had died when she was only twelve leaving her Mom to look after four daughters. Her elder sister had taken up much of the household responsibility which allowed Ellie to concentrate on study, meaning she wasn't there to help out so much. Which created a fair bit of tension between them, and Ellie was still trying to make amends.

"Where's the patient?" She asked to change the subject.

"He's just..."

"Hey you" Aston cut him off as he stuck his head around the corner of his room.

Their flat was so much nicer than her dorm at the University. "I still can't believe you guys got this place." Ellie had helped them move in and added a few feminine touches where she could, even taking Harrison and his daddy's credit card to Ikea to buy curtains, rugs, lamps and some pictures to brighten up the place.

"It's great that you're here Ellie, I'm so excited about this! I have been thinking about it all day."

"A bit too deeply so you said earlier!" She said quickly.

Harrison laughed. "LOL, yeah man. I heard that too. I bet Ferris was pissed!"

"Yep, he wasn't best pleased, but I managed to convince him it was the after effects from last night!"

"Aston I'm not sure we should do this. I'm worried that you'll end up catatonic or something." Ellie thought she should at least try to take some moral high ground.

"Look I think it'll work, and I've been thinking about what you said, about it being more me than the hypnosis. I'm sure it's something to do with the spotlight attention meditation. I was solely focussed on my inner thoughts and mind when he was trying to put me under, and that's what I think triggered this window opening and my soul to reboot."

"Hang on. You think your soul rebooted — are you mad?" Ellie had a problem with regression, reincarnation, and the whole past life thing. She was raised a Catholic by her mother, and they still attended mass when Ellie visited.

"That's the only thing I think could explain it Ellie - it was like I was there like I said before, and after watching the thing over and over I reckon that this wasn't a regression. He pointed to Harrison "We watched heaps last night trying to suss out how it happened, and they were different right."

Harrison nodded.

Ellie was turning off the idea even more now "Look I don't mind trying hypnosis and was happy to play along but messing with reincarnation and past souls I'm not sure I'm up for that."

"We need you, Ellie!" Aston looked a little crestfallen.

"You don't need me. You've never needed me, Aston." Ellie wasn't sure if she should have said that, she tried to deflect a little "you two seem to have this figured out between both of you. What exactly do you need me for?"

Aston looked a little puzzled as if he was trying to work out what Ellie's little slip up was about. "I...I...I" he stumbled, she knew he was flustered especially when he started stuttering "I...I'd rather have you here, just in case, medically I mean."

"Medically' medically!" Ellie's short temper was about to get the better of her, "So I'm nursemaid am I?"

"I didn't mean it like that." Aston was starting to raise his voice.

"Well, that's what it sounded like, I'm the bloody medic you said" her temper had taken over, and she took the way out Aston had just presented. "I'm off!" she turned on her heals.

"Elle your part of our team — we need you, I was getting palpitations last night when I came around, Ellie! Ellie!"

Aston's protests didn't resonate, and she kept on walking out of the door, making a point to slam it behind her. She couldn't believe she'd had two arguments, with people she cared about, in the same day.

Aston didn't do arguments, although Ellie had run him close on numerous occasions, she had a temper shorter than a fuse on a Roman candle and it was easy to light. His reluctance to get drawn into arguments stemmed from having to listen to his parents as a child. They would argue for what seemed like hours while he and his sister would cower under the bed clothes, pillows as earmuffs. Aston was glad in a way when his father disappeared; the conflict cease fired and his mother seemed so much happier once they had moved back to London. He had vowed to himself never to be like that when he grew up and preferred to walk away or concede rather than evoke memories of his childhood nightmares.

"Let her go" he stopped Harrison from opening the door. "She's well within her rights; I was a little unsubtle."

"I was more worried about the door and the neighbours, what brought that on? Probably a bad time, you know."

Aston shook his head "Don't."

"And what was that 'you never needed me' comment? Maybe it's hormonal."

"Harrison" Aston curtailed his friend's sexist dig but he was a little puzzled by Ellie's left field comment, but he didn't want to get into it right now though. He and Ellie had never got anywhere near romance as far as he thought, he'd fancied her early on but knew she was into older guys. He always thought she saw him as more of a brother, and when they found out they shared the same interest in extreme sports, the sports became something to do together. They would frequently try to get one over on each other, who could be more radical or daring, the mountain biking became rock climbing which turned into abseiling and was due to become hang gliding.

"We're just good mates," he didn't mean to say it out loud.

"Not anymore my friend," Harrison was laughing.

"She'll be all right, I'll call her tomorrow. I'm just pissed off we may have to put this off for now. Her Med' school training would have given me more confidence should anything go wrong."

Harrison was keen to try and solve the problem as always, "I've been thinking about that and I reckon we can hook up something to monitor your vitals if you're that worried. I've got a sportband we can use that, connect it to your phone and I'm sure I can hack something together in a few days to monitor brain activity." He started fishing about in one of his desk draws.

Aston was still thinking about what had just happened."I'm gonna text Ellie just to say sorry" he typed out the message a few times deleting words and phrases until it read okay in his head before he sent it.

"Sorry Ellie don't get cross at me — it's an adventure I'd rather do with your support, help and perspective — call you tomorrow, if I'm not shipwrecked! :0)." He thought a touch of humour may help but didn't want her to dwell on their spat without him reaching out in some way.

"Look" Harrison had found the Sportband "try this on and we'll see if it works," Harrison's confidence was starting to bring Aston's focus back on the regression.

"Right, you're right" he shook his head to clear his thoughts. "Let's just do it!" He said with a wry smile. The wristband blinked into life, returned a pulse rate of just over 55bpm, Harrison checked the App. "All working. You can go for a run or we can give this a shot."

"Cool. Let's get started."

"I'm just going to check the video again to see if we can see anything." Harrison was taking the lead, "I recorded the sounds yesterday to try and isolate out what the hypnotist was saying from the background noise but I reckon it's worth checking the visuals he may have done something else."

"Not a bad idea bro."

"That's a bit weird."

"What?"

"It's gone — the URL's not working, I'd added it as favourite but looks like the video's been taken down off YouTube."

"What do you think happened?" Aston was partly relieved he was no longer viral but also, a little miffed as it would have helped.

"I guess someone complained or the film infringed on some rights management law or something. Or the bar staff probably didn't want anyone to see how many people they let in that night."

"It's not our night. Do you still have the sound recording?"

"Yep on your phone, check out Hypno playlist, track one."

Aston scrolled through his playlists, "What else is on here? There's about fourteen tracks."

"Some of the hypnosis preamble stuff we found yesterday plus some relaxing ambient sounds, thought they might be handy — hey they nearly put me to sleep!"

Aston played track one. It was weird listening to his replies but Aston found himself repeating it back. He stopped the track and turned to Harrison.

"This could work."

"Too right it could!"

"So instead of you trying to put me under like yesterday I think we just use this and see where it gets us."

They debated how best to set things up. If Aston was going to be under, where would be the best place for it to happen. Harrison thought it a little weird doing it in Aston's room with him lying down on the bed. Aston suggested setting up his yoga mat in the lounge and using the classic cross-legged Lotus meditation position which he believed would give him the best chance to go under. The logistics debate ran for the next 15 minutes until they settled on Harrison's idea of a therapists couch type scenario using the reclining sofa chair.

Before they began, Aston checked his messages; no reply from Ellie. It was a shame she wasn't there but it was her choice and his worries re medical support were somewhat relieved by the Sportband. "Remember if anything goes wrong call 999 then try and revive me."

"I think you're being a little too cautious but I've got you covered man."

"Okay, pass me the headphones, we don't want us both going under."

Harrison handed over his headphones, Aston plugged them into his phone, lay back on the recliner and pressed play. He crossed his arms and held his thumb and forefingers together applying a little pressure to help his focus. For the second time in a matter of days, the hypnotist's voice began to lead Aston into hypnosis.

"I need you to find the release form for Christ's sake! Is it too much to ask?"

Leonardo Desangé was annoyed at his assistant; he was starting to lose his temper and then she asked him which one.

"Which one, which one!" he exploded. "The bloody regression from the end of the show last night that's which one. Jesus!"

He was due on stage in 30 minutes and was still thinking about the kid from last nights gig at Oxford University. It had distracted him at the office earlier and had played on his mind for most the day. 'The Battle of Trafalgar' he thought to himself 'odd, very odd,' the regression hadn't gone as planned and the kid put up some strong resistance, and the trigger points were wrong when he went under. It was also unusual to get so much intricate detail; specimens are usually quite vague even if they get to a past life event. Most don't even have the brain capacity to get close to it, let alone give a frank and intimate recollection of a definitive end of life event.

He'd never gotten a chance to speak to Giselle about it and now when they had his assistant was too worried about her costume to find the release forms from last night and help him.

'The boy could be another one?' He thought, starting to calm down. He'd seen the YouTube video which reaffirmed the complexity and depth of the regression, that was before he'd ordered it to be taken down, that exposure was unfortunate and potentially embarrassing for him, he was glad he sorted it out quickly. After the show he would get in contact with the kid on some premise, that is he thought, as long as she finds the form. For now, he to had to get ready for his performance.

He looked at himself in the dressing room mirror, the glow of the halogen bulbs around the edge of the frame exposing every detail in his face. At least this venue had a decent dressing room; most were dreadful. He'd been doing the hypnotism act for a long time now. It was a hobby, a game really, that tweaked his amusement, he'd used it as a method for manipulating people, the passers-by, the flotsam of life, but every now and again he discovered someone, a soul that interested him, a potential candidate for higher study or possible recruitment. "He could be another shifter, Giselle. It's vital we find the form. I want to speak to him." His voice softer now, his accent caressing her name as only the French could.

As he sat and applied his stage makeup he looked at the lines on his face and thought of the time he'd been here. Not bad for someone over two centuries old he thought. A long time ago Leonardo Desangé had been taught a secret, a very powerful secret. One that had given him the ability to shift his soul. He could control his mind in such a way that he was able to self-regulate his bodies regenerative balance therefore controlling the cells ageing process. He had hardly aged since learning of the secret during the Opium wars in Canton China over a hundred and fifty years ago. A complex and intense meditation method gifted to him by an adversary that had saved his life. As well as controlling the ageing process soul shifting gave him the ability to shift mentally back in time, he could regress his soul to revisit his earlier life, learn from experiences and even influence future states.

Desangé had abused this secret ability to establish, and become the head of, a small but incredibly powerful global investment company. The firm had made its fortune benefitting from what he had coined as "outsider trading" on presumably unforeseen economic events, stock markets fluctuations and money market collapses. He had used his ability to shift back in time and manipulate the market. Short selling specific stocks and currencies, placing long positions on entities just before a major breakthrough or profit reports. They had been doing this for the past hundred years and had now amassed a billon dollar empire. The company inexplicably being able to foretell the stock market, economic conditions, political swings and major incidents, the first being one of the only businesses to profit from the Wall Street crash in 1929. The forerunner to many investment miracles ever since that despite being investigated by authorities were seemingly infallible and legitimate.

Over time, he had imparted this secret on a select few, his generals and confidants, identified after taking part of a hypnosis show or, as in the case of Giselle, souls he had met and during his travels around the globe. Each thoroughly scrutinised before receiving the chance to join him. Most welcomed the opportunity without question, those who did not would not live to tell their tale as Desangé could not tolerate rejection or risk exposure.

"Giselle did you find the forms from last night Mon Cherie?" his mood had softened to a dead calm.

"Here they are Leonardo" she kissed him placing the forms on his dressing table. "But I'm not certain which is which."

He started flicking through the forms and said: "I think this kid could be of interest and he may be our next little study, someone we can manipulate and possibly learn from, I think he could become a new and potentially important member of our group."

"Sounds interesting and I'm glad you've calmed down" she kissed him again as the stage manager knocked the door and called five minutes.

"But it will have to wait until after the show," she opened the door. "By the way, I've got the blank forms for tonight." She winked and headed for the stage.

"Merde, merde" his temper returned as he called after her. "The little shit used a false name! Here under the heading regression, the name given is Michael fucking Mouse."

Aston listened to the hypnotist attempt to take him under, the French accent seemed more prominent now than when he was face to face. Harrison had done a superb job isolating the vocal, and the clarity of Bose headphones made it feel like the hypnotist was actually inside the head he was trying to hypnotise.

Aston tried to remember at which point he'd tried to block out the hypnosis; he wanted to emulate the night before exactly, 'right here' Aston recognised the staircase and responded by focussing on his mind with the spotlight attention technique as before. The trigger worked and Aston started hearing a sound he recognised, it was a blues rhythm with a rock guitar track that was unmistakeable, 'was that Hendrix?' For a moment he thought he was hearing sounds coming from the university club the night before, the chatter of voices, clicking of glasses, but they didn't allow smoking and he could sense the tobacco smoke in the air. The music suddenly changed and his ears filled with John Coltrane's Giant Steps, it was complete and began overtaking his senses, drowning out all other sounds nothing like the muted music from before. Giant steps got louder and louder racing up and down the scale. All of a sudden Aston was pulled out of his transient state. It was his phone ringing, he saw a shocked looking Harrison staring down at him, his heart was racing, he shook his head took a deep breath and looked at his phone Ellie was calling. He answered.

"I'm outside, I'm sorry for storming out but you know how I get."

Aston was still trying to get his breath and couldn't speak.

"Aston, Aston - are you there?"

"Yes!"

"Are you okay, you sound like you're out of breath? What were you doing? Let me in I'm at the door!"

Aston could hear the echo of her voice by the door. He turned to Harrison, "It's Ellie, can you let her in."

"Coming now Ellie," Aston said trying to get his breath. He hung up the phone and checked the heart monitor on his wrist. Harrison and Ellie came through the door Aston was still wired up and Ellie had a horrified look on her face

"Is that your heart rate?"

The wristband was now reading 180 bpm and was down from just over 200.

"Either you've been exercising too hard or your heart is in Arrhythmia." Ellie rushed over to him and felt the artery in his neck, and she checked her watch. "Well, the wristband is working, Aston how did this happen?"

"I have no idea how it happened Ellie, but we were in the middle of a regression when you called. It's like last night my pulse was racing when I came out of the hypnosis. That's why I wanted you around, you understand these things and can monitor the biometrics."

"Well, I guess it's a good job I came back, I got your message." She smiled and her face lit up, " But you need to be careful, max heart rate is 220 minus your age and that's during heavy physical exercise. Harrison, did you track this thing?" She took off the Sportband and waved it at him.

"What do you think? Of course, it was hooked up to his phone!" Harrison grabbed Aston's phone and pulled up the app. He scrolled through the data and then checked the phone call. Wow, that's odd, at the exact time of the call the heart rate jumps from normal around 55bpm right up to 210. It's like coming out of the reboot, jump starts your heart or does something."

"Reboot, not again. What's with this rebooting? He's not a bloody computer H!" Ellie was starting to look cross again "You're seriously messing with the unknown here and it's not something you can fix by turning it off and switching it back on again."

"I'd call it a window to the soul but rebooting the soul does kinda sum up what were doing." Aston defended his fellow tech head. "Anyway don't take it out on H, he was here to help me after all." The sudden realisation that they had in fact managed to open up the widow on another soul hit him. "It worked by the way, right until your call, I was starting to experience another soul."

"What?" Ellie looked shocked.

"We did it?" Harrison high fived Aston.

"Yes, we did, although it wasn't the Battle of Trafalgar it was some nightclub, and I think it was the sixties."

"The sixties? How do you know that?"

"Well, I could be wrong because it wasn't entirely clear, but I think Jimmy Hendrix was playing."

"Hendrix? Seriously? That's cool! But it could have been a DJ or even a jukebox so you could have been in the seventies?" Aston could tell Harrison couldn't quite believe it.

"Maybe so, but I'd swear he was actually on stage. I wasn't there long enough thanks to Ellie and John Coltrane here" he waved his phone.

"Yeah you might want to put it in flight mode next time!" Harrison laughed.

"Sorry," Ellie apologised.

"You weren't to know Ellie; the good thing is I think we've cracked it. I see what I need to do now and Harrison, I believe tech is your department, you might have thought about that before."

"This is exciting man — we did it! And I reckon I can sort out a better way to monitor your heart rate and maybe brain activity as long as I can get the equipment. Give me a day or so as I need to ask a few questions but I think I can get it rigged up by Monday."

"And you are going to need some expert medical assistance from now on. I may not agree with this and the ethics involved, but I'm damn sure I'm not going to let you kill yourself. Count me in!"

"That's bloody marvellous you guys. I think that calls for a celebration. Fancy a pint?"

Deep down Aston would have liked to try again but thought better of attempting to push things especially now Ellie was on board, 'let's give it a day or so then the adventure starts' he thought. The image of the club flashed in his mind, the sixties! His mind started racing again he now had a whole new raft of questions and possibilities. Where better to discuss them than the pub he thought, he put his arms around his friend's shoulders

"The pub — first round on me!"

CHAPTER THREE

I Harrison woke with that all too familiar numbness in his head; the pub had gotten pretty messy, and they'd made it home just after midnight. They had both stayed up well into the night discussing what their next steps would be. Aston buzzing with the knowledge and potential of what he'd discovered and Harrison believing his friend had genuinely uncovered something outstanding and the more they discussed it, the more convinced he became that the right application of a technical solution could correctly monitor and help control the reboot process. Once Aston had crashed, he had stayed awake trawling different websites and posting on numerous forums. Harrison was wary of keeping the reboot process a secret but still needed to give enough detail to find a plausible solution. The mixture of the late hour of the night, and the amount of alcohol consumed, finally got the better him, but just before his eyelids fell closed, and he slipped out of consciousness, he had written four letters on the back of his hand, TDCS.

Harrison reached for the headache tablets to clear his head and noticed the letters where he had etched them. The drinking had become a bit of a habit for him, especially since he'd gotten to Oxford. It was a release more so than an addiction, having a very successful parent who expected his son not just to follow in his footsteps, but create an even bigger footprint on the world, was a burden he found hard to bear. The parental pressure explained his eagerness to answer everything and the need to find a technical way to solve every problem. The need to prove himself and create that killer app or invention that would impress his family and especially his father. The alcohol gave him a valve that allowed a release, but one he knew he had to keep from overtaking him.

"TDCS," he said to himself "too much Harrison, you're starting to erase brain cells." He picked up his phone and pressed the home button, and Siri sprang to life with a beep. "Search for TDCS," it was easier than typing, and he'd grown fond of her voice. "Transcranial direct current stimulation (tDCS) is a form of neurostimulation which uses constant, low current delivered directly to the brain area of interest via small electrodes." Siri quoted the first line from Wikipedia.

"Shit yeah!" Harrison jumped out bed.

"I'm sorry I didn't get that," Siri responded still sat on his bedside table.

Harrison's drinking hadn't obliterated too many brain cells, as his memory came flooding back. Transcranial direct current stimulation was suggested to him on a forum very late last night. He thought it too much to remember so had written the acronym on his hand. The technique had been developed a hundred years ago for patients with brain injuries, but after joining some forums he had been in contact with a guy involved in recent studies on healthy adults. He reckoned that these tests had seen good results whereby brain stimulation using TDCS had improved cognitive behaviour such as attention span, language skills, memory and coordination.

He checked to see if Aston was still around but he wasn't in his room or the lounge, no doubt out on his bike or jogging somewhere. Harrison didn't get the fitness thing, his idea of a workout was going ten rounds on Tekken on his Xbox.

He shot down two quick espresso's in succession to further clear the fog in his head. He fired up his Mac Pro computer and began researching all the latest blogs and articles about TDCS. Harrison used his fathers trusted name along with his own Apple Developer ID status to get on a trial for one of the latest products due for release. He had just completed signing up when an out of breath Aston came through the door.

"You're up?" Aston pulled a pint of milk out of the fridge. "You were dead to the world an hour ago, snoring your head off."

"Your fault Mr 'let's go down the pub' you know what I'm like and my heads only just growing back."

Aston downed a pint of milk then noticed the tech device on Harrison's monitors "what you got there? Looks very Star Trek."

"That is a transcranial direct current stimulation headset."

"Trans-Siberian currency what the..."

"Transcranial direct current stimulation and this baby might be able to give us ultimate control of your soul reboot."

"What? How?"

"It's not that complex. TDCS is a form of neurostimulation using electrodes to supply a mild electric current directly to the brain. This little device has an anodal electrode and a cathodal electrode. The current flows from the anode, through the skull and brain to the cathode, creating a circuit. If positioned to a particular area of the brain we can improve focus and stimulate cognitive behaviour."

"So you think shooting a current through my brain will help do you? I'm not so sure?"

Harrison could sense his friend wasn't entirely convinced but was keen to show him more.

"Look it sounds pretty cuckoos nest I know, but look at the results these guys have produced." He showed Aston the results he'd received from the forum. "These guys have been using these headsets, and it's improved their gameplay by 45%, no one can get near the scores without the headsets on."

"Okay, I can see that but how does that relate to the reboot." Aston was still not convinced.

"It's not just the current that I'm thinking of Aston. If we can create some control software that can moderate the level of stimulation and also send data to the right area of your brain. We could more or less suggest a precise date in time, to influence which soul you open."

"Yeah I can see where you're coming from," his interest had been sparked about the date.

"We hook this sucker up to your phone or iPad and capture and display results from sessions, and we've got a device that we can monitor all your vital signs, stimulate your brain and control the process."

"So you think you can get this set up for tomorrow as we planned?" Aston was on board, although Harrison knew he might need help with the software but he had someone in mind. The issue was there was no way he could get it done by tomorrow, so he came clean.

"I know I said I'd get it done for tomorrow but I reckon if the headset gets here as promised, they told me 48 hours when I ordered, it would then only take a few more days to code up the software and application. We'd need to test it, so I reckon in a week we could have it sorted."

"Hey no pressure H, a week would be cool, but I still want to try a reboot again tomorrow with what we have already and with Ellie here."

After Aston had gone to hit the shower, Harrison sent an email to his computer science professor under the premise of a new thesis he was looking into based on TDCS. He knew that the professor would be able to help him, but it was just a case of leverage, and Harrison believed he had some.

The following day as planned, with Ellie watching on and Harrison now satisfied the Sportband Bluetooth connection was working, Aston pressed play to start the hypnotist recording.

"Hang on" yelled Ellie so he could hear.

He paused the recording as she grabbed the phone.

"You need to be in airplane mode, so no one calls" she smiled, Harrison winced embarrassed they'd both forgotten what happened just a few days ago.

"Thanks Ellie, I told you that you were needed," Aston winked then gave Harrison the thumbs up and pressed play.

The smooth French voice filled his mind as he waited for the right trigger point to start spotlighting. The steps came and his meditation led him down them, focussing on nothing but the back of his mind, the cerebellum he'd learned in biology, controls muscle and he'd been taught that spotlighting on this area relaxed his entire body. For the third time in a week the trigger released, and his subconscious unlocked, his senses flooded and Aston started to pick up his surroundings just like the other day.

The music was the same, rhythm and blues mixed with rock, it was Jimi Hendrix, the guitar playing was unmistakeable, the electric sound was filling the room he was in but it seemed to be coming from elsewhere, a stage nearby perhaps. The music muted the other sounds, chinking glasses, snatched conversations, excited shouts and laughter, were all intermixed with the backing track of Hendrix's guitar, cigarette smoke filled his nostrils, so alien to him it stood out from other more familiar smells from his surroundings, he was definitely in a club or bar or possibly both. Loud laughter and the hint of dark perfume came at him getting instantly stronger, a kiss planted on his lips and he tasted the sweet sticky lipgloss.

"Darling, how wonderful to see you!" The girls accent was well-to-do London if a little staged. His blurred vision cleared and he was taken aback by the beautiful face that pulled back from the kiss, her short crop of blonde hair under a peaked cap, thick black eyeliner accentuating her bright blue eyes, her red lipstick smudged around her broad smile.

"Another Martini?"

He nodded.

"Well, I'll need money then darling?" She held out a hand, and his hand went for his wallet. Aston was there experiencing this in the first person perspective, but he was more of an observer. He felt strange watching as he handed over a pound note, his first thought being he'd need to give more.

"Ooh ta" she kissed him again, and he watched her head to the bar. Her tasseled tan suede leather waistcoat swayed as she walked away in her very short skirt sitting atop her long legs. A model figure to go with her looks.

Aston looked around and took in his surroundings. He was in a group of people in an overcrowded bar, which was obviously a section of a larger music club. The vibe was intense, the noise was cranked up, the drinks were flowing, faces were smiling, laughing and everyone including his soul seemed to be smoking. He was undoubtedly in the sixties, late sixties possibly. The moustaches, bell bottoms and paisley patterns of the guys shirts were a strong hint, and the mixture of short skirts, kaftans and flower power frills of the girls were unmistakeable. With an interest in soul and jazz, Aston had a soft spot for the swinging sixties. He loved Motown especially, so he was more aware of the era, unlike many kids his age who may have only heard of the Beatles from their parents. He was part of a large group who were all sat in a booth centred around a small Formica-topped wooden table. They were obviously enjoying themselves judging by the empty glasses. The band must be playing in another part of the bar or next door, as the whole place was packed.

"Hey Warwick" a guy next to him got his attention shouting above the noise. "Are you and Amy going out now?" Aston's attention fixated on his handlebar moustache.

"We're just having fun, Nigel." Aston was a little taken by hearing his soul's voice; it was subtly Scottish and rather rasping and deeper than he expected. Amy returned with the two Martinis.

"Wow it's really packed tonight" she handed one to him and they clinked glasses." Hendrix is something else, he's out of here, I can't believe I arrived late. Hey Nige" she kissed him and proceeded through the group, Aston noticed another girl in the group hand her something which she quickly put in her bag. They were part of a close-knit group who, as far as he could establish, all seemed intent on having a good time.

'So this was the swinging sixties' Aston thought. It was really odd experiencing the soul of someone else, a little voyeuristic.

"Warwick did you get that gig at the Lyceum, Shakespeare wasn't it?" Another question from the group directed his way.

"Yes, Twelfth Night, and I start rehearsals next Friday, some American director, but it's booked for a three-month run, so I'm happy."

"And I'm due to play Maria if all goes well," Amy cut in wrapping her arm around him. "Come on darling, let's go see Jimmy."

Aston's souls date led him through the crowd past the bar and through a corridor, the walls covered with bill posters. He was at the Marquee club judging by the name on top of all the posters, he recognised some out the band names as they passed by them, The Who were prominent, Manfred Mann, the Stones, he also knew some Jazz names amongst them. The posters not only told him where he was but also when, it was 1967 the date was 24 January, The Jimi Hendrix Experience was headlining and Syn supporting. They pushed on through the crowds, Aston could feel her hand holding tight pulling him with her to get a view of the band. Hendrix was playing on the stage at the far end, its striped canopy standing out behind the band. It seemed tiny, nothing like the big arena concerts Aston had become used to, this was more like a university venue. Aston was amazed, in awe of the sound, to experience Jimi Hendrix first hand, well second hand he figured, but his performance had such energy and his electric guitar playing was mesmerising. Amy shouted in his ear "look there's George, and apparently all the Beatles are here. Over there I think" she pointed, Aston thought he saw them but also saw another face he recognised. Amy broke his train of thought as she kissed him once again and said," I love you, Warwick."

Aston had no control of the actions of his soul but at this time he didn't mind he was happy playing pseudo third wheel, at what he would class as the gig of a lifetime. Hendrix ended his set with Purple Haze, and the climax set the crowd into hysteria. After screaming at the stage and in his ear Amy said something that, couldn't be heard over the melee and led him out of the gig. On the way out his soul pulled Amy aside to indicate the need for the toilet and he ducked inside the crowded facility. Aston was initially surprised at the cleanliness, then realised it was due to the attendant who was keeping the place tidy and orderly, even with the masses needing relief after the gig. Aston got his first chance to see his soul face to face as he checked out his appearance on washing his hands. Aston studied his face, trying to guess his age, late thirties he thought, his souls pale appearance, thinning hair, greying at the sides, and dark rings under his tired eyes pointed to that, or either he'd had a hard life. Despite this, he was a good looking guy, kind of suave, a bit Ewan MacGregoresque Aston thought, or maybe the goatee got him thinking that way. Warwick washed his hands, then ran them through his hair pulling the fringe forward as if to cover the receding hairline, smiled checked out his profile then lit a cigarette, and left a tip for the attendant and walked out. Back in the corridor, Amy was waiting with a big smile, looking very pleased with herself. She planted a longing kiss on his lips then said, "Come on Warwick you're taking me home." Aston was beginning to like the swinging sixties even more.

"This is my favourite time of day" the hypnotist, Leonardo Desangé lay back on the rug next to the roaring fire in his penthouse suite, his head on an ornate carved wooden block, his hands holding his antique Opium pipe over the oil lamp he'd used for almost a hundred and fifty years. He inhaled the vapourised opium and passed the pipe to his assistant.

"Mine too" she sighed as she inhaled "and I love this pipe" she passed it back to him and stretched her naked body against the thick pile of the rug.

"It's been with me for a long time." He pulled another long hit on the pipe keeping an eye on the drug inside the chamber which he held skillfully above the lamp, the vapour filling his lungs and the drug infused his nervous system. "I took it from Li Wei Lim."

"The Canton that saved you? You've mentioned him before, but I don't know the history, tell me." Giselle asked as she gratefully took the pipe handed to her.

"The Canton saved my life and freed my soul shortly after. He was the one who gave me the secret to soul shifting. The same man also taught me the pleasure of the opium pipe."

"It's empty. More?" His assistant handed back the pipe and watched intently as Desangé refilled the Opium chamber, placed it back over the flame and then drew a large intake, his eyes glazed and he recounted the story of his saviour, his teacher and the man he betrayed. Outside the Thames embankment penthouse, a ship sounded its horn, and the sound sparked deeper memories from his past.

"He pulled me from the water after our ship, the Arrow, had been captured in the straights of Canton during the Opium wars in 1856. I had been thrown overboard during the fighting and left for dead by the captain and crew. I cannot remember exactly but somehow managed to grab hold of battle debris and had floated down the river before being found by Li Wei Lim and his brother. They found me washed up on the bank half drowned, but they breathed life back into me somchow. The brothers took me back to their village in the hills where, with a mixture of opium and local medicines, they nursed me back to health." Desangé took another long burst from the pipe. "I lay in a fevered state for weeks until I gradually gained strength. The village was remote and, as I was presumed dead, the English didn't send out patrols or try to find me at all. Lei Wei was an educated man, he spoke English very well and had been trading with Western travellers for some years. The addiction to Opium was not affecting his village unlike the rest of mainland China. Instead, they used it to gain energy and enlightenment, assisting transcendent meditation. Lei Wei taught me many things during my time in the village, not just how Opiates can help healing by relieving pain but also how pure, good quality opium can energise a person both physically and mentally.

I asked him to teach me the art of meditation, and after some time he showed me how to focus the power of the mind and turn it inward, mettant en lumière. This was core thread that led to the secret, spotlighting, unlocking the power of your mind to keep your cells regenerating, to staying young and living forever, the cantons in the region had kept this secret for generations." Desangé passed the pipe back to her.

"Well, merci to Lei Wei and his brother, and thanks to you..." she kissed him seductively "...for sharing the secret with me master."

"I'm a little more careful who I select to pass on my secrets to. He was a fool and had no idea what power he held and what could be achieved with it, look at this place, look at where we are today." Desangé sat up, he was feeling energised by the high quality Opium. "When he taught me, I was astonished, it was unbelievable. I said to him that this was a powerful secret, to live through time and shift between time was something that could have massive impact on the world. He and his ancestors had no context from which to imagine the opportunities this could have, living in a remote village why would they."

"They didn't understand the power of being immortal?" Giselle looked puzzled.

"Not quite immortal, death could still take them just like any other, illness or accidents cannot be avoided but this was a secret to a life that lasts for longer than any man. History has spoken of times when men lived beyond the normal lifespan some say immortal but the bible speaks of men, who've lived for 960 years."

"Methuselah."

"Right," Desangé was enthused by the Opium coursing through his body and mind "Just think of travelling back a thousand years to experience previous lives, previous souls. I think Lei Wei only gave up part of the secret. His teachings constrained the shifting within my own souls timeline, but if what the boy has experienced is true, this could open up endless possibilities for our business. We could influence history on a completely different level, change the world as we know it."

"The boy?"

"Yes, the boy at Oxford who witnessed the battle of Trafalgar. This is why I need to find him. If we could shift beyond our own soul like he claims, we would have power beyond anything I imagined when I first discovered the secret. Lei Wei knew power was something that drove me."

He turned towards the fire, noticing it was burning low and dropped another two logs into the flames and watched the fire take hold.

"He realised what I was thinking and tried to spin a tale and belittle what he had given me, but I knew what this meant, the possibilities, and I saw a path I could follow, this was my fortune, and I would never forget."

"So what happened after."

"The following day I was annexed, shut out by Lei Wei and his family, from the entire village. They told me to return to the West, find passage back to Hong Kong or Kowloon Bay and forget about what I knew, forget the village that had become a kind of home and the people that saved me. I argued with Lei Wei and during this argument he threatened me, he threatened to shift back and leave me in the river, to take back the secret. I knew then and there, I had to act if I wanted to keep the secret, harness that power and live forever. I knew it was his time to die."

"He looks so peaceful when he's sleeping, okay when he's — hang on what would you call what he's doing?" Ellie looked from Aston to Harrison, her expression prompting a swift response.

"Transcending? No rebooting. Well, I'm not quite sure what to call it either, but you're right he does look very peaceful." Harrison checked the monitors, "His vitals seem stable enough although his temperature is up a little from when he went under."

"Yeah his REM activity is picking up, it is like he's asleep"

"Do you think we could suggest something, technically he is under hypnosis."

"Harrison!" Ellie was shocked.

"Aston when you wake you'll have a desire to clean the flat from top to bottom."

"You're wicked" Ellie punched him in the arm.

"Oww! That hurt."

"Well stop it, we're supposed to be looking after him."

"You've changed your tune, I thought you didn't want to be nursemaid?"

Harrison had a point, but Ellie wasn't going to rise to his provocation, she cared for Aston but didn't want them to take her for granted. If he wanted her to be a part of this whole adventure then she wanted to feel like it wasn't just a safety net, she wanted to contribute. Her father had taken her mother for granted when Ellie was young, even more once he fell sick and before he died he had expected to be taken care of, without gratitude, or a show of respect. Ellie was always wary of this in men she got to know, which is partly the reason she'd reacted to Aston's comments the way she did.

"His heart rate is normal, and his breathings okay" she checked the monitors to deflect the comment. "It is a little warm in here which may explain the rise in temp."

"So Ellie where did you go on Saturday when this all started?"

'Cheeky git' Ellie thought, she wasn't about to tell him her business, yes they were friends but he was not even close to being 'bestie' material. What was he thinking, like she would tell him her secrets! "You don't want to know" she deflected.

"I'm not prying Ellie, I was miffed you didn't say hello to me on the night but I remembered Aston was curious that's all. You think I'm being nosey now don't you, sorry, I was just making conversation."

"I didn't see you H, else I would have said hello you know that." She rubbed his arm where she'd punched him.

She did feel bad that she hadn't said hello but she'd arranged to meet her sister who she hadn't spoken to for two years. It was a major breakthrough for her sister to agree to meet, and the time was not Ellie's choosing, hence why she had to bail from the show. The meeting hadn't gone as she had planned in her head, her sister still harboured the resentment that had grown following her fathers untimely death. He had died of stomach cancer when she was in her teens leaving her mother to provide for Ellie and her four sisters. Being the second eldest meant she had the chance to study while her older sister looked after the household. Ellie always tried to help out but her mom had pushed her to be the academic achiever, and as this led to college and then university, it also led to her sisters animosity and resentment. While Ellie was taking exams and getting rewards, her sister had to take a far more responsible role, looking after her siblings, taking care of the household and foregoing her own education. The meeting started well enough, a quite drink in the Emillion wine bar, Ellie had been positive, asked the right questions and they were getting along, but a passing comment from an admiring student towards her seemed to prick her sisters temper. Much like her own it didn't take much and this had led to a row that neither of sisters egos would back down from. The night had ended in tears for Ellie as her sister had left her without resolving anything. She had left a message with her mother and gone back to her home feeling pretty awful.

"Ellie, Ellie I think you should look at this." The tone of Harrison's alarm broke her reverie. "His eyes are going crazy."

Ellie looked at Aston; his eyeballs were moving at an accelerated rate.

"Now that's rapid eye movement and then some."

"What's are his other vitals?" Ellie had been part of an REM study and had never seen eyeballs move in this way.

"His heart rate is slowing, but his temperature is the same as before." Harrison looked at both the computer and the mobile display to double check. "Now I wish I had the TDCS set up, we'd get a reading on his brain activity."

"TDCS what's that?" Ellie grabbed Aston's wrist to manually check his heart rate.

"Transcranial direct current stimulation, but it's not gonna help with this."

"What? Never mind, what can we do, wake him up?"

"I think that would be bad Ellie, what's with the slow heart rate is that okay?"

"It seems to be settled at 40bpm which is a little flat but not..."

Ellie stopped mid-sentence when Aston's eyes suddenly stopped moving.

Amy grabbed his hand with a laugh and led Aston's soul Warwick out of the club. Aston was a little reluctant to leave especially as it sounded like Hendrix had come back on for an encore. Having no control of his soul's actions he was powerless to intercede. They stopped to get their coats, Amy wrapped herself in a fur of some description, as Warwick donned a classic trench. They passed a couple of the friends from the bar earlier Amy said:

"We're off to mine to get wild, want to come along Warwick's driving."

Aston was slightly concerned about the wild statement when the friends replied.

"We know where there's a party on Amy, and then we can all get wild." This girl was the one Amy had taken something from earlier. Amy replied "Great" kissed Warwick then said, "you don't mind a foursome baby."

"Hell no, the more, the merrier!" Warwick replied. Aston, who had not had much experience or luck with girls, would have raised his eyebrows if he could. He felt somewhat alarmed, slightly apprehensive but also quite excited by the prospect. They came out into the cold and bright lights of London's Carnaby Street and the narrow streets alive with people. Aston was trying to absorb everything. He'd been there a couple of times himself, but the modern trappings, neon signage and shop fronts were gone, the street had less flash but seemed to have more style about them, a cool understated feel with the shops concentrating on clothes and fashions rather than brand names. He could see the psychedelic influences of the times reflected in the colours and fabrics on display.

A couple of scooters zipped passed them "bloody hippies" one shouted. Aston noticed the Mod symbols on the back of the parka coats; their days were behind them holding a grudge against change as well as holding on to the past he thought.

"Warwick, where are you parked? It's freezing out here!"

"Just around the corner, hope your okay squeezing in back?"

"Not a problem Warwick as long as it warm."

It was getting cold Amy held his arm tight as they turned the corner.

"He we go" Warwick pulled the keys from his pocket standing next to the silver DB5 parked between an old Ford Anglia and Mini, he opened the door.

"Nice wheels, Amy your man's got style."

"Very Bond isn't he" she kissed him on the cheek and climbed into the back. "Kate and I will get cosy in the back seat," Kate jumped in, and Warwick let her partner into the passenger side.

"So how long have you had the Aston?" Kate's partner asked as he sat next to him.

"About a month, paid for from my last gig, did a world cruise, 2 hours work a night, nine months travel around the world; you'd be amazed what you can save with all your expenses paid." Aston was severely impressed with the car. His father had named him after the very same model, his favourite from the Bond movies; Aston preferred the modern models especially the Vanquish but as a marque, the Aston Martin had no peers.

Warwick turned the key, and the engine sprang to life, the throttle giving volume to the roar of the cylinders. "The names Warwick, Warwick Scott" he shook Kates partners hand "So where are we going?

"Paul. Head for Knightsbridge, Kensington Mews our friends are having a house warming."

"Anyone I know Kate?" Amy enquired from the back seat.

"Yes, the Moxleys."

"Fab, now they know how to have fun. Warwick you'll love them too, put your foot down and turn the heater up."

Ten minutes later after negotiating the busy London streets, they pulled up in a secluded mews the windows starting to steam.

"This should make sure we are up to speed with the party," Kate handed a small blue pill to everyone.

"Dexies! You're a blast Kate, love you." Amy popped hers and then kissed Kate full on her lips. Aston again felt slightly nervous as Warwick popped his pill and opened the car door. They made their way to number 11a whereby the sound that was coming from inside meant the party was in full swing.

After a while banging on the pillar box red door, it opened, and a turban-clad Indian dressed in full garb welcomed them in. His attire reminded Aston of his toga party days, but at least, this looked more convincing. He welcomed them and gestured for them to follow. The house was decked out like an Indian palace, muslin sheets, mock statues of gods, a large Vishnu being the centrepiece. The sitar music combined with a more modern back beat provided the backing track, the powerful incense providing extra ambience to the obvious guru inspired theming.

"Kate, Amy how great you came, how did you like my swami? Isn't he super?" The hostess who was slightly worse for wear greeted them, with what Aston was beginning to realise must be a swinging sixties style greeting, kissing both girls full on. "Paul so good to see you again." Another kiss. "And we have not met," she faced Warwick with a big smile, "Amy is this your new man? He's delicious."

She kissed him very furtively and then continued to introduce a whole host of other guests scattered around the house, some on cushions, some dancing, some obviously too high to notice. It seemed there were people everywhere.

The drinks were flowing, and the drug consumption was increasing, after a short while Amy grabbed him "I want you lover — I want you now" she kissed him and passed a pill of some sort into his mouth which he swallowed.

"You are a wild one," Warwick said.

"Let me show you how wild!" She replied as she led him upstairs.

For a moment, Aston wasn't sure if he was actually experiencing a previous soul or whether he was just dreaming. The band, the girl, the car, now this, it could be this was just his vivid imagination playing out a very, very good dream, he wasn't sure but was sure he was going to let it continue.

The only room not occupied was, what seemed to be the hosts main bedroom. Amy didn't seem to care and pulled him in. "Has it kicked in yet?" She asked I think mine's a dud; I can't feel a thing. Ah well never mind, come here, lover." She pulled him close kissing him then turned with her back towards him. "Unzip me I'm all naked underneath" just as his hand started to release the tension at the top of her dress she pulled away. "Oh my! Look what the Moxleys are into, I never knew!" Amy had spotted something on their dressing table and picked it up. She held up a small vial of something at him "Opium, the Devils" she said, "well the least they can do is share don't you think."

Aston was hoping Warwick would be the voice of reason. If he were in control, he would have said maybe let's just stay as we are and have some fun, but it seemed Warwick was unable to say no to this girl or maybe had a similar taste for the extreme as Amy did. "Any needles nearby?" He replied, which was probably not what Aston would have said given the fact that he'd just consumed an LSD tab and before that some Dexedrine plus all the alcohol. Aston was trying to find a way to take control and maybe put a stop to this, but his mind was somehow starting to be affected by the drugs consumed.

"Ah ha," Amy twirled around with a needle and syringe procured from the cupboards she been routing through. "Let's do it! I've never made love with opium, how about you?" She proceeded to fill the syringe with half the vial. "Sounds like a rush sweet lips."

'No,' Aston thought that's not a good idea, he was definitely not dreaming now, or if he were it was a nightmare. 'How can I get out, if only I could control his actions?' He felt powerless. Warwick and Amy were now intwined on the bed, Amy was naked, kneeling over him, opium syringe in hand, about to give Warwick a shot, one Aston wasn't sure he would recover from.

CHAPTER FOUR

The REM had stopped, but Aston's eyes were now wide open, his retinas rolled to the top of his head, Harrison looked at Ellie and then at his friend, Aston's eyes were weird and it was freaking him out a little. They hadn't discussed bringing him back out. The thought just never occurred to either of them,

"I wasn't prepared for eyes and irregular heart rates. I just thought he'd come back of his own accord."

"So what can we do?" Ellie asked him. Her face was panicked "I could give him an adrenalin shot."

"That might be our last resort Ellie, but I'm not sure what his mental state would be. What am I saying? How the hell would I know, I'm not a psychologist!"

"His heart rate is slowing, and his temperature is increasing."

"We need to bring him out just like a hypnotist would," he snapped his fingers, nothing. He clapped his hands, still nothing. "Arise — wake up — I release you! Fuck this is crazy. Wake up Aston" Harrison pulled out the headphones and shouted in his ears. "Hang on. I might know how we can fix this, in fact, I'm pretty sure I can."

"How? Because I'm pretty sure medically I can't." Ellie looked hopefully at him.

"Well, we were playing the French hypnotist dude soundtrack to induce the reboot so maybe he's the only one who can bring him out of it!"

"Well, I hope you know his address, and he lives close because if his heart rate drops anymore, I'm using the adrenalin."

"No, we can run the track forward and play the part that brings him out."

"But didn't Aston come out of his regression by falling off the chair, that's how it looked to me!"

39

"Damn it, you're right — hang on, we might be able to pull something off the internet." Harrison jumped on to his computer and searched for 'the hypnotist' in an attempt to find some video footage on YouTube, Vimeo or something. After a while, he turned to Ellie. "Nothing! I can tell you where his next gig is but that's it, that's weird, we might be better off finding his address the phone book." Harrison now wished they had waited until he had the TCDS system set up, at least, he could try to stimulate some brain activity and monitor what was going on. He contemplated calling the professor just to get an opinion but figured it would take two long to explain the circumstances. He couldn't believe there's wasn't anything about the hypnotist on the internet it was very odd.

He pulled up some hypnotism scripts that he had found with Aston a few nights before and flicked through to the final chapters he and Ellie tried different phrases but nothing seemed to be working. Harrison tried a French accent which didn't work at all but alleviated the tension a little as Ellie broke into laughter, if only for a few seconds as Aston's heart rate started to increase setting off the monitors.

"Pull up that copy of Aston's YouTube video there may be something at the beginning from the group before him."

"You may be right Ellie" Harrison pulled up the file and just before Aston got to the stage, there was a snippet right at the beginning from the previous group of girls who were made to believe they were kittens. If Harrison remembered correctly, it was at the opening frame you heard the click of his fingers, and him say '...and awake' in the distinctive French accent.

"I think I can enhance that and play it back full volume through the headphones."

"Worth a shot as I can't use this now with his heart rate this high it would kill him." Ellie gestured to the adrenalin shot.

Harrison quickly pulled the clip into Final Cut Pro and isolated the soundtrack, he illuminated the background noise and enhanced the actual sound, he got the clicking fingers and the 'and awake' and exported them to an MP4 audio file.

He pulled the headphones from Aston's iPhone and plugged the jack into the computer and pressed play. Then pressed play again. Nothing, Aston's eyes didn't even flicker.

"Bollocks" Ellie swearing took Harrison by surprise. "Sorry thought that would work for sure."

He tried again half-heartedly hoping for third time lucky.

"There must be something" Harrison knew there was a solution to this and was determined to find it.

"Pass me that iPad and switch his phone off of airplane mode, I want to try something."

Ellie gave Harrison the iPad and grabbed Aston's phone switching it from airplane mode. Harrison pulled up Aston's photo gallery and changed the settings to flash the images randomly at 4 per second. He held the iPad directly in front of Aston's eyes and started the slideshow. The images flashed in Aston's face and wide open eyes.

Ellie looked over quizzically; Harrison tried to explain. "This should provide some visual stimulation to his optic nerve, all you need to do now is plug his phone into the earphones and call him. If this doesn't work, we call the ambulance and deal with the consequences."

Ellie plugged the earphones back in his phone, picked up her own and in a weird twist of logic, dialled her friend who was lying directly in front of her.

"Here goes." Harrison looked at Ellie she glanced back at him, and they both looked at the monitors. Aston's temperature was now reading 44 degrees, his heart rate was just tracking passed 195 into 200, Harrison winced as it hit 205, he held the iPad firmly in his hand and looked up at the ceiling for inspiration. The heart rate monitor pulled his attention back, as it started to flatline when Aston's heart suddenly stopped beating.

Aston watched aghast as Amy found the vein in Warwick's arm. He was utterly unable to do anything to stop her. He could see where this was heading, but at a loss to how he could prevent it. He was just an observer, as she injected the opium, he noticed the small trace of blood enter the vial and then saw it expelled as she pushed the syringe down slowly, releasing the drug into his bloodstream.

"This will be a trip," she said.

Warwick sighed and breathed out "oh yeah" as the opiates hit his central nervous system "LSD and Opium, I believe you've just created a new cocktail."

Aston inwardly grimaced as Amy smiled, she kissed Warwick longingly, then using the same needle, skillfully injected herself. She lay back alongside him taking in the moment of ecstasy as the drugs coursed through her, then said: "LSD, Opium and me lover, come here." She rolled on top of him and threw back her hair. Warwick didn't respond "Warwick? Warwick? You cannot fall asleep on me now, Warwick, no!"

Warwick hadn't just fallen asleep he'd slipped deep into unconsciousness.

At the start, Aston thought this reboot experience was going to be a lot less intensive than the regression on the ship. It had begun so well, seeing Jimi Hendrix on stage, the close attention of the sexy, if a little crazy model girlfriend, the sublime car. He always thought being in the swinging sixties would be a blast, but he had never imagined it would lead to where he was now.

Aston knew he had to try to gain some control, but his own mind was becoming cloudy, could the drugs be affecting him because from what he could fathom his soul had just fallen into drug-induced unconsciousness. Aston suddenly realised he had an element of control, but his host was totally lifeless, if not he felt sure he could try and move his arms and legs, his whole body in fact. For a fleeting second, he contemplated enjoying the experience with Amy, but he felt the drugs that were in his souls body were now starting to affect his own mind. He also had the sickening feeling that his soul wasn't just unconscious but could be slipping into a dangerous drug-induced coma or worse, overdosed at the hands of his lover and could well die. Aston struggled to contemplate the seriousness of his situation, and questions raced through his head. What happens if his soul dies while he was in a reboot? Would he still be experiencing his mind, his last thoughts and possibly his death?

Would he be able to return back to his present life, or would his own soul die alongside his former soul? A wave of paranoia flooded his mind; the drugs were now starting to affect his own thinking. They were not just affecting his mind but, strangely enough, his body as well. He felt his heart rate galloping, thumping at a million miles an hour, or then again, was it his or was it Warwick's heart rate. The drug-fuelled paranoia again playing with his mind, or was it?

His mind's eye suddenly began to see images flash in front of him, psychedelic colours, visions from out of nowhere, or out of the future, or were they his own past. Amy's protests and noisy attempts to arouse Warwick were starting to be faded out by the sound of jazz, it was John Coltrane, and it interweaved into his thoughts, getting louder with each image that flickered like a strobe light in his head. They were pictures of his parents, his cousins, his holiday in France, his childhood in Hong Kong, and his friends. His friends, 'Harrison, Ellie, Harrison' the sound of Coltrane grew progressively louder as if calling him, the images flashed brighter, and they ran through repeatedly, louder, brighter, louder, the sensory attack was too much, causing his mind to shut down completely.

Aston jolted onto the bed, but not the bed in the Moxleys room; this was the massage bed in his flat in Oxford, he caught an image of Harrison and Ellie staring back at him, it flashed in his mind for a single second, and then everything went black.

Ellie saw his eyes open for a split second. "Did you see that, his eyes moved."

"What?" Harrison was still holding the iPad.

"You did it, it worked. His eyes moved, I swear it, he's back, show me the monitor." The heart rhythm had just spiked, if only a brief jump up from the flat line, it was definitely something. "See!

Ellie's training kicked in and she began emergency CPR. She banged down on his chest, beating his heart in a panic, with Aston back it would be crucial to get his heart beating and him breathing again as soon as they could.

"Call an ambulance genius!" She shouted at Harrison, who seemed to be basking in the glory of bringing Aston back.

"Now" Ellie yelled louder. Then started mouth to mouth giving him breath then helping him breathe. This was the first time she'd kissed Aston since she'd known him, the thought lingered for just a second, she counted the number of ribs up from his sternum and started compressions. "One, two, three, four, five..."

Harrison had got through to the emergency services operator and was giving them the address.

"Tell them it's a cardiac arrest after a hypnotic state and to get here quickly."

"Okay, yes cardiac arrest, male aged twenty-two." Harrison rolled his eyes, obviously struggling at the inquisition on the phone.

"How much time will they take?" Ellie said as she switched from breathing to compressions.

"Ten minutes tops."

"Ten minutes! He could be gone by then."

"Just get here as fast as you can." Harrison hung up the phone "What can I do Ellie?"

"Four, five, six, seven, eight... What's his temperature?"

"Back to normal. What's normal again?"

"Between 37 and 42," Ellie said as she stopped mouth to mouth.

"Normal then."

"How long is that now?"

"Maybe two minutes, three almost, could be four." Harrison was not helping her.

"Jesus H, how long have we been doing this two or four minutes, check the monitors, my compressions will register on them."

"Three minutes, thirty seconds — Sorry Ellie I..." Something caught his attention, and he pushed passed Ellie.

"What are you doing?"

"Why don't we use this?" Harrison held up the adrenalin shot Ellie had with her, she had placed it on the couch next to her when she'd called his number on her phone.

"Oh shit." Ellie ripped open Aston's shirt and then grabbed the shot.

She pushed out a little adrenaline to ensure there were no air bubbles in the syringe, then she stabbed the needle down into his chest cavity and administered the small dose straight into his heart and stepped back.

Harrison looked at her wide eyed in amazement, and the moment seemed to hang silently. It was only a second though when the silence broke, and Aston sucked in a massive breath, grabbed hold of the side of the bed and seemed to straighten his entire body, then collapsed. The monitors jumped into life at the same time the sound of an ambulance siren enveloped the flat, the blue lights streaming through the gaps in the curtains.

Ellie let out a huge sigh of relief and grabbed Harrison, hugging him tightly. "Thank god you saw that H, why didn't I think of that at the start!"

"Ellie you were great, I'm the one that didn't know what to do, I didn't even think to call the ambulance."

They both looked at Aston, who was breathing, and the monitors affirmed his beating heart although he was still unconscious.

The door banged and the bell rang as the paramedics made it to the flat entrance, Ellie dashed to let them in and recounted what she had just done. "Four minutes CPR after cardiac arrest and then an adrenalin shot to the heart."

"Why did you wait four minutes?" The paramedic asked as he applied an oxygen mask to Aston.

Ellie looked at Harrison, "I forgot I had it with me, else I would have used it sooner of course." Harrison winked at her.

"So what on earth were you doing on a massage bed to induce a cardiac arrest or should we leave that for the Police?" The paramedic looked around at the monitors, unhooked the wristband and headphones and looked again at Ellie and Harrison for answers. They looked at each other as if they were eight years old, both wearing guilty expressions. Ellie finally said, "You'll need to ask him when he's conscious. We were just helping as part of his experiment." Harrison gave her a look to indicate he thought she'd said too much.

"Well let's get him to hospital and we can ask him," the paramedic looked at his partner suspiciously as they transferred Aston on to the portable gurney.

Ellie grabbed Harrison's arm, "I'll go with them, you meet us there, and I guess we should phone his mother."

CHAPTER FIVE

Without opening his eyes, Aston could sense an intense white light. His senses had taken in some extremes in the last few days and hours meaning his orientation was a mess. The bright light made him question exactly where he was. He was lying down, that was apparent, but he wasn't sure whether he was still within his former soul. His sense of smell gave him a good indication as to his location, as the air had that unmistakeable carbolic cleanliness that only hospitals seemed to have. 'I made it to a hospital then' he thought. A vague recollection of an ambulance hit him, but he was still unsure if that was him or his previous soul. He opened his eyes then quickly shut them, the searing white light leaving a blur in his vision. It did prove he had control, so it was a good chance it was his own body. He took a deep breath to try and focus, the sharp pain halting the intake, burning his chest 'I don't remember doing that.'

"Take it easy Mr North, you've broken a couple of ribs, so breathe gently."

Aston opened his eyes again and turned his head to see the nurse reading his chart next to his bed. He noticed the green fabric screens pulled around them and a heart monitor beeping rhythmically next to him.

"Your girlfriend may have saved your life, but she almost broke your heart, well your ribs anyway. I'll go tell them you're awake and also let the doctor know."

"She's not my girlfriend." Aston lay back and closed his eyes, the events of the reboot running through his mind. The fact he'd regressed to his former soul still felt like a monumental accomplishment. The fact that he seemed drawn to traumatic events in former souls lives somewhat disturbed him. He was grateful for whatever Harrison and Ellie did to get him back, the broken ribs aside he didn't feel too shabby. He couldn't wait to see them and talk about his experience in the sixties. His excitement instantly diminished when his mother opened the screens followed by the nurse and judging by the white coat the doctor. He suddenly felt like a child again.

"What on earth were you doing Aston? The doctor tells me you had a cardiac arrest for gods sake. We also need to get you a private room." Aston's mother leaned in and kissed her son, as she looked down her nose at the small cubicle "Did you not tell them you had health insurance?"

"It was an experiment mother, something for computer science class." Aston lied thinking on the fly but hoped Ellie hadn't told her what had actually happened.

"An experiment?" The doctor questioned, "That's interesting, you flatlined after your pulse hit almost 210 bpm. If it wasn't for your friends you'd be laying in the morgue son."

"Oh my god!" Aston's mother looked at him with a death stare that he thought, could quite possibly put him in the morgue.

"It wasn't anything untoward we just wanted to monitor a deep hypnotic state, and I guess we got our wires crossed." Aston hoped being a little truthful may help appease the medical staff. Ellie stuck her head around the curtain.

"Hey Aston, how are you feeling?"

"Here's the girl you need to thank, your other friend the Asian guy assures me this young lady saved your life."

"Thanks, Ellie" Aston winked.

"Sorry about your ribs."

"I've got others! Sorry, you had to be put in that position, told you I needed you." Aston's mom picked up on the last comment and looked at Ellie as if she sensed something untoward between them.

"So this deep hypnotic state, were there any drugs involved?" The doctor quizzed him further, looking at the chart.

Aston rolled his eyes, if only they knew what drugs he'd experienced during his 'trip.' "No, we just meditated into a trance-like state, must have been something we did that triggered the heart arrhythmia."

"This was no regular arrhythmia Mr North, what I can't explain is why your body is showing signs of drug withdrawal, but our tox screen shows nothing but the adrenalin shot Miss Cole administered to save your life."

Aston's mother looked even more horrified at hearing this. "What on earth are they teaching Oxford students nowadays."

"Mother I'm sure the seventies were far worse than today. We took nothing doc honestly, maybe your charts or readings are wrong."

"Well, I'll get the nurse to run some further blood work, but it's an unusual case even without the added drug mystery."

Aston was happy the doctor decided not to push any further with the questions. He was also glad his mother followed both the nurse and the doctor out of the cubicle pushing for them to move him to a private room.

"What the hell happened?" Ellie beat him to the opening question.

"Oh my god Ellie you're never gonna believe it, the guy odeed on LSD and opium, his naked girlfriend injected..."

"Naked girlfriend?" Harrison swished through the cubicle curtain.

"Who was naked? It was your soul's girlfriend wasn't it, was she hot?"

"H! Good to see you made it." Aston said.

"How are you feeling? Back in the land of the living again."

He raised his hand to receive a high five, but Aston failed to reach his arm as the pain pulled him back, the broken ribs stopping any momentum.

"Felt better H, but what a trip, thanks for getting me back in time."

They both helped Aston sit up in bed, Harrison paying rather too much attention to the heart monitor connectors while Aston recounted the whole story back to them. He was a little freaked out hearing about the REM and CPR when Harrison and Ellie reciprocated with their side of events but felt very glad he had friends he could trust with his own soul.

"Your 10.30 meeting with Elliot has been delayed, Leonardo. He'll be here in twenty minutes, so I thought you'd like coffee" Giselle handed him his decaf latte.

"So where's Elliot, why the delay?" Desangé stood up and looked out of the window of his investment companies London office. They had recently moved to the seventeenth floor of the Gherkin building, in St Mary's Axe, and he still enjoyed the view from the bustling heart of London. He took a sip of the coffee and recognised the taste.

"Is it from Alessandro's?"

"Yes, just as you like it, a double shot."

"I hate delays, is he with the Chinese still?"

"Yes I know, that's why I bought you coffee, I told him to call if they need more time."

"Fucking Chinese, I shouldn't have let Elliot get involved, if it weren't such an important trade, I wouldn't, you know how I feel about dealing with them."

"That reminds me. You never did finish the story about Lei Wei from last night." Giselle brushed her hand through his hair.

Desangé snorted, "I'm not sure if we have time, or if I'm of the right mind to tell."

"Please Leonardo, it meant a lot to me that you told me about him at all, I'd love to know how you got him back."

He knew she was tweaking his ego but last night had been the first time he had shared his story for a long time, she was in the inner circle now since she had the secret, and knowing the full story would be a test of loyalty.

"Well he got what he deserved, you can't give someone knowledge that leads to all this and threaten to take it away." He raised his arms and gestured to the office.

"So what did you do?"

"After the village cut me off and Lei Wei threatened my life I knew I had to kill him, I thought about going back and just slitting his throat in the dead of the night. A risky strategy being as the man, his family and the entire village were experts in Kung Fu.

I was staring out into the bay and saw a clipper flying the British flag, lucky for me they were on a search and destroy mission. It struck me that the method of my meeting Lei Wei could provide me with a way to destroy all of them. I tracked back to the bay avoiding the main route to the village, as I knew they would keep a lookout. I was mindful of leaving a trail so I could find my way back. It took me some time to explain to the British soldiers who I was. I told them of how I was captured and tortured by Chinese rebels based in the mountains. I made up a plausible story how I'd escaped and negotiated passage back to Europe in return for showing them where they were. They were eager to have some Chinese rebel casualties to report back to their generals in Hong Kong."

"Did you go with them back to the village?"

"Of course, they followed me back along the trail. We waited until the middle of the night then the British slaughtered everyone, and I made sure Lei Wei knew it was me who had led them to his village. I looked him in the eyes when I identified him as the leader of the rebel gang and made sure he was last to be killed."

Desangé drank the last of his coffee and noticed Giselle hadn't enjoyed hearing the end of the tale. "What's up my dear, had you forgotten my black heart?"

"No, no, I didn't expect you to kill everyone."

"The British were unmerciful they burnt the entire village to the ground as a message to other rebels. It did mean that I was now the only person who knew the secret, or so I thought at the time, my only regret is what else burnt within that village."

"So you think there were more secrets?"

"I think there may have been some further history kept there, some teachings that could have given more light into the power they had shown me. I didn't get time to go through the smoking ashes straight after, but I went back later in life to check. I couldn't find anything it was just charred remains that the undergrowth had started to reclaim."

"Did you think about shifting back and returning."

"I contemplated it but was conscious of being identified. What people call fate or Karma is often misrepresented. A souls imprint on the world can have many traces, and I didn't want to trigger or release any potential threat by returning there."

"A déjà vu dilemma."

"It's no joking matter, Giselle. Once you've shifted a few times you learn that returning to the scene of a crime, even before it's been committed, is not a wise thing. Elliot can tell you stories of how a few of our early trade manipulations almost backfired, the lighter you tread back in time, the better for all."

"Less is more, I understand. So how often have you shifted?"

"Enough, but limitations within your own lifespan are restrictive. This is why the Oxford boy interests me so much, and I think Lei Wei knew shifting between souls was possible. He said to me before he died that the power I thought I held in my grasp was only small in comparison to the time of men."

"You think the boy has something?"

"I'm positive, and that's why I want you to get a team searching the Oxford campus as soon as possible so we can find him and get him to 'share' with us." Desangé emphasised the word share with his hands and smiled: "I only need a few moments back in his mind, and I can find out exactly what he knows, I might even ask him to join us, he could be a valuable asset to have around."

"You want me to go there?"

"Yes, as you've met the boy you'll be best placed to recognise him, follow him and get his correct name and address, so we can pay him a visit. You can go after we finish tomorrow's show."

The phone on his desk started flashing; he pressed the intercom. "Mr Desangé I have Mr Dempsey for you."

"Elliot, tell me you're finished with those damned Chinese?"

"All done, although they want to meet us both in a few days, otherwise the trades in place for the fifteenth, 20 million fully funded as you asked.

"Good."

"It makes sense for us to use them, I know you're reluctant but having this Yen trade on the books gives us leverage when they announce the deal. I'll be with you in about ten minutes and tell you the full story."

Desangé smiled, it was satisfying to get a large deal locked in just before a major market announcement or political deal. The big gains may come from shifting back and changing positions following stock crashes or upheavals, but it made sense to have these regular bankers in place that they could just reverse by shifting back in time once the announcement happened.

Aston winced as he felt the ribs in his chest. He'd spent the night in the private room courtesy of his mother's health insurance, but despite the quiet and more comfortable surroundings, he'd not managed much sleep, although once again he felt quite rested. The lack of sleep was not because of his chest pain and the difficulties breathing. He'd spent most of the night thinking about his next reboot and ways he could control it. His mother had left him around half past seven. After bullying the hospital into providing the room she was adamant he'd be coming home with her once discharged, so wanted an early start to get his room ready. He'd protested and complained that he would miss too many lectures, but his mother had called the Oxford student admin and arranged for him to cover any lectures and studies, online.

After she'd left, Harrison and Ellie had stayed on until nine o'clock, Ellie was mortified she'd broken Aston's ribs and was even more concerned that he was going to die if he tried it again. He had managed to convince her that not trying it again was not an option, but Aston was as eager as ever to try to get the process perfected. Together with Harrison they had talked about better control of the beginning of the reboot and ways in which they could improve coming out of the process. Ellie was central to this discussion and had some good ideas how using suppressant drugs might help control the heart rate. Harrison was convinced the transcranial direct current stimulation monitored by an app he'd been working on would, in theory, give them enough control getting in and out of the reboot. They had also discussed the control that Aston needed when inside the soul of his former lives, if only he'd been able to influence actions and decisions he could have avoided some of Warwick's rather hedonistic choices. This led to Harrison embarking on a Google quest to find out more about Warwick and whether he had died that night from an overdose. They learned that Warwick Scott had continued his run at the Lyceum during the summer of 1968 to some decent reviews, so it appeared Warwick had survived that night somehow, although they found no mention of Amy in the cast list. They laughed having found an old casting photo of Aston's former soul looking very suave in the early seventies. Ellie had said he was kind of her type which led to an awkward moment between the two of them when Harrison mentioned the kiss of life. He then brought the mood down when he found a short obituary in the Daily Telegraph of 1993 for Warwick, who had succumbed to lung cancer in the early hours of 25 January aged 62. The article reporting the sad news of the passing of a much-admired character actor who graced the stage of many a West End and provincial theatre in the early to mid-seventies who given better breaks or less indulgent vices may have rivalled the names of his day. He apparently died leaving no dependents after a year-long battle with lung cancer and had been buried with a simple service in Christ Church in Hampstead Heath attended by a small group of old friends.

The sudden realisation that Warwick's death exactly matched, to the day, Aston's date of birth had chilled him, and as he looked at his friends, he knew they too had realised the enormity of what he had discovered. This was his previous incarnation, a real thread between the past and the present, proof of this could have profound repercussions across all beliefs, all religions and societies as a whole. As they looked at each other and back at Harrison's iPad, the nurse put her head around the door and called time on visitation. That was nine o'clock and Aston recalled he had sat alone for around an hour after, troubled, thinking about the implications of his discovery, he had tried meditating but failed to find focus, something he thought was understandable. He had finally fallen asleep while watching TV, choosing to escape his own thoughts watching some crime scene investigation drama. It worked to a point, but Aston had woken around two in the morning and since then, had been trying to reason with his own thoughts and find a solution to gaining control of the actions of his soul when in a reboot.

It was now morning, and as the fractured ribs had curtailed his regular exercise routine, he was sat back in bed waiting for whoever to check up on him so he could get himself discharged. The nurse came at seven o'clock with, to his welcome surprise, an attempt at decent food for breakfast. She also gave him hope that the doctor would be along to check on him and discharged him, albeit into his mother's care. 'It may be better to stay in the hospital' he thought, but when the doctor arrived, Aston was just glad that he gave him the go ahead to call her.

His mom answered and much to his surprise she walked into the room just after picking up.

"That was pretty quick Mom, even for you."

"Funny Aston, they told me last night you'd be discharged in the morning so I thought I'd get here early just in case you had any ideas about heading back to Oxford without me."

"I am an adult Mom, so I could have discharged myself." A wave of realisation hit him that he could have done just that. "Damn!" he said aloud and putting his hand to his forehead.

"Are you okay?"

"Yes, mother." He may have been an adult, but his mother still had that control over him, as most parents do, that brought out the inner child. "I'll need to go back and pick up some things, especially if I'm staying a while." It suddenly dawned on him that being at his moms would scupper any plans to reboot again. "How long am I supposed to be staying with you?"

"Aston don't worry it'll only be for a week, maybe even five days as I've got a shoot coming up and I may have to leave on Friday. So you'll be back with your friends soon enough. I've asked the lovely Ellie to pick up some of your things from your flat, and she'll bring them over tomorrow."

"Okay great I'll give H a call and let him know what to give her." Aston wasn't quite comfortable with Ellie picking out clothes for him, let alone having her sorting through his wardrobe and drawers to find them.

As he followed his mother out of the hospital, he dialled Harrison knowing full well it would go through to his voicemail as it was only eight o'clock.

"H it's me, look Ellie is coming over later today to pick up some clothes for me while I'm at moms. I really don't want her picking out my pants and socks so can you grab a few pairs of boxers and socks from the bedside draw plus my black jeans, a couple of tees, my Adidas hoody from the wardrobe and my black converse boots. Throw them in my gym bag plus my razor and stuff. Any probs give me a callback. Oh and H..." Aston checked to see if his mom could hear him. She was signing something at the front desk, so he had time. "...I think I've worked a few things out with the reboot, Facetime me later, and we can discuss next phase. Hope the TDCS stuff arrives soon as I want to get it controlled so we can avoid further trips to the hospital, cheers and thanks." He hung up as his mom came back over.

"All sorted, we can leave now" she ruffled his hair, and he pulled away shyly. "Great..." Aston rolled his eyes and said to himself "...this may be a long week."

Harrison laughed as he listened to Aston's voicemail 'poor blokes getting it from both sides, his mother and Ellie' he thought. He was thankful he had little complications in his own life, his dad was happy to fund his son's lifestyle and apart from the regular summer and Christmas holidays he spent with his family, they didn't demand any extra time from him.

It took him two minutes to gather Aston's things together. He dumped the bag by the front door in readiness for Ellie's arrival and sent her a text message asking what time she planned to come to the flat. He checked the post in the lobby as the TCDS package was due in today, but nothing arrived. Online the courier tracking ID, once he found out how to retrieve it, told him it had reached the local dispatch office. He was excited, this confirmed it should be in his hands later today. Harrison was distracted by the couriers request for feedback, he duly obliged but doubted if they would get the sarcasm. After about twenty minutes of surfing the usual suspects online, he decided to jump back into the Apple IOS development centre and update the user interface he'd been working on for Aston's reboot program. He was struggling to find the right way to utilise Airdrop so the app could take data from multiple sources and had left a post on a forum overnight. The hope was one of the worldwide group of developers or even maybe one from Apple in Cupertino would have replied. They had, but for once Harrison was a little baffled how to incorporate the solution into his app development.

After a couple of failed attempts and much keyboard mashing, he decided to follow up the email he'd sent to the only person he knew of that might understand, David Ferris, his computer science professor. Ferris an American had been at the heart of Silicone Valley during the tech boom of the nineties, he'd worked with Steve Jobs at Next computers before becoming an academic, giving lectures in computer studies at Princeton for ten years before being lured over to Oxford. He didn't suffer fools gladly and was known for his temper but had great connections and the top tier of graduates from his classes, managed to secure placements with some of the largest tech companies in the world. Harrison found him holed up, as usual, in the University computing laboratory. It was one of the most advanced university suites in the world, which Ferris had helped to set up with a little help from Larry Page at Google, another reason he'd been persuaded to move to Oxford.

The professor was surprised to see Harrison around campus so early. "You've either been up all night, or you've got another app in development Mr Ng."

"Very perceptive Professor, it's the latter, and I need your help on this one." Being one of the top students in his class had some perks and Harrison was lucky to have a good relationship with the otherwise abrasive professor.

"What is it this time? Wearable tech again or are you looking at in-car operating systems integration?"

"No, this one has a little bit more soul," Harrison couldn't avoid being cryptic. "I'm working on something with Aston North."

"North? He could probably do with your guidance, maybe something to help him concentrate in class more."

"Well, this will kinda help him focus." Harrison smiled at the professors observations and preceded to explain his problems with Airdrop and his inability to get it to accept multiple sources. The academic was keen to understand the data sources and their use, but Harrison was trying not to give too much away. As he knew he would, the professor spotted the error. Harrison had sought to transpose the code for one link into multiples but needed an include that would never have been apparent to anyone without the experience the professor had. After that it just led to more questions, he wasn't letting up with the sources.

"So your analysing four incoming data sets and transmitting data based on this section of the code. These are biometric data sources are they not?"

Harrison couldn't help but answer. "Yes, I'm using a number of devices to monitor heart rate, temperature, respiratory and brain activity, which I'm influencing with transcranial direct current stimulation" he knew he'd let on too much.

"So that was what that email was about, is it for North? What on earth are you two doing? Is this anything to do with him missing tutorials and lectures this week? I think you need to tell me, Harrison. I don't mind helping you with CS code and solutions relating to study, but I'm not aiding students who are messing with their health and especially influencing brain activity using direct current."

Harrison knew Aston would be mad, but he'd dug himself a hole and continued to tell the professor the whole story. He could tell from the professors reactions and subsequent questions that he may have said too much. To his credit he did offer a few positive solutions, one being adapting the fingerprint security scanner on the iPhone to pick up the heartbeat, something the professor had been working on for a medical app of his own. The conversation then turned to ethics something Harrison wasn't expecting.

"Have you or Mr North thought about the religious implications of what you are doing?"

"I know that I haven't Professor, I've never really given much credence to the church whichever denomination it is."

"Well maybe you should, reincarnation or whatever Mr North thinks he has uncovered isn't something that many religions, including my own, buy into. My diocese would take a discovery of this magnitude very seriously."

Harrison was slightly taken aback by the sudden switch in his mood, the tone of his voice changed dramatically and never thought a man of science, especially computer science, would be deeply religious. His phone vibrated signalling an incoming call, and he was quite glad of the distraction. Showing the phone to Professor Ferris as he walked out, he took the call outside.

"Ellie glad you called, how can I help. It's the bag isn't it, you're on the way there aren't you. What time will you be there?"

"Yes H as ever you answered your own question" Ellie replied. "I'll be at the flat in about 30 minutes."

"Cool, you've saved me from a rather awkward moment with Ferris, details later." He checked his watch it was half past one. "I'll be there at two okay."

"Okay" Ellie sounded a little confused, but he hung up so he could make his excuses and get away from the now slightly odd professor.

As Harrison opened the laboratory door, he could hear Professor Ferris was on the phone himself as he caught the tail end of his call.

"...I'll give you more detail this evening — no I can't the student will be back any minute — I just thought you should know that's why I called. Yes — what these kids are doing isn't right, they're into past life regression and trying to prove reincarnation of the soul. Yes reincarnation, I know how you feel, that's why I called, I wanted to check you were okay to meet. I'll try to get more detail and will see you later." Harrison heard him hang up, so he pushed the door fully open and re-entered the room.

"I've got to go Professor!" It was all he could do to stop himself reacting to what he'd heard.

The professor was suddenly excessively keen to help, but Harrison made his excuses, grabbed his bag and made a hasty retreat. The knot in his stomach was starting to grow knowing Aston wasn't going to like what had just happened.

CHAPTER SIX

"Mom do you have a wifi connection?" Aston hadn't stayed at his mom's new house since he'd been at university. Before that he'd taken a year out and travelled through Europe, Australia and America, so he hadn't lived with her for close to 3 years now. She had managed to move all the stuff from his room from their old Finsbury Park home into the swanky Knightsbridge flat, which was very handy, and he had to admit that after seeing the new place he may be inclined to visit more often. Just so long as the broadband internet access is reasonable. He'd been stalling visiting her since starting the second year, so his mom had secured a moral victory in getting him back.

"It's written on top of the modem thingy in the study!"

"Thanks, Mom."

"You should be resting Aston. The doctor said no physical activity for the next few days" she was in the doorway with a concerned look on her face.

"I'll just get this code into my phone so I can FaceTime the guys and see what I've missed at Uni." What he meant is that he can catch up with Harrison and find out how the tech was coming along and discuss the next reboot. It was his first thought once he'd woken up and checked the time. He'd been asleep for over eight hours which was very unusual, and he felt like he'd missed half a day of his life then smiling to himself realised that may be something he should get used to now.

"Okay you do that, and I'll make us a cup of tea. You should also speak to Ellie and check what time she's bringing your clothes tomorrow."

He'd been stalling that call as well, not only was he a little wary that his Mom was trying to match-make but felt weird that he kind of owed Ellie for saving his life now. Added to this were a mixture of pride, his own feelings about her and the confused messages she was giving him. He knew she could be the perfect girl for him but was he ready to commit during his second year at University. "Too intense," he said to himself. I'll phone H instead, he'll know when she's coming.

He connected the wifi, 'four bars not bad considering the position of the modem' he thought, he was tempted to use the free wifi options that listed. "You should tell your neighbours they should protect their networks mom."

"What?"

"Nothing, doesn't matter" H would have a field day with these he thought.

"Would you like anything to eat?"

"No mom, just tea's fine...maybe later."

The call was dialling as his mom bought him the tea, including a couple of chocolate digestives.

"H" his friend's face came through on the screen just as he bit into a biscuit.

"Hey, you're looking better I see. Getting looked after by mom?"

"Hmm, all good" he managed with his mouth full. "Just got up actually."

"Spot of tea, darling." Harrison continued his wind up.

"So what's new your end?" Aston was keen to focus his friend and stop the joke and the posh accent before he got carried away. "New tech arrived?"

"You bet. Got delivered about an hour ago, it's awesome...hang on." Harrison's head disappeared from the screen, and Aston could hear the scrabble of wires, and plastic, the rustle of papers then a loud thud, and the screen jumped, Harrison swore and then reappeared rubbing the back of his head. He was wearing a headset made up of two V-shaped arms either side of his temple with circular nodes at the ends of each V. He tried not to laugh, but the fact that Harrison had bumped his head on his desk just tipped him over the edge. "Aw fuck that hurt, sorry, I was too eager to show these bad boys off." He turned to show the side and the back were connected a little like headphones. "What do you reckon? I know they look a little freaky, but it has blue tooth connection and check out the back." Harrison pulled off the headset and showed him the housing at the back contains the battery and CPU "Google glasses but with a view into the mind!"

"Let's see if they work first, but have to admit they look good. I was expecting mini sponges and a copper wire, but again you've surpassed my expectations. How long does the battery last?"

"It says 12 hours full use in the promo material, but that may need testing, and we would only need full function at the start and end, I need to play around with it some more and work on the app integration, but I got some great tips and advice from Professor Ferris." Harrison's face reddened as he inadvertently mentioned the Professor in his excitement.

"What did you tell him H, please tell me you didn't?"

"Well..." Aston knew something was up. It was so much easier to tell when someone's hiding something over a video call.

"H you bloody better not have, this needs to be kept between the three of us. Come on you know. You heard how weird the doctor was about this." Harrison's facial expression gave the game away. "Not him of all people. He's a dick and I don't trust him, and he bloody hates me."

"What can I say, I needed a solution to be able to get this working in time Aston" he waved the headset at him "I didn't go there with the intention of telling him, it came out as we were problem-solving. I wasn't to know he was all religious and shit."

"What? — What do you mean religious? What did he say? I just meant he wouldn't be able to keep it quiet."

Aston's face went white as Harrison told him about the telephone call the Professor had made.

"What the fuck! Who the hell did he call?" Aston tried to remain calm, but he knew his voice was getting louder. His mom called out to check all was well. He lowered his voice, "Look I'm sorry, it's not your fault, well not entirely, we've got a few days before I'm back at Oxford so let's see if he says or does anything. Do you think you'll get the TDCS tech working by then?"

"I'm sure I'll have it ready by tomorrow and Aston. I'm as pissed off as you are, trust me. I'm really sorry."

"Look H, I couldn't do this without your help, so it's not a drama. Let's hope Ferris doesn't make it into one. Let's aim to try another reboot when I'm back, say Monday night, and then we can show him and his mystery mate the truth."

"I'll send you the link to download the app on your phone so you can see how it's going, you'll need to change your Apple ID to the dev one we set up, though."

"Okay, can't wait, just don't send it to anyone else," Aston said with a wink. "Oh yeah, I almost forgot, did Ellie pick up the bag and what time is she coming?"

"Yep, she's got your bag and said she had to be in London early, something about seeing her sister. She said she'd be at yours around midday."

"Cheers H saves me a call, maybe I'll just text her instead. I'll speak to you tomorrow."

He hung up the call and shouted down to his Mom "Ellie's coming over at midday tomorrow Mom."

"That's perfect I'll be back from my coffee morning by then."

Aston rolled his eyes at the thought, then smiled as that might give him an opportunity to be out when Ellie arrived. He finished his tea and sat up on his bed, folded his legs into the Padmasana pose and began his meditation routine.

19a Cadogan Square, Knightsbridge, Ellie checked her phone again, yep she definitely had the right address, she felt a little awkward as she rang the intercom again. Looking through the grand glass entry doors she never realised Aston's mother was so well off, a far cry from her own roots, still no reply, she dropped his bag on the floor, 'Typical, I wonder where he could be? Probably asleep or meditating.' For a moment, the idea that he might have attempted a reboot on his own crossed her mind. She started typing out a text message to him, just as the sound of footsteps came from behind her. She turned to see Aston's mother. She looked like a star, her flawless complexion shone in the daylight, although casual, her styling seemed straight out of the pages of Vogue magazine and was that a Louis Vuitton Capucine bag she was holding. "Hi Mrs North," Ellie said, "I'm so glad to see you, and I hope you don't mind me saying you look absolutely incredible, is that a Capucine?"

"Thanks my dear" she kissed her on the cheek, "yes it is, got it just last week, but we can talk more inside, why hasn't Aston let you in?"

"I've been waiting here about five minutes I was just about to text him when you arrived." She finished the text adding - I'm with your Mom, where are you - you git!! and pressed send.

"Well that won't do, he's probably sleeping, at least, I hope he is." They looked at each other both thinking about the reason they were here. "You don't think he's had another episode?" Ellie grabbed Aston's bag and followed his mom into the grand hallway, who had now started to run up the entrance staircase not at all slowed down by her heels. They reached the front door of the apartment Aston's mother had the key in the lock when Ellie's mobile pinged, by the time she got her phone out to read his reply, his mom was already holding the note he had left in the kitchen.

"He's just popped out," they said in almost unison.

"The little shit" his mother added "don't think I've ever made it up those stairs that quick before. Especially in these heels! I'm so sorry for my son Ellie, far too much like his father."

"I'm used to it Mrs North. He's the same at Oxford."

"Would you like a cup of tea? Please call me Helen, I think we're passed the formality, especially after my son's latest little stunt."

"That would be nice Mrs N... Sorry Helen." Ellie wasn't going to get used to being on first name terms with his mother anytime soon, but she made an effort all the same as she was starting to like her. "Where should I put this?" She lifted Aston's bag into view.

"Oh just leave it there, we can pop it in his room later, or Aston can sort it out when he gets back. Do you take sugar?"

"No thanks."Ellie looked around the kitchen. It was exactly what she would have expected in a million pound plus Knightsbridge apartment. It was immaculate like a show home but nicer, it looked like no one lived there, all things had their place with no clutter, she knew Aston would soon mess that up.

"Let's take these into the sitting room shall we." Aston's mother handed her a mug, she had been expecting a china cup and saucer, but unflustered Ellie followed her through to a quite astounding room, dominated by the floor to ceiling sash windows, that had a view of the fenced off gardens Ellie had peaked into on her way there. The furniture was immaculate, very opulent with a range of fabrics in neutral tones that enhanced the look, yet still had a homely feel that complemented the decadent styling. She was a little apprehensive to sit down hoping not to spill her tea but followed Aston's mothers lead, placed her mug on the ornate glass coffee table and perched on the edge of the mocha coloured sofa.

"This is an exquisite home, Helen." Ellie still felt a little awkward being so personal, but when in Rome she thought.

"Why thanks, Ellie, very sweet of you to say, Aston didn't even mention it. I can't believe he isn't here, so rude! Now that's two compliments you've given me today. I should thank you for bringing Aston's belongings with you. I do hope you didn't come to all the way to London just to deliver my sons clothes."

"Oh it's no bother, I was already planning to head up today, it was a free day at Uni, and I had some things to sort out, plus I got to check out the sales."

"Probably best to do it before the weekend, Oxford Street is murder nowadays on the weekends, especially when the sales are on."

"You must enjoy the location. Being so central to everything."

"Well, you're welcome to stay at any time my dear, I now consider you a close friend of the family. So tell me more about what you and Aston were up to that got him into hospital."

Ellie was a little shocked at the sudden change of topic and somewhat taken aback trying to think of what to say. "I — I guess I should leave that explanation to Aston." She managed to rescue herself, or so she thought.

"Well he's been very aloof, spun some yarn about a science experiment and hasn't said anything else on the matter, I was hoping to get a chance to speak to you about it. I'm a little worried about him." Ellie could sense that his mother was reaching out to her, and her own inner conflict about what he was doing saw an avenue for release.

"Mrs North, sorry Helen, I can tell you what I know, but your son has been quite forthright with Harrison and me about keeping this a secret so I must implore you not to tell anyone else."

Ellie took the last sip of her tea and then gave Aston's mother a very simple overview of the events from the last week. As the story unfolded, she kept edging closer, and when Ellie reached the part about bringing Aston back to life with the adrenalin shot, her face turned a weird shade of pale and Ellie thought she was about to faint.

"Oh my god. What on earth does he think he's doing. I don't believe it! I know he told the doctor it was a hypnotic state but transcending souls. Ellie, my dear, you have to stop him."

"I don't have that influence over him. I voiced my objections and only agreed to help so I could be there to make sure nothing went wrong."

"Well, it's a bloody good job you stuck by him. You know I blame the nanny in Hong Kong, she was always teaching him about meditation, taking him on temple visits and schooling him ancient Chinese and Buddhist ways!"

"He has mentioned her to me before; Grace wasn't it?" Ellie was intrigued about getting a little more information about Aston's childhood so wasn't afraid to probe as his mother seemed willing to offload some issues.

"Grace Li, his father hired her, I did think it made sense, and I wasn't in the right mind having to put my career on hold after I moved out there for him. Aston got far too close to her, and she to him for my liking. One of the positive outcomes of us leaving Hong Kong was breaking that bond. I'm sure he would have become a monk if we had stayed any longer. Just wait 'til he gets home I'll give him a soul reboot."

Ellie started to get concerned that his mother would make a big scene when he came back, and Aston would blame Ellie for letting her know. She began to backtrack and deflect the blame.

"Helen, it wasn't something he planned to do, it was the hypnotist show that led him to discover that he could. He was a little reluctant to get involved with that, to be honest."

"Well, Ellie I'm going to put a stop to this even if I have to hypnotise him myself!"

Aston stopped his run to check his messages. Ellie had got there okay, he smiled to himself at her tone and sent a quick reply, although the thought of his mom and Ellie spending time together wasn't that appealing he was rather glad that he didn't have to rush back straight away. He had rather hoped his mom would be back in time especially after she said she would only be out for the morning, and he wasn't sure what to say to Ellie if he was by himself. The whole life-saving thing still played on his mind. He would be forever grateful as she'd saved his life. He felt indebted to her, and that changed the dynamic of their friendship now, and if he was honest, it dented his ego somehow, but he wasn't sure why. He'd hoped the run would clear his head and give him a fresh perspective and so far it wasn't working.

He'd woken late, and his ribs had felt a lot more comfortable, he'd missed his exercise regime for the last few days so felt compelled to get back into it. He'd managed most of his usual reps without too much difficulty and felt the need for a run to stretch his legs. He didn't have his usual running gear, but thought the sweatpants, trainers and T-shirt he'd worn from the hospital would be sufficient. He wasn't planning on running too far and knew a change of clothes would be with Ellie on his return so after writing his Mom a quick note in the kitchen he had grabbed the spare key, his phone and headphones and left the apartment at a gentle pace. Within five minutes he was into Hyde Park, it was enormous compared to the grounds at Oxford, he felt so much better and decided to extend his run and try a complete lap of Hyde and Kensington Gardens. It was such an impressive place, steeped in history. He headed North and in no time had rounded speakers corner, as he jogged he was intrigued by the diversity of people that he passed. He'd skirted around the top of the Serpentine and the Italian Gardens, then stopped for a second debating in his head whether to do a lap around the lake. His jogging app told him he done almost two miles. 'Maybe a little too far to do both' he thought, so he stuck with the plan and set off towards Kensington Palace. As he passed by he began to imagine the people in the park in different period costumes and how the landmarks would have looked back then. As he rounded the bottom corner, he could see the Albert Hall looming in the distance and then realised that he could soon have the ability to actually experience those times. At the memorial, he slowed down to a walk and turned around to take it all in. Aston wondered whether any of his other former souls were London based, Warwick was here, so it may have been a possibility. The voice on his jogging app pulled him back to the present day announcing he had covered 3.5 miles in 20 minutes. His thoughts went back to Ellie and realised that it would be best to head back and save her from his mother or maybe the other way around. He sent her a text to tell him he was just around the corner and apologised for being late then started for home.

Ellie and his mother together still played on his mind as he crossed Carriage Drive into Park Close heading for Knightsbridge and home. On the corner was The Wellington club, a large poster with a familiar name on it caught his attention. He almost ran past it, but the face stopped him, he turned and took a few steps closer. It was the same poster that had promoted the hypnotist show at Oxford. It was the face of the French hypnotist that triggered a memory from somewhere other than the show. He stared at the poster trying to think where he'd seen it and took a photo of it just in case it came to him later. Then it hit him. It was just a few days ago, but it wasn't his memory it was Warwick's. He had seen the same face in the Marquee club talking to the guy they thought was one of the Beatles. 'How could that be, is it his relative or is my mind mixed up' he thought?

He didn't hear the footsteps behind and was about to turn to head home when he was suddenly lifted up by his arms. "What the fuck?" He turned his head left and then right, to see two stone-faced burly looking guys in suits and ties holding him up, the grip locked his arms and elbows to his sides. He couldn't move.

"What the fuck are you doing?!"

They didn't say a word or even look at him, just carried him quickly towards the door of the club. They pushed their way through, Aston's legs swinging about as if his was still running in mid air, they carried him into a darkened room. Someone was following behind them who clicked the lock on the door, turned on the lights then said: "It's okay, let him go." Aston recognised the French accent straight away.

CHAPTER SEVEN

Leonardo Desangé finished his ritual, he regulated his breathing, uncrossed his legs, let his mind filter back to a relaxed state and stood ready to face another day. It was 8 am, the hour he spent meditating, spotlighting attention to focus on and accelerate the twelve natural meridian lines, it was something he had been doing every day for almost two centuries. This acceleration technique was intrinsic to increasing the bodies regenerative process, stimulating the cells to reproduce at twice the normal rate and thus deflect the ageing process. This technique was the gift he'd been given by Lei Wei and for just a moment, thoughts of his old master came back to him. The reminiscence was fleeting and soon dismissed as his modern day life took over. He planned his day in his head, as he'd taught himself over the years 'success comes to people who plan and strive for it.' Today he had to visit the Wellington club to check on the stage and lighting for his gig that evening. He also pre-played out the afternoon meeting with the Chinese investors he had agreed to, following their significant investment. His mantra was to focus on imagining how the key milestones on any business day would play out; he liked to strategise how he would encounter any issues or scenarios.

Just a few hours later, he was thinking again about his morning's plan. He had definitely not foreseen what was happening at a little before one o'clock in the afternoon, or more precisely who would be involved, and he had definitely not planned what he was about to do next.

"It's him! I'm certain of it."

"Who Mr Desangé?"

He leaned into the front of the car and pointed to the youth peering at the poster through the club window. "That boy there, staring at the poster, it's him the kid from Oxford. We need to detain him. I want to speak to him, he may have something for us and could make a good shifter." The urgency in his voice prompted his companions attention.

"Detain him?" Elliot said confused, "But we have the Chinese meet in at three o'clock?"

"This will not take long Elliot and for gods sake they can wait! You and Nigel grab him, carry him to the club, and I'll follow you. If he doesn't oblige, I'll erase his memory just to be safe. Nigel pull up slowly just opposite."

As they approached Elliot gestured to Nigel indicating how he planned to grab the boy by his elbows, the kid seemed to be transfixed with the poster which made their surprise snatch easier. Desangé checked around to see if anyone noticed before following them through the main door into the Wellington club.

Positioned just off Kensington Avenue, the club was small, exclusive and only open to private members. The Wellington club often had small bands, comedians and entertainers most days of the week. This evening it was scheduled to be the return of the successful Hypnotist. The club was the last in a small venue run that had proved quite lucrative for him, running for the past three months it had uncovered a few potential recruits but also gave him the chance to exorcise his demons by manipulating and humiliating the English middle class. The small but exclusive club was as conservative in its decor as it was its patrons. Desangé followed his driver, and his trusted advisor passed the sparse entrance hall and cloakroom. He then ushered them left into the main bar and through to the extra function room, which he usually used as a makeshift dressing room. He was sure no staff had seen them and closed the door.

"Bonjour Mon Ami, it appears fate has dealt me a splendid hand." The boy looked very nervous, wide-eyed and seemed to be staring right through him. "I'm sorry for the dramatic treatment, but I've been eager to speak to you since we last met."

"Mon Ami?? What are you? Deluded or something! You don't just snatch people off the streets!" The boy was irate, still rubbing his arms from the snatch, but didn't break contact with his eyes. It was if he was studying him.

"Look I'm sorry, no harm done. You are okay now, yes?" Desangé gestured to his arms." I just wanted to talk about your hypnotism. You remember me from Oxford, no?" The nod of the head gave him, at least, a little encouragement. "You are okay are you not? Would you like a drink? Nigel get him a drink." Desangé pointed over to the makeshift bar and the stack of Coke cans, and the driver passed one to the boy. He opened the can took a sip but still didn't look away. Desangé was keen to get this done quickly so laid his cards on the table. "I think you have a talent, one I believe could be useful to our group."

"You can stick your group, I'm not buying this okay, just let me go" the kid was not calming down.

"Mon Ami, just relax, and listen to what I have to tell you — now take a deep breath." The kid took a breath as instructed. "Now take second," he did as instructed. "This might be easier than I thought" Desangé started to smile as he continued with the opening line from his act. "Good, that's good — now imagine yourself..."

"You're a fool if you think that's going to work on me anymore." The kid was obviously not going to succumb to hypnosis on verbal command. "I'm not going under that easily. You should know that, as you said — I have talent. I'm gonna call the Police. Right now!" The kid searched in his pocket for his phone and looked perplexed when he couldn't find it.

"Nigel!"

Leonardo's driver had the phone in his hands. He walked up to the kid and grabbed his hand. He pushed his index finger onto the home button to activate the fingerprint ID scanner. The driver then tossed the unlocked phone towards his boss. Desangé looked at the phone and then took a picture of the kid.

"Fingerprint ID, so secure, I do admire this new technology, whatever next?" He read a few of the texts looking for what he needed.

"Aston! This is interesting" he searched the phone contacts. "Aston North in fact."

"Look just give me back my phone, let me go, and I'll listen to whatever you have to say."

The kid was still staring at him intently but sounded genuine. Desangé tossed him his phone, he had the information that he needed and hoped its return would instil some calm into young Mr North. The surprised look had gone from his face, and he seemed to have at least accepted the situation.

Desangé was still a bit bemused at his stares, though, almost as if the kid recognised him. He looked at his watch, fifteen minutes if Aston North wasn't interested in what he was about to tell him, then the plan would be to hypnotise him, get at the information needed and then silence him one way or the other.

Aston was trying not to panic, how could he work his way out of this, but even more worrying was how come the guy who had just kidnapped him could have possibly been at the Jimi Hendrix gig back in 1968. It was definitely him, and he hasn't aged at all. Aston had been studying his face trying to rationalise another explanation, as well as having to fend off his attempt at hypnosis. He pressed his ribs to send a shot of pain to clear his head, 'be calm, cooperate or at least try to give that impression.' He caught his phone after the hypnotist threw it back. 'When did they lift that' he thought 'great now he has my details.' He told himself to stay calm, just hear him out and maybe call the police or get a message to H while he's talking.

"We have your talent too," the hypnotist said. "But much more refined, your ability to achieve a deeper state while under hypnosis opens up possibilities you can't believe. If you join us, I can show you — I can teach you."

Aston activated his phone inside his pocket and started to text his friend, then stopped short as the hypnotist said something that instantly sidetracked him. All of a sudden he knew the answer to why he'd seen him at the Hendrix gig.

"We are soul shifters Mr North, we can shift back in time within our souls lifetime. The experience you had under hypnosis at my show made me believe that you too could have that ability, and possibly more given the right mentor. I can make your mind more powerful than you could imagine, give you a gift that was bestowed on me a long time ago."

Aston thought for a while and whether it was bravado or just plain one-up-man-ship he played his own hand. "I'm in no need for a mentor, and I don't want your help, I've realised the power of what my mind is capable of." The hypnotist's face seemed to darken slightly. "I've harnessed what you only uncovered at the show all by myself and guess what?"

"What Mr North?" His frown became just that little bit darker.

"It turns out that you're not the only one who can shift back in time. In fact, that's why you found me here, I recognised your face, not from Oxford but from London in the sixties."

"That's impossible" the henchman to the left seemed shocked, "you couldn't have been alive then..."

"Elliot shut up, let him talk — I told you he had talent," a slight smile had replaced his frown "go on, Mr North, please go on."

Aston wasn't sure whether he should continue or try and make a break for it, the guy called Elliot had stepped away from the door to be closer to his boss. He decided against it but was conscious he should try to move a little as he spoke.

"I used the experience at your Oxford hypnosis as a starting point and..." He was a little reluctant to spill all the details "...and I guess I rebooted to a former life. It was January 1968, the Marquee Club. Hendrix was playing. I saw you brown nosing with the Beatles entourage. I see you still like small venues."

"That's fascinating" the hypnotist ignored the sarcasm. "This reboot as you call it, did you have any help?"

"Purely my own skills, I don't need any help."

"You're wrong Aston, with my help you could fully understand how to control this reboot, and how it can lead to incredible power and enormous wealth. If you join us, we can show you your true potential."

"I'm pretty certain I can realise my own potential, and I think I'm going to have to reject your offer, I never really got into the whole gang banger thing, just not my scene."

Aston's quick witted and sarcastic comments had landed him in trouble before, but he couldn't help himself sometimes. Although judging by the faces of the two men opposite he may well be in more trouble than he initially thought. He had managed to make a few small steps to his left and was now in line with the door.

"I think I'll let myself out" he turned on his heels ready to grab the door, but the big guy Nigel blocked his path. Aston had failed to notice that he'd moved to block the door, literally bouncing off him and ending up sat in a heap where he started.

"I think I say when you can leave Mr North" the hypnotist tone and demeanour had changed dramatically.

Desangé was incensed, yes this kid has something, but his stubbornness and contempt irritated him, but he was intrigued by this past life story and the fact their paths had crossed.

"So good of you to decide to stay Aston" the boys face didn't register the party of sarcasm. "So tell me more about the Marquee club, who else did you see me talking too?" The boy didn't answer. "No, not so willing to converse now. Okay, tell me why you chose to shift back to that moment and what was your past life doing there? Was this another random past life experience or did you select this for a reason?" Desangé remembered the gig. Hendrix had pulled an audience of the London elite not just musicians but from the entertainment world, big business, politics, and industry. He was there with a major client who was about to take a fall, but they couldn't know that.

"So were you there for the gig or were you there just to follow me?"

"Why would I be there to follow you?" The kid looked puzzled, but at least, he was starting to get something out of him. "I'm still trying to figure out how you could be there? You haven't aged, what's with that?"

"That is the second element of shifting. You see - I've been around for a couple of centuries, I'm able to counter and control the ageing process, a gift given to me and one I only share with those who show the ability and have the foresight to benefit from it. Tell me why you were there Mr North, and then let me show you what your new found ability could do."

He seemed to hesitate, considering his reply but eventually the kid replied. "It was a random reboot, shift or whatever you want to call it. I saw you, and I wish I hadn't because if I hadn't, I wouldn't be here and would like you to let me go, else I'm calling the police and as for joining your merry band of immortal weirdos it's still no with a capital N!"

Again the kids brashness fuelled his temper, Desangé knew he had to draw the line.

"You have one chance left Mr North. I don't want to do something you might regret. I'm offering you the opportunity to be part of a life-changing venture, and I honestly believe you have a raw talent that will mutually benefit both of us. You can either remember this moment as a milestone or, I can make sure you forget it ever happened and a lot more besides."

The kid was still sat on the floor smiling at him "I'm sorry exactly which part of no couldn't you grasp, or would you prefer me to translate for you."

Elliot was livid "Enough is enough, are you going to let this little shit goad us like this?"

"You're right Elliot, and no I'm not" Desangé walked directly towards his antagonist, he maintained eye contact as the boy stood up but he had no time to react. Desangé raised his forehand and very quickly applied a sharp snap of his wrist that directed enough momentum to Aston's forehead and uttered "sleep now." The kid fell to the floor lifeless. His conscious state entirely switched off with the combination of the simple trigger word and the sharp jolting movement to his brain.

"Why didn't you just do that twenty minutes ago?" Elliot looked at him and rolled his eyes.

"I wasn't a hundred percent convinced it would work but as you correctly pointed out his goading was becoming too tiresome. It's a back door hypnosis method I install in most of the people at my shows just in case they get out of hand. Works well wouldn't you say!"

"Very handy, you'll need to share that one! Now can we go?"

Desangé contemplated getting into the kids mind there and then to see what he knew, but he would need more time and privacy.

"Yes okay, Nigel stick the little bastard in the car, and we can deal with him later."

Desangé followed his two counterparts and their captive out to the car. The side street was seemingly empty, so two men carrying a boy by his shoulders didn't attract any attention. They shoved him into the back seat; his unconscious body slumped up against the rear door.

"Hang on one-second" Desangé turned back towards the club.

"What's up?" Elliot enquired.

"I'm going to tell the manager to cancel the show. You may also want to call the Chinese and tell them to reschedule our meeting."

"This little shit better not screw up any more of my plans." Elliot pulled out his phone and dialled. Desangé walked away and didn't see Elliot take a vicious swipe at the boy with his elbow. Neither did he hear his subsequent groan as a trace of blood trickled down from the corner of his mouth.

The elbow hit him hard, the pain coursed through his body. He couldn't contain the moan, it took all his mental strength not to cry out, he gritted his teeth and tasted the blood as his lip split inside his mouth. He had been expecting something along those lines back inside the club a few moments back, as the hypnotist approached him. Although when he had raised his hand with an outstretched palm, Aston felt certain it was the rapid induction hypnosis method he'd seen a week ago, coming his way. He made an instant decision and feigned going under, hoping that the hypnotist wouldn't try to check that he was totally unconscious, he knew he couldn't fake it if they had checked by burning him with a match or a sticking him with a needle. He'd also gambled on the fact they would try to move him once he was under, for, now it seemed to have paid off.

With his eyes tightly closed he relied on his other senses and heard footsteps approaching the car, which from what he could smell seemed new and the sizeable leather seats he was on meant it was probably a high-end model. For a moment, his male curiosity as to the make of the car tempted him to grab a quick sneak, but the brevity of the situation he was in tempered that thought as the hypnotist opened the car door.

"What happened to him, is he bleeding?"

"I think he may have caught his face on the door frame getting into the car," Elliot lied, "he's still under, though."

"No bother really, deservedly so, can you believe what he said in there. I've half a mind to kill the little shit and dump him in the Thames as we cross it. He now knows too much about us, but as we've got things coming up, I figure I'll just erase his memory when we get back, and then leave him to work out which life he's in. Can you believe he shifted back, quite remarkable, but if he's as stubborn as he makes out he's just not going to be any use to us. What do you think Elliot? Think he was genuine about the Hendrix gig?"

"I don't care, let's just get out of here and sort the Chinese out. Personally, I'm for the Thames, but it will have to be later, we need to be back in the office."

Aston knew time was not on his side, he needed to get out of here and the sooner, the better. Just after they had pulled away, the car jolted to a stop which pushed Aston forwards into the seat in front of him.

"Should we put his seatbelt on?"

At least, someone showed some concern for him. Aston figured it was the driver.

"No need really, he won't be here that long — hopefully." The snide comment raised a laugh, and Elliot shoved him sidewards, so his face was pressed against the car window. The nudge was exactly what Aston needed, it now gave him an opportunity to open one eye without being noticed, so he could possibly work out where he was and hopefully see a way out.

Although not being used to the area, Aston was soon able to get his bearings. A road sign for Brompton Road swung into view as they turned right and as they moved slowly through the congested traffic he could also make out the bright green flags on the side of Harrods department store. It wasn't too far from his moms, so making a break for it, now, would be his best bet. Aston caught a glimpse of the traffic flow behind them in the mirror, momentarily he was distracted as he saw the elegant bonnet and realised it was a Bentley Continental. 'Very flash, probably the only time I get to ride in one, and I'm a bloody captive' he mused. In the same instant, Aston saw his escape in the mirror. Coming up in the clear outside lane was a black cab travelling at some speed. Aston hoped that the Bentley wouldn't have child locks, and as he had no seatbelt on, the element of surprise was on his side if only he could time it right. A seconds slip and he may just be doing the hypnotist a favour by throwing himself in front the of the cab and being splattered all over the road.

Aston manoeuvred his hand slowly onto the door release, he could open it without giving any hint of movement or warning to his captors. He stole a last look at the black cab in the mirror which was almost on them, took a deep breath and counted to himself, 'one, two, three,' then pulled the release. Aston used all the effort his cramped muscles could muster and pushed open the door. With the forward momentum in his favour, he dived across the road to the opposite side. In his head, the split-second escape lasted much longer as the world around him seemed to slow down. His timing was sublime, he held the Bentley door wide open for a microsecond, his hand released it just as the cab smashed straight into the door, the glass shattered exploding into the air. The door ripped off its hinges and careered forward, spinning onto the tarmac and the screech of back cab's brakes seemed to mute all the other traffic noise. Aston rolled to the opposite side of the road and jumped up, normal time was now restored. A double decker bus was just beginning to pull away towards Hyde Park, the driver knew to keep his schedule despite the collision in his mirrors. Aston bolted towards it as it picked up speed, he leapt on the back end, jamming his figures into the gaps in the coachwork for grip, holding on for all his worth, his feet scrambling to get balance on the bumper. His rock climbing skills tested to the max as he held on for dear life. The bus gained speed, his fingers strained in the gaps, the skin tearing on the sharp edges, but somehow Aston held on as the number 11 carried him towards safety. He could hear his former captors screaming after him, he strained to turn his head enough to see the chaos he'd just created. The Bentley minus its door, the cab driver standing over the wreckage and the guy called Elliot starting to run towards him. The bus seemed to slow, but he heard the hypnotist yell some French expletive and his pursuer gave up the chase.

It only appeared to be a few hundred yards down the road when the bus pulled to a stop, Aston released his grip and jumped off the back, his fingers ached, balling them into a fist hoping to restore the feeling. 'I'm certainly raking up the war wounds' he thought to himself. Conscious that he wasn't as far away as he'd like, and after a quick glance back down towards Harrods to see if anyone was following, he sprinted across the road and headed back towards Knightsbridge and 19 Cadogan Square.

CHAPTER EIGHT

Ellie jumped up at the sound of the door opening, she'd exhausted all avenues of meaningful conversation about half an hour ago and was contemplating her own escape from Aston's mothers having given up on him coming back. She followed his mother towards the door expecting her to give him a severe rollicking, not only for being over an hour late, which he deserved but also, and this made her slightly nervous, about what Ellie had told her about his recent hospital stay.

Ellie was taken by surprise when she hugged him, but when he looked up from his mother's embrace and smiled at her she too realised he'd been in some sort of trouble. His bottom lip was swollen, there was a nasty contusion on his forehead, he certainly looked like he'd been in a car crash. She sat open mouthed, as did his mother, as Aston told them he'd been clipped by a cyclist courier while running back to the house and had then fallen head first into a parked car. His poor mother wanted to take him straight back to hospital for a full checkup, but as Ellie thought he might, he managed to persuade her otherwise. As they walked back to the kitchen, he turned to her and said: "It's good to see you Ellie, and thanks for bringing my stuff, I think I'm gonna need the extra clothes now."

Once again her nurturing instincts kicked in as she helped tend to his wounds.

"Just sit down, it looks like I'm turning out to be your very own private nurse!"

Aston's mother looked up a little-taken aback from the suggestion, she handed over the first aid box and left the kitchen. Aston smiled at Ellie as she got on with her task, luckily the kit was reasonably well stocked with proper gauze and dressings, not the standard band-aids. Ellie kept quiet as she tended to his injuries, after cleaning the wounds she applied the sterile dressings to his face and then on his hands, at which point she started to

73

get an idea that there may be more to his story than he was willing to say.

"Aston, these wounds aren't from a fall off the kerb are they, tell us what actually happened? Your hands are pretty shredded and your lip. Have you been in a fight?"

"It was the hypnotist!"

"What?" Ellie said a little too loudly, and his mother overheard.

"Is everything okay?" Aston mom called from the other room and poked her head around the door.

"It's fine Mom - I was just telling Ellie about Harrison." He lied and his quizzical expression at Ellie indicated she should play along.

"Oh him, I'm not sure he's a good influence on you, he's a little shady for my liking." Aston rolled his eyes as his mom walked back out of the room. "I'll draw you a bath Aston so you can get cleaned up."

"Thanks, Mom."

Ellie was still trying to process the fact Aston had been attacked by the hypnotist and with his mother out of the room, Ellie probed a little further.

"So what the hell happened?" Ellie said in a whisper.

"I was on my way back, and as I jogged passed a club I saw a poster promoting his show, I stopped to take a closer look and recognised his face. He was at the club Ellie."

"Is this when he attacked you?"

"No not at the club with the poster, the hypnotist was at the Marquee Club, in the sixties, I saw him during the reboot."

"You didn't mention this before."

"I only realised after seeing his face on the poster. I was staring at his picture when the bastard jumped me."

"What!" Again Ellie said this a little too loudly but thankfully Aston's mother didn't here over the noise from the bath.

As Aston recounted his story her mind was in overdrive, she knew this whole thing would be dangerous, but she was initially concerned about his mental and medical state from the regression and hypnosis. She didn't imagine for a second that this would lead to a maniac, soul shifting, insider dealing criminal.

"You have to go to the police with this Aston. He could have killed you."

"I can't, what proof do I have. You have to admit it sounds a bit far fetched, telling you now I'm not sure I can believe myself, and I was there."

"What about the accident, there must have been witnesses? It was outside Harrods for gods sake surely the Taxi driver would have seen you?"

"I guess, but it would be my word against his, he could create any number of credible stories to explain it away and what do I have? Kidnap, hypnotism, time travel and rogue traders, they'd ridicule me or lock me up for being on drugs!"

Ellie laughed then stopped herself realising the brevity of the situation. "So what's your plan? We can't just carry on as normal, go back to Oxford and wait for him to snatch you again!"

Aston's mother shouted that his bath was ready

"I guess I'm going to have a bath, and then work out what to do." He grinned, no doubt thankful for the distraction.

"That's not funny Aston, this is serious, we need to go the police, I'm worried about you." She said gently touching the dressing on his face.

"I know you care Ellie and I'm stoked that you're with me on this, but we're going to need more proof. Can you hang around? Maybe we can phone H when I get out and see what he thinks."

The thought of waiting around with Aston's mother wasn't appealing and she was conscious that the other reason she'd come up to London was to meet with her sister Jessica. She pulled out her phone from her pocket to check the time, she hadn't noticed the message come in from her sister asking when she would be arriving. "I have to go Aston but I can drop by on my way back from my sisters and we can talk then, it will be late this evening though."

"No that's cool, I could probably do with some rest."

"You should have let your mom take you to the hospital just to be on the safe side."

"No need, I've got my private nurse remember."

"Don't push your luck."

He held out his arms for a hug and smiled, Ellie went to hug him back but remembered the broken ribs that she had inflicted. "How are your ribs?" She placed her hand on his chest and he grimaced with the pain. "Not good then, you really need to rest Aston. How about I come back tomorrow, I can stay with Jessica tonight and then drive you back to Oxford, we can maybe figure out how we tell the police all this on the way back?"

As ever, Aston was noncommittal on the police. "The drive back sounds like a plan, I reckon I can persuade mom to release me. I'll try and speak to H and get his thoughts on how we go from here. I'd really like to find out more about this guy before we go to the police."

His mom stuck her head around the door reminding him that his bath was ready. Ellie took the opportunity to say goodbye and make her own getaway. As she was getting into her car she picked up a text from Aston ' thks Ell, couldn't do this without you, say hi to Jess from me. Glad you two made up.' She started the car, if only it were so simple, her sister might be talking to her now but they we nowhere near as made up as he thought.

Leonardo Desangé sat at the boardroom table, the rearranged meeting with the Chinese had gone very well. The deal was signed, the trade agreed, and the dates were now locked in which made Elliot euphoric and there had been no mention of the delay. Elliot had managed to push it back to five o'clock which allowed them time to sort out the mess with the Bentley and the taxi cab. Desangé massaged his temples as he replayed the events from earlier in his head.

He felt for sure the kid was under, if only he had tried to get inside his mind at the club he would have known. How he had escaped was another matter he'd take up with Elliot, but having to watch the kid get away was as maddening as his refusal to join them. Having to persuade Elliot not to chase him down or shoot him in the street wasn't easy, but the attention around the crash needed to be minimised and quickly, damage limitation was the priority, and it required all of them to deal with it.

Convinced he'd run someone over the cab driver was distraught but he was quite easy to pacify, and such a weak mind accepted the suggestion that it was just the car door being opened by mistake from the wrong side onto oncoming traffic. Desangé had thought about suggesting that it was the cab drivers fault but thought it best to accept responsibility as there were more witnesses involved. They had exchanged insurance details before the police arrived, so it was then just a case of getting Nigel, and Elliot's statement along with his own. A busybody old girl almost complicated things when she butted into the conversation, raving about the boy running off but luckily the police were keen to limit their paperwork and were happy just having the statements from the occupants of both vehicles. With the reports complete it became a formality for them to set up the necessary cordon, direct traffic around the incident and wait for a tow truck for the two vehicles and the mangled door. Elliot had called the office, and they had sent a car to pick them up. They left Nigel to handle any issues with the tow truck, and both had headed back to the office to get ready. On the way back Desangé had kept an eye out just in case he spotted Aston North but knew the kid would be long gone.

During the journey, Elliot had gone off about Leonardo's obsession with this Aston North. He was adamant about dealing with him and suggested shifting back to just before the Oxford show and either stopping the kid from taking part in the show or snuffing him out after it. They'd argued to the point that he had threatened Elliot not to do anything rash, this was a problem he had uncovered and a path he felt that only he could resolve. Elliot eventually backed down but warned Desangé not to let this become a major distraction in their business. He knew that the China deal opened up a massive investment stream for them to exploit, and like so many money motivated men always wanted greater wealth and security.

Elliot was a natural which is why Desangé had partnered with him when they met, his knowledge and insight in the aftermath of the Wall Street stock market crash in 1929 was key to where they are now. He knew to stay out of the consequent bear market to help hide their gains, and his connections in the underworld meant they could further supplement and build their wealth by financing black market enterprises. This background would often lead Elliot to choose a more final, often violent solution with the least consequences or loose ends. Another reason they got on so well, but on this occasion, Desangé had to disagree with his close friend.

Elliot raised the subject again after their Chinese business partners had left, "I need you to be clear of mind leading up to this trade, you know that timing will be paramount, enough distractions with this kid Leonardo. This whole deal could have been blown today because of you, sort your karma, sort the kid out or I'll sort it out for all of us."

Desangé knew he had a point about the kid but for him this was personal, and until he knew the complete truth he couldn't let it go. He walked around the boardroom table to the small bar and poured himself a brandy, he savoured the taste and looked at the label. It was his favourite Napoleon vintage, and it reminded him that there was a connection between him and Aston North he couldn't ignore. After meeting him again and hearing the revelation about his ability to reboot his soul and the story of their paths crossing in the sixties, he knew. He took a large swig and poured another brandy. If the boy could physically encounter his former lives, then not only would this open up new uncharted territory and potential avenues for shifting, but also uncovered a deeper connection between them that the boy couldn't know. The regression at Oxford where Aston North experienced his former soul's death at the battle of Trafalgar was also the day Leonardo Desangé was born.

The rain was torrential but Aston kind of enjoyed it, he felt it somewhat cleansing, and it reminded him of Hong Kong during the monsoon. He looked across at Ellie, who was transfixed, totally concentrated on what little she could see of the road ahead. The wipers on the Mini were going at full tilt, but it was still almost impossible to see out of the car, the rain forming a continual river flowing over the windscreen. The abnormally dark storm clouds made it feel like a late evening rather than midday which made driving the short trip back along the M40 to Oxford all the more hazardous.

"You okay there Ellie?"

"No, shush I'm concentrating, I can't see shit."

"You can still talk and drive."

"No, not unless you want to craaaash." They were getting overtaken by an articulated lorry, the spray from the eighteen wheeler making matters worse. "Oh shit," Ellie was not enjoying the atrocious conditions.

"Keep it straight, keep your distance and we'll be fine," Aston was smiling still looking at Ellie.

"Back seat driver!" she looked at him and glared for a second. "Don't distract me; your safety depends on it."

"It's not like were doing a hundred miles an hour Ellie," he looked over at the speedometer. "You're only doing fifty!"

"There's nothing wrong with being cautious. Safety checks save lives."

"You're so safety conscious, always a stickler for caution. Do you remember tandem skydiving last year, I'm amazed you managed to jump out the plane!"

"That's not fair. Thought I said no talking, I'm trying to concentrate" she said with a hint of the smile he was hoping to see.

"What was it the instructor called you when you questioned his own safety routine!"

Ellie was not taking the bait her concentration couldn't be broke.

"The triple check chick wasn't it? I remember he wasn't too impressed" Aston laughed.

"Well, you would have jumped out alone, probably without a chute! Mr throws caution to the wind. And that guy asked me out afterwards. You don't remember that do you." Her concentration broken she came back at him. "And if it wasn't for my caution and triple checking you might not be alive, remember who saved your life last week!"

Not quite the playful response Aston was trying to prompt, but her tone wasn't hard or aggressive. He always had trouble reading her, though she could be more deadpan than him at times. He knew it was a clear signal not to goad her anymore and had to admit since the life saving his feelings towards her had changed. Aston felt closer to her, more connected but didn't know if it was gratitude or whether he felt in her debt, or was it something else. He did know that the instructor had asked her out because the guy asked him for her mobile number first that's why he remembered the nickname. Aston had refused to give him the 'triple check chicks' number out of some friendship loyalty premise, which on reflection was probably jealousy. As ever though he avoided any discussion of feelings and told her what was really playing on his mind, another reboot.

"I'm going to do it again Ellie. I'm going to reboot again when we get back, and I'm going to need you to help me and possibly save me again." He waited for the reaction, nothing. "I know you think I'm mad, but I reckon there's a deeper meaning to this. If those guys are willing to kidnap me because of this, then I can't stop." He looked over, and she was concentrating again or seemed to be. "It kinda proves these reboots are for real don't you think?"

The rain had slowed a little, but the traffic was heavier than before. The road noise, the wipers and the pounding rain combined to make a wall of sound outside the car but inside the silence from Ellie was deafening Aston. They hadn't spoken about the kidnap at all. Ellie had asked how he'd managed to talk his mother into letting him go back so soon, as apparently she had been quite vocal about him staying with her for a while. That surprised him as his mom seemingly bought the story he'd concocted about having to prepare for a midterm paper, the fact that Ellie was driving him also helped, she no doubt thought Oxford may be a little safer after his story about being knocked over on the busy London streets. From Ellie's reaction, he got the feeling they may have discussed his adventures a little more in depth than Ellie or his mom had let on but had changed the subject before digging any deeper. Although switching to questions about Ellie's sister hadn't proven to successful either that was just before the rain started, and Ellie had been pretty quiet since then.

"So you'll help right?" Aston thought a direct question might, at least, get something. He was wrong.

"F-f-f-for fucks sake Ellie, say something" his stutter underlined his frustration.

Ellie hit the indicator and pulled into the hard shoulder. She stopped the car and turned to face him, her face was not giving a hint of emotion.

"Aston, I'm not going to argue with you when I'm driving in this" she gestured to the window. "You know damn well I'll help you, I'm your friend aren't I, and I'm in too deep now. I may not agree with what you're doing, and I know you're risking your neck, but I'd rather be around to be the safety chick" the half smile reassured him some more. "We can go over this later, and I'll even try to talk you out of it, but let me get us back to Oxford in one piece at least and please stop hassling me you know my driving's terrible."

"Okay, okay, I'm really sorry and thanks, Ellie, thanks for being you, and being my friend." She accelerated and indicated to get off the hard shoulder. "Oh and thanks for saving my life, just don't kill me getting back on the motorway." He expected a punch, but the smile on her face told him he was at least back in her good books.

CHAPTER NINE

"They look awesome but will they work?" Aston was stood in front of the mirror in his apartment looking at the TCDS headgear Harrison had just placed on his head. They had set everything up yesterday after Aston and Ellie had got back from London and Aston was ready to jump back into another soul reboot.

"What do you think Ellie?" Aston asked.

"How many volts will you be putting into your head?" she asked.

"It's Amps, not Volts. That's right H?"

"What?" Harrison looked up from his screen and took off his headphones.

"How many amps go through these things?" Aston asked.

"It can typically deliver up to two milliamps" Harrison replied.

"I take that's milli as in millimetre, not million, else we might as well call an ambulance right now!"

"Ellie made a funny" Harrison quickly cut her off.

"You said typically two milliamps, what have you done?" Aston removed the twin V-shaped headset from his head and looked at the battery unit in the rear that appeared to be modified judging by the electrical tape that held it together.

"I made a few modifications and from my tests I can double the amperage to get four milliamps which still kinda sounds lame, but it will help — trust me."

"I've just escaped from one guy who was trying to get inside my head, and now I'm letting you control my mind. What did you do install a new power source!?"

"I pulled the lithium battery and the processor from my old phone and hooked it up to the headset, obviously needs refinement, but it works fine so these can now stimulate, monitor and receive data."

"Will this help us figure out how we can influence the date of the reboot?"

"I'm still working on the software code, I thought we might be able to send data but that's not worked out, so I'm thinking if we can suggest the date as part of the hypnotism recording to get you under. The additional direct current stimulation at that trigger point may help, but I think it's you who ultimately has that power. It pains me to say this, but the tech can only go so far."

"Just as long as you don't fry my brain. So are we good to go?"

"Are we doing this now?" Ellie said looking somewhat surprised.

"Why not?" Aston looked to Harrison his eyebrows raised expecting support.

"I'm ready if you are?"

Aston thought Ellie was going to try to delay things, but she nodded. "Just let me check my stuff and I'm happy" she started checking over the medical kit borrowed from the Nursing school yesterday. She pulled out a mini defibrillator which got both Aston and Harrison's attention. "No broken ribs if you crash this time Aston. Yes, boys this little lady packs a few more volts than your headset!"

"Okay we now know Ellie is ready" Aston threw Ellie an impressed look and nodded. "Let's get this going." He handed Harrison the headset, "I just need to pee first" and headed to the bathroom.

They had decided to forego the massage bed and opted to use Aston's room just in case he was under for longer. Harrison was waiting for him when he returned.

"I'm excited" he rubbed his hands together.

"Me too I've been working on pulling all these monitoring sources into one app so we can control it all from one screen."Harrison showed him the iPad and the app that displayed heart rate, temperature, bar graphs to indicate brain activity, and time elapsed."It will work on your iPhone; I'll set it up while you're under."

"Thanks H, that looks awesome - I'm impressed - let's see if it all works."

Ellie came in as he lay on the bed "You know we might want to think about a saline drip to keep your fluid levels stable."

"That's not a bad idea" Harrison replied as he attached the headset and headphones on Aston's head. "You'll need this too" he handed him the Nike Fuel band.

"I don't intend to spend that long under but it's a fair call just in case it gets interesting - you never know I could end up back in the sixties with Warwick and Amy."

"Yeah you'd like that you pervert" Ellie laughed.

"Well, it's a random chance this time. Hopefully, we'll get the date suggestion to work next time, but I want all the sordid details this time if you do meet up with Amy, just avoid the drugs if you manage to get control." Harrison connected the two inputs into the jack he'd brought and then plugged in the iPad.

Aston had thought about the possibility of gaining control so he could influence his regression. It was one of the things he was eager to try out as it could open up a new dimension to this, give it more of a purpose but didn't want to contemplate the implications. He figured it must be possible, but wouldn't know how until he was back under.

"Hey, whatever happens, I couldn't do this without you two. Thank you, I mean it, I'm in your debt and your hands. Now let's see where I end up."

Harrison pressed play on the iPad and set the TDCS to full power. Aston closed his eyes and shuddered as the hypnotist's French accent spoke to him once again.

It came easy, this time around. His stimulated mind grasping the trigger point with enhanced eagerness and again his subconscious flooded with the senses from a previous existence. The sound of a radio in the distance, a sports commentary of sorts but Aston couldn't distinguish the game they were playing. The clink of glasses being picked up was unmistakable and for a second he thought he was back in the bar, 'was he with Warwick again in the sixties?' The acrid smoke of stale cigarettes nauseated his senses. He was in a bar, but this smelt different, and the bitter nicotine taste filled his mouth and his lungs as he inhaled. His blurred vision cleared and Aston found he was looking around a bar room, but this was definitely not the sixties. The bartender clinking more glasses as he placed them on the shelf above the bar. His slicked back hair, trim moustache, white shirt and waistcoat reminded Aston of a character from Boardwalk Empire. The two guys standing at the bar with their backs to him wore suits, one brown, one navy pinstripe, and their fedora hats tipped slightly on the heads. 'Very gangster' Aston thought and then he saw the unmistakeable Thompson's machine gun held at the side of the pinstripe-suited man. He must have rebooted into the late nineteen twenties or thirties. There were two other groups of men in the bar from what he could see. Two waiters or bartenders, so it seemed, as the were dressed to match the one putting away the glasses, were listening to the radio commentary. "Bottom of the eighth," said the announcer and Aston heard a crack of a bat against ball. "Foul ball," said the announcer met by groans from the crowd.

"Damn it! We're down by five" one of the men yelled.

"Should have never sold Ruth to those damn Yankees, we've been played off the park by everyone since" the other bartender replied.

The other group were old timers, grey-haired with thick set weathered faces, and all crowded around a small table playing dominoes from what he could make out. This group was also the source of the smoke as it seemed, a thin cloud was suspended above them slowly amassing its volume from the butts in the ash trash and those loosely attached to the lips of the players.

"Now Babe Ruth he could play" one of them interjected into the baseball discussion. "Knocking! Jimmy - you're up - when you've finished discussing the Red Sox with the hired help." Aston noticed that he was actually in control of his thirties soul, as it seemed it was his conscious decision to look back from the table playing dominoes, to the guys listening to the game. He looked down at the small round table in front of him, the empty glass on the mahogany surface sat next to a folded newspaper. The main article heading declaring 'mob racket busted wide open' grabbed his attention. In his mind, he reached out for the paper, and the hand of his soul followed the request. He turned the paper over to see the Boston Globe masthead; he checked the date, Wednesday, August 18, 1931. He was in the thirties, but he was in the United States. Aston also noticed there was blood on his hands, his white shirt cuffs, peeking out of his suit, were stained with specks of blood. He checked both arms and looked down opening his black double-breasted suit to inspect his midriff, and the shirt inside had splatters of blood too. 'What on earth' Aston thought, noticing the handgun holstered neatly inside his jacket. Curious to know more, he reached into his inside pocket and pulled out the wallet of his former soul. Opening the leather wallet, he saw a white ivory card, an auto licence dated 1928, issued to Peter Latchford of Elm Hill Drive, his was born in 1904, he weighed 170 and was 6,2.

"Hey, Latch" the gangster in the brown suit called out.

Aston's attention turned away from the drivers licence towards the two men who were now walking towards him, a bottle of bootlegged Bourbon and glasses in hand.

"Latch, tell John what you said to me, he wants to hear it first hand."

He put back the wallet as they sat down at his table, Aston was interested in what his soul was about to say, although somewhat distracted by the machine gun placed on the table with the drinks. He stared at the wooden handle and rounded magazine clip an icon from the old gangster movies his dad used to love.

"Latch come on" his compatriot raised his voice starting to get a little aggressive "John needs to know where Joe was taken out."

"What," Aston thought and then heard his soul say it at the same time. His mind started to race, if he was in control of movement and voice how would he know what had gone on before him, he had no way of being able to answer the brown suited man's question and couldn't tell John anything.

"Come on Latch snap out of it, I know it wasn't your fault, Tell John where you were and how Joe wound up dead."

Aston looked at the paper searching for inspiration or a name but then realised that the brown suited man knew what had happened so any lie by Aston to cover himself would be rebuked on the spot. If he couldn't answer him and his soul would be in deep trouble.

"Come on Latch I'm only gonna ask you one time" it was John speaking now, and he put his hand on the Thompson just to dial up the pressure. "I need to hear how this happened, where he was taken out and how come you survived and came back here covered in blood?"

Aston's time was running out; he needed to relinquish control of his soul's actions, but he didn't know how to. Could he reboot back, perhaps wake himself up, he realised he never really had any control of this and started to regret jumping back into this so soon.

"I, I, I..." All Aston could manage was his usual stutter, the pressure getting to him and his own reactions coming out in the soul he'd regressed to.

"Latch what's a matter with you? You're starting to freak me out here?" The gangster grabbed him by the shoulders and shook him, he raised his arm backwards ready to strike, and Aston closed his eyes in a vain hope of shutting out the situation.

He felt the hard slap, and the jolt brought some clarity to Aston's mind, he reached into his childhood memories of Grace and his nannies Buddhist teachings, 'focus not on the distractions in life, let your mind be neutral and your inner calm will shine through.' Aston had practised this so often it was second nature but how would it relate to his subconscious state? He knew for certain that his only option was to give it a shot and deal with whatever played out.

"It was near the South side of Huntingdon Avenue, not far from old South Church" Peter Latchford responded.

The technique had worked, Aston was still part of his soul, and his senses could still pick up everything as before, but Latch was back in control of his own actions.

"They hijacked us. I picked Joe up at home as arranged and we drove to the drop point. Joe told me to wait in the car and got out to meet with Solomon as arranged, but the Fox brothers showed up. They had a few words, and I think Joe knew it was a trap. He started running back to the car, waving at me to get it started, I opened the door for him, and then they started firing. He was almost in the car when he took one square in the back. I swear his heart exploded, it was like a nightmare. Look at me Jimmy, I'm covered in his blood. Give me that drink!" He grabbed the bottle and poured a glass of the Bourbon then downed it in one.

"We need to find Solomon, Jimmy. Find out what the hell is going on and get those bastards for what they did to Joe." John turned to Latchford "so how come you made it out of there Pete? With the bullets flying you seem relatively unscathed apart from Joe's blood splattered on you."

Peter Latchford poured another shot of bourbon and replied "I was lucky to be in the car, that's why! When Joe went down, I hit the gas, spun it around, put my head down and got the hell outta there. I managed to knock one of the bastards over who tried to stop me getting out of the alleyway. Go see the car John it's parked right around the street. The back windows out, the front lamps smashed in and there's bullet holes all over, ain't that right Jimmy?"

"That's right John - Latch came straight to the club that's when I called you. He reckons the Fox boys have got together with someone on the outside of the seven families."

"Okay, I'm buying the getaway car story, shame we had to slap some sense into before you told us. But you've done well and thanks for coming directly to us Latch." He turned to his offsider. "Jimmy when you find Solomon set up a meet and we'll work together on how to sort the Fox boys out once and for all."

"I know where Solomon is John" Latchford offered. Aston wished he had the ability to google Solomon and find out who he was and what he was caught up in.

"What? You know where he'll be right now?"

"Yeah I think so, Joe said he'd either be in one or two places. He wasn't at the Huntingdon Avenue meet so he should be at the Cotton Club. We should try there, but for all we know Solomon may be in on this?"

"We need some backup. Jimmy, go get the boys and well meet back here in fifteen minutes, I'm gonna call Sonny from Atlanta and see what he knows. Peter get yourself cleaned up as I'm assuming you wanna come along."

The two men stood and walked away in separate directions, Peter stood, poured another shot of Bourbon, and walked to the bar. As he downed the glass, Aston thought now would be a good time to try to regain control of his soul's actions. Shifting his focus from calm, neutral thoughts, to the chaos of Peter Latchford and what was around him, and immediately found himself back in the consciousness of his soul. He put the glass down on the bar and asked the bartender where the toilets were.

"Same place as last week Latch! Down the hall and on the left."

"Don't suppose you have a spare shirt back there?" Aston asked he thought he'd best do as directed before John came back.

The bartender looked him up and down and then reached under the bar to his left. "Here you go, but you're gonna need to switch collars" he tossed the white shirt to Aston, who caught it and tried to figure out what he meant. He felt the collar of his own shirt and found the button to the back, he realised that back then starched collars were separate from the main shirt and walked towards the toilets.

Aston stood in front of the mirror looking at his former soul. It reminded him of when Warwick had visited the bathroom during his last reboot. Although this time the face staring back at him was younger, with a pale complexion, brown eyes, and brown hair, slicked back and parted on the left. His face spattered with traces of blood, which was also on his suit jacket as well as his shirt. Aston opened it, and the blood stains were only noticeable on close inspection, but the white shirt underneath was laced with the crimson blood of whoever this guy Joe was. Aston's attention was taken away from the blood and any thoughts of Joe's demise when he noticed the holstered gun under his arm. He stood back from the basin and tried to draw the weapon as he'd seen so many times in movies. His hand caught in the holster on his first attempt, on his second, the gun got stuck under his armpit. He tried a third time and clumsily drew the gun out, but it was no way as slick as he'd first imagined. The snub-nosed gun was heavy for its size, a six shooter and Aston tried to pop out the revolving cylinder. It didn't budge until he tried it the other way and managed to flip it out, he span the bullet chamber and flicked it back into place as he'd seen done countless times on TV shows. His reflection caught his eye, and his play acting ceased as he realised that this was actually real, the blood stained shirt that he'd come in to change a stark reminder.

He put the gun back in the holster and took it off. He turned on the cold water tap and ran his hands under, removing the blood. Aston carefully wiped his hands dry before removing the buttoned down collar, and taking off the shirt. He looked at his soul's body which seemed in good physical shape, all but for the large round scar on his shoulder which looked like an old bullet wound. The pitted scar tissue felt strange to the touch, and Aston wondered what his soul, who was only in his mid-twenties had been through and what lay in store for them both. He was just finishing getting his suit jacket on when he heard Jimmy's call.

"Latch, you in there? Come on we're rolling."

"On my way!" Aston replied nervously.

He threw the bloodied shirt in the trash on his way out of the bathroom and walking up the corridor Aston opted to zone out of his soul and become a spectator to whatever was about to happen.

Aston had thought of his dad as he'd climbed into the old Ford sedan. The runner boards, sweeping wheel arches and curved bonnet for some reason made him recall his father's dodgy impressions of Bogart from the black and white gangster movies. His dad would watch them over and over, and now Aston was seeing one first hand or was it second hand, but there was no mistake he was smack in the middle of a real-life gangster experience. The reality check of how this story could end up brought Aston's brief recollection of his early childhood to an abrupt end. His former soul Peter Latchford was in the back seat of a traveling party of three cars. The sparse functional interior trim a stark contrast from the plush leather of the Bentley Aston escaped from a few days before. Every bump and pothole accentuated by the car's suspension or lack of it, which given that he now shared the limited space with two burly gunmen, made the journey far from comfortable. Aston practised taking back control over his former soul who was now in possession of a Thompson's machine gun handed to him as they left the bar. Aston was examining the iconic weapon when the car hit a sizeable pothole in the road and lurched to the side. The jolt took Aston by surprise, and his finger slipped pulling the trigger and the Thompson's clicked as if to fire. The safety catch engaged and stopped Aston from wiping out those around him. The gunmen to his left gave him a disgusted look as Aston released his trigger finger and zoned back out to leave Peter Latchford back in control of his own fate.

The cars pulled up to a halt just shy of their destination, the Cotton Club, located just two blocks away. Aston watched as John climbed out of the lead car and made his way over to the second vehicle He leaned into the open window, "Pete..." a tram car rattled past and stopped him talking, the noise as the coaches clung to the rails just too much. Once the last coach had gone he continued "so you think Solomon could be in on this?"

"John, I don't know, but it's kinda weird that the Fox brothers knew what time Joe was meeting him and all. We need to be careful, maybe go in hard around the back of the club."

"I'm not sure Pete, Sonny said he'd heard a rumour someone was causing trouble in Boston" he paused for thought. "Jimmy!" John yelled towards the third car and gestured to Jimmy, who slowly opened the car door and ambled over. "Jimmy I want you, Pete and the rest of the boys to go around the back of the club. Me and Danny will pull up out front and go in as normal under the guise of looking for Solomon, so we don't arouse suspicion!"

"Okay boss" Jimmy replied, "I guess you are the boss now Joe's bought it?"

"Give me five minutes and after that come in heavy, guns blazing if needs be?" John went to leave then turned back. "Pete I hope you're wrong about Sol's involvement in this - I've known him since we were kids, and I'm gonna be pissed if he's cut a deal with the Fox brothers. He knows Joe and I control bootleg production and can't expect me not to retaliate."

Aston suddenly realised what his soul was involved in, bootlegging illegal whiskey was big business in the thirties. He had covered the Great Depression in his history classes at school not to mention the many US TV dramas on the subject.

John had got back in the lead sedan and despatched two of the gang members to ride along with the rest. The two stood like sentinels on the runner boards either side the car Aston was in, they held on to the door pillars with practised ease as the cars pulled out, did a U-turn and made for the back of the club and via the narrow alleyway two blocks down. There wasn't much room for the cars to get through and the tight fit made the sentinels hanging on to the outside look a little uneasy. The narrow alleyway led to a wider clearing and the back entrance of the club, from what Aston could make out. It was off to the left-hand side judging by the number of bins and the trilby-wearing guard. He was talking to the driver of what looked like a delivery van, and as his soul turned around to look back down the alleyway, Aston noticed two other cars parked on the back wall by the alley entrance. They pulled up to the right of the van, and the two runner board mounts jumped off before they had fully stopped. They went straight for the guard and the driver, the first knocking the guard to the ground with a vicious swipe of the butt of his Thompson's gun. The second aiming his through the open window at the face of the driver who timidly got out of his cab to receive a similar crack to the skull which put him on the floor alongside the guard. The rest of the gang were out of the cars waiting, and Jimmy pulled out his pocket watch to check the time, he held up his arm "two minutes and we go in." Aston was suddenly aware his former soul was becoming a little agitated, in fact, Peter Latchford started to back up a few steps putting a little distance between him and the rest of the gang. He lifted his machine gun and quietly pulled back the firing pin to engage the magazine. Aston heard the doors of the cars behind him open and noticed the tarpaulin covering the back of the delivery van begin to lift. Aston's mind raced 'oh my god this was a double cross all along,' and realised his soul had set it up. Aston wasn't the only person who noticed what was happening "It's a trap!" Jimmy shouted just as the bullets started flying. His men had no time to react before they were cut down by the rival gangs indiscriminate hailstorm of bullets.

Aston had played his share of World of Warcraft but before him the blood and flesh he saw torn from the men he was just riding along with bore no resemblance to the digital destruction his Playstation controller had reaped. For a split second, he thought about rebooting out of this mess, but the shock realisation that he, as Peter Latchford, was firing on his own men pulled him back. Without consideration for the consequences, he took control of his former soul's actions, spun around and began to return fire in an attempt to protect some of the gang from slaughter.

CHAPTER TEN

Ellie checked Aston's pulse, his body had been jittering and his head twitching a lot in the past hour, and although she trusted the technology Harrison had set up she wanted to check the old fashioned way just to be sure. She let go of his wrist, looked up at Harrison, the iPad display he was holding was correct - 80 bpm, a little high for resting but nothing of concern. Touching his hand also served to reassure her own feelings, and she thought maybe Aston might pick up on it wherever and whenever his subconscious might be.

"Apart from that last twitching spell he's been pretty stable don't you think?"

"Yeah his vitals have been in and around the norm, brain activity is massive, though." Harrison showed Ellie a quick graph with the swipe of his finger. "We should probably test on a regular sleeper as a comparison. It will help towards the study paper." Harrison continued, Ellie frowned at him. "I'm maintaining current flow at around three amps through the headset, and it's holding up. Look." He flicked another graph across the touch screen.

"You really should get out more!" She taunted, laughing.

Harrison pulled the iPad away "Whoa that's deep girl, I get out, I do my fair share of socialising, and before you say it, it's not all online."

"H, I wasn't going to say that, but there's nothing wrong with being a geek!" Ellie laughed again and dodged the crumpled up sweet wrapper he threw at her. Harrison's phone went off, the Apple logo glowed neon blue. "Now that is cool, you need to do my phone" she smiled.

"Oh and now who's the needy geek, hang on." Ellie waited as he picked up the call, after a few moments he looked at Ellie and said: "it's a friend, see social butterfly me, I need to check something in my room, is that okay?"

"Sure, say hello to her from me" Harrison swatted his arm dismissing her sarcasm as he left. "Needy geek?" Ellie said it aloud so he would hear. "No wonder you two get on so well" she spoke to Aston knowing he couldn't. After a minute of silence, Ellie took to her mobile, clicked on the Facebook app icon and waited for her news feed to update. A knock at the door startled her. It was loud and quite forceful, and she turned to face the door Harrison had just walked out of expecting him to appear as it was his house. Nothing. A minute went by, judging by the time on Aston's monitor and the door knocked again with the same forcefulness, apparently someone expecting immediate attention. Ellie walked over and stuck her head through the door of Harrison's room.

"Did you hear that? Are you expecting someone?"

Harrison looked up from his call, seemingly startled by the intrusion. "What no...no I didn't and no not expecting a soul!" He smiled with the pun.

"You want me to answer?" Ellie was hoping Harrison would hang up and sort this out as it could be awkward.

"Do you mind Ellie, I'm almost up here but if you could sort it that would be awesome! Tell them to get...Well you know" he went back to his call.

Ellie walked out shaking her head 'light weight' she thought and headed for the front door. She peered through the spy hole; it looked like a salesman, but the guy had his back to the door. 'Just tell him no thanks and you're done' she said to herself and opened the door. He must have turned to knock again just as the door opened, he stumbled and almost fell through the door. Ellie was a little taken aback "I'm so sorry about that." She said apologising. The man stood on the doorstep, he was blonde, blue eyed and sported a full beard. A bit nerdy but the suit, and tie made him presentable.

"How do you do?" He spoke very well, and Ellie detected a hint of an American accent.

"Good thanks, how may I help?" Ellie thought she'd follow his polite lead.

"I'm hoping to catch up with Harrison if I may." 'That explains the nerdy beard' she thought, 'probably one of his tech groupies, although he looked a little older and quite cute.' Ellie released her hold on the door and allowed him to step inside.

"I'm a friend of Professor Ferris, and he mentioned I might be able to find you guys here."

"Harrison's on a call, but he shouldn't be long."

"Is Aston here?"

"What? Do you know both of them?" Ellie thought his tone was a little pushy.

"I know what they have been doing."

"Sorry?!"

"What they have been doing together, Professor Ferris told me and I'm here to persuade them to stop."

"Excuse me?!"

"Mr Ng and Mr North are dabbling in past life regression and writing a thesis to prove reincarnation of the soul."

"What are you on about?" The realisation that she had just let someone nobody knew into the flat struck, and Ellie's heckles raised.

"They are undermining the foundation of faith, to even suggest one's soul can be reincarnated is deeply offensive. God creates every man uniquely, and every human soul is different and valuable. The very notion of reincarnation taints this individuality. A soul isn't a vehicle travelled for eternity; a soul cannot be reborn, a soul..." Ellie cut him off.

"You sound like the asshole Mr whatever your name is. I think you should leave."

"I'm not going until I've put an end to whatever your friends are trying to prove. There is no endless cycle of death and rebirth. Hebrews 9:27... 'Just as man is destined to die once, and after that to face judgment.' Evidence that a man only dies once and is then judged before God on the life he has lived."

"Evidence you call that evidence, and what about women you sanctimonious prick." Ellie started pushing him back toward the door. The man stood his ground his body strength matching the strength of his belief.

"You will be judged along with your friends."

"Judge this you lunatic" Ellie took a swing at him.

He caught her mid swing and grabbed her wrist.

"There is but one life on Earth, and then, given our earthly deeds and practices, we either go to Heaven or Hell."

"You go to hell" she kneed him straight where she had been taught. He grabbed her and pushed her away, Ellie fell hard back against the wall, winded, her legs gave way, and she slumped to the floor.

"Hang on C" Harrison heard Ellie's heated argument with whoever was at the door. "I think I'm gonna have to call you back little one — yeah, you too." C was Harrison's little secret although it was becoming increasingly hard to keep her from his friends. He felt bad not telling Aston about her although the two had met, albeit briefly, just before the semester started. They had met for coffee and were ordering when Aston walked in to get his takeaway. He never realised that she was with Harrison and stood and chatted to him ignoring her completely. C stood for Celia, who was a yummy mummy, at least that's how he liked to describe her when he wanted to wind her up. Her husband was a real estate agent who, obsessed with making his over inflated fees, had no time for his wife or family which led her to seek adventure elsewhere. That adventure transformed into a habit for roulette and subsequently placed her next to Harrison at a roulette table at the Oxford Grand Casino. Harrison's appetite for a drink often landed him at the casino after hours and again unbeknownst to his friends spent much of his spare time and his father's allowance playing the odds. After jointly playing the same combinations and riding a winning streak they struck up a friendship and had been seeing each other for about six months. She had recently declared her love for him and ended most of their calls that way, but he still couldn't say the words.

"You too C, I have to go — yes I'll call you later." Harrison hung up; the commotion was getting louder downstairs.

He quickly checked Aston's stats, his temperature and pulse were normal, but his brain activity had just hit a high point. He had no time to increase the current or do anything about it as he heard a yell and a crash. Ellie was in trouble.

He burst through the door phone in hand.

Ellie was on the floor by the kitchen wall and a geeky looking guy in a dark suit, and a full beard was staring straight at him.

"You need to get the fuck out dude before I call the police."

"Harrison?" The guy somehow new his name."You need to stop what you're doing."

"You need to seriously get the fuck out!" Ellie had stood up her face red "Ellie are you okay, what did he do?"

"No, this lunatic barged in, he said he knows you."

"Professor Ferris told me what you are doing with Aston North. Is he here?" Harrison looked back towards the door behind him. "No - now get out before I call the police" he waved the phone at the guy. 'Ferris and his phone call, I'd forgotten that. I can't believe he told him where I live.' Harrison's mind was racing, what could he do if they call the police they'd have to wake Aston and explain everything.

"Where is he, back there? You both need to stop; you are undermining the foundation of the Catholic faith. To suggest a soul can be reincarnated is preposterous and blasphemous."

"You've got five seconds to get out."

"One is not born again in an endless cycle of death and rebirth. Upon death, good men that pass judgement are reincarnated into the next life with God, but it is in an entirely different state, our eternal lives with God are set apart from our earthly souls."

Harrison had had enough preaching he tapped his phone once then three times again. Holding it up to his ear, looking the geeky looking guy directly he rolled his dice. "Emergency, yes, police please" he hoped his bluff would get this nutter out of the flat. "You need to leave now." Harrison paused "yes police. I'd like to report an attempted rape, yep number 57, Cowley Road. It's the flat above the Tick Tock Cafe." Their zealous intruder suddenly lost his confidence."IC1 male, early thirties, blonde hair, dodgy beard wearing a dark suit, white shirt, and tie."

Harrison held the door of the flat open. "Go and keep going they may not be able to catch you!"

"Your sins will be judged, young man."

Harrison spoke back into his phone "I think he's got a knife, please come quick, 57 Cowley Road, my friend she's in trouble send an ambulance as well, please."

The intruder raced passed him and down the entrance stairs. Harrison yelled after him. "Tell Professor Ferris if I see you again he's getting a child molesting complaint that will make his Judgement Day happen sooner than he'd like."

His heart rate was racing, the adrenalin of the situation heightened his senses. He sunk to his knees and looked at Ellie, who had done the same.

"Jesus, where did he come from?"

"You heard him knocking. He just went off once I let him through the door. I tried to push him back, but he shoved me and that's when you came in."

"Bloody Professor Ferris, he's to blame for this. I overheard him telling someone on the phone after I'd asked his help on an issue I had with the tech. This guy must have been the one he told."

Harrison stood and walked over to Ellie, crouched on the floor, he offered her his hand to pick her up.

"Are you okay Ellie? I'm so sorry. Did he hurt you?"

"No, but I'm telling the police when they get here."

"They're not coming." Harrison braced himself for the backlash. "I was bluffing."

"What? What if he hadn't left. What were you thinking!"

"Sorry Ellie, I wasn't, I panicked and thought a bluff would work."

"Bloody Hell Harrison, that's a big gamble. He could have killed us."

Harrison looked out of the window. "The good thing is that he's gone now, and if he comes back we will call the police, promise."

"If he comes back I'll be the first on the phone don't you worry." She managed a smile and Harrison felt relieved she didn't go mad at him.

"I'm sorry I let the freak in the door. He said he knew you. How did he know where you lived?"

"Ferris must have told him, the fucker. He did go a bit weird the other day after the phone call."

Harrison continued to tell Ellie the full story about how he'd asked the professor for help and had to tell him what it was for and then the phone call he overheard at the computer suite.

"Bloody religion why does it make people so crazy? Too many gods, that's the problem. They should realise it's all noughts and ones!"

"Noughts and ones? Oh, I get it when the lights out then nothing." He was impressed she got the reference many didn't. "You're an atheist. That makes sense." She looked at him eyebrows raised. "You do know I'm Catholic, are you pigeon holing me in the crazy farm too? A little faith is all most people are after we're not all extremists."

"Yeah but it's those that cause all the grief! Make all the noise. They just can't get on with their own lives they have to involve others. Our bearded freak just now is the perfect example."

"I'm not disagreeing H but let's not go there. It's made my mind up though. I can't do this anymore, and I'm leaving just as soon as Aston wakes up."

Harrison stopped her and bolted for the stairs."Holy crap Aston, his brain activity was off the charts. We need to check he's okay!"

Aston stared up at the Thompson machine gun raised in the air. It's barrel still smoking. The silence seemed as intense as the gun fire that had stopped moments ago, the echo's of bullets gave way to the groans of the injured. He remembered getting off a couple of rounds, and he may even have taken out a couple of the ambush gang before the warm end of a handgun muzzle touched his neck. The words that broke the silence turned him cold."Toss the weapon Latchford. I told Mr Solomon you were a man who shouldn't be trusted." No, it wasn't the words the sent his mind reeling, it was the accent, the soft, subtle toned French accent. 'It couldn't be' he thought, he threw the Thompson's to the floor and wished he could turn around, but the gun at the back of his head kept his eyes fixed ahead of him.

"You almost followed the plan to the letter Latch! What changed your mind? Did you think that John persuaded Solomon to switch sides? You want to go inside and talk to them? I think you should." The muzzle of the handgun urged him forward, "Let's go find out."

'It's definitely him, the accent was unmistakeable' Aston thought as he slowly walked past the scene of the ambush, his feet treading in the blood of the dead. The surrendered gang mates had been herded against the far wall behind the truck. "Don't worry about them Latch" his French antagonist taunted, "they'll be joining us or joining you six feet under."

They walked through the kitchen entrance and through into the club. John was sitting at a table, the left side of his face looked broken, bloodied and bruised, Aston saw the body of Danny lying on the floor behind him. John stood "Latchford you double crossing bastard, you get Joe killed and led us to this slaughter. You, the Fox brothers, Solomon, and that French fucker can all go and fuck yourselves" he spat straight in Peter Latchford's face.

"You should be nice to him John, and sit back down" the commanding voice came from the right of Aston. "I hear Peter had a change of heart at the last minute isn't that right Leonardo?"

"It's true Charles, your little patsy upped and switched back to the old side, killed Franko and would have taken a few more down with him had I not been keeping my eye on him. I told you I didn't trust him. Sit down Latch." Aston was shoved towards the table and finally got the chance to see the man he knew as the hypnotist. He sat staring into the face that had kidnapped him a few days ago, it was exactly the same, he hadn't aged just as he said. Aston had thought the whole 'countering the ageing process' the hypnotist had told him about was bravado, some pomp to give an air of invincibility, but now it's truth was literally staring him in the face. 'What did he call it the second stage to shifting' this was getting way too deep and not what Aston had expected when he set out and he was starting to get a little freaked out and scared. What was the hypnotist links to him and his former souls, how the hell were they connected?

"So Peter why the change of heart?" Charles Solomon asked.

Aston didn't hear him his head was spinning with the consequences of his ties to the hypnotist.

"Peter?"

Aston turned to face the gangland boss just as the hypnotist smashed the butt of his gun into his cheek. Aston reeled with the force and winced from the pain and he lost control of his soul.

"He's a copper Charles, I know it" the hypnotist hit him again.

"He's no copper, he's just a rat bastard, Joe treated him like a brother for the last two years."

"No one asked you, John!" The hypnotist pointed the gun in his face "I'd be quiet, or you'll be joining this one dead at the bottom of the Charles River."

Aston recalled a similar threat the hypnotist had made to him about throwing his body in the Thames, and he knew he had to get out. It dawned on him that he wasn't sure exactly how to reboot out, what did he have to do? What control did he have to get back? He had previously either been brought back by Harrison or fell back after the explosion at the battle of Trafalgar. Could he just jump back by waking up from this nightmare? The conversation in the Cotton Club was getting heated, but Aston wasn't listening he was desperately trying to establish how he could return back to his own soul. It then struck him that his own actions may have just altered the destiny of how Peter Latchford dies, so in fact, his soul may not be his to return back to. Aston needed to clear his mind, meditate out, find some blank space amid the chaos. He raised his hands to his head in an effort to stop the noise in his mind. Peter Latchford did the same. Aston was back in control of his former soul and suddenly back into the Cotton club confrontation.

"He's a cop Charles, take a look at this."

The hypnotist threw a wallet on the table where Peter Latchford sat. The gold Boston police shield shone out from the leather backing with numbers 1553 under neath. "I've been trailing officer 1553 since you and I met, he's been undercover for over two years apparently."

"What?" John's disgust at Latchford was evident even through his facial wounds.

"Yes, I thought his double-cross idea was too good to be true, so I had him checked out with some friends of mine back home."

"So you're the guy Sonny warned me about!"

The hypnotist shut John up with another blow from the butt of his gun.

"Atlanta's ours too now John. Sonny will find out soon enough. Isn't that right Charles?"

"The bootleg liquor business needs new direction and Sonny will find out he's going the wrong way. The Fox brothers are heading there to let him know."

"So the plan hatched by you and the Boston PD to get Mr Solomon to show his cards and to get evidence to arrest my good friend isn't going to work." He turned back to face Peter Latchford. "You see your DCI at Boston PD is actually my DCI at Boston PD, he's on our payroll, so they are currently waiting for Mr Solomon to show up at Fort Point. Which is where we'll be dumping your carcass later today as planned."

Aston found his blank space just as the hypnotist placed the gun to Peter Latchford's forehead. Aston looked back at the hypnotist, a final stare through the eyes of his soul, the cold black pupils he looked into flared as if they recognised something for a split second. His concentration fully focussed Aston's mind as he attempted to jump back into the blankness, his last sensory experience of his former soul was the click of a revolver trigger mechanism. Then nothing.

Aston opened his eyes, his bedroom ceiling a welcome sight. He sat up just as Ellie and Harrison rushed through the door.

"Oh my god are you okay? You're not going to believe what just happened!" Ellie got in before Harrison could say the same.

"I think I am, but you're never gonna believe what just happened to me."

CHAPTER ELEVEN

"I can't do this anymore Aston." Ellie knew she had to tell him. "It's getting far too dangerous, not just for you, but for all of us. That nutter could have had a knife, you've been kidnapped, you've had a heart attack for gods sake, and I haven't even started on the regressions you've been involved in. If you count the first one you've died twice by the sounds of things and almost suffered a heroin overdose."

"But Ellie, can't you see we're on the verge of a breakthrough. This hypnotist guy is after me because our souls are connected somehow. We need to keep going and find out what it's all about and then uncover this maniac."

"Aston he's a bloody gangster and from what you're saying he's immortal. You're bloody lucky you're not dead already. From what you've just told us he murders people for kicks, and I thought he was an asshole as a hypnotist. It's not just him anymore it's also Mr suit and tie god squad who wants to put an end to us also. It's scaring me Aston, and I'm sorry, but I'm out - I just can't do this anymore."

"She does have a point; the guy freaked me out a little" Harrison chipped in. At least, he was now seeing sense. His support gave her the confidence. She was mad at Aston, but she had to tell him how she felt and thought if she made this gesture he might be persuaded to go to the authorities rather than try and figure it out for himself.

"I stayed, at first, to make sure you didn't kill yourself but it just got way too dangerous and the sooner you tell the Police about this, the better."

"That's just it I've got nothing to tell the Police. They'll just look at me and think I am the lunatic."

"That's also true, point each!" Harrison was doing his best at being the mediator.

"If I hadn't been there and done this myself I'd probably laugh this one off as a University prank. Without some evidence we've got nothing, so I've got to try again, and I need you, Ellie, like you said, to stop me killing myself."

"Hey what about me" Harrison was trying to diffuse the argument, but Ellie wasn't finding it funny.

"I can't Aston I just can't, not anymore and if by going I'm stopping you kill yourself then maybe that's a good thing." Ellie grabbed her car keys off the kitchen bench top and brushed past Aston as she made for the door.

"Ellie come on, d-don't do this" Aston grabbed her arms and turned her to face him. For a second she thought he was going to kiss her, but he just held her arms and looked straight into her eyes. "Once more that's all we need to get some evidence. P-P-Please?" That boyish stutter and cute smile weren't going to work. She knew she had to leave, and she had to tell him.

"Let go, Aston, let me go. Look I love you, and I don't want you to get hurt. I'm not going to stand by and let it happen, you know that's not me. So this is me saying goodbye." She wrenched away from his grip, opened the door and ran down the stairs.

"Ellie!" Aston called after her.

On the street she clicked her key fob, and her car lights flicked on, she didn't think to look around in case anyone was watching, she pulled the door open and sat in the Mini. 'Why am I crying' she thought and moved the rear view mirror. Ellie looked at her face and wiped the tears from her cheeks. She knew why. Ellie was happy to have him as a friend but was her feelings deeper. She thought the extreme sports were his adrenalin release, and if she was honest, they were hers too, but the past week and the whole reboot thing was way too dangerous. He seemed ignorant of the danger and was obviously too close to it. She was too close and hopefully he'll get the message now, but she knew how to get away from it if only for a short time.

She started typing a message on her phone 'Sis it's me hope you don't mind if I come a day or two early. On my way. Love Ellie.' It wasn't an easy option, but it was safer than here. They had arranged the visit when they met a couple of days ago. She just hoped her sister didn't mind and would reply before she got there.

Out of the darkness, two hands slapped on the rear window. Ellie screamed almost jumping out of her skin.

"Ellie" it was Aston, she exhaled a deep breath in relief.

"You bastard, what do you do that for? I thought it was the weirdo from the church, Aston you scared the shit out of me, what the..."

"Ellie, I'm sorry! Let me in" he tried the passenger door. "Don't leave, let's talk, come to the pub and I'll buy you a pint."

Ellie started the car. "Sorry Aston, it's just not that simple. I need to get out, look at the state I'm in. I was supposed to be going to Jessica's next week, so I'm just gonna head there early." She reversed out of the parking space. Aston stood looking a little forlorn. "I meant what I said. You need to stop this for your own safety and sanity."

"I'll call you" he shouted.

She hoped he wouldn't but knew she would pick up if he did.

Harrison watched from the window as Ellie pulled away and drove down the street. "Damn" he slammed his fist against the window sill. He'd hoped Aston had a chance of persuading her to stay but totally understood her reason leaving as the incident had really shaken her up. He felt guilty not only for the fact it was his big mouth that led to this, but also if he hadn't been on the phone he could have prevented it. 'If only I had answered the door' he thought to himself, he also made a mental note to call Ellie and apologise properly, maybe once she's had time to reflect she might change her mind.

"Bloody Ferris" his thoughts turned to how to get back at his professor. He never took him for a god-squadder and would never have guessed he'd get all high and mighty. 'Probably brought up in the American Bible belt. Well, he'll get what's coming to him I'll make sure of that.' Harrison had been working on a new virus with a few of his close internet hacker friends and as payback, his Professor may just get to be the first victim. He just hoped that his crazy church group members were connected online as this particular strain can infect any connection be it via social media, email, instant message, video call or any internet protocol connection.

The sound if the door bell brought Harrison back from his cyber plotting. Aston had not taken his keys, so Harrison had to let him back into the flat.

"You okay?"

"Yeah didn't think she'd up and leave like that."

"Neither did I, but she had a point, it was getting a bit out if control. She was shaken up by Ferris's bearded Bible basher."

Aston took his alliteration the wrong way. "Glad you can joke about it H if you hadn't gotten Ferris involved he wouldn't have been here."

"Hey no fair man, I'm as pissed off about what happened as you and Ellie" Aston had struck a chord "I'm gonna get Ferris back and then some but don't ever think I'm not taking this seriously."

"Sorry H, she's got me wound up, and I don't want to lose two friends in one night." Aston did look pretty down, but Harrison had a solution which for once was not technical.

"Pint?"

"Splendid idea! Possibly the best way for men to deal with a crisis. The pub sounds like a good plan."

Harrison grabbed the iPad before they left as he wanted to review the reboot data and see how well the TDCS had worked.

"It's my round I think. Same again?" Aston offered. Their crisis summit wasn't going as planned. In just a small window of time, they had managed to solve nothing, forget about their troubles and consume three pints, three whiskey chasers and a packet of crisps.

Harrison gave him the thumbs up "Get another pack of crisps, smokey bacon this time." He turned his attention back to the reboot data he'd been trying to look at in between the drinking. The data extracted was comprehensive enough. Over the three hour period, Aston's heart rate had remained almost constant at around 120 beats per minute which is 60% maximum heart rate for his age. His breathing rate, which Harrison had added this time around by counting the rise and fall of his chest via a sensor, was almost treble the average adult at 45 breaths per minute. His body temp had dropped to below 36 degrees Celsius, which was odd considering his heart rate and breathing were considerably higher.

As well as stimulating Aston's brain activity the headset also measured it using delta and alpha band frequencies used in EEG. Delta activity was recorded at the front of the scalp and Alpha measured from the rear sensors. The data presented was picking up some huge fluctuations over the three hours. Aston had gone over what had happened, and they had worked out that when Aston was in control of his soul's action, the activity was 87% higher than when he wasn't and at times of stress it was triple the normal rate.

Aston returned with the drinks and pointed out something Harrison had been struggling with getting his head around.

"It looks like the sensors failed just as I booted back."

"That's just it the sensors are still working, you've still got on your wristband. See if I look at them now they're still sending data!" He showed Aston the current readings. "Obviously, your heart rates slowed with alcohol consumed!"

"So what about the gap when I came back?"

"Well, either your whole heart stopped, and brain activity shut down at the same point, or there was something else happening. It could have been a power surge, but I've checked, and the one sensors that did register was temperature and look it's the only time it peaked above normal."

Harrison looked at his friend who had put down his whiskey chaser.

"So what are you saying H?"

"I want to check the data on my main computer, but the only explanation is that you died, well flatlined on two fronts at least, just before you booted back. Or to look at it another way, exactly when your soul Peter Latchford was murdered."

"That's not good. Not good at all. Do you think we could find a way of controlling this?"

"Like I said without checking the data I can't be sure, but I'm guessing no" Harrison downed his whiskey and banged it on the table.

"Thank god Ellie didn't find out she'd have freaked."

"Yes, but without her when we do this again you could be in a lot more danger." Harrison downed his pint. He stood up and waved the empty glass "Fancy another?"

"Go on then" Aston stared at the iPad data, the consequences of his situation sinking in. Ellie was right he needed hard evidence to prove the hypnotist's involvement and something he could take to the authorities. He also needed to find a way to get Ellie back on board because if Harrison was right, his own life was at risk.

Harrison came back smiling carrying more drinks and a packet of crisps clenched in his teeth. Aston rolled his eyes, "It's a good job my tutes not until tomorrow afternoon."

Elliot came bounding into his office beaming like Carroll's Cheshire cat; he was obviously ecstatic. "The Chinese are astounded! They are convinced we have unparalleled genius and insight into the markets and begged to know how we predicted the trade report announcement."

"If only they knew our little secret Elliot. Insights are all well and good but to be able to change the trade once the embargo has been announced does have its benefits. Here's to you!" Leonardo Desangé poured his counterpart a cognac and raised his glass. "Did you shift back personally?"

"Had to, this was too important, and as I placed the original orders, I thought it kept the risks to a minimum. I knew the US, and Australians would sign the Free Trade Agreement but wasn't sure what restrictions they would include around Chinese trade. Once we had them, then we knew which markets and stocks to increase our position on. We are now looking at a $40 billion upside and the Chinese think we are magicians!"

"Close I suppose. I am the Hypnotist!"

"Well, maybe now you should think about giving up on that little sideline."

Desangé smiled at his friend, they both knew that wasn't an option he was going to take. He chose to ignore the subject.

"$40 billion that's a bloody good upside, just in trade fees alone. It certainly beats the liquor business wouldn't you say." Desangé had noticed Elliot looking at the picture of them both standing next to Charles Solomon and the Fox brothers on the boardwalk in Atlanta.

"Those were good times. Simpler. If someone stepped out of line, the next day concrete boots."

Desangé knew he was referring to their business dealings with the

Boston and Atlanta crime families which were necessary but very brutal, even for him.

"I think we got out at the right time. Solomon should have listened to you."

"He was never an investor, he preferred risks he could relate to."

Elliot had offered Charles Solomon an option to join them on New Year's Eve in 1933. He declined, preferring to remain in the liquor business and a month later was gunned down in his own club.

"He would have enjoyed being part of a $40 billion upside instead he got what he had coming."

"If he hadn't of got taken out by the Family, I seem to remember the Feds were all over him. Another good reason for getting back in the markets. It would have been hard to run away from the heat Solomon had attracted. It was bad enough after you shot that undercover cop a few years before."

"Him, I told you and Solomon he was a rat. He definitely got what he deserved. Like you said simpler times." They clinked glasses and downed another brandy. "The liquor certainly tastes better nowadays!"

The intercom interrupted their toast to the past and brought Leonardo's present into focus,

"Giselle to see you Mr Desangé."

"Send her through."

Desangé hadn't spoken to Giselle in a few days, as she'd been in Oxford looking for Aston North. He last talked to her after he retrieved the details from the boys phone and he was hoping she brought some news.

She too came striding into the room with a big smile, she walked directly towards him, ignoring Elliot's presence and planted a kiss on the mouth.

"I've missed you."

"I can see" he wiped off the lipstick with the back of his hand.

"We've found him, Leonardo. We've found the boy. Not at the address you gave me, the contact details must have been from last year. I spent a day trying to get access to those halls of residence but eventually persuaded a very kind boy studying there from Singapore to let me in."

"I hope you didn't break his heart" Desangé knew how persuasive she could be.

"She probably broke him in" Elliot added much to the annoyance of Giselle.

"Well, I accessed the residence office and found Mr North's new address."

"I thought we weren't wasting any more time on this?" Elliot asked.

"I said it wouldn't interfere with the Chinese trade and it hasn't. Giselle has his location so now we can go and remove this little distraction.

"So now you want to Google him?" Aston glared at Harrison, who was still dressed in his clothes from the night before and looking a little worse for wear.

"After the pub last night you weren't interested at all."

"I wasn't?"

"Ooh no, you were off to the land of Celia! Who is this mystery woman? You said you had to go and visit her. She needed you. That was until you passed out in the street!"

"What I don't remember..." Harrison held his head.

"I don't know how you got so wasted. You only had what I had right?"

"Ah...I may have sneaked in a few more shots when I ordered!"

During the short stagger back to the flat, after being kicked out of the pub, Harrison had become engrossed with his text messages and this girl and despite Aston's request to focus on how best to search for details on Peter Latchford he was oblivious. He seemed determined to tell the empty streets all about her in his alcohol induced state. Aston eventually managed to get Harrison off the street and through the door of the flat in his semi-comatose state and left him slumped in the lounge.

"You may want to lay off those shots next time my friend. You may also want to check your texts as I think you may have sent stuff you also don't remember!"

Aston had tried searching online on his own for references to Peter Latchford but after a few dead ends succumbed to sleep as the drink took its toll on his consciousness.

He had woken early, once again more refreshed than he would have expected. That fact the each time following a reboot his sleep and recovery was so heightened hadn't gone unnoticed. He had breezed through his daily routine, something that he usually struggled with after a session in the pub. He felt a distinct clarity of thought after his meditation which provided him with clear perspective to work out what he needed and wanted to accomplish. After his run he'd picked up two coffees, figuring Harrison would be in need of one if he were to provide the level of help Aston required.

"So check your phone, get your head clear and we can then piece together what records or evidence there is of what happened to Peter Latchford. I'm hitting the shower." He left Harrison, perched on the side of his bed, his head in one hand, his coffee in the other.

"Oh and you can tell me more about Celia later on!"

When he returned, Harrison had already begun the search.

"Google returned nothing, so I created a dummy Ancestory.com account, and I've dug up his death certificate and his birth certificate."

"Get out. Really!" Aston was always surprised that Harrison could seemingly find a solution to a problem so quickly. Today's attempt was somewhat remarkable especially with the hangover he'd had ten minutes ago.

Aston pulled up a chair. "So what do we know?" Harrison showed him the screen.

"Peter Latchford died August 18, 1931."

"Yeah it was a Wednesday, I was there yesterday!"

"He was born..."

"1904 - I saw the guys driving license" Aston interrupted.

"In New York March 16, 1904. His father was called Phillip, who was a policeman. His mother was Maria, maiden name Ellis." Harrison finished and turned to his friend. "So we can assume that your other soul. What's was his name?"

"Warwick Scott"

"Warwick right. That he was born in 1931. Around the same date!"

They both said it together. Harrison began typing.

"Here's his birth certificate. Born Wednesday, August 18, 1931."

"That's two souls going back over 100 years. Wow."

"The bad news is we've now hit a dead end!" Harrison half laughed at his impromptu joke. "Sorry didn't mean it that way!"

"What do you mean?"

"Look" he showed Aston the screen "this is all the people who died on March 16, 1904," he started scrolling through the list of over 500 names.

"It doesn't matter though H. If we can get it to work we may have the date for our next reboot and we can find out that way!"

"Of course, as long as I can get a date variable built into the suggestion mechanism. Shouldn't be too hard. I may need a clear head to get into it, though!"

"Let's see what else we can find on Latchford. I tried some of the old newspaper archives last night but couldn't access their image database."

"Now that is something I can do with a hangover! Where do we start?"

"The Boston Globe is as good a place as any, then maybe the New York Times."

Harrison rubbed his hands together and started typing. He began with the Globe and after a couple of minutes had hacked into the papers Proquest archive system. They found a story of a mob shooting two days after the event. It had made the front page, but there was little detail, and there were no images, apart from a stock shot of the outside of the club and one of Charles Solomon smiling to camera. Aston felt the hairs tingle down the back of his neck as the image popped up.

"That's a poor piece of journalism, and they've not mentioned any of the people involved or the scale of the killings. It was a bloodbath H, and they've made it sound like Solomon's exacted revenge on a rival gang of bootleggers."

"We can try the New York Times. That should have more detail and could have an alternative angle."

"Yeah we'll try that next I just want to check the obituary section." Aston had thought of where he could search for detail on Peter Latchford and the obits sounded like a good place to start.

"Look at least a couple of weeks after the murders," he asked.

Harrison found a small piece four days after. It read 'In memory of a loving son, cut down in the line of duty and taken from us in his prime of life. You will live on in our hearts forever. Phillip and Maria Latchford.'

"Is that it?" Harrison was a little bemused. "I thought he would have warranted at least one from the paper itself."

"Nice though," Aston thought for a second what his parents might write about him.

"Hey look" Harrison brought back his focus. "They got more on the New York Times."

"You really don't mess around H. Did you hack this one too."

"No need, they have guest access. Although I might need to get access to the supporting content and images."

The New York Times had much more detail, at least, a thousand words and a couple of shots of the aftermath. The headline read 'Solomon suspected in Boston gangland gunfight' and the article mentioned the Fox brothers, the Cotton Club and the deaths of four members of the Boston bootleg liquor gangs. They also referenced the earlier slaying of Joseph Magri. The images showed the exterior of the Cotton Club's rear entrance and the bullet-riddled walls and an interior shot of a bloodstained bar area that Aston recognised only too well.

"Shit that's where they shot me, him - you know, shot Latchford."

"The pictures credited to Abel Wolinksky maybe I can hack in and search some of his file footage. Let's see" Aston watched as his friend utilised his multi-screen set up to source elements to access The New York Times archive database, pulling code from one to the next then back to the login page. "I'm in... Now how's the best way to get what we need. Yes, just a standard database utilities software. Here!"

"Cool," Aston again in awe of his friend's abilities taking minutes rather than the hour or so he would have taken.

"Wow!" There were file shots that evidently they couldn't publish. The morgue shots showing two of the victims on the slab were pretty gruesome.

"That's him" Aston pointed Harrison to a thumbnail image of Peter Latchford's dead body his head wound gaping. The full detail opened up of Aston's former soul, his head ripped open where the bullet exited his skull, the two friends look away then at each other.

"Shit that's sick, and I mean sick dude. That's horrible."

"Damn that's not funny even in black and white" Harrison felt flustered at the sight. "Close it and let's just check what else is there." Aston was after some evidence to link the hypnotist to this but couldn't see anything.

There were pictures of all the major players in the Boston crime families. The Fox brothers, Charles Solomon, John and Joe Magri back in the bar where Aston had begun his reboot. There was also some shots taken at the Cotton Club in full swing. Harrison opened the full image "I wonder who the band was, could be someone good." They scrolled through a few shots taken of the group and the crowd from the stage area.

"Fuck!" Aston put his hand on the mouse to stop Harrison selecting another shot.

"What is it?"

"There on that table. It's him!" Aston pointed to a group of men, sat enjoying the show, drinking champagne, laughing and smiling. He placed his finger on the screen below the face of the man that hypnotised him ten days ago and completely changed his life.

"The hypnotist," he said, "and he's sat with one of the bloody guys that helped him kidnap me!"

CHAPTER TWELVE

Harrison couldn't focus during his lecture. He still had the image in his head of Aston's former soul laying in the morgue with a gaping hole in the back of his skull. He thought he'd seen some blood and gore in his time but the graphic detail of the mess the bullet left still made him grimace. The image of the hypnotist he and Aston had found earlier that morning had given him an idea. He didn't want to mention it to Aston just in case it didn't work but once his Applied Epistemology lecture finished he knew where he was heading. He realised the theory of knowledge class could possibly be crucial to his philosophy double major, but his concentration was lost very early on, and no end of metaphysical questions about time, causation, necessity, and truth, even though science related, would do nothing to help him focus. The lecture should be posted online later in the week, but attendance was mandatory for these early classes. His mind was not only on the images but also on the numerous ideas he had to repay Professor Ferris for yesterday's visit by his religious friend. He just hadn't worked out which one would be more appropriate.

The lecture finished and Harrison was first out of the auditorium and made his way to the Wolfson Building and Oxford's famous computing laboratory. He was confident that, as his lecture finished after five o'clock, there wouldn't be as many staff around to question his movements. Access into the building was easy, Harrison had made a copy of one of the staff swipe cards a few months back, partly to see if he could, but also just in case he needed any out of hours access to the more powerful computers kept in the lab. The door latched clicked as the cardax system light turned green and Harrison eased through the main doors. He almost didn't notice the two admin staff still at work, who were sorting out a large LED display screen in one of the classrooms on the ground floor. Only just managing to avoid them, as they carried the screen out of the room, Harrison took the stairs down to the basement levels meaning additional security access points, something he'd planned to avoid by using the service lifts.

The basement access to the computer lab had keypad access, he just hoped the code hadn't changed since he was last down here. Harrison input the code he'd seen Professor Ferris use six weeks ago, the led light remained annoyingly red, "Damn it" he said under his breath. The University had a 90-day automatic password change policy which was apparently followed by the door access system. He pulled out his phone and was about to text Aston when he remembered an old security hack he'd used countless times on systems he'd needed to bypass. "SOS," he said to himself he pressed the numbers 1001001 to reflect the binary version of the Morse code standard. The lock opened, and the green light signalled him through.

The computer lab had some very sophisticated kit, as well as hosting the main Oxford systems and servers, the lab had probably the best online connectivity and processing speed, which rivalled most government intelligence departments.

Amidst the banks of multi-screen arrays, Harrison found the one he was after. He'd been shown this on a tour of the building during Open day a few years back. The tour highlighted that Oxford had developed facial recognition software. They were quite proud of the fact that they had pioneered the program which was now used by some government agencies. Harrison pulled up a chair and switched on the computer and screen. He smiled as the software loaded, he'd used Professor Ferris's access which ironically he'd lifted using a keystroke-sniffing trojan that Ferris had helped him with. He pulled out the microdrive from his pocket and inserted it into the USB port. The drive contained the hypnotist picture which had required some retouching and cleaning up within Photoshop to give it the resolution and clarity. As Harrison uploaded the image file, he crossed his fingers and hoped it was enough to be compatible and get accepted.

'Enter database required' the program asked.

"Great I'm in" Harrison selected the Oxford image database, another reason for coming to the lab was the direct access and speed of the computers, he could have hacked his way in, but by being directly on the servers, he could utilise computational power his own hard drive could only dream about.

After what felt like an age, but was in reality was only five minutes, the software returned a couple of matches. Harrison sat bolt upright and stared at the results, the first dated back to 1844 and the second 1945. Two facial image matches almost a hundred years apart. 'Go figure' Harrison thought, he clicked on the reveal image icon under the 1844 result. The hypnotist's face was instantly recognisable, even with the moustache. He was posing in what looked like an old, early photographic studio. He wore a morning suit jacket, a cravat and waistcoat and the sepia tones of the image reminded Harrison of an Instagram filter.

"Aston is going to be one happy bunny" he said to the empty room as he saved the picture to the USB drive and clicked back to access the 1945 image. The crowd scene was a stark contrast to the staged older shot, and it took Harrison a while to spot the hypnotist, who was smiling along with the hundreds of excited Parisians celebrating the end of the war in front of the Arc de Triomphe. There were some soldiers mixed in with the crowds, but the hypnotist was wearing civilian clothes, a smart suit, tie and a trilby hat tilted ever so slightly on his head. He had a smug grin, and a tall Asian girl had her arms wrapped around him.

'Arrogant shit' he thought. The face was identical to the other picture, despite the century difference between them. Harrison went back to the portrait shot just to check, 'it had to be the same man, this software doesn't lie' he thought to himself. He saved the other image to his USB drive and was about to set in motion his plot against Professor Ferris when he had an idea. "Passports! What if I could run a check against the international passport records?" He would only need to edit the facial recognition software to enable it to access a different database. 'That would be easy' he thought the hard part would be to break into an airline's secured passport network and stay in long enough to allow the software to find a match. Difficult but not impossible. Harrison pulled over another display, connected the cables and reset the display settings so he now had two screens to work on. On the first, he accessed the settings files of the facial recognition software, and on the second he set in motion a brute force attack script to attempt multiple username and password entries to the passport verification systems. The code for the facial recognition software was a little harder than imagined but after ten minutes Harrison was ready to input the database ID. He killed the exhaustive keyword attack, which had done its job and locked out all known user id's for the passport database. The next step required no programming skills, the trick was to call the right number help desk number and obtain a password reset pretending to be a user desperate to get in. He called British Airways head office first.

"Are you having an issue with passport verification?"

"My phones are starting to light up, which airport are you in?" The help desk sounded flustered and didn't ask for a name. Timing was everything.

"I'm at Heathrow, and I need resets for all my operators" Harrison could sense the frustration, panic and urgency he'd created. He heard the operative typing away on the other end of the line.

"Okay done, the passwords password, upper case P and the ss is 55."

"Cool, can you confirm the user id's just so I make sure everyone changes theirs." It was risky, but it paid off as the help desk relayed all the user id's back to him and even got Harrison to read them back.

Harrison waited five minutes before trying the first ID. He got into the system, reset his password when prompted and using this new access ID set the facial recognition search in motion. He sat watching the program flick through the images and wondered how long it might take. Behind him, the noise of the cardax system unlocking the lab door broke his focus.

"Harrison?" The familiar tone of Professor Ferris's voice spun him around on his chair.

"Hey Professor, I've been waiting for you?" Harrison wasn't sure what to say, but as he stood up, he reached behind to turn off the display screen power.

"Who let you in Harrison?"

The sight of the professor fuelled Harrison's anger, he could feel his heart rate increasing as he anticipated the confrontation. He paused, took a breath and quite calmly replied.

"One of the guys upstairs working on the presentation displays. He said he knew you were on your way and that you wouldn't mind."

"Where you working on something?"

"No, I was just on the internet, incredible speed down here, connectivity is awesome." He continued the lies, trying to think of something plausible to say without getting angry was getting harder. He reached behind his back trying to locate the USB key so Ferris wouldn't notice.

"It's not really designed for that Harrison." His smile somewhat condescending as only teachers can. "This equipment costs millions of dollars, sorry pounds. How can I help you?"

Harrison's fingers found the USB key, but he couldn't hold back his frustrations.

"Well, I think you can start by not giving my address out to members of your 'reincarnation is the devils work' brigade!"

"Excuse me." The professor's smile vanished.

"No sir I don't think I can, or will excuse you. A member of your church group broke into my flat the other day and assaulted my friend, and I hold you entirely to blame."

The professors face turned a little pink, unable to hide his embarrassment. He went to speak, but Harrison cut him off.

"Do not deny it Professor I heard you on the phone telling someone, probably the dickhead that came. You told him about what Aston and I were working on."

"I may have..."

Harrison didn't let him finish. "What's bugging me is how did he get our address? You must have accessed student records and gave them to him. You know that's a serious offence? I wonder what the Vice Chancellor would say if he knew. Or the police?". This was one of the ways he thought he could get back at the Professor but thought a the threat was more powerful.

"It would be your word against mine, boy" Ferris sounded harsh. "And I know whose side Professor Stirling would choose."

Harrison was taken aback by the Professors stance, he'd enjoyed a good relationship with him and being on the other side shook him.

"I think you should leave now Mr Ng before I report you for trespassing and misuse of university property."

Harrison made for the door, as he reached the safety of the half opened entry he turned to have the final say.

"This is not over Professor, you know I'm in the right and what your friend did was inexcusable."

He closed the door staring hard at the professor, turned and bolted up the stairs.

Ellie had hoped she'd avoid having to go back to Oxford, she'd only checked her diary on arriving and realised she needed to attend a practical assessment the following day. She had no other commitments that couldn't be done online which meant she had to travel all the way back just for the hour long assessment. It was lucky for her it only started at four o'clock in the afternoon, and once out of the way she had a clear three weeks with the holidays coming up.

Her sister Jessica had been great, just what Ellie needed, a female shoulder. Having burst into tears as soon as her sister opened her door, Ellie had offloaded all her pent up frustration in floods of tears. She'd apologised again for the fallout between them that had lasted for the best part of three years until they met last week when Ellie was in London. Jessica had practically raised the family and given up a blossoming education following their dad's death when Ellie started achieving, she had the opportunity to excel and got the scholarships and a subsequent chance at University. Ellie had foolishly forgotten her sisters sacrifice one Christmas, making a joke about her grades and lack of ambition that prompted one hell of a fight and two and half years of cold shoulders and unanswered messages. Over a couple of Gin and Tonics, Ellie told her sister all about the night's traumatic events, after which she had wanted to call the police. Ellie persuaded her not to and then felt compelled to tell her all about Aston's soul rebooting, about her saving his life and about her feelings toward him. They had stayed up into the early hours, and Ellie had fallen asleep contented to have part of her life fully restored and having offloaded her frustrations about Aston North.

As she walked back to her car, relieved the assessment was over, she was thinking about the next few weeks away from Oxford when she saw

Harrison running toward her. For a second she thought about turning away so he wouldn't see her, but her good nature and the fact he looked a little stressed changed her mind.

"Harrison" she called out and waved at him.

"Ellie..." He paused to catch his breath. "What are you doing in here? You had a class you couldn't get out of right?"

"Close, but what are you running away from? - I'll let you answer." She knew he wouldn't get the sarcasm towards his habit of answering his own questions.

"Me?" he looked back behind him towards the building he was running from. "Just had a run in with professor Ferris."

"And?" 'Why did men always need that extra prompt to get more detail' she thought.

"I told him I was going to tell the VC about him giving out student details to his crazy religious friends. I also told him how the guy went mad and assaulted my best friend." Harrison looked her in the eye "Sorry Ell" threw his arms around her and hugged her. "All my fault and I didn't get the chance to apologise properly with Aston and all that."

"Thanks, H it's cool really. I got it out of my system. We're good honestly. Now let go before it gets awkward" she smiled at him as he let go.

"You're the best Ell. Oh, and guess what?"

"What?"

"We found him. The hypnotist. Got his picture and everything." Harrison looked back at the computer lab building again as if he'd forgotten something.

"What is it?"

"Nothing. I — no it doesn't matter." He pulled out the USB key from his pocket. "It's here I've got two pictures of him almost a hundred years apart, it's freaky, and I reckon we can trace him." He looked back again.

"What is he in the building?" Ellie felt a little scared for a moment.

"No. No, it's Ferris. I just remembered I left something on, I'm sure it will time-out though. It's nothing. Look I'll show you the pics." Excitedly he pulled his laptop from his Crumpler bag, flipped the screen and stuck the USB drive in the port. Ellie found herself a little transfixed at the images of the hypnotist. That the man she'd seen at the bar less than two weeks back could be the same man staring back at her in these old pictures.

"Isn't that his assistant? The girl with her arms around him, I'd swear that's the tall Chinese looking assistant from the show."

"You may be right, I didn't notice. It's proof though Ellie, proof that we can use to identify him - don't you think?"

Ellie was fixated on the images, she had kind of felt on the outside of this whole reboot scheme but seeing the hypnotist's face, on pictures back in time, gave it a sense of reality. Third party accounts of a mystery man who for all she knew may have been part of Aston's subconscious, were difficult to get a sense of, but seeing the hard evidence for herself Elie all of a sudden felt more involved.

"This one looks like it was taken in a photo studio. Do you know when they were made?"

"That one was 1844, and the Paris shot was 1945."

"Wow! What did Aston say?"

"I haven't told him yet. I've literally just found them searching on the Oxford systems." Once again he looked back towards the buildings.

"Wow, he's gonna be thrilled."

"Look, Ellie, I need to tell you that he was really, really sorry about last night. He was pretty cut up after you left. So was I, I'd hoped he'd convince you to stay."

"Well, he knows my number and tell him, if he wants to grovel, I'd be willing to listen. I'm staying at Jessica's and am off for the next three weeks, so I might even be persuaded to help catch this guy." She tapped on the image. "He looks like he needs locking up."

Aston still couldn't believe he had a copy of birth certificate of Warwick Scott in his hand. He also couldn't believe the time of birth he was looking at. Warwick was born within minutes of Peter Latchford being murdered. "Minutes" Aston said to himself, "three minutes to be exact." He had requested the birth certificate from the GRO website yesterday, registering under a surname of Scott, which was easy once he'd set up a new email account. Ordering the copy of the certificate had been simple, he'd opted to use the express post delivery option, and he was surprised it did turn up the 'next day' as promised. He'd returned that afternoon to find the official government branded envelope waiting for him.

He knew Harrison could probably have found an online version within minutes but somehow having the certified copy made it more tangible and kind of personal.

Looking at the time got him thinking, and Aston suddenly wished he'd ordered the death certificate as well. He picked up the phone and dialled his mother. After the usual pleasantries and enduring his mother asking him how he was, he dodged her question about whether he was still involved in the 'reboot nonsense' and got to the point of his call. "Mom can you send me a photo of my birth certificate."

"What on earth for darling?"

"I'm taking part in a Psychology study, and they're keen to know what time I was born."

"You don't need the certificate for that. I remember both you and your sisters quite clearly. You were both born just after midnight almost exactly the same time. Three years apart but your timing was spot on, your father thought it was lucky, but he hadn't been in labour for a whole day."

"A little too much info mom" he really didn't want to go near the thought of his mom in labour.

"Can you still send me over a picture of my certificate if you get chance mom." Aston still wanted to see it with his own eyes.

"Hang on Aston and I'll get it now if you like."

"Thanks Mom" he heard her place the phone down and could hear draws being opened. He thought back to the obituary they had found on Warwick's death 'succumbed to lung cancer in the early hours of 25 January.' It's close but if only he had requested the death certificate as well.

"Hello Aston, are you still there? I've got it."

"Yes, Mom."

"Exactly five past midnight, you popped out, see I told you. Do you want to Skype me and I'll show you?" Aston loved that his mom had a grasp of digital technology.

"No it's okay mom, just message me a photo of it. That would be cool thanks."

"Okay darling, now you're sure your feeling better, I'm worried about you. When are you coming over next?"

"I'm okay Mom. It's almost end of term so I can get up to London in the next couple of weeks probably."

"That works, but I'm on a shoot on the fifteenth for a few days so anytime after then. Love you and say hello the gorgeous Ellie from me."

"I love you to Mom." Aston hung up the phone, his mom's comment bring back his last conversation with Ellie and her speeding away from him. 'I should give her a call and apologise' he thought.

His mobile pinged to indicate a new message. His mom had sent through the image of his birth certificate with her customary smiley face. Distracted away from thoughts of Ellie his attention turned back to Warwick North and how to find his time of death.

He pulled up the GRO website and logged back in to order the death certificate as he pressed send he thought of Harrison and how he could probably get the details a lot quicker. He picked up his phone and face timed his best friend.

Harrison's face popped onto the screen "Hey man I was just gonna call you."

"Beat you to it then H. Where are you? Your lectures finished right?"

"You just missed Ellie dude."

"What? Thought she went to her sisters?"

"Nah. Well yeah, she did but she had a class in the afternoon so she had to come back. I bumped into her on my way out of the computer lab. Holy crap that reminds me I found him."

"Found who?"

"The hypnotist."

"What?"

"Facial recognition my friend, I borrowed the FR software and system from the lab and ran a trace using the picture we found. Pulled up two results, a hundred years apart.

"Fuck really?"

"Oh yeah, one in a photo studio in 1844, the other in Paris 1945," Harrison said excitedly. "We've got evidence my friend, evidence that he's been around for at least a couple of centuries."

"That's awesome and kinda trumps my news. What are the pictures like? Are you heading back now?"

Harrison described the two shots in detail making Aston strangely eager to see his nemesis again if only in photographic form.

"I've emailed them over, but I'll be back in 10 minutes. What was your news? You've found a link between Warwick and Latchford?"

"Nope, I've got Warwick's birth certificate and the time of death and time of birth are real close, like three minutes."

"Wow, how did you get that? Hacked into Ancestry.com no doubt!"

"Old school - had the Government registry office post them."

"You know I could have got that online! Did you get his death certificate too? We could check yours and see how close you are to Warwick!" Aston smiled at the similar thought process.

"Exactly why I called you H. Thought you could save the postage costs!"

Aston's phone pulsed to indicate incoming email.

"The pictures are here. Great work H. I'll see you in ten minutes."

"Oh Aston, Ellie saw them, and I think she might be persuaded to help out again."

"Cool. See you soon." Aston hung up and didn't quite take in what his friend had said. The face of the hypnotist was looking directly at him, once again hauntingly staring into his eyes. His eyes were drawn to something else in the silvery toned image, Aston spotted a monogram on the camera equipment the hypnotist rested his arm on. He pinched the image to zoom in revealing what appeared to be a name but he couldn't make it out as the text was reversed. He sent the picture to his Gmail account and reopened it in Photoshop on his laptop, after flipping the image he could read the monogram perfectly. The name on the camera was Antoine Claudet.

Leonardo Desangé wiped the sweat from his brow, the workouts he needed to maintain his physical condition seemed to be getting harder, although he knew it may just be the repetition over the years that meant they dragged on. He had tried so many different techniques in his time, and he'd experienced a number of personal trainers. Giselle was one of the best, he looked admiringly at her tight physique as she completed the Bikram yoga warm down stretches. They had met by chance on the streets of Paris following the Nazi retreat from France. He had been there to profit from the aftermath of the war and got caught up in the celebrations. He'd been attracted by her physical prowess more so than her beauty but he was also intrigued by her Cantonese heritage, mixed race was so very unusual back in the forties. She had fallen for his elegant charm, bemused by his experiences and knowledge of China and after a few years together in Paris, she followed him to London where she soon became an integral member of his inner circle.

He was glad she was back from Oxford and even more pleased that she had located the boy. "You're positive we have the boys right address Mon Cherie."

"Yes, I saw him in the local bar close to the address he shares with his Chinese friend. I followed them and it's definitely him, they live together" she continued her stretches.

"Strange they can afford a house together outside the usual student residence."

"I did a little extra digging, and the apartment is rented, paid for by the other kids wealthy father."

"That's nice for them but means another memory to manage or body to dispose of, depending on what his friend knows."

Desangé had lost count of the number of memories he'd taken across the years, people who hadn't quite been ready to understand what he had to offer, or clients who had questioned his methods and ethics. The lives he'd taken were fewer in number, but anyone who threatened to expose his past or obstruct him from achieving the goals he wanted was swiftly dealt with and disposed of. The boy Aston North fell into both categories, his revelation about witnessing him in the sixties was a definite threat which could expose him, and also, his ability to reboot his soul and shift into past lives was something Desangé wanted badly. Over the last few days he had been thinking of the immense potential such an ability could bring and it was now his new number one goal.

"I'm going to get this North boy to give us his secret and his little friend could be leverage."

"Leverage?" Giselle asked quizzically.

"North's reluctance may be a little easier to break with his friend experiencing a little, shall we say — pain."

"I do love your darker side!" she kissed him. "Shower?"

"I'll join you in a minute. I need to make a call."

Desangé pulled his towel around his neck walked through the hallway and went through to his private study. The study reflected his own character, stark but sophisticated, the room very minimal but for the grand old desk on which the phone and his personal computer sat. He preferred the secure line he had installed in his study for making certain necessary calls. He lifted the receiver and dialled, as he waited for the call to connect he picked up the only other object on his desk. The elegantly framed picture was there to serve as a reminder of where he started from. His younger self stared back at him through the daguerreotype photograph. As an assistant to one of the pioneers of the photographic industry, he had enjoyed four years learning the trade and capturing the likenesses of well to do London families. He smiled to himself remembering the taking of this shot, he had set up a crude timing mechanism on the Daguerre camera obscura that allowed him to open and close the lens with his foot much to the annoyance of his boss, Antoine Claudet. Disgusted at his assistant's lack of respect he had sacked him on the spot, an act that turned out to be a catalyst for his commission into the British Navy, his fighting in the Opium wars and the journey to immortality and soul shifting.

"Hello," the call connected just as he was about to hang up.

"Nigel, this is the mobile I gave you for emergencies is it not?"

"Yes, Mr Desangé."

"Well in future I expect you to be a little more prompt in picking it up, and maybe have the courtesy to answer a bit more politely than hello."

"Sorry Mr Desangé, I was just..."

Desangé cut him off "I don't care what you were doing. Listen, I need you to organise a team of guys for this weekend to head up to Oxford. We're going to snatch someone so we'll need a van and an overnight stay somewhere quiet to interrogate them."

"Similar to the broker who double crossed us last month?"

"Correct, you're not as slow as you make out Nigel. But I'm hoping it won't get as messy. There will be two kids, and one of them is a tricky little bastard, so make sure you pick your top men."

"Yes Mr Desangé, should I let Elliot know?"

"Absolutely not. If I wanted him involved, he would have been the one calling you Nigel, by no means, is Elliot to be involved, this is just between you and I. Got it?"

"Yes, Mr Desangé."

"Call me back when you've got the team together and sorted out the details. I don't want any fuck ups on this like last week in Kensington."

Desangé hung up the phone and noticed that he'd turned the picture face down on the desk in his frustration. As he placed the frame to its rightful place on his desk, the charred edges reminded him of the night he had retrieved it.

After returning from the Orient with his new found secret, Desangé had forgotten all about his photographic past until reading about Claudet's death in newspaper obituaries. It was 1867, and there was an exhibition in Claudet's Regents Street 'Temple of Photography' Desangé had visited out of interest and noticed his own 'likeness' as part of the exhibits. He knew he had to remove such a prominent trace and reference of him, so he had waited until the exhibition closed, and in the middle of the night set fire to the building. In a moment of vanity, he stopped and returned for his own Daguerreotype, only just saving it and himself from the flames and smoke.

"Are you coming for a shower?" Giselle's voice brought him back to the present day. He turned to see her standing seductively in the doorway wearing only a smile.

"Well, when you put it like that, how can I refuse!"

Aston sat back in the First Class train seats Harrison had managed to change their allocation and upgrade. He'd stopped asking how he did these things but always enjoyed the unexpected extras. Although the journey time to London was just an hour, it still felt good to travel in style, especially after what seemed like a very long week.

With only a few classes in the run up to half term it had dragged. He had finished his unit assignment on data structures and algorithms early and without the help of Harrison much to his friend's surprise. The rest of his free time he spent researching Antoine Claudet and 19th-century photography. The man was a pioneer in the field, making him a prominent figure of the time. He was world renowned and had invented dark rooms using red light to help develop his daguerreotypes and even toyed with the creation of moving imagery. Aston had found images of Queen Victoria, Napoleon, the Duke of Wellington and Charles Babbage. The latter would come in handy for his upcoming unit on the history of computing. By the end of the week, Aston was almost certain which time in history he wanted to reboot to next. He hadn't seen much of Harrison, who had locked himself away developing the reboot application to enable them to influence the specific date of the regression. Aston had tried to get Harrison to explain how it worked on the odd occasions his friend had emerged from his room. He'd been very reluctant to give any detail other than mentioning enhancing brain activity and looking into additional suggestive stimulation mechanics, which Aston took as a he hadn't quite worked it out yet.

Aston saw Harrison approaching with two cups of coffee balanced on top of each other and what looked like a sandwich in a bag between his teeth as he tried to open the carriage door.

"Are you okay there H. Do you need a hand?" Aston stood to take one of the cups from his friend.

"Cheers," he sat down dropping the sandwich in his lap. "We may be able to travel in style but I don't hold out too much hope that the drinks and food will be of similar quality."

"It's not that bad if a little on the cold side."

"Do you want any BLT?" He held up the limp sandwich. Aston shook his head and Harrison took a large bite. "So...did you decide...on a date?" Aston could hardly make out the question as Harrison devoured his breakfast.

"I think we should go for 1844. It gives us the best chance of finding more about the hypnotist as we know where he'll be or at least a good idea of where he had that picture taken."

"I agree, if you chose Paris during the war it would be bloody hard to find him unless we got the exact day that shot was taken. Although I reckon we could get close based on the image and the date, Paris was liberated."

"You are forgetting Warwick would be 15 years old in 1944 and there's the little matter of World War Two which might make it difficult."

"Fair point, that would be tricky."

"But, if you think about it, and I've had a bit of time to think it over, my soul must have died in the battle of Trafalgar, which means my next soul would be 39 in 1844."

"Decision made then, 1844 it is."

"Let's hope the date additions youAnyhow work then. You seemed to be taking enough time this week."

"It'll work but it's reliant on your mind as well Aston. I've not just been working on that I've also been laying the groundwork for our little trip. Ellie took a lot of persuading, you owe me big time for talking her around and for letting her use her sister's place."

"Yeah I know, I know, I owe you both and I promise to make it up to you."

"I'm sweet Aston it's Ellie you need to work on. Have you figured out what you're going to say to her?"

"Not yet, I might just wing it."

"I told you to call her or at least text. It's gonna be awkward." Harrison's inflection on awkward was followed by the announcement that the train was approaching Paddington station.

Aston stressed about what he would say to her all the way to Stratford Station on the tube. The girl he had known as a friend for so long was now possibly more than a friend, girlfriend potential. She had said she loved him, he'd kind of got over his feelings for her a while back, or had he? Maybe it was always an underlying possibility that the two of them never acted upon.

Awkward wasn't the word but how should he handle it? Play it cool 'just say Hey Ellie and walk in' he thought or maybe just come out with an apology and tell her how he felt. The debate raged on within his head all the way up to the door of the address Harrison had been given, and still without an answer, he found himself ringing the door bell.

Ellie opened the door, that smile took him back to the first time he'd seen her. He knew instantly how he felt, but not what to say.

"Hey, Aston." She kissed him on the cheek "H, how you doing, come in. How was the trip?"

"Yeah okay, the walk from the station was the worst," Harrison replied dropping the bags on the floor. Aston was dumbfounded, Ellie was the one playing it cool. They followed her through the hallway and into the kitchen.

"You two should really think about fixing that car."

"I'm holding out until dad buys a new one" Harrison was still doing all the talking. Aston found himself staring into space trying to think of a way to handle this.

"I do need to pee though Ellie, where's the loo?"

"Upstairs on the left, and put the seat down afterwards!" Ellie turned as Harrison pounded up the stairs. "You want a tea?"

Aston had thought of a plan, 'actions speak louder than words' he thought and as he really didn't know what to say, he pulled Ellie toward him and kissed her.

For a second his plan worked, their lips pressed together, Aston felt there was a spark, then there was pain. Ellie slapped him, hard on the face and stormed out of the kitchen. Aston followed her as she headed for the stairs.

"I thought that was what you wanted?" He called after her.

She turned halfway up. "You don't get away with it that easily Aston, you should know that! And besides, I'm still mad at you for not bothering to call me — and getting Harrison to do your bloody grovelling."

Aston felt the sting on his cheek and the knot in his stomach. "Look I'm really sorry, I-I-I didn't know what to say but I feel ..."

Harrison appeared at the top of the stairs looking rather sheepish having interrupted the argument.

"Let's just get on with this bloody reboot, find the hypnotist so we can get the psycho locked up where he belongs — and then we can deal with how you feel!" Ellie barged past Harrison and slammed the bedroom door behind her. Aston looked up at his friend somewhat confused. "This is why I don't understand women!"

"What did I miss?" Harrison walked down the stairs and pointed Aston to the hall mirror. Aston saw the red hand print on his face. "You don't wanna know H! You don't wanna know."

Harrison reached into his bag and pulled out the TCDS headset "Okay then, so where do we set up?"

The slap wasn't discussed for the rest of the morning while they got things set up for the reboot. Ellie had emerged from the bedroom after about half an hour and Aston decided it was in his best interest to keep out of the way at least for a while. Her conversations were mainly directed towards Harrison and Aston was kind of glad that the outburst had served as a catalyst for them all to concentrate on the task at hand.

They had set up in Ellie's sisters spare bedroom, which she had been using as a home gym, so it was clear of clutter and furniture. Aston wasn't opposed to using the yoga mat to lie on, he'd been using one for the past ten years, but Ellie and Harrison had significant doubts. Not only would being at floor level make it harder to help and monitor him but also they were worried how long Aston would be under. They thought it could take a while for his soul to get to London, from wherever Aston rebooted into. Their options were limited, though it was either that or the kids room which had a small cot bed or the main bedroom which is where Ellie was staying. Ellie found a suitable solution by way of a fold out sun lounger stored in the garden shed. Watching Harrison trying to unfold the bed and the metal legs did bring a moment of light relief to the morning. Ellie even managing a brief smile and a chuckle which didn't go unnoticed by Aston.

He also noticed a wry smile when she emerged with an IV stand and kit that Harrison had persuaded her to bring from the teaching hospital supplies.

"Are you sure that's necessary H" Aston asked.

"Look if you're in a regression for over eight hours we'll need to keep up your fluid levels up. Right Ellie?"

"He's right and we actually had this discussion last week, the reboot could go on for a few days. In which case keeping your mind and body hydrated will be critical and one thing I'll be keeping a close eye on."

Aston was tempted to make a joke about her keeping a close eye on his body but chose not to "Okay, I agree, it does make sense. Will one bag be enough?"

Aston knew that there were no guarantees that his 1840s soul had any connections to Antoine Claudet or even if he would be in the same country or continent for that matter. Aston did know something. He was confident that the photographer offered the best chance of finding out something about the hypnotist's past and he had a feeling there would be some link back to his own soul. What he did know for certain was the name and address of the studio in London from the reference off the Wikipedia page plus the numerous articles online. Between 1841 to 1851 Antoine Claudet operated his studio on the roof of the Adelaide Gallery, which they now called the Nuffield Centre. This was behind St. Martin's in the Fields Church, London so he had a prominent landmark to head for during his reboot.

"Now the only thing we need is to guarantee the date I reboot back to. You're positive it's gonna work H?"

"I'm kinda confident but this is the beta test remember."

The app looked impressive, it displayed all the inputs from Aston's vital signs, had the amperage from the TCDS headset plus the brainwave activity and in the right-hand corner had the numeric display for the year selected.

"So how does it work exactly?" Ellie asked.

"It was Aston who put the idea in my head." He looked at Aston who stared back. "You'd been talking about other hypnotist regressions you'd read about where the hypnotist specified the destination." Aston looked puzzled.

"Well, looking at the data captured from the previous reboots, I've managed to isolate the increased brain activity just before the regression. I've set up the TCDS to increase the amperage to the frontal nodes at this time. Using this timing sequence, I've reused the trick we used to get Aston out of his earlier reboot. Whatever date we add into the application, I programmed it to display flashing images of the year we input."

"Shame we didn't have a pair of Google glasses."

"Next time Aston, I'm still waiting for my developers kit. I've also added the date into hypnotist voice track which triggers at the same point. That wasn't so simple as I had to sample his recording to make sure it was similar and then synthesise it to repeat the date during the hypnosis."

"Wow H you certainly don't do things half-arsed," Ellie said smiling. "Let's see if it works. Aston, you ready?" Ellie took his arm, applied a tourniquet, and having found a suitable vein, wiped his forearm with a sterile swab. She looked at Aston and paused as if to say something.

He smiled back and whispered, "I'm really sorry Ellie."

"I know, me too" then inserted the needle and cannula into his arm.

"Ow," Aston exaggerated the slight pain.

Ellie winked "See, I said I'm sorry too. Any how, that didn't hurt you wimp." She applied the sterile tape to keep it in place. "All done, I'll connect the saline IV once you've been under for a few hours."

"Right then let's do this" Aston carefully laid down on the camp bed, the springs twanged ominously but it didn't collapse. Harrison placed the TCDS headset on his head, hooked up the monitors and turned on the wristband Bluetooth connection. The app started to register his vital signs and Aston put on the headphones and turned his own phone to flight mode.

"Are we ready?"

Harrison typed 1844 into the iPad. "All set mate, the rest is down to you."

"Let's see if it does work." He turned to look at his two best friends and knew he couldn't do this without them. "Thanks, H." He turned his head and looked at Ellie and mouthed sorry and closed his eyes. A mixed feeling of trepidation and excitement came over him and then he shut his mind off to all thoughts and concentrated on the voice of the hypnotist in his head he was aiming to uncover. The date flashed in his mind's eye, picked up by his optic nerve perhaps, the voice encouraged him there also, and once again Aston rebooted his soul into the unknown.

CHAPTER THIRTEEN

Aston certainly felt like the reboot had worked but his confused senses made him think otherwise. He couldn't see a thing, having rebooted into complete blackness, he could tell his eyes were open but just couldn't fix on anything. There was no sound apart from an odd scratching above him, or was it below? He was totally disoriented and felt like he was in some sort of void. Aston knew he was in another soul and felt he could get control of his actions if he wanted but his instincts waited until his other senses started to filter through. The smell receptors hit him next, it was acrid, like burnt sulphur, filling his nasal passages and lungs as he inhaled each shallow breath. Then his sense of touch, his hands were braced hard against something, it was cold and hard pressing against his palms but it felt as if his hands were covered in a soft powdery substance. He could also feel specks, of what felt like powder. He felt the tiny molecules land on his face, in his hair and in his open eyes, the sharp stinging sense of pain was finally enough to trigger Aston to take control. Without thinking, he focused his mind, closed his eyes and as he got control pulled his hand to his face, a reaction to try to stop the irritation. He immediately lost balance, his footing went from below him and he dropped like a stone, straight down around eight feet, he dropped into the lightness.

The light penetrated his closed eyelids, the smell was still lingering but not as profound as in the pitch darkness, he tentatively opened his eyes, wary of where he might be. He looked around, he was sitting in the foot of a large open fireplace, surrounded by soot bags, brushes, extension poles. The clouds of soot were settling inside of what looked like a living room.

"Are you all right guvnor?" The muffled young voice came from above him, high above him inside the chimney flu.

"I'm alright lad keep on climbing." His soul responded the fall must have returned control. "I'll be sending the brushes up in a mo, shout when you're near the top."

Aston beamed inside, at least he was in London, the accent was unmistakeable. He found it easy to take control back from his former soul.

"Where are we?" He called up to the voice in the chimney with a hope of establishing at least some idea of his whereabouts.

"In the bloomin' chimney ain't I Mr Daniels."

"No what road?" Aston had half expected a cheeky comment as soon as he spoke.

"Old Kent, o course, same as most days. Have you forgotten somefink?"

Aston didn't bother to reply and started for the main door of the room, he had his bearings now and knew where he needed to be. The room had a light covering of soot where the clouds had settled after his fall, the dust sheets only covered so far and looking back as he opened the door Aston saw the boot print trail he'd left behind him.

As he made for the main entrance down the hallway, the housekeeper came out of what looked like the basement stairs. She looked quite daunting, her black outfit and the stern look on her face added to her dour demeanour.

"Have you finished already?" She snapped. "What was that crashing I heard from downstairs?" She stepped passed him avoiding contact "wait there Soot, you're going nowhere until this is finished."

Aston had no intention of hanging around, for one he had no idea how to sweep a chimney and as for cleaning that soot filled room he didn't even want to think about it.

"Oh my Lord and stars, what on earth..."

Aston quickly closed the door and the problem behind him. He was immediately confronted by another issue as he experienced the hustle and bustle of the nineteenth century London street in front of him. There were men pushing carts, horses pulling wagons and carriages even cows being led down the road. He realised that he had no idea how to get about in the Victorian age, he couldn't just jump on the tube, or hail a black cab. He looked down the steps, there was a horse and cart stood at the side of the muddy road, the sign said Daniels Soot Oh Sweep. He thought that might be an option but had no idea how to ride a horse, let alone drive a horse and cart. 'How hard could it be' he thought.

"Oi sweep get back in here and clean up this bloody mess!" The housekeeper took the option away from him. He bolted at the sound of her shrill voice and thought for second she was chasing him but it was just her manic cries carrying after him.

As he ran Aston thought he could possibly make it all the way to the centre of London but after a couple of minutes his breathing became tight and he stopped. A sensation Aston hadn't had before, he put his hands on his knees and started to cough. He realised that his soul wasn't anywhere close to his own fitness and looking at his feet he thought that hobnail boots were definitely not made for jogging. Catching his breath Aston smelled the vile stink in the London air. He'd read about the over population and lack of adequate sewers contributing to the 'great stink' of the Thames but this was overpowering, how could people live with this. He thought of jogging again but the boots and the unnecessary attention a chimney sweep running would attract led him to decide it wasn't worthwhile. For a moment he thought he may have run the wrong way down Old Kent Road, but the site of St Paul's in the distance reassured him. He longed for Googles street maps and his mobile so he could work out the distance required and plan his best route. He had a good idea of the London layout but he'd usually been a passenger in someone's car or taken the tube when he visited. On the roadside at the next street junction, the nineteenth-century equivalent told him 5 miles to Westminster. The milestone buoyed him on, Aston realised how lucky he was that his soul actually was in London, he knew there was a chance and had hoped before the reboot, but in reality, he could have been anywhere in the world. He knew he would never have stood a chance of getting here and was surprised he hadn't spoken to Harrison about it. But with each step now he was closing in on finding Antoine Claudine and possibly discovering what he needed to trace the photographer's assistant and help uncover some truth and background of the hypnotist.

Ellie turned to Harrison. "I've just thought of something. We have no way of knowing if the date trigger thing has worked?"

"Fuck I didn't think of that." Harrison looked at Aston, who was deep in his regressive state. "It must have worked! If it hasn't he'd reboot back again. Surely?"

"Well didn't you discuss that?"

"No. We didn't talk about much all week, we never spoke about the reboot until earlier today. I forgot to go into the alternatives in the scramble of trying to get the concept working this week."

"Did you not think it might be important?"

"Like I said I was busy and we really didn't get to see much of each other and it didn't come up on the way here."

"What is it with guys and meaningful conversations? Is there a gene missing that avoids them!" Ellie rolled her eyes.

"So did you see the game last night?" Harrison avoided Ellie's hand swipe at his attempt at humour.

"You know I know you're a nerd don't you. So your talking football just won't cut it, more likely to be a keynote speech from Larry Jobs or some other tech CEO."

"Don't dare..." Harrison held his hand up to stop her and Ellie laughed, she knew how to press his buttons. Mixing up Steve Jobs and Larry Page was a sure fire way to do it.

"You want a cup of tea?"

"Of course. Has sister dear got any biscuits?"

"As long as you tell me about your new girlfriend."

"What about Aston? No, it's okay, I've set up a warning if the readings go beyond the average peaks, so we'll know if he's in trouble."

Ellie and Harrison spent the next 20 minutes discussing his relationship with Celia, Ellie's relationship with her sisters and managed to avoid talking about Aston, the reboot process or the hypnotist. Ellie was more comfortable with him since they had bumped into each other on campus earlier that week. She saw a different side of him now and was about to open up about her feelings for his best friend when they heard a knock at the door.

It felt like déjà vu, Ellie and Harrison were both startled by the knock at her sister's door. Ellie knew it wasn't any one calling for her sister or for her, she quizzically looked at Harrison. "Tell me you never told anyone you were coming here!"

"No way, not after last time, that was why we came, right?"

"What about Aston?"

"If he did, he didn't tell me. But why would he and who would he tell? Outside of you and me, he's not got many other close friends."

The knocking got louder and more obsessive and Ellie knew this was trouble.

"You don't think that lunatic from the Church followed us. Sorry, you?"

"Fuckin' better not be." Harrison picked up a kitchen knife.

"H that's not intelligent." The knocking continued and Ellie picked up a knife too. "Just to be safe," Harrison smiled and nodded towards the door.

"Only one way to find out."

"Thanks, H" Ellie was suddenly losing the new found respect she'd found in Harrison. "Who said chivalry is dead!"

"Ellie it's your sister's house, it could be the neighbours. I'm right with you if it's not."

She led the way through to the hallway, peaked through the spy hole, breathed a sigh of relief and put the knife down on the side table.

"It's not the Jesus freak" she whispered to Harrison. "Who's there?" She shouted to the gentleman still knocking. He stopped.

"Miss, I need to speak to Mr Ng. I know he's there. Please open the door!"

"What the fuck?" Ellie turned to Harrison "Who the hell did you tell this time?" she whispered frantically.

"No one, I've got no idea, honest..."

"Open up Miss it's the police." The smartly dressed guy held his identity badge to the door. Ellie slipped on the security chain and opened the door, the identification card peaked through.

"My names Agent Baker, I'm here to find out why Mr Ng would be tapping into the secure passport database and using facial recognition to match records."

Ellie poked Harrison in the chest with her finger, rolled her eyes and said: "Well I guess you'd better come in then."

Ellie took the security chain off the door and let the officer in.

"Thank you, Miss. Sorry, I didn't catch your name?" The officer had a stern but calming tone. She thought he was probably mid-thirties, quiet handsome in a way, great skin but then most Afro Caribbean's had good complexions. Ellie warmed to him and didn't even consider not giving her name. She smiled like only she could "Elisha Cole, but my friends call me Ellie." Her charms instantly had the effect she was used to.

"Thank you. Miss Cole" he said returning her smile. "Mr Ng, I presume." He looked at Harrison.

"Yes." Apprehensively he engaged the officer. "My friends call me H but you can call me Mr Ng."

"I think I'll call you Harrison, and I'll try to make this quick." Ellie noticed his tone getting sterner after Harrison's quip. "Harrison, I'm with MI6, and I don't normally tell people that until it's too late, but with you, I'm making an exception." Ellie switched her gaze to look directly at Harrison, who had done the same. She excised her best death stare and then they both quickly looked back at the MI6 agent.

"Harrison I'm here to ask you how you managed to access some very heavily secured systems. How you had access to facial recognition software that is restricted and also why you were looking for this guy?" The agent held up his phone, on which he had a picture of a passport photo. Ellie's mouth dropped open as she stared very intently at the picture and then turned to Harrison, who was similarly opened mouthed, transfixed by the modern day passport image of the hypnotist.

Harrison couldn't believe the passport he was looking at. He also couldn't believe an actual MI6 agent was standing in front of him. The very fact that a government agent knew exactly what he had been doing at the computer lab was also spinning him out.

'How could I be so stupid,' he thought to himself. 'Using the Oxford servers was my first mistake and not shutting off the passport search was another. Schoolboy errors that I would never have made on my own system. Damn Ferris.'

"I take it you know this man?" The far too suave looking, and a little arrogant, MI6 agent asked. Harrison had no answer. None that would make any sense. In his head, he ran through a couple of options, but neither had a favourable outcome from what he could envisage. He needed to try to deflect the conversation.

"Can I ask how you knew where to find me?"

"You'll no doubt be aware that mobiles have GPS."

"Yes, but how did you get the SIM id to be able to locate the exact address." Harrison knew that you could track a mobile exactly just by the mobile signal. "Professor Ferris told you my number, and you contacted my carrier, right?"

"I'm not at liberty to tell you, but we didn't need your Professor. The stunt you pulled with the airline gave us your mobile details. Now back to why you went to so much trouble to find this man's passport details." The agent shook his phone a little just for effect.

Harrison knew he'd royally screwed up, another schoolboy error using his own mobile. 'Why didn't I call from the computer lab phones!' He was desperately trying to think up a plausible excuse that could explain why he needed the hypnotist passport without bringing Aston into it.

"I can tell you Agent Baker." Ellie cut in.

"Ellie no." Harrison objected but knew it was too late. This was her opportunity to get the authorities involved, something she had wanted to do for weeks. He understood her, but his abject mistrust of authority still made him sceptical and anxious of what she was about to say.

"H, it's better to tell them now because whatever story you were going to construct would only delay things and land you in deeper trouble."

"You should listen to your friend Harrison."

Over the next twenty minutes, Harrison tried his best to be helpful as Ellie told the agent what she knew, or at least what she thought she knew. He added a few facts where he could, but tried to limit the level of detail they were giving to him. Whenever possible he tried to keep the conversation directly away from Aston and to her credit Ellie never let on that he was currently in the upstairs bedroom.

The agent seemed very interested to know more about the hypnotism act but without Aston's side of the story, Harrison couldn't go into too much detail. He got the impression, though, that this was completely new information to his investigation and decided that it was about time that the agent gave them some information.

"So Agent Baker, you now know everything we know about this guy. How about letting us know something. Why is he of interest to MI6?" Harrison thought there was little chance of a direct answer.

Agent Baker smiled, went to say something then stopped himself. He seemed to think for a while and then spoke. "It's a little tricky as this is one element of a wider ongoing investigation. This man is one of a number of suspects thought to be the brains behind a network of insider traders. These traders have ties to international money launderers and have committed multiple counts of significant stock market fraud involving billions of pounds. The man has been under investigation for a number of years, but there has never been any evidence, he's always come up clean. The case was on a watch list and was due to be closed but your hack into the passport database triggered a flag at GCHQ, and it landed on my desk to follow up." Harrison was intrigued and from the look on Ellie's face she was to and Harrison knew Agent Baker could sense their anticipation for more information.

He continued "This is why I'm talking to you now and from what you've told me this information about the hypnotist show, and what did you call them, the 'soul shifters'. If that's true, and I can prove it, it could be the key to establishing his direct involvement in some very dirty trades. I could open the files restart the investigation, and it might eventually get him locked up."

"Agent Baker, are you able to tell us who this man really is?" Ellie was direct, and her smile certainly helped facilitate the answer.

"I guess it's not going to harm the investigation, and you would be better off in you knew who this man really is. His name is Leonardo Desangé."

"So are you working on this on your own? You're just following up a cold case based on new evidence."

"Well, it's not a cold case Harrison, when there are billions of pounds involved these cases never go cold. But yes am I working independently on this line of inquiry."

"So can I confirm you're not here to arrest me for hacking into the passport database." Harrison felt he needed to ask for clarification.

"Harrison?" Ellie obviously thought he was a little too cheeky.

"Hey we've cooperated, and I'm sure Aston will be able to help too." Harrison glanced at Ellie "when he gets back I mean."

Agent Baker smiled and nodded, Harrison knew he was in the clear. "You're quite safe for now Mr Ng, but I would stay clear of government sites for a little while and yes, please make sure Mr North contacts me as soon as he gets back."

Aston regretted not researching more about London in the 1840s. The monuments and buildings he thought would help him navigate, weren't built or were in construction. London without Big Ben and the Houses of Parliament just felt wrong. The building work next to Westminster Abbey gave no hint of the iconic structure it was to become. It was only when he passed the Abbey he realised exactly where he was. The hustle and bustle of the London he was experiencing was as vivid and evident as it was in his own time but the Victorian version was wildly different. The horse-drawn carriages of all shapes and sizes replacing the modern transport modes and they seemed to be increasing in number, along with the myriads of people on foot, as he got closer to the Thames. The stench was also increasing in intensity. He'd stopped a number of times to catch his breath and even tried using the inside of his jacket, pulled over his face as a mask to try to limit the pungent odour. Aston knew he'd never get used to it and was hoping it would be behind him once he'd crossed Westminster bridge. The sweeps outfit seemed to be an excuse for people to stop and say hello and to ask him to wish them luck, it was apparently deemed a worthy profession in the early Victorian community.

As he crossed the Thames, the foul stench was at its worst, a quick glance up the river along the embankment was all he could manage. The chaos of the roads and traffic was nothing compared to those navigating the river. Boats of every size and description were bustling up and down the banks and from what he could see from the sewer pipes the contribution to the smell was never ending.

The stink did subside once he passed Westminster and he did notice an upturn in the quality of the clothes worn. Especially top hats, he wasn't sure if he'd not noticed before but as he walked up Whitehall towards Charing Cross, the number of gentleman wearing top hats seemed to triple. He started to feel a little conspicuous in the sweeps garb, a number of the coach drivers who passed by were giving him looks as if to question his status. He remarked to one morning suited pedestrian who had looked him up and down like he had just climbed out of the stinking Thames, "What's up don't you think they get chimneys cleaned in Downing Street." The gent scuttled passed and Aston smiled to himself enjoying the curt cockney accent. Five minutes later he was stood, again dumbstruck, staring in awe at Trafalgar Square. The monument to Nelson appeared to have just completed construction, it was cordoned off, and apart from the odd Mason here and there, it was completely empty. The statues were pristine and the brand new stone looked at odds with how Aston had grown used to seeing them. One of the masons came through the cordon and saw Aston staring up at the column.

"Pretty sight ain't it."

"Magnificent, I've never seen it like this before."

"Well it's taken four years to put it together, quite somefink I'd say. You want a quick look around Soot?"

"Can you? That would be awesome." The Mason gave him an odd look at his reply and Aston thought to himself to be mindful of his choice of words.

The Mason led him behind the cordon and Aston got a firsthand view of the Square. He listened intently as the Mason told the ins and outs of the build, the issues faced, problems with fountains, statues that weren't due to be finished, and the delays in removing the scaffold around Nelson's column, all things that were incomplete for the launch tomorrow.

Aston felt privileged to get a guided tour, his friends wouldn't believe him and thanked the Mason for taking the time. He also asked him if he knew of the photography studio based in the Adelaide gallery behind St Martins church. The Mason said he'd had no call for that new fangled technology and preferred a proper artist and craftsmen.

He did show him the quickest route passed the church which led to Adelaide Street. On the way there, Aston noticed the bill posters promoting the illustrious public opening tomorrow, 1 May 1844. At least now he knew the day and date he was in.

It didn't take him long to find the gallery and Aston nerves were on edge as he made his way up the stairs to the roof studio. Knocking on the studio door, Aston suddenly realised he had no idea what to ask. He couldn't tell the man the truth as he'd have the door slammed in his face or could even get his soul locked up in an asylum. Hearing footsteps approaching Aston scrambled around for ideas. He could be a long lost friend but what if the hypnotist was there, he'd be found out immediately. The door opened, and Aston led with the easiest and only option.

"Alright guvnor, I'm here to discuss sweeping your chimney. We have a deal with the gallery, and they said to give you a knock."

"Excuse Moi."

"I'm here to sweep your chimney."

"But I know not of this and where are your brushes?"

"Let me in and I can have a look-see, then give you a price. Then I'll go and get me gear!" Aston stepped forward hoping the Frenchmen would agree. "You can even take me picture if you like!"

Claudet looked bemused but let him in. Aston strode forward confidently, he really didn't know what on earth he was going to say when he found the chimney. He just hoped it would give him a chance to engage the photographer in a conversation and possibly mention his assistant. The light filled the studio from the glass-covered ceiling, Aston looked up and said: "Great light in here does that help reduce the exposure time?" For a second he'd forgotten where he was and not thought about what he was saying.

"Yes, of course, that why we chose this place, but how do you know of exposure times?"

Of course a lowly chimney sweep could never be educated enough to know about the photographic process. What on earth was he thinking to say that. Aston thought of an answer that would help pacify the old photographer and help himself.

"I'm sorry guvnor but that was what your assistant said last time I came around."

"That imbecile. Zut Alors. I might have guessed."

"He seemed a nice bloke, French like you, very knowledgable." Aston tried to push some buttons.

"He was no artist, a pretender, and he knew nothing about the art. He is no longer in my employ for that reason." He was obviously still aggrieved for some reason. "The chimney is this way sweep." The Frenchman huffed and strode through the main area into a dining room Aston recognised it from the photo of the hypnotist posing with the equipment.

"When did your assistant leave?"

"I do not want to discuss him." Claudet wasn't happy and obviously a little guarded about his former assistant. "Just look at the chimney, name your price and then get your brushes" he said rather sternly.

Aston stuck his head into the small fireplace pretending to know what he's doing, looking up reminded him of his earlier encounter albeit this chimney was a lot smaller but still as black as pitch. He prodded the sides and a bank of soot dropped off the chimney walls and hit the fireplace floor and released a small cloud.

"Imbecile, look what you are doing! Get out now."

"Needs a damn good clean Mr Claudet, that's why it's dropped. You don't want that to drop during a sitting and it's a fire hazard." Aston thought he even sounded knowledgeable as he spun his lie to try to rescue the situation. "I can do it for..." He realised he hadn't the first clue about pre-decimal currency let alone pricing in Victorian times. Aston glanced around and saw a stack of posters advertising Antoine Claudet's daguerreotypes for four shillings and sixpence.

"...Four shillings." He guessed. The French photographer scratched his chin, as he thought for a while. He to glanced at the posters on the sideboard.

"How about I take your likeness and in return you sweep my chimney. It will be an interesting portrait for my collection, and you will have a miniature to show your family."

"You have yourself a deal." Aston wiped the soot of his hands on his clothes and offered to shake the photographers hand. After a brief pause, he obliged.

"Oh, Mon Dieu." He looked at his hands covered in soot. "Wait here I will get cleaned up and get my equipment.

Aston knew this would allow him more time to quiz the photographer about his assistant and was quite excited about his soul being captured for posterity.

Aston noticed the monogram on the camera obscura as the photographer set up the shot, it reminded him of the picture that had led him here. He avoided being direct while the shot was being taken, which seemed to take an age, and he could see that Mr Claudet didn't care for intrusions or conversation during the session. He bided his time until after the shoot and offered to help him with his equipment.

"Mr Claudet do you still use an assistant." Aston asked as he handed him the box of exposed plates.

"Normally I have a two or three that help around the studio but not today. As you know, one has recently been dismissed, and the other is unwell."

"That's unfortunate, was he with you a long time, your French assistant."

"Desangé was older and agreed to be learning the trade on a five-year basis but although he showed some skills Mr Desangé was too set in his ways and was destined to take another path."

'Leonardo Desangé' Aston smiled he had a name finally. "Shame he didn't stay with you, are you still in touch with him?"

"I'd prefer not to talk about the matter. I shall process these plates and then I suggest you should honour your end of our agreement Mr I'm sorry I didn't get your name?"

"Daniels" Aston knew he needed more than just his name but thought it best to change the subject before alienating the photographer. "Mr Claudet how long does it take to process the plates and create the images?"

"You seem to be well versed on the methods of photography. Odd for a sweep or was this something my wayward apprentice told you too."

"No sir, I'm just keen to educate myself where I can, it gets that way when you spend so much time working in the dark."

"Interesting that you mention the dark, the plates need to be developed in darkness, your eyesight may well be suited to working in the dark room. Most assistants struggle with chemicals in the darkness, and it leads to accidents and wastage."

"Surely the red light helps them?"

"Red light?" Mr Claudet looked at him puzzled. "Why red light, what do you mean, there's no light..." He stopped mid-sentence and Aston could see he was working something through in his mind. Aston had read that Claudet had pioneered advances in the use of red lights in darkrooms.

Antoine Claudet's eyes lit up. "...Mon Dieu of course, red light! It is the far side of the light spectrum. It should work. I do not know why I haven't thought of this before."

Aston realised what he may have just done but the photographer wasn't angry he just looked so pleased as if he'd thought of it himself.

"How do you know of this, is it used in the chimney to help you see? I cannot thank you enough for this idea. You should have your likeness for nothing and I will pay for your services."

"There is something you could tell me?" Aston saw this as an opportunity to find out more about the real reason he was here.

"Ask away my friend, I am indebted to you."

"I need to find your assistant, Leonardo Desangé."

The smile dropped from the photographer's face and the pensive look returned. "If I tell you, you must promise not to give him this idea of red light."

"I just need to speak to him, it has nothing to do with photography Mr Claudet I assure you."

"I think you may not be able to find him, I have his last business address, he'd established his own studio the swine. He was to be commissioned into the Navy to take photographs so I think he is on his way to China. He had the gall to ask me for a reference for his work." Claudet went over to his desk and leafed through a few papers. He found what he was looking for and handed it to Aston.

He read the note from the Navy commission which included Desangé's last known business address in St Mary's Axe, his date of birth and details of his commission for fighting in the Opium wars. It was effective 3 April 1844.

He had hoped to find the hypnotist but at least, he had his name, an address and a date of birth. The latter was of most interest, 21 October 1805. Desangé was born on the same day as the Battle of Trafalgar. Aston realised the significance of this and was certain he couldn't dig any further on the subject. As Claudet started to complain about his apprentice, he closed his mind and searched for the blackness, he rebooted back leaving behind a very bewildered sweep with an even more confused photographer.

Leonardo Desangé held up Giselle's hand and took the applause as normal. The hypnotist had again wowed the audience, this time at the rearranged gig in the Wellington Club, Kensington, and he felt energised by the reaction. This adulation, as it always did, fed his own ego and was a high he found not many narcotics could replicate. It was the main reason he continued to put on the shows. To some degree, this show also made up for missing the North boy at Oxford, and as a bonus one of the nights participants showed some potential as another soul to convert, or at least a mind to manipulate.

As he walked back to the dressing room, the man approached him wanting to talk more. He was middle aged, early forties, well spoken and quite handsome, a black guy but that wasn't an issue now as it was in his day. Giselle warmed to him as she had during the show but Desangé wasn't the jealous type. He told him to wait for ten minutes and then come back to the dressing room to be taken out of hypnosis with the other participants.

The guy was the last of the volunteers to visit the dressing room, and Desangé was quite pleased as the club was closing which meant no more intrusions. The man had been very susceptible to hypnosis and gone quite deep even though he was early on in the routine as one of three who made up the barking dog routine. Desangé chose to fake the backing out of hypnosis routine as he thought he might be able to use it to delve deeper during their talk.

"So Mr Desangé how long have you been hypnotising people?" Desangé was definitely not expecting the man to know his name.

"Well, you appear to know my name, but I'm not sure I got your full name. Paul was it? Giselle, do you have his volunteer form?"

Giselle handed him the form, she was a little more organised nowadays after the Oxford shows.

"Mr Baker. Can I ask how you came by my name?"

"You've been on our radar for a while Leonardo, and it's Agent Baker." Desangé was a little taken aback as he pulled out his MI6 credentials from his jacket. He was surprised that he revealed himself so early in their conversation. His first mistake."

"Am I under investigation Agent Baker?" he kept a straight face and waited to hear how this would play out.

"Not yet Mr Desangé but I wanted to meet you in person and be the first to let you know, that we now know where you are, and this little charade you have going, so you'll need to be on your game."

"Well, may I ask exactly what it is you think I'm doing? It's surely not my act that's got MI6 concerned."

"I'm not at liberty to reveal the nature of the investigation Mr Desangé, but I like to introduce myself to my adversaries before the battle commences. I feel it gives me the edge and allows me to sit back and watch you make mistakes."

"Well Mr Baker, I would love to play your little game, but I do feel it's me who has the edge." Desangé clicked his fingers. "Sleep." The agents subconscious took control of his body, his head dropped, and he fell into a hypnotic state.

Desangé picked up his phone and dialled.

"Nigel! Well done for picking up first time. You still have the van from Oxford. Yes?"

"Yes, boss. It's due back tomorrow." His henchman confirmed.

"Well, we can make some use of it. Pull it around to the rear doors of the Wellington club in twenty minutes. Call me when you're outside."

Desangé hung up the phone and turned to the unconscious agent. "Mr Baker when I click my fingers you'll awaken and answer my questions truthfully. Nod if you understand." Agent Baker nodded his head.

"Have to say I thought this guy showed promise earlier, maybe I'm losing my touch. Must be that damn kid."

"Don't be too hard on yourself Leonardo. He seemed genuine to me too." Giselle handed him a drink. "Heres to a good show and it looks like we get to have some fun after as well."

They clinked glasses, and Desangé took a sip. He then snapped his fingers, and Agent Baker sat up in the chair as if he hadn't been unconscious.

"Mr Baker I'll need you to hand me your phone." The agent reached into his jacket pocket and gave up his mobile." Desangé popped the back off the phone and extracted the SIM card. "You'll not be needing this anymore." He dropped the SIM and the handset into the ice bucket." Any other tracking devices or gadgets?"

"No Mr Desangé."

"So Mr Baker, what am I being investigated for?"

"The investigation is based on international money laundering and illegal trading activity."

"What evidence do you have?"

"The are a number of multi-million-pound trades against the market linked to a holding company that has links to you and a number of entities to which you have joint ownership."

"Why did you come here today?"

"You've been a suspect for a long time but following a strong lead from a separate line of enquiry, I discovered your hypnosis sideline and traced your schedule to the Wellington club."

"Who was this lead and what did they tell you?" Desangé looked at Giselle quizzically as he asked the question.

"It was an Oxford student who led me to you." Desangé and Giselle both mouthed 'Oxford' as Agent Baker continued. "His name is Harrison Ng, and he managed to access the Governments passport database which is behind a series of very secure firewalls. Once he had access, he managed to perform an illegal search using a specialist facial recognition software using a picture of you. This search triggered a flag, and I followed up as a routine enquiry. Little was I to know that after a short interrogation, Harrison and his female friend Elisha Cole would uncover your apparent ability to shift back in time. This evidence coupled with our previous enquiry strongly suggests you had the means to manipulate market decisions and affect large-scale stock market fraud."

"Well Mr Baker, I think you're about to find out that it's not just the stock market I can manipulate."Desangé clicked his fingers instantly returning Agent Baker to his state of unconsciousness.

"Oxford," Desangé said to Giselle. "Had to be linked to Oxford."

"I know, and you know who's living with Harrison Ng in Oxford?"

Giselle paused for effect. "Aston North!"

CHAPTER FOURTEEN

"Aston, Aston? Aston! — He's not responding."

Aston could hear her voice, she sounded stressed.

"His heart rate is racing he's about to go into cardiac arrest if we don't get him back."

"What can we do? I can up his TDCS current to see if that stimulates him."

Aston recognised his best friend voice. They both sounded close, but he felt like he was outside of his own soul. It was weird a bit like when he was observing his former souls but without being able to see.

"Hang on this might work." Aston wondered what Ellie could be proposing. He heard a loud slap. His eyes opened, and he could feel the sting on his face.

"Owww, good god Ellie." He rubbed his cheek to try to take away the pain.

"Oh thank God. Aston, you're back. Your heart rate went off the charts look. Show him the display Harrison."

Aston could feel his heart racing, but it didn't feel abnormal, more like a hard day's workout. He looked at the iPad display that Harrison was holding, his heart had been approaching 400 beats per minute.

"400 that's not good right?"

"No shit, that's at the maximum limits for tachycardia." Ellie had her stethoscope on his chest. "It's so strange, your heart sounds normal now." She placed it back around her neck, 'like a natural' Aston thought. He held out his arm for her to remove the IV needle and cannula. " Tachycardia can be brought on by severe stress, so for some reason when you reboot back, your body is fighting it or something, and it causes the heart rhythm to go bananas."

"Okay, but did you have to slap me, that's twice in one day!"

"Well, you should be used to it by now." Ellie raised her arm playfully. "I guess it was either that or Harrison zapping you with more AC current. I thought slapping was faster."

"Well, thanks," Aston said sarcastically. He also thought it was a good time to change the subject away from his health. "So it worked H, the time additions worked. I rebooted into 1844, just as we'd planned, well I think it was your planning."

"We figured it had worked as you would have come back relatively quickly if it didn't. How was it?" Harrison seemed a little subdued.

"You won't believe it. I only rebooted into someone's chimney flu, it was pitch black, I thought I was blind for a moment. I was a chimney sweep, Mr Daniels at your service guvnor, what do you make of that?"

His friends didn't quite get Ashton's attempt at a cockney accent. "What time is it? I'm starving." He suddenly felt famished.

"It's late, but I can rustle something up," Ellie said smiling. " Cheese on Toast?"

As they had made their way to the kitchen, Harrison turned to Aston at the top of the stairs. He paused as if to say something important but then seemed to shake it off, then he said "Bloody lucky you rebooted in London. I was worried about where you would end up."

"I know, good job it was the Old Kent Road, so I didn't have too far to go!"

"I bet it was kinda freaky seeing London back then."

"It's was awesome but oh my god, the smell!"

Aston continued to give his friends the full details of his latest adventure, his journey through the streets of eighteenth century London and his meeting with Antoine Claudet. They had devoured two rounds of Ellie's cheese on toast by the time Aston got to the crucial part of his story when he revealed what Claudet had told him about the hypnotist.

"Don't you think it's a little strange that his date of birth is the same day as the battle of Trafalgar?" Aston really thought his friends would be a bit more into the details. "What if the significance of the battle I saw in my regression is more than we thought. Guys? You don't seem that bothered. Have I missed something?"

"Aston" Ellie spoke first. " We found out about Leonardo Desangé about an hour after you went under."

"What! How could — I don't get it?"

"We had a visitor. A government agent. MI6 actually." Harrison said.

"What the fuck!" Aston's mind was racing with a hundred and one questions. "How did the agent know who Desangé was? How does he know about us? What was he doing coming here?" Aston could see his friends trading looks as if to decide who should say what. "Hang on. What did you tell him?" Ellie instantly blushed but said nothing. Harrison spoke.

"It was my fault, remember the search using the facial recognition software last week when I used the Oxford computers. Well, I triggered a red flag at GCHQ or something, and I obviously didn't cover my tracks so well. I'm sorry Aston it was stupid."

"H. Hacking 101, hide your IP, you taught me that."

Harrison apologised repeatedly as he went through their meeting with Agent Baker. Aston sat a little shell shocked, occasionally shooting daggers at Ellie as Harrison told him the whole story.

"Aston, don't look at me like that. It's out there now, so that's a good thing right? The authorities are on our side. They now know he's a hypnotist, and I think they're going to arrest him." Ellie seemed relieved, but Aston felt let down, he couldn't quite get his head around why his friends had betrayed him.

"So let me get this clear. The MI5 guy asked you why you were looking for Desangé, and you just out and told him about the whole reboot, soul shifters, and hypnotist thing."

"He was MI6, but yeah."

"He was going to arrest Harrison for hacking into government computer files. We had to tell him and quite frankly I'm glad we did. It's too dangerous. We were looking after you."

Aston had kind of figured that Ellie had been the instigator, she would have gone to the police a few weeks ago if he hadn't objected. She was looking after herself more like. He was feeling quite resentful to both of them and needed to find a way to process all this.

"Look, I can't handle this right now. My heads spinning, it's late." Aston checked the kitchen cooker clock, it was after 2 am. "I'm feeling really tired. I'm going to try and get some sleep. We can continue this in the morning. Okay?"

Aston made for the door and the stairs before they could answer. "I'll take the camp bed again H" he called out as he raced up to his room.

Aston didn't really need to sleep, he just lay on the camp bed and listened to a few muffled conversations downstairs. It wasn't long before he heard, judging by the noises made, first Ellie, then Harrison head back to their respective rooms.

He stared at the ceiling, trying to work out what he should do next. He certainly didn't want to spend tomorrow being interrogated by some MI6 agents. He'd hoped that by using the address Claudet had provided, he and his friends would be spending the day planning how they could track down Leonardo Desangé. The address he'd intentionally failed to share with his friends after they broke the news of their own visitor.

As he lay there, another nagging thought played over and over in his head. He'd mentioned it briefly to his friends before they stressed him out. It was a thought that had blossomed when Claudet had shown him the Royal Navy draft paper with Desangé's date of birth on it. If his own soul had died at the Battle of Trafalgar, there might be a very strong link between the two of them. The more it swirled around in his head, it dawned on him that the cannon explosion he'd witnessed during his regression, might well have been the one that killed Desangé's previous incarnation too. He tried to shake off the idea, as it was a bit of a long shot given the amount of souls that died that day. But, if it was true, it could seemingly tie both him and the hypnotist together, two souls linked by that significant event. He tried to sleep but couldn't, his mind jumping between the betrayal of his friends, especially Ellie, who he thought was back onside now, and the horrible thought of this link between his own soul and that of Leonardo Desangé'. He contemplated meditating to clear his thoughts but was too afraid of what or where that might lead. He just couldn't get off to sleep and on hearing the first calls and tweets of the birds greeting the dawn, he got out of the camp bed, laced on his Nikes and opted for the streets to save him and headed for a run. 'No trouble sleeping in there' he thought as the sound of Harrison snoring echoed in the hall as Aston crept passed his friends room and down the stairs. Closing the door as quietly as he could, he strode out into the grey morning mist, sucked in the dawn air, pressed play on his iPhone and set out on his run.

"Nigel, listen I said pull the around the rear entrance, that's not out front." Desangé turned to Giselle holding his phone to his chest "can you believe this guy!" He returned to the call. "Look I don't care if you cannot open the gate, use your influence, intelligence or brute force and pull the fucking van around the back of the club in five minutes. And Nigel if you don't you'll be joining my guest at the bottom of the fucking Thames!"

Five minutes later Agent Baker stepped into the back of Ford Transit van parked awkwardly close to the beer barrels and bottle bins behind the Wellington club. Leonardo Desangé was right behind him followed by his assistant Giselle. Before he got into the van, he turned to Giselle. "You take the car back to the apartment, and I'll see you in a couple of hours. You'll need to dispose of this somewhere on your journey." He handed her the agents mobile and SIM card and stepped into the van closing the door behind him.

"Well, Nigel I'm so glad you joined us. You know where we're going, right? You spoke to our friend at Tate & Lyle Sugars?"

"Yes, boss he's meeting us at the gate on Factory Road in twenty minutes. He was glad to be of service again."

"So he should, his shareholding would have never been where it is without our help."

Desangé had helped a select number of associates obtain significant shareholding in various high profile companies. These companies were carefully chosen to offer leverage in the stock exchange and commodities markets. The trade in sugar may not be where it was 100 years ago, but the factories position on the Thames came in handy on a number of occasions. Its proximity to the Thames barrier meant whatever was disposed of could be guaranteed a good swell and strong current to enable it to travel far enough downstream to make its drop off point virtually untraceable.

Nigel turned the ignition as Desangé clicked his fingers, both the van, and the MI6 agent sprang to life.

"Agent Baker I need you to tell me a little more about your investigation."

"What would you like to know?"

"Have you spoken to your fellow officers about your line of enquiry?"

"No?"

"You may just have saved your own life. Nigel, we may not need..."

"I have filed a written report with the section house listing my line of enquiry, the potential suspect's ID and the location where I would be observing and engaging the suspect."

"Most unfortunate, Nigel stick to the plan."

In the twenty minutes, it took to get across the city, Leonardo Desangé had managed to extract every scrap of detail from Agent Baker about his investigation. He knew he had become a little arrogant over time at the success of his latest investment company. There had been a few in the last century, and this investigation was an indication that it was probably time to change again. His arrogance had led him to not realise that the questions he'd faced by the securities commission about his trading activity would be noticed higher up. Beating the market a few too many times and then goading the commission with cast iron proof of legitimate trades had been too enjoyable. No one had ever been able to prove it wasn't legitimate. Shifting had been far more lucrative than he ever imagined when Li Wei had told him of the secret. But because of this one agent, he would now need to close all the loopholes, transfer assets and restart the company elsewhere, something he hadn't done since the nineties.

The most annoying fact was that the investigation was about to be closed down until the kid ran the passport database search and triggered the red flag.

"If those kids hadn't been looking for you I wouldn't be here." Agent Baker said just as they pulled up to the factory road gate. He placed his hand on the agents forehead and said "Sleep." The agent fell back unconscious, and Desangé opened the doors of the van to greet his associate.

"Lord Sugar!"

"Don't call me that." The associate grimaced as he shook Leonardo's hand.

"You know it's true, this little investment has almost got you into the upper house." Desangé looked over at the massive Tate & Lyle signage on the iconic blue and white refinery buildings.

"Another minor problem you need our help with Leonardo?"

"Yes, but the less you know, the better. Are we all clear?"

"The security guard knows not to interfere, and the lights and cameras have been killed on the main docking wharf. Does Nigel know the way?"

"I'm all good Mr Desangé, right after the gate on to the central warehouse and out under the loading area. Straight out over the river towards the giant blue cranes. Easy?"

"An elephant never forgets eh Nigel!" Desangé and his associate laughed.

"Well don't forget this favour, I may need a boost to my portfolio soon Leonardo. Sugars not as sweet as it used to be."

"In good time, come and see Elliot and me at St Mary's next week and thanks again." Desangé climbed back in the van, pulled the sliding doors closed. Once through the factory gates the route was just as Nigel remembered and they pulled up to the main docking wharf.

"Nigel don't get too close to the edge and kill the lights."

"Now Agent Baker time for a swimming lesson." Desangé pulled open the van's doors. The were on the edge of the dock with the Thames tide lashing the side of the dock. The lights on the flood barrier station in the distance to the right. He placed his hand on the Agents forehead and said "Agent Baker you've been a big help, but I need you to do one last thing for me. When I clap my hands, I want you to dive into the water and swim as fast as you can. A boy is drowning somewhere by the barrier, and you're going to save him. Have you got that? Nod if you understand." Agent Baker nodded. " One other thing." Desangé smiled sadistically. "When you hear me whistle you will become that boy. You'll be heavier than lead, unable to stay afloat, but you know a secret agent is going to save you, so no need to shout and don't worry if you go under. Have you got that? Nod if you understand me." Desangé got out of the van and looked at Nigel and winked as the agent nodded. "You have to love the power of hypnotism." He clapped his hands and Agent Baker dove straight into the cold, dirty water and started to swim.

"Will he be able to hear your whistle out there?" Nigel asked.

"Of course, I'm not going to let him get too far, watch."

Desangé put his two little fingers in his mouth, folded the end of his tongue and blew, very hard, the high pitched whistle echoed out the twenty or so metres that Agent Baker had swum. He stopped, thrashed about a little. Desangé turned to his driver and said: "See, what did I tell you, works like a charm." They both watched as the agents head turned frantically looking for his saviour, he held up his arms in a last hopeful gesture as he succumbed and slipped beneath the waves. Desangé smiled wryly to himself as he imagined the agent coming out of his hypnotic state for a brief moment of terror before he drowned.

Aston's running app told him he'd completed fifteen miles, and he was closing in on his original start point. His head was clear and apart from the lack of actual sleep he felt relatively good. During the run, he'd released the tensions built up from the anger of his betrayal by both of his friends. He'd rationalised Harrison's part in it and was sure his friend would have allowed himself to be arrested rather than give up information to the authorities. Aston was still mad at him for making mistakes and not covering his tracks but reckoned that his flatmate could not be held responsible for the breach of trust. Ellie, on the other hand, he couldn't forgive, he knew she would have jumped at the chance to include the authorities when they turned up. The maddening thing was that he thought she was back on side, and they were working things out. The kiss was a mistake, a large one. Aston had spent a few miles trying to figure that out, figure her out, in fact trying to figure her and him out. The slap, actually both slaps were another thing, plus the arguments before that. He'd never spent this much time thinking about her, and he'd definitely never considered their relationship or its status, and he was a very long way from updating his Facebook status. She'd well and truly deleted him metaphorically when she told her tale to the authorities.

He could see the reason for her to tell but was surprised at himself for not confronting her about it last night. He couldn't figure out why he wouldn't do that, in the past they would have argued it out, but now his reactions were becoming irrational. "Get a grip Aston," he said aloud trying to get some perspective back. One thing he did know for sure was that his feelings about her had indeed become somewhat confused.

Aston shook off that train of thought and focused on his primary objective, finding more about Leonardo Desangé. He decided that he wouldn't share one vital piece of information that Antoine had given him, the hypnotist's original address. Aston hadn't told them last night, he was going to, but he'd intentionally held it back, thinking it would be where they could all investigate first.

The crisp cold air had clarified his thoughts, though, and he felt it was better to go it alone for a while partly out of spite for the betrayal but also to stop anyone else from being hurt or getting pulled into this world he'd uncovered.

Aston stopped just outside the house, someone was at the door. In an instant his mind ran through a number of scenarios of who it might be, then he noticed the milk cart on the other side of the road. The milkman busied passed him on his morning deliveries, he said good morning and a relieved Aston nodded back to him and watched him for a while until he jumped back into his milk cart and trundled down the street. He thought it was the MI6 agent back again to question him, something he wanted to avoid or at least delay as long as he could. His friends had provided enough information already, so Aston thought a few more days wouldn't hurt and maybe if the address pans out he could even help them find Desangé.

As Aston got to the door, it dawned on him that he didn't pick up a key. He tried the door but knew it was locked, latched from the inside. It was still quite early so he couldn't rightly knock and wake both of them up. For a moment he considered it, they had let him down so he could justify getting them up early. The nice guy in him decided against it, he chose to text Harrison.

'H I'm outside, no keys - can you let me in! :0)'

He just hoped that H was sleeping with his phone next to him like he did when he was at home. While he waited for a response, he checked out the side entrance to the house. Although it was semi-detached, the side boundary was shared with the next building. Aston tried the fence to see if he could get over but figured it would be difficult without making a heap of noise. On his way back to the front door he tried the door handle on Ellie's mini parked in the drive, but that was another thing he was locked out of. Aston checked his phone then tried his friend again.

'H still outside, get up and let me in! ;0I' he sent it twice for effect.

The double text worked as his phone sprang to life.

"What are you doing outside you crazy bastard?" Harrison sad laughing. "It was weird I was dreaming you were trying to contact me from a reboot and bloody woke up to my phone buzzing. You do know it's only six o'clock? Of course, you do you've probably not been to sleep. Meditating or running, I'm guessing running."

As ever his friend knew him too well.

"H just let me in before we wake the street." Aston hung up and stood by the door waiting for his friend. He heard him thump down the stairs and recalled his mother chastising him as a child doing the same. "You sound like a heard of elephants H" Aston recited his mother's analogy when Harrison opened the door. "I was trying not to wake you both up."

"Dude you woke me from an excellent sleep, even if the dream was a bit weird. Cut me some slack, I'm not the one pounding the pavement at the break of dawn and forgetting my keys."

"Fair point."

"What's going on? You guys know it's only six o'clock I take it?" A rather tired looking Ellie appeared at the top of the stairs. Aston thought she still looked good in her pyjamas and ruffled hair.

"Sorry Ellie, my bad, forgot to take a key on my run."

"I thought we were being raided by the bloody secret service."

"Sorry, Ellie that was me and the stairs," Harrison replied sheepishly. "Go back to sleep."

"Right." Ellie closed the door behind her.

"I'm making coffee if you want one H. Not quite Bean standard, but I think I saw a Nespresso machine yesterday."

"May as well, let's check it out."

Aston found the machine and the pods and they sat down at the breakfast bar.

"What on earth were you doing jogging at four in the morning," Harrison asked.

"Had a lot on my mind, couldn't sleep. I was kind of pissed off about the secret agent, to be honest."

Harrison shrugged his shoulders. "Sorry dude. I wish it hadn't happened. I feel bad if it makes you feel better."

"H, I'm pretty sure you weren't the first to tell all, and to be honest I don't blame you. In the same situation I'd probably do the same, especially if someone else..." Aston looked to the ceiling. "Had confessed all first."

Harrison drained his coffee. "At least it's out now, if MI6 are on the case then we've got nothing to worry about. They'll lock him up so no need for us to bother with him. We can get on and explore the past, I'm so glad the date modifications worked. When are we doing another one?"

"Soon, I've got to go and see Mom." Aston lied, he wanted to go to London and check the address Claudine had given him. "Maybe when I get back to Oxford in the week."

"Are you going to contact Agent Baker today?"

"Not today, it's Sunday after all, and I'm going to get off soonish so that Ellie doesn't badger me all day." Aston hadn't forgotten their promise to the agent that they would tell Aston to contact him as soon as they saw him. He figured the guy can wait for a few days.

"You could go see him in London. Check out the secret service building. Now that would be cool."

"Yeah maybe." Aston couldn't think of anything worse than being interrogated in the spy centre of London. He finished his coffee. "H, can you tell Ellie I went to Moms. Not sure if I want to see her, and we'd only end up arguing. So I reckon it's best if I get out of here. I'm gonna finish my workout and hit the shower and then head to London. Is that okay?"

Aston knew it would be and left his friend, albeit a bit bemused. After finishing his workout, he showered and left without saying another word to either of them.

"I had no choice, Elliot. It's done. No, I know it wasn't the most sensible of options but like I said it's been taken care of." Leonardo Desangé put the phone to his chest to mute the call and turned to Giselle. "I think he sometimes forgets who's in charge." He went back to the call. "Elliot listen, I never called you last night because I knew how you would react. You forget I've been doing this for a little longer than most." Desangé listened as Elliot berated him for last nights removal of Agent Baker and the position this now left the company in.

"Leonardo there's always a way out of these things so I need you to listen." Desangé paused for effect and was surprised his friend, and business partner waited for him to speak. "The agent gave me all the details of the two kids before his demise. All we need to do is get the team on the case right away and track them. It should not take long to identify their previous souls, then we just shift back kill them and the problems solved." Desangé paused again to allow Elliot to respond. "Yes Elliot, just like the Wall Street broker who double crossed us. If we remove the kids, then nobody gave evidence to the agent, he never filed a report, and we don't get MI6 climbing all over us."

Desangé had used this method many times over the years to cover up any intricate deals, remove evidence or to just simply change history in his favour.

By shifting back in time and killing the targets former soul before they were supposed to die, it permanently shifted the destination of the soul. The targets body still exists as a person, but without the original soul any memory is inherently erased, they would have made alternate choices and led an entirely different life.

"It easier this way Elliot. There's just too much evidence if we go back a few months and kill them or him." Desangé rolled his eyes in a show of exasperation to Giselle.

"Elliot even if we have to shift back a century it will still have the same effect. Trust me I've done this a number of times."

Desangé mouthed to Giselle. "He hates not being in control."

"So Elliot if you can start the wheels in motion and get our best shifters to start tracking back. The first kid is Harrison Ng. He's male, his date of birth is 29 August 1992. The second is Elisha Cole, a female and her date of birth is 5 March 1993. Got that? Great. Oh and Elliot, I want you to help me do this, it's been a while since we had a little fun together."

"No fair. Are you forgetting me." Giselle complained.

"No, you're shifting isn't perfected yet and I need to keep the circle tight so the fewer people involved, the better."

"Okay Elliot? I'll see you in the office tomorrow."

Desangé hung up the phone.

"Is the vinotherapy bath set?" He asked Giselle.

"Sure is, do you want me to join you?"

"Your skin is far younger than mine my dear, I think I'll take this alone."

"No fair twice Leonardo, you know it was me who got you into this."

He knew she was right, but he wanted the time alone to bask in his glorious idea. As he eased himself into the warm bath, he recalled the story Giselle told him about when she had worked in a vineyard on the outskirts of Paris before the Germans invaded. The owner had educated her on the restorative powers of vinotherapy after she commented on his wife's perfect skin. He said that she was over fifty and swore by the beauty therapy process where the residue of wine, grape seeds, stems, and skins, is soaked into the skin. The wine residue contains powerful antioxidants, minerals, pectic, sugars, tannins and vitamins, all of which are fundamental to the skin's well being.

Desangé had discovered her bath time indulgence a few years ago and after confronting her, she admitted she hadn't believed that spotlighting attention technique would help her skin regenerate and explained the benefits of vinotherapy. The thought of lying in a bath of wine appealed to him so he'd joined her and had been surprised by the results and since then had adopted it into his own regenerative routine.

CHAPTER FIFTEEN

He knew it was a bit of a long shot, but Aston wanted to physically visit the address first rather than Google it, he hoped it would give him a feeling, a second sense maybe. He'd spent Sunday at his mothers so avoiding the Internet and search engines had been relatively easy. She was very pleased to see him, and Aston had been happy for the distraction of just listening to how her latest TV movie shoot was going, along with the gossip from her social scene. Aston had enjoyed being looked after for most of the day, and they'd spent the evening watching the latest acts on X factor much to his mom's amusement. He had to agree with her that celebrities were a lot classier back in her day. His Mom had only mentioned the subject of the hypnotist briefly during the whole day and was 'ever so pleased' that it was all in the hands of the authorities. Aston had embellished the details somewhat to avoid detailed interrogation.

As he stared up at the building, he started to wish he had investigated the address on the Internet. The address given by Antoine Claudet was no longer a photographic studio. It was now one of the most eye-catching buildings in London, the Gherkin. He knew Saint Mary Axe rang a bell, but the tall glass towers of London's financial centre had hidden the curved tower quite well until he turned from Leadenhall Street on to Saint Mary's.

So much for a second sense, nonsense he thought to himself, it seemed another dead end. He jumped on Google to get some background as to what happened to the previous buildings. Wikipedia had details about the Baltic Exchange building that was demolished following an IRA bombing in the early nineties. That building was built in 1900, but he couldn't find anything more that could help him. Maybe he should have bought his friends. Harrison would probably have the building blueprints by now along with the census data listing all occupants. The atrium and surrounding area were buzzing with people milling about, a regular Monday bustle for the financial capital. Aston imagined what it might have been like back in 1844 and was regretting rebooting back so soon. 'Maybe I should have checked it out after Claudet had given me the address.' If this was to be a dead end, then at least, he was going to have a look around, and as he stood in line for coffee, he heard two tourists talking about the fabulous views from the restaurant at its peak. He decided it would be a shame not to use the sight-seeing opportunity, even just for the experience alone. Perhaps there might also be some information about the site inside. Aston hastily took his coffee from the barista and made his way through to the rather magnificent main entrance. He smelled the fresh coffee aroma through the hole in the plastic lid. There was something about that initial waft that added to the coffee experience. He looked up, just before taking his first sip and almost dropped the cup to the floor. Perplexed, Aston went rigid as just to the right of him Leonardo Desangé walked up to security at reception, swiped his card and made his way to the elevators. He was talking intently on his mobile phone stood to wait for the doors to open. Aston moved closer to the reception card access barriers, literally ten or fifteen feet from the hypnotist, who had his back to him so Aston felt no danger of being discovered.

"Do you have a pass, sir?" The security guard startled him with his question.

"Erm, no I was hoping to get up to the restaurant?"

The doors pinged as they opened, Aston couldn't take his eyes off the hypnotist even though the security guard was up close.

"Have you got a reservation, sir?"

Desangé got in the lift. Aston knew if he was the other side of the barrier he might just be able to see what floor he was heading for.

"Of course, I'm meeting my Dad for brunch." Aston had a knack for lying on the spot and sounding utterly convincing.

"I'll swipe you in sir, enjoy your meal."

Aston thanked the guard as he hurried through the barrier just as the elevator pinged as the doors began to close. His line of sight was slightly obstructed, but Aston got there just in time to get a brief glimpse of the buttons inside and the light on button seventeen shone like a beacon as the doors closed on his nemesis.

There were four companies listed as occupants of the seventeenth floor. Aston had taken the next elevator up to the restaurant on floor thirty-eight and waited for ten minutes before venturing down to seventeen. As soon as the information panel had flashed up the names of the companies Aston instinctively knew which one it had to be. Trafalgar Investments stood out by a mile. The coincidence was all too apparent, and Aston knew this must be the front for the hypnotist and his network. He'd been able to scout around as the four companies shared the lobby space. Trafalgar Investments were by far the largest of the business, they took up a third of the office space and had a very opulent reception with what Aston thought was a Matisse taking pride of place behind the reception desk. There were two double doors to the right and a couple of glass booths or offices on the other side of two leather Chesterfield sofas. They naturally attracted a high-class clientele judging by the decor, but surprisingly Aston found no one in attendance. He'd ridden the elevator back up to the restaurant and back down again, and the receptionist was still nowhere to be seen.

Feeling brave Aston decided to find out more about the company, on his first visit to the reception he'd noticed the corporate promotional material on the gilt coffee table between the two sofas but didn't want to stay too long, but now he felt he'd take the chance. Aston had leafed through some the stock market review documents headlining Trafalgar's economist's viewpoint plus a number of the product brochures but found no reference to Leonardo Desangé at all. He was starting to question his choice when he opened an investment magazine, and there was an article bookmarked promoting Trafalgar Investments. In a group shot taken in the foyer, Aston was currently standing in, Desangé was front, and centre and his hypnotic stare seemed to be following Aston as he moved the page. Somewhat taken by his discovery and a little transfixed Aston was surprised all of a sudden when he heard the handle turn on the two large internal doors. He crouched down in an attempt to hide himself, the small leather sofa offered little in the way of obstacles between Aston and the doors that were now opening. He was bound to be discovered.

"...and another thing" Aston heard a male voice say to the other, that interjection delayed them entering the reception, the doors wavered and gave Aston enough time to dart into a small opaque glass meeting room adjacent to the other doors that were now swinging open. He was just able to hide under the desk before the two men stepped through.

Aston could hardly move under the desk let alone twist around to see who they were, as they continued their conversation. He didn't need to see though, and the hairs stood up on the back of his neck as he recognised the distinct accent.

"I'm meeting them in five."

Aston wondered what to do as he listened to the hypnotist voice that he wished never heard. He needed evidence, so although cramped, Aston managed to get his phone out of his pocket and press voice record as the other man replied.

"Leonardo, before you go. I've just got news on the other matter you had the team look into. They've found something you're not going to believe. The two kids Elisha Cole and Harrison Ng well..."

Aston nearly dropped the phone hearing his two friends names.

"Hold on, not out here, my clients might arrive" the hypnotist opened the door to meeting room next to where Aston was hiding. His heart skipped as he thought they were going to open the door of his hideaway and find him.

"So tell me the good news!"

"Well, we had a little luck. A twist of fate you might say. The tracers had established the identity of their past souls back through a couple of generations but decided to go back a little further. One of the team ran a background check on the names and they crossed."

"What! Their two souls met before?"

"Yes, right here in London, back in 1888, September 29 to be exact. Do you believe that?"

"Incredible, maybe they are kindred spirits."

"Not really, they were both in an incident outside a pub in Settlers Street, Whitechapel. We were lucky that it was on public record."

"So we can kill two little birds with one stone. Perfect."

"I know and guess what..."

The phone rang on the desk above Aston, drowning out the chilling conversation. Startled he banged his head on the underside of the desk. He could not believe what he had overheard, his blood ran cold with the thought of his friends being murdered. The ringing stopped, and Aston's focus immediately returned to Desangé's conversation.

"Really, that's fabulous. See if they can get more detail but even so that would give us a perfect window of opportunity. This is going to be easier than I expected."

"When do you want to do it?"

"Sooner rather than later don't you think? I've a meeting at lunch but after that, we can shift back together, silence our two little birds and this little problem with MI6 will be forgotten forever."

"Just you and I then, I like it. Oh, you should get going Leonardo, if you want to meet your clients."

Aston heard the two men leave the adjoining office.

"I'm going to check that phone, see who called."

The door opened, and Aston was no longer alone. The man span the phone towards him, picked up the handset and tapped a few numbers. Aston looked at the opaque glass facing his side of the desk. There was no reflection, so he couldn't see Desangé's colleague but also it meant the man couldn't see Aston cowering under the desk, holding his breath.

The man hung up the phone, turned and opened the glass doors. Aston heard him hit the light switch, which was odd as the lights weren't on. The reason became crystal clear as it apparently controlled the smart glass for both offices. Aston was left cramped under the desk, now facing a clear glass wall which was in full view of the rest of the Trafalgar Investments office.

Harrison had travelled back to Oxford yesterday afternoon on his own. He had known Ellie wouldn't take the news about Aston leaving early very well, but didn't expect to spend most of the morning having to listen to her complain about Aston's rudeness and lack off respect for authority. He just wished his two friends would finally realise how they felt so they could get back to normality. Although all of their perceptions of normal had become very skewed since the hypnotist show. If only he hadn't dared Aston to take part in the show, this term would have been a lot less stressful. As a distraction he'd contemplated dropping in on Celia but when he checked she was spending Sunday with her husband and couldn't get away to meet him. He'd spent the evening playing World of Warcraft and taken out his frustrations on a virtual killing spree against countless enemy foot soldiers.

Harrison woke early and as he'd planned was now back in the Oxford computing laboratory. The fact that his error had led to MI6 getting involved still rankled in the back of his mind, and he'd thought of a few ways to make amends and prove to his friend that he could still be trusted.

The first thing he'd prioritised was to retrieve the stored passport search files that had triggered the MI6 investigation. They would at least provide more background into the hypnotist and maybe give them some insight as to what the authorities knew. Retrieving them from the computers memory was relatively easy even though it looked like the search history had been erased. He used a trick the professor had shown him to capture previously deleted hard drive files and was surprised whoever had tried to get rid of the history hadn't done a more thorough job. His thoughts turned to Professor Ferris for a moment as he had yet another reason to get back at him. Not only had he obviously helped Agent Baker's investigation and given him his mobile number, but he still hadn't repaid Ferris for setting his maniac church friend upon them. Harrison's grand plan for revenge on his professor would have to wait; he wanted to do that in his own time, but there was a small payback included within his next priority. He planned to utilise the computer labs power and network to hack into the historical records of births, deaths and marriages and this time he wouldn't be so careless with the IP address. This time, he'd be using the Professors own IP address to cover his tracks.

Before Aston had left for London, he'd mentioned that he wanted to know more about the souls he had already rebooted into. They had written down all the details that Aston could recall so they could narrow down the search. The ease in which he had found records for all three surprised Harrison, the information available on the net was growing and with a few backdoor hacks to ancestry sites and local parish records he had everything he could have hoped for in no time at all. He was glad because his next task was proving more a little more difficult.

Harrison wanted to find out more about the two officers at the Battle of Trafalgar that Aston thought were connected. His friend had been sure he'd experienced the death of his own former soul but was also convinced that, after finding out Desangé's date of birth was the same day, there was some chance it wasn't a coincidence.

Finding out if it could have been both of them was proving to be a harder task than just hacking into ancestry.com and pulling off a few birth certificates and documents. It had taken Harrison a substantial amount of time to access the official Naval records. He was being additionally cautious hiding his identity after last time as well as linking his actions via numerous IP's back to Ferris's laptop. There was some information on the sailors that died on the official Battle of Trafalgar website, but the information required meant he needed to dig deeper. Harrison had been thwarted by the Royal Navy triple firewall but had managed to get access to a mid-tier administrators email and under the premise of a security breach had given clearance to the Professors own Oxford email account. Once inside the network as the professor, he still needed to locate the correct naming conventions for classified historical manifests. Luckily Harrison had stumbled upon an online training module that outlined the Navy's common vocabulary which given his access, led him straight there. Archived as Classified in confidence, historical records, Trafalgar, 1805 he finally found what he was looking for. The was an account of the posthumous court martial of a gunnery lieutenant aboard the Belleisle. The account outlined the incident that Aston had described back in the student union bar, but it was recounted by an observer, another gunnery officer and the detail was a little sketchy. Harrison read the trial documents intently, the officer on trial was James Pierce. His actions led to the death of three ordinary seamen and the severe injury of another two, one of those losing both legs at the knee. Harrison stopped when he saw the name of the other officer James Pierce had been charged with, gunnery sergeant George Pierce.

"His brother," he said to himself. "Aston was right." It wasn't just a date of birth his soul had in common. Aston and Desangé's former souls had been blood relatives blown apart at the Battle of Trafalgar.

Harrison knew Aston would want to know this and quickly, so he copied over the files relating to the trial, including the two brothers records of service. Together with the other records collected earlier there was too much to email so, he created an encrypted zip file and uploaded them to a private DropBox account. Sharing it with Aston and Ellie, the message read "Check out files in here - massive connection between Aston and hypnotist former souls at Trafalgar. H."

Before closing off the computer, he thought about Ferris and having used his email address to access the Naval records he thought he'd have some fun. Harrison checked his watch, wary of the time he'd spent in the lab knowing that during the breaks at the end of term breaks some staff would be back on campus, and he'd been lucky so far.

Ferris was a Google man through and through and had linked his Oxford email to his own Gmail account so Harrison could access everything from the professors Google Plus circles to his browser history in Chrome. 'That should give me enough things to play with' he thought. He started snooping through his contacts, Larry Pages personal email address caught his eye along with other high profile industry heads and as a plan formulated in his head around Trojan viruses he saw the subject line of another email that completely sidetracked him.

'Who the hell was Schindler Whit and why was he sending emails with my name on?' Harrison opened the email thread and quickly realised that this must be the bearded church guy who had turned up and confronted Ellie and him at their house. The thread was proof that the man was still stalking all three of them, Aston included. Harrison was getting more irate with each line and couldn't believe the Professor had been feeding him contact info in a hope to stop their supposed anti-religious experiments. The latest mail was unopened and had attachments. Harrison clicked on the image attachment icon and saw Aston coming out of Ellie's sisters, and the next saw him greeting his mother in London.

Aston exhaled a long controlled breath, his was doing his best to combat the panic. Being caught by Desangé wasn't something he'd thought about when he'd stepped into the lift an hour ago. He knew he had to do something, the meditation may have staved off his initial panic and helped him avoid the thought of the cramped position he was in, but Aston was sure it was just a matter of time before he was going to be seen. Some heads had turned his way after the glass switched from opaque but as he wasn't spotted Aston supposed that no one was looking out for someone squeezed under the desk.

His phone pinged, Aston grabbed at it to try to stem the noise, then waited a few seconds to see if it had attracted any attention from the office. He checked the screen it was a Dropbox notification from Harrison, 'a massive connection' he thought to himself 'well I've got an even bigger one in the making right here for you H.' Intrigued, and unable to move, he started to open the files. His phones connection speed meant it would take a while to download the large zip file, and all Aston could do was watch and wait as the count ticked down from three minutes 30 secs. After two minutes watching the download progress the phone suddenly burst into life with a FaceTime call from Ellie. Aston thought that the distinctive noise must have been heard as he quickly pressed the answer button to silence the phone.

"Elle," he said in a whisper.

"Aston, are you there? I can hardly hear you."

To him the volume was deafening, he knew someone would hear, but he also knew this could be a chance to get some help. He hurriedly turned the volume down to a minimum.

"Ellie shush."

"Don't shush me, I've called to apologise..." Her face filled the screen, and her voice seemed to fill the office. "...and to ask if you'd seen Harrison's files?"

"Sorry and it's me who should apologise but listen, I'm in a bit of a tight spot of my own." He whispered.

"Where are you?"

"I'm sort of in his office." He moved the camera the best he could to reveal his haunched image crammed under the desk.

She laughed "Oh Aston that's so... Hang on. Did you say his office?"

"Yes, his office."

"My God Aston, you know he's out to get you and you go there alone."

"I didn't expect to get stuck like this and yes, I'm regretting going it alone, but now I need an escape plan, Ellie. Without the authorities if possible, I'd prefer he didn't know that we are aware where he works."

"Aston you need to make sure you get out in one piece, this man has already tried to kidnap you, remember."

Aston was more concerned about the conversation he'd just overheard about Desangé's plan to kill his friends. He figured he couldn't tell Ellie that right now fear of scaring her, but if he didn't make it out of there, he might never see either of his friends again.

"I know, that's why need a diversion or something Ellie, it's only a matter of time before someone finds me."

"I'm already on my way into the City so I can be there in about twenty minutes. I can cause a commotion or something in reception."

"That's perfect, it's on floor seventeen, Trafalgar Investments." The thought of his friends being in danger prompted him into a decision he knew he should have made sooner. "Oh and Ellie text me the number of that MI6 agent, there's something he needs to know."

"Okay Aston will do. It's about time. "She winked at him. "You hang on, I'll be there soon."

"Thanks Ellie and I'm sorry."

"You can apologise properly when we've got you out of there."

She hung up, and Aston peeked out into the office to check if there was any sign of him being seen. There were still the same staff sat at there desks busily doing whatever Desangé employed them to do. Aston wondered if they knew the truth about their boss. Were they part of his group of 'shifters' or just regular investment staff and brokers? His phone pinged as the number for Agent Baker came through from Ellie. 'They're going to find out soon enough' Aston thought as he tapped the number and pressed call. He wasn't sure what he was going to say exactly but knew it was time for him to let someone else know what he'd found out. The disconnected service message was a little strange for a supposed MI6 agent, but he held on while it transferred him. Aston was even more uncertain what to say if someone else picked up. How could he explain this? Where would he start? The call answered "Government services how may I direct your call" somewhat flustered Aston hung up.

It did prompt Aston into action. He could wait for Ellie to help him but there was a chance that Desangé would just capture both of them. The government services message reminded him of a 999 call, 'Call the fire brigade' he thought. That might still mean a wait and it wouldn't guarantee that they would come to the right floor as the building services would no doubt check and confirm there wasn't a fire.

"Building services," Aston said out loud as he suddenly realised what he had to do. He Googled the primary 30 St Mary's Axe building management number and dialed.

"We've got a fire here on seventeen!"

"What, I'm not getting any alarms on my monitors."

"I know the alarm I've just broken didn't go off that's why I'm phoning."

"I'm sorry that just will not happen, not in this building."

Aston rolled his eyes, not believing he'd got the jobsworth on shift.

"Look if you want to risk the lives of the hundreds of staff then by all means come up and check the fire alarms, but we're coming down the emergency exits if you report it or not. What's your name because it's going in my floor warden report!"

"Okay, okay, seventeen?"

Aston hung up as he heard the fire alarms wail around the office. The brokers in the office were slow to get up at first some frantically typing some, checking desks for possessions. Aston heard the shout of 'is this a drill or for real' but eventually all the staff reluctantly started to leave the office. Aston took his queue and rolled out from under the desk and bolted for the reception. Unnoticed in the evacuation he joined the crowds of grumbling office workers filing down the drab interior concrete staircases and out on to the concourse.

Ellie got off the tube early at Bank station and made her way to the Gherkin building as quickly as she could. As she rounded the corner Ellie was surprised by the number of people there were outside the building. 'It wouldn't normally be so busy' she mused. The sirens, she thought were just everyday traffic noise, were now getting louder. She turned and saw a first and then a second fire engine turn onto the road behind her, lights blazing to match the sirens. Their appearance drew great applause from the crowds around the tower as Ellie realised what all the crowds were there for. Concerned she called Aston.

"Are you okay?"

"Hey Ellie, yeah I'm out of the office."

"That's great, where are you, safe?"

"I've just come out of the emergency exit, think I'm on the south side, hang on." Ellie waited for Aston to find his bearings. "Yeah I've come out of the exit on to Bury Street side. Do you like my diversion?"

"Considering you didn't want to get the authorities involved you seemed to have engaged the fire brigade and a few police from what I can see!"

Aston was laughing "I took a leaf out of your book. Sorry, I should have listened to you earlier."

"Hah quite, if only you had." Ellie felt relieved he'd finally seen sense.

"Oh, and I tried to call that Agent but it didn't connect. All I got was a weird voicemail."

"That's odd I thought that was his personal mobile, maybe it's switched off."

"I'll try again later but Ellie I've got something really important I need to tell..." He broke off abruptly and then Ellie heard him say in a serious tone "Oi watch it mate, who do you think you..."

Ellie heard scuffling and a few grunts. It sounded like a struggle or a fight. There was another voice, but the microphone seemed muffled somehow.

"Aston take your finger off the phone." She said more to herself. It shifted but the sound was still a little muted. Ellie then heard a voice she was sure she had heard only a few days ago, then she was convinced as he was uttering something about blasphemy.

"Aston! Aston? Are you okay?"

The phone call cut off and Ellie started running to the other side of the tower. The isometric diamond pattern seemed to spiral like a kaleidoscope in her peripheral vision as she raced around. She couldn't remember what Aston was wearing but strained at the crowds to see if she recognised him amongst all the people.

It seemed to take an age to get to the other side, but she couldn't see him or any commotion. Ellie turned in a circle.

"Aston" she shouted. People's heads turned to look at her distress.

"Are you okay Miss." A gentleman asked but Ellie ignored him.

"Aston" she shouted again turning more heads. 'This was definitely Bury Street' she thought, she ran to the street and checked the road sign, then looked up then down the road. At the end of the street, she saw a man bundling what seemed like an unconscious Aston into the back of white transit van. As he shut the doors, he turned, and Ellie instantly recognised the same man who had threatened her and barged through the doorstep in Oxford. She started running but watched helplessly as he quickly got in the drivers side door and pulled away. Ellie reached the corner and stopped to catch her breath, disappearing down the main road she saw the van carrying Aston off to god knows where.

Aston came to in a state of panic. The last thing he remembered was a bearded guy interrupting his call to Ellie and remonstrating with him about challenging Christian beliefs and reincarnation.

"One is not born again in an endless cycle of death and rebirth. Death awaits all of us because all of us are sinners, Jesus' sacrificial death on the cross has freed us from this."

Aston's reply seemed to flame his temper "Actually I can prove that the soul is reincarnated! How would your God feel about that!"

"Liar! For the wages of sin is death, but the gift of God is eternal life in Christ Jesus our Lord. You must be held accountable for your lies and sins!" The man had then grabbed him and tried to wrestle him to the floor. Aston had pushed him off, turned and started to run away but he wasn't ready for the blow to the back of his neck that knocked him out clean.

From what he could make out he was now in some sort of cellar, he was sat on a makeshift mattress, there was a blanket next to him. The walls were dark, dank and as cold as the hard stone. The only light came from what looked like a modern day replica of an oil lamp. He got up to see if it was connected but with no lead he figured it must have been battery operated. He turned around to see a large wooden door at the far end and a stack of wooden benches or pews at the other. 'Am I in a Church?' he thought, trying the door, wherever it was he was locked in.

"Hey is there anybody there!" No one answered, just his voice echoed around the dark cellar.

He felt his pockets front and back, no phone, no wallet. He had no idea what time of day it was, but it felt like he had not been unconscious for too long. His whole body ached especially his neck where his captor had knocked him out. Aston tried to massage away the pain in his neck, but his own concerns and predicament were secondary. He was way more concerned about the threat to his two best friends. What he'd overheard Desangé and his colleague discussing, played over and over in his head, they were shifting back to kill Ellie and Harrison later that night. Aston felt sick at the thought of losing them and felt wracked with guilt that his actions, his decisions had got them into this. He knew full well he could have prevented this by either cooperating with Desangé or going to the authorities sooner. The black thought that he may have killed them himself hit him. He kicked the door in frustration and yelled "Let me out of here! I need to help my friends."

He sat down, held his head in his hands and sucked in the dank air. The realisation hit him that if he didn't reboot back to 1888 in the next few hours and at least try to save his friends, he would never see them again. That single clear premise took over his thoughts, he only had one chance to save them, he knew the date and the location, he had to try whatever the consequence.

Aston knew he had never rebooted without his friend's help and what that meant. No safety net, no one to bring him back or revive his heart, given his lack of success to date he knew what that could mean. Without his phone, he also wouldn't have any of the technology Harrison had set up for him. No way of trying to monitor his heart rate or vital signs. More importantly, he didn't have the latest application they'd used to influence the date and time of the reboot. Out of habit Aston dabbed his pockets again, being without his device felt odd, it isolated him from his friends even more. Lack of a phone or a way to get in contact with them or his family wasn't something he'd experienced for a long time. Aston remembered his dad had ensured he'd had mobile phones from an early age growing up in Hong Kong, although his nanny had kept them from him more often than not. The thought of her gave him a seed of inspiration, her encouragement, and teaching of meditation and Chinese culture may well have had something to do with how he'd got to be where he was now. Aston then realised that maybe it was the one key that might turn into a solution.

The hard stone floor was hardly conducive to meditation let alone achieving the total alpha mind state he'd been taught. He folded the blanket up to use as support for his head and laid out on the cold floor. It was very different from his previous reboot environments, but then again it may just help his concentration.

"Wish me luck guys," he said as closed his eyes. As he began to clear his mind the randomness of what he was about to do struck him. Trying to reboot his soul alone was massive. If he thought he was taking a risk with the previous reboot, then this took the proverbial biscuit in terms of unknowns. But he had no other options, if this didn't work Harrison and

Ellie, his best friends would be dead. If it worked and he managed to save them he might well end up dead when rebooting back with no one hear to resuscitate him, but he was out of options. Closing his eyes he focused on nothing but the date and the blackness, it was surprising given the events of the past few hours that his mind could achieve this state. He crossed his arms and held his forefingers to his thumbs as he'd been taught many years ago and took the largest leap of faith in his short lifetime.

CHAPTER SIXTEEN

Leonardo Desangé once again opened his eyes to the nineteenth century. As his senses took over his distant souls body, his memory cells began to fire, bringing back the sights, smells and the tastes of his earlier life. He was ready for the dizzy, light-headed sensation that he knew would happen. He steadied himself, placed his hands on the nearest wall and drew in a large deep breath. He wasn't ready for the taste of the smog or his lungs reaction to it. The semi-toxic, filth-laden air filled his lungs and triggered a mild coughing fit. He bent over to try to ease the discomfort but wasn't able to control the coughing.

"Are you okay? You're here then old chap?" Elliot slapped him on the back in an attempt to help.

"Yes — I'm here" Desangé managed to splutter out between coughs.

Elliot continued to slap him on the back. "Is that helping, I had the same when I shifted, thinks it's the air quality mixed with the disorientation from the drop in blood pressure when you shift."

"I'm quite alright, just sucked in too much filth trying to clear my head rush."

"I know the bloody smogs dreadful but have to say the smell from the Thames has improved." Elliot stopped slapping. "You seem to be over it now."

Desangé straightened up, his face red but his coughing and breathing were back to normal. "Thanks, Elliot, did it take you long to get here and find my old self?"

"No like I said before we shifted I knew my old self was staying in Kensington, so finding my way to your home in Oxford Street was simple. Persuading your soul to join me for a drink was easy to, it was like old times, we were reminiscing just before you shifted. Shame we weren't indoors as it may have been a little easier for you. This fogs a proper pea-souper as they used to say." Elliot mocked a cockney accent.

"Shall we hail a carriage?" Desangé kept his focus on the task at hand.

"I'd rather not walk in this, and if we get there sooner, we can get a good idea of the lay of the land."

"I still think we're a bit light handed for this Leonardo. If we had another couple of guys, it would make it a lot easier."

"It might sound simple Elliot but you know how hard it is to coordinate these things. Shifting back over a century means the logistics get complicated especially the more numbers involved. Travel times, rendezvous points, it all gets a little more complex the more people we bring along."

"Yeah, I take your point. I guess we could ask some of your own guys from now to help out?"

"No loose ends Elliot and this will be more personal, I know your penchant for a little violence now and again. Think of it as a reward for pulling off the China trade."

Elliot laughed and whistled for a carriage. "Why thanks Leonardo. I suppose killing prostitute and her punter will be kind of fun and it shouldn't raise too many eyebrows or questions from the present day coppers."

"No, you're right it will make the murder a little more discreet."

Desangé thought to himself that it was somewhat fitting that his young nemesis friends were once a prostitute and a drunk. He wasn't surprised that two souls would weave throughout time, the mortal and religious called it many things but during his long lifetime and from shifting back and forth he had exposed these twists of fate so often. Something he'd experienced first hand on a number of occasions. Their status here and now would make it all the easier, and he would take great pleasure in telling Aston North what his friends were before he removed them from existence.

"That kid and now his friends had caused us enough problems, and I am quite looking forward to removing the headache once and for all."

The horse-drawn carriage pulled up next to them. The hooves clanged off the cobbled streets and echoed in the foggy air.

"Whitechapel. Settles Street" Elliot instructed the driver as they climbed aboard. The suspension springs creaked as they settled into the hard leather seats and closed the carriage door.

"I don't miss this, thank God for the twentieth century and motorised transport!" Elliot said.

"Yes, that's an investment we missed out on, maybe we can pick up some shares in Benz or Ford while we're here." Desangé laughed.

"It's good to hear you talking business again Leonardo. So once this is done we forget about the other kid and move on to shaking up the market once again."

"Elliot, once this is done I want one more crack at getting into his head and finding out exactly what he knows. Then we get rid of him and go after Wall Street."

"Good, It will be good to get you back to doing what you do best."

Desangé smiled to himself 'this little trip back was becoming all the more pleasurable and definitely worthwhile' he thought.

For a moment Aston thought he was actually floating on air, as had happened before his mind took a while to process what his senses were receiving. His vision perspective was about eight feet off the ground, it was blurred, or was it mist he saw as he slowly moved forward, it felt like he was gliding. The confused state led him to think he'd failed and just meditated to some dark corner of his mind or possibly experiencing an out of body vision. But, as his senses adjusted he knew he'd been successful, and a wave of relief surged through him, he'd definitely rebooted, but he had no idea where. Two horse heads appeared, and as his hearing cleared, the clopping of hoofs on cobbles echoed all around, deafening him with their intensity. Aston also felt the leather reigns in his hands and then realised he was in charge of the two impressive black horses pulling a carriage. His soul was the driver riding on top, and as the carriage pulled to a halt Aston concentrated hard and took over his soul's control and started to look around, he needed to get his bearings. The grey mist appeared to be fog, it deadened other sounds from the street now the horses had stopped, but then one unmistakeable sound told him where he was and informed him of the exact time. Six loud clanging chimes, one after another, from the famous bell of Westminster's Houses of Parliament. Big Ben sounded six o'clock out across London, and Aston knew where he was, although trying to find out which borough he was in would be tricky with this evening fog.

He spun around on top of his carriage hoping to get a sense of where he was. On the other side of the street Aston saw a chimney sweep packing up his brushes, he smiled to himself at the coincidence then called out "Oi Soot."

The sweep looked up from his brushes "Good evening to you."

"Good evening" Aston had one of his questions answered. He thought about being ambiguous but decided to ask the direct question as he knew time wasn't on his side. "You wouldn't happen to know which street this is?"

"Heavens above, that's rich coming from a cabbie. This is Wilton Place, Belgravia of course. What's a matter lost your way of something?"

"It's the fog old chap, just lost my bearings, trying to find a fare."

"Well best o' luck with the rest of the night, this pea souper's gonna stick around for days if you ask me." The sweep picked up his brushes and made off up the street. Aston again smiled to himself remembering his last reboot but the severity of the task he had to do brought him back down to earth. He was sure he didn't know the way to Whitechapel from Belgravia.

What he did know was that St Paul's Cathedral was close to Whitechapel, if only he could see through this thick, stifling fog he might be able to use that as a reference point. He needed to get to Settles Street in the East End of London. 'That's it' he thought to himself and almost said it out loud 'the East End - I can just go the opposite way to the sunset!' Aston looked again to the sky and the foggy mist. He knew it would be pretty damn difficult to navigate that way. "Fuck it," he said out loud this time.' I've got to try even if I have to ask someone at every bloody street corner, I'll just ask for the quickest route.

Aston was about to turn the carriage around, he needed to be in the East End as quickly as he could, so even if he couldn't drive, taking the horses was his only viable option and made sense. He leaned over the side of the carriage to check if it was empty. As he did, he saw the door of the house he was parked outside open. The gentleman dressed in black with a cape, a top hat, cane and carrying an odd-looking case closed the door very methodically behind him. He continued toward Aston then muttered "Hello driver, glad you found the place from my instructions." Aston quickly thought of what he had to do and switched control back to his former soul as the man continued. "I need to get to Whitechapel driver and I need to go by way of Westminster Bridge."

'Fate' thought Aston.

"And driver I need to stop at St Thomas' hospital."

"Right O guvnor" Aston heard his carriage driving soul respond.

'Of course' Aston thought 'why didn't I think of that! My souls a driver, he's been doing this his whole life probably. I just needed to find a way to ask him! But this is so much better, as long as the man doesn't take too long in the hospital, we'll make good time now he's driving.'

The man with the black caped and the odd looking case opened the carriage door and climbed aboard. He banged his cane on the roof. "Drive on. Drive on."

With his soul now in charge of the carriage he flicked on the reigns signalling for the horses to pull off.

Aston started planning what he would do once they arrived in Whitechapel and the passengers left. He figured it would be relatively easy for him to take back control of the carriage from his soul. Then all he had to do was locate the pub in Settles Street and find his friends. 'Oh shit,' he thought, 'shit, shit, shit' Aston cursed himself for being so stupid. The sudden realisation that he had no idea what his friends' former souls would look like struck him like a dagger in the heart. How could he be so mindless? He had no way or no chance of being able to recognise Ellie and Harrison's former souls.

"Harrison you are not going to believe what's happening!" Ellie held her phone tightly to her ear. She was trying to keep an eye on the small grey van which kept dropping in and out of her vision behind whatever vehicle pulled in front of her taxi. She was also trying to stay calm and not scream again at the driver for lagging too far behind. The driver had warned her time and again for being too frantic, so now having Harrison to vent on helped enormously.

"The lunatic from the church just bundled Aston into a van outside the Gherkin."

"What? — What was Aston doing at the Gherkin? Hang on? — What were you doing there? Harrison for once sounded totally confused.

"He was investigating the bloody hypnotist. On his own I might add. I only found out when I called him. That reminds me I need you to track his phone because I'm scared I'm going to lose him. Well, the driver might lose him... He's turning right up there!" Ellie tapped on the glass divider in the taxi and gestured to make sure he saw.

"Can you track him, Harrison?" Ellie ignored the driver's protestations. "Now!"

"Okay, okay! It's pretty simple, I know his Apple ID, so just bear with me."

"Where's the van?" Ellie questioned out loud to herself as well as the driver. "I'm paying you to follow him. For gods sake, I think he's lost him."

"Ellie I've got him, he's on my find my iPhone app. Where are you?"

"What street is this?" Ellie knew the driver was close to pulling over and kicking her out so she corrected herself, knowing Harrison had him helped calm her down a little. "Sorry, I don't mean to be short. Where are we now?" She smiled. It helped as always.

"We've just turned on to Royal College Street, just near St Pancras Hospital."

"Did you hear that?"

"Yes, yes I did. He's just turned into Prince of Wales Road, not far from you so you haven't lost him, Ellie."

"Carry on to Prince of Wales Road. We've got him on a tracker so we can't lose him now. Thanks, driver."

"Ellie, I know who this guy is, and I think I know where he's taking him!"

"What? — How?"

"His name is Schindler Whit, and I've got a sneaky suspicion he's taking him to Christ's Church on the edge of Hampstead Heath."

"Schindler who? And how the hell do you know where he's going? Ellie asked somewhat perplexed.

"Yes, well it is was an informed guess! I found an email from this Schindler guy to Professor Ferris. Can you believe Ferris has been feeding him our contact info from the school files. What an arsehole!"

Ellie kept an eye on the road as she listened to Harrison recount what he'd found on his professor's email account and how he'd traced this Schindler Whit back to Christ's Church in Hampstead.

"How quickly can you get here?" Ellie asked after he'd finished his story. She knew she would need help and Harrison was the only one who had witnessed this Schindler guy's exploits back in Oxford.

"What about the authorities? Are you gonna call Agent Baker?"

"As soon as you agree to come I will, yes!"

"I'll be there when I can Ellie but I'll need to borrow a car from someone. It'll take way too long on the train."

"Just get here H. Aston needs you." Ellie used the nickname Aston used to make her point.

"I'm there Ellie. I'll keep you up to date on the tracker via text. Shame you're an Android else I could hook up the app, and you could track him yourself."

Ellie ignored the dig but was relieved her friend was confident and also on his way. She was about to dial Agent Baker when Harrison's first text re Aston's tracker pinged into her phone.

'Aston turned left into Fleet Rd still on route to Hampstead.'

'Thks H c u soon' she replied.

Agent Baker was her next call. They needed help, and at least she wouldn't have to try to retell their story to some random copper who, she was certain would take some convincing. Ellie recalled Aston's comment about not being able to get hold of him as she listened to the disconnected service message. She held on while the call was transferred. Ellie was hoping to hear the agent's voicemail and was surprised when a female voice answered: "Government services how may I direct your call."

Rather strange an operating service answered a MI6 agent's calls she thought. "I'd like to speak to Agent Baker please."

"Agent Baker." Ellie heard a question in her tone. "One second I'll transfer you."

"Hello, Miss. Can I ask where you got this number?" A male voice answered sounding officious.

"Is Agent Baker there?" Ellie was somewhat rattled so went on the offensive.

"I'm afraid not. He's been out of contact for a couple of days. I'm sorry I didn't get your name?"

"What? Is he missing?" Ellie started to get a little suspicious and wasn't about to give them her name.

"We were hoping you might be able to tell us where he is. Miss Cole."

Ellie hung up the phone. 'How did they know my name?' Her mind raced, she stared at her handset wondering if it had been traced. Was she beginning to take Aston's sceptical view of the authorities. What had happened to Agent Baker? What had Aston got her into? She needed help or advice, a sounding board to vent her frustrations and none of her friends were around.

"Which way now, Miss?" The cab driver asked.

Ellie only had one choice.

"Head for Hampstead Heath, Christs church."

She then dialled the one person close by that she knew she could now count upon.

'He's been there a while!' Aston was waiting for his client, who ten minutes ago had jumped out of the cab on arrival at St Thomas' hospital as instructed. His patience was wearing thin, and he weighed up the options of taking control and leaving his souls client to get another cabbie. A few minutes later and Aston was working out how he could navigate a horse and trap through fog-filled London. He'd decided to take control just as the gentleman returned. Most probably a doctor Aston thought, judging by the case, which now seemed heavier to carry based on his awkward looking walk, the case weight pulling him distinctively to the left. Aston thought the doctor was waving at him but realised he was signalling another man who appeared on the other side of the cab. Swinging around to see the rather poorly dressed man. A full beard, deep-set eyes, and Aston also noticed his Eastern European sounding pigeon English. The men embraced in a cordial greeting before the new passenger opened the door for his compatriot and took the bag from him. Aston heard him thanking the doctor and mention their night's work or something to that matter. The thud on the ceiling indicating it was time to move on.

"Brick Lane, driver." The well spoken Doctor ordered.

Aston left the control to his cab driving soul, who snapped on the reigns, he studied the man's technique as he skilfully navigated the cobbled route. Seemingly ignoring the thick fog, plus the other horses and carriages that all of a sudden, or so it appeared, had converged on the main streets of London. As he started to get accustomed to the ride, his own thoughts began to focus on his task. How he was going to work out which pub on Settles Street the incident, that he'd overheard Desangé discussing, had occurred. He hadn't had any time to research it online and hadn't thought to contact his friends for help either before being kidnapped. Harrison would have found it in no time at all. He didn't even know how many bars there were on Settles Street for one.

The journey to Brick Lane was quicker than Aston expected. Thankfully the fog was beginning to clear albeit only slightly, but it was enough for Aston to revel in the sights of some of the monuments he knew from modern day London. In the misty twilight, the Capitol didn't fail to surprise him. Even with the burden of the task that lay ahead, he found himself taken aback seeing Tower Bridge being constructed in the distance as he drove along the Embankment and travelling past the monuments and new buildings gave him a taste of Victorian Britain first hand. After passing Tower Hill, the East end squalor was also an eye opener for Aston. He was sure that he had never seen a program that came close to depicting the conditions these people survived in. Passing a few of Whitechapel High Street pubs spewing out the hard living inhabitants pulled back Aston's interest to focus on a plan on how to identify his friends. The taverns they passed were open with big doors and large fronted windows and from the elevated position of the cab Aston reckoned he would be able to keep an eye out of some these places to see if Desangé was in there. From what he knew, he wouldn't have any difficulty recognising him so as long as there weren't too many pubs to keep tabs on.

As they turned into Brick Lane Aston began to worry. It seemed everywhere he looked he saw a pub or drinking den of some kind.

"Brick Lane Sir!" His soul called out as he reigned in the horses to a halt. Aston couldn't quite make out the quick murmuring of conversation between their passengers in the carriage below. Something about rendezvous after midnight but then the carriage door was opened, and the two men alighted. The doctor tossed up a handle full of coins, and as Aston's soul grabbed them between his gloved fingers, he said. "There's double that amount waiting for you. We just need you to keep it confidential and agree to meet up at midnight. Same place."

Aston thought it a little strange but rationalised it remembering the hassle of getting a cab late at night in London. He was just glad they were leaving and didn't care about the return fare. It meant that he was free to save his friends. He watched the two men walk away then gained control of his soul. His knowledge of London's street wasn't even close to that of a cabbie, and he realised he didn't have a clue where Settles Street was. He rummaged around in the space around the driver's seat in the vain hope for some type of map. Nothing! What he wouldn't give for a GPS system or access to Google maps right now he thought. A passer-by caught his eye so Aston asked for directions knowing full well that the answer would be loaded with sarcasm or wit of some kind.

"You should know mate, being a cab driver and all. Head for Commercial Street" the man pointed down the street that the carriage was facing. "It's that way, and it's the fourth street on your left!"

"Thanks." Aston thought about trying excuse his lack of knowledge but decided just to be cordial. Besides he had another pressing issue, he now had to work out how to drive the horses. Aston had never really got on with horses, too much power and far too little control in his opinion. The need to get where he had to be and be able to use the carriage as cover gave him enough incentive to overcome his equine fears. 'How hard could it be?' He thought to himself as he picked up the reigns. He had observed his soul as he'd driven the streets en route and he knew the horses were accustomed to their role, and a quick flick of the reigns got them moving. Aston was thankful his destination was only a few streets away.

There was only one pub on Settlers if it had been Brick Lane he would have been in dire straights as he passed about twenty on route. Aston managed to stop the horses and positioned the carriage across from the Bricklayers' Arms and from his lofty position he could see inside. All he could do now is wait.

The pub wasn't that busy compared to the ones he had seen on Brick Lane, but there was still a fair amount of activity going on. Aston was getting cold sat up in the carriage and after being pestered by yet another punter looking for a fare into the City, he decided to go inside. He climbed down from the carriage, fished the coins out of his pocket from the earlier fare and headed into the Bricklayers Arms.

Leonardo Desangé sat in the squalid pub in Settles Street. Basically, it was a back street gin house full of, what he thought were, societies cannon fodder. Low life's with little purpose, drowning out their miserable existence in an equally miserable bar with whatever intoxication they could afford. He thought of the boy who had been the catalyst for him being back in this wretched part of the East End. What would be Aston North's reaction if he knew what low life scum his best friends souls once were. Once this deed was complete, he would ensure that North knew every intricate detail of their final hours and how he had joyfully, and painfully for them, removed them from their miserable existence. The irony that the kid wouldn't be aware of this, as his friends would no longer be who they were, kind of added to his enjoyment of what he was about to do.

He'd been watching the prostitute cavorting around for the past half hour, pimping herself from one drunk to the next. He was certain it was her from the Swedish accent, which he experienced first hand when she stumbled his way offering her filth for a shilling and a glass of gin.

He'd pushed her away, and now she was in the draped over of some other punter who had bought her drinks.

He turned to Elliot, who was also stood staring at their quarry.

"What other information was in the archives about this tart?"

"Just her name, the fact she was a known to the police as a prostitute and her Swedish nationality."

"And the guy?"

"Just his name from the press coverage of the incident and police report. We obviously tracked the death and birth records to match them to those two kids."

"So we know their age and parentage?"

"Yes, but we couldn't get any address details from the census data. So this is our best shot at finding them, the fact they are together on this day makes it a hell of a lot easier and timely too."

"Yeah, and I'm going to enjoy this one all the more. We just need him to show himself and we're set."

"Yes Leonardo, it's a relatively straightforward plan and judging by the dregs we have in here, no one will care who's who."

"This could be him now."

Desangé's attention was taken away from the prostitute as a carriage driver walked through the door. He too seemed to be taken aback by the bars inhabitants. He was new to the bar and similar to how Desangé had behaved earlier, took a little while to get used to the surroundings. Desangé watched him, hoping he might make a move towards the whore. For a brief moment, he thought he could be the guy, but when he avoided her advances and apologised, Desangé knew it wouldn't be him.

He turned to Elliot, "Not going to be him then."

"I think you're right. Far too meek to be cavorting with our little tart."

They both laughed, and he noticed the driver look up briefly at them both before finding his own quiet corner to watch the people from.

"This could be a long night." Elliot said.

"I know I was hoping I'd have blood on my hands by now." Desangé's patience was starting to strain. He checked his pocket watch, they'd been watching this rabble for over an hour.

"Another one?" He said picking up his glass. Elliot nodded, and Desangé made his way to the bar.

He caught the barman's eye by waving a note in the air. A little arrogant and it did bring undue attention his way, but he wasn't prepared to mingle with these drunken barflies longer than he needed. Drinks in hand he turned away from the rabble and made his way back to his friend.

"Did I miss anything?" He handed Elliot his beer.

"Possibly, look." Elliot pointed to a gent, drunk and accompanied by another prostitute. "He could be our guy."

The man was way past sober and revelling in the lurid attentions of his female companion, which had caught the eye of some the locals. One of them being the far from charming Swede, who instantly took offence to a rival taking her stage and benefiting from a cashed up punter. Evidence of this wealth on display as the man started waving white notes at the barman.

Desangé and Elliot watched with glee, knowing that their prey was now together, as the resident whore took matters into her own hands. As the other girl was distracted by the barman's drinks, she slipped in and kissed the gent full on the mouth. The gent obviously wasn't picky and Desangé assumed was also dumb as he reciprocated her advances just as his own whore turned to witness the new found liaison. The ensuing cat fight consumed much of the bar area, and Desangé knew his timing needed to be precise, but he did garner great pleasure watching two prostitutes go at it like two wildcats. He nudged Elliot as the fight threatened to spill into the street. More drunks were being drawn into the melee as the hissing combatants pushed over tables, smashing glasses and spilling gin, whiskey and beer around them. This was the incident that led to the arrest so he knew the police wouldn't be far away and when the fight spilled through the door Desangé made his move, shoving past the group of bystanders watching by the door. His plan was to intercede, split them apart and drag the two souls down a side alley, murder them both to make it look like they killed each other. The whore and her punter in an argument about money, both to blame and no one would be any wiser or care much either.

Elliot pulled two men away pushing them back into the bar.

"We're the law, detectives hunting the Ripper case so break it up and be on your way now, hop it!" Desangé grabbed the two girls, separating them, shoving the other prostitute to the opposite side of the street. " Get on your way miss." He hissed, keeping a firm hold on his prey. "Think yourself lucky you're not coming down the station." Taken aback, she swore at him and seemed to contemplate fighting back. Desangé stared hard, and she finally took his advice and scurried off up Settles Street.

"You got him," Desangé asked his accomplice.

"He's secure." Elliot had the gent in an arm lock much to his annoyance. "You can't arrest me, I haven't done anything" he protested.

"Breach of the peace" Elliot replied and led him away towards the alley. Desangé followed dragging the prostitute by the hair as she spat and hissed her anger at him he turned and said: " you're coming with me bitch."

Aston had clocked the hypnotist and his right-hand man shortly after he entered the bar. Seeing the man who had become his enemy turned his life inside out and was now threatening his friend's lives and not over reacting was difficult. He'd waited, biding his time, trying to keep an eye on the two men while people watching in the most surreal pub experience he'd even seen. The chaos of the crowded streets he'd seen on the way, was now crammed into the bar. The drunkenness, the noise and the diversity of

Victorian societies underclass staggered his senses, and the distraction made it difficult for him to keep focussed.

The mouthy girl bouncing around the pub from punter to punter caught his attention, she was not much older than he was. She wore a bright red bonnet that she pulled up and down to the amusement of some of her targets. She looked like she was going to latch on to him, but he avoided eye contact and said sorry which seemed to do the trick. He noticed that the hypnotist couldn't take his eyes off her which got Aston thinking that she could be the one who was Ellie's former soul. Now as he followed the fight, the hypnotist and his partner in crime outside he was certain, and one of the other two men in the fight must be Harrison's soul. Aston watched from just inside the door as the two went about their plot. He thought about confronting them during the fight 'safety in numbers maybe' but thought better of it as they were masquerading as police.

As Desangé and his offsider dragged Ellie and Harrison's former souls into the alley, he knew what he had to do. It was their lies about being the police that gave him the inkling of an idea and when he stepped outside of the Bricklayers and noticed two bobbies in the distance on the corner of Settles Street he knew it would work. They were probably the real policemen who were meant to break up the fight, had it run its course, but now Aston could use them to his advantage. Aston remembered the whistle in his coat pocket that he'd found driving the carriage. He assumed that carriage drivers used them for protection, and he knew it would now help his friends.

He blew the tin whistle as loud as he could, two shrill bursts that cut through the street noise. The police started running towards him.

"Murder" he shouted at the top off his voice. "Murder" then he blew the whistle again for added effect. The two bobbies were with him in no time, and he didn't give them time to stop. "Down there" he pointed down the alley "quick." The irony of him finally using the authorities was lost in the moment as Aston joined them in pursuit.

Desangé had his hands around the neck of Ellie's former soul as they came upon them.

"Unhand that woman" one of the bobbies yelled and struck Desangé with his truncheon. The swiftness of the bobbies Victorian London crime fighting tactics seemed to take them by surprise. His accomplice panicked and shoved his own captive towards the policemen and made a break for it. Aston's quick reactions took over even in his cab drivers soul, and he spun and with a swift sweep of his left leg taking the guys legs from underneath him as he rushed past. The man crashed head-first into the hard brick wall, Aston went to restrain him, but the man was out cold. Desangé had released the prostitute and was now grappling with the two officers. He was putting up a good fight until Aston and the other gent waded in and helped the policemen overwhelm him. They finally bundled him to the floor next to his unconscious accomplice, and the police cuffed them both of them together.

"Thanks for saving me. They said they were going to kill us." Said the gent thankfully shaking Aston by the hand.

"Don't mention it H" Aston stopped mid sentence realising his mistake.

"Who's H?" The gent looked puzzled.

"Never mind, sorry you remind me of someone. Where's the girl?"

Aston was now concerned for the whereabouts of Ellie's former soul. He looked around, she must have taken off pretty quickly during the fight, but Aston wanted to check she wasn't harmed.

"Where does this alley lead to?" Aston asked the gent.

"Comes out just behind Berner Street by the Jewish club I think."

"I need to check she's okay. Can you help me find her, it's important?"

"Of course" The gent nodded naturally grateful Aston had just saved his life.

The two police had officers had other ideas. "You'll need to come with us and make a statement sir." Said the first officer.

"She's probably just a prossie who's too scared of the police and has run back to the workhouse," said the other.

Aston was not about to let Ellie's former soul go without checking she was safe, especially after all he'd been through. "I have to find her, I'm sorry but this gent will answer all your questions officers." He said patting him on the back. "But take good care of him" and darted up the alley.

Aston ignored the calls behind him and hoped they wouldn't try to stop him. The police did seem a little bemused by his concern for a common prostitute, but he was intent on finding Ellie's former soul. He needed to be sure she wasn't injured from the fight but also felt an overwhelming desire to tell her to look after herself so he and Ellie could enjoy the future together. Aston surprised himself with that thought. Maybe he should tell Ellie the same thing when he got back. He reached the end of the alley and Aston found himself in a back street that must have been a dumping ground or junk yard. There was rubbish strewn everywhere and the smell reminded Aston of the Thames from when his reboot as a sweep. As Aston stumbled about in the dark unlit side street, he dreaded to think what he was treading on, or in. Soft mud or something underfoot, if only there was a street light he might have been able to see footprints from Ellie's former soul. The noise of the nearby club, raucous and loud, drew his attention so he followed the sound. It was easier to use to find his way in the darkness, and as it got louder and closer, he found another alley. A distant street light at the other end provided a visual beacon for his search. Aston assumed she would have followed a similar path if she had any sense, she would have known her way around and couldn't imagine her hiding in the dark back street. She was probably back on the game, touting for more punters in the warmth of the club. He darted down the alley towards the light. He came out on Berner Street according to the street sign and the entrance to the Jewish club. He made his way inside.

Once again he was overawed by the sites and sounds of life in the late nineteenth century. This club was teeming with a broad mixture of people and either celebrating the end of the day or trying to forget their grim existing both seemed intent leaving their worries behind at the bottom of a dirty glass. Aston worked his way around the club searching for a glimpse of the girl. Another fight broke out in the corner of the snug bar, and he hoped that she was again the instigator but this time it looked like the argument was over a game of cards judging by the aftermath. She wasn't in here and it seemed he'd been searching for a good half hour, maybe the policeman was right she had gotten scared and gone home. Aston decided to try a few more pubs and clubs before giving in, he circled back the other way around the club just in case and made his way to the entrance.

He took one last look around the club before stepping through the door. Something odd caught his eye as he looked out across the street opposite the bar. Aston noticed a man crouched over something or someone lying in what looked like a builders yard. It was someone, not something. 'No' Aston was immediately concerned and started to run over.

"Someone help, this woman's been hurt bad" the man yelled.

Aston started to slow down as he got closer and could now see more detail. The mans hands were covered in blood, he was kneeling next to a body of a woman.

'Oh no. Oh no, it can't be her' Aston worst fears were realised when he saw the distinctive red bonnet that Ellie's soul had been wearing. At the yard entrance he stopped dead, his own mind retreated back on itself not wanting to face the reality of the horror before him.

The cab drivers soul took back control, and although bemused as to where he was, he immediately tried to help the man who had found the girl.

Aston could still see through his former soul's eyes as the two men tried in vain to help the girl.

"I've just found her, lying there," the man said.

The girl's neck was slashed open, there was so much blood all around her matching the colour of the bonnet but also a spray of red roses on the ground next to her. The cab driver used his whistle to raise the alarm, bringing more people out of the club and the surrounding houses.

"Keep back" the driver tried to stop people getting too close.

"Did you see anyone?" He asked the man who had found her.

"I think I disturbed them, I was coming back to lock up, but by the time I'd got to the gate they'd vanished. Probably made it out through the other entrance."

"They? There was more than one?"

"I can't be sure but I reckon so" the man replied.

"Oh my god" a woman screamed behind them and they turned to see the mass of people that had started to gather around them. Aston, in a chilling out of body experience, watched as increasingly more people crowded around the corpse of the former soul of the girl he'd fallen for, the soul who would now be lost from his.

Within a few minutes the police were there and began to take control of the mayhem. They quickly ushered the crowds back behind the yard entrance gates and a white sheet was placed over the lifeless body of the girl. Not that it stopped the crowds of people peering through the metal railings trying to catch a glimpse of the body. The whispers and gossip about the rippers latest victim had already started as the Police started interviewing those, who they thought were close to the scene.

After answering a few questions the cab driver checked his pocket watch and explained to the police that he had a fare to pick up at midnight. The officer took his name and address, Andrew Porter of Lollard Street and let him leave.

The name of his former soul hardly registered with Aston, who was still in shock. He couldn't come to terms with the consequences of the death of Ellie's soul and continued as a passenger, his mind spinning, as Andrew Porter made his way back to the carriage.

Aston tried to rationalise what the hell had happened. There were so many questions that he had no way of answering about her death. His first thought was towards Desangé and Aston tried to figure out if he'd had a hand in it. There was a chance he could have slashed her just as she ran away, but that wound was far too deep for her to have made it that far. Aston dismissed that idea as they would also have seen or found the knife when they subdued him. If he was involved, it must have been an accomplice, someone else in the bar or waiting at the end of the alley perhaps. For a moment, Aston considered whether Desangé had shifted back in time again, but again that would have been difficult handcuffed and in police custody. Unless he returned later but that too seemed impossible given the timings although what did Aston know of how soul shifting worked he just wished that he'd never met the bloody hypnotist.

It didn't take long for Andrew Porter to get back to Brick Lane, it could only have been a little after twelve but the fare he had picked up earlier was waiting. He was very agitated and acting all high and mighty.

"We had an agreement damn it. You know I cannot abide tardiness." He said chastising the cab driver. "We must leave for St Thomas' immediately, these instruments need to be returned." The old man clutched the bag close to him somewhat over protective of them.

"Apologies for being late sir." Porter replied. "There was an incident in Berner Street. Young girl taken in the yard across from the Jewish club, very nasty. The Ripper again, some were saying."

"Most unfortunate. Look I'm very keen to leave right away."

"Is your associate from earlier joining you sir?"

"No, no," he said dismissively. "Let's get on." The man reached into his black coat pocket and retrieved a purse and tossed it to the driver. "Your fee as before." He quickly climbed aboard the carriage.

"Right you are sir." Porter replied.

He pocketed his fee, picked up the reigns and leaned over to release the hand brake. Out of the corner of his eye, he saw a small red object thrown out of the carriage and land in the gutter. It was a the crushed head of a red rose, the petals still vibrant under the street light.

The sight of this brought Aston out of his depressive state as he remembered the scene from Ellie's soul's murder.

The fare banged his cane on the roof "It's time to go."

Aston thought about taking back control and confronting him but as Andrew Porter flicked the reigns to spur on the horses he knew he had to leave too. With his will and his heart feeling as crushed as the rose, he closed his mind and rebooted back to face the new reality now waiting for him.

Leonardo Desangé's cold eyes stared straight through his associate Elliot, he was furious they had been caught and was certain he knew exactly why they were currently locked in a cell in Whitechapel police station.

"It was the look the cab driver gave me, it was exactly the same look that fucking kid gave me in the club in Kensington. It was the look, Elliot. I stake my reputation on it."

"I'm not even going there until we are out of this place, Leonardo, I'm damn well annoyed enough without having to listen to your hypothesis, however, unfounded or baseless on fact."

"It had to be the kid interfering, I've seen it too often now not to be mistaken. I just can't work out how the hell he knew."

"Exactly, he couldn't have. Your paranoia about some stupid kid is severely affecting your judgement. I don't want to talk about it lets just think of a way out of here."

Elliot had a point, they did need to get out of the station to be able to shift back to the present day. Desangé knew it also needed to be without little or no consequence else time and history for their soul's journey could be damaged. The longer they were locked up, the longer they were shifting, so the possibility of the more damage occurring from unplanned interactions was greater. This was something he'd learned through the years, and he didn't want any further problems.

Desangé had almost fashioned an escape shortly after they had been arrested. He had managed to hypnotise a weak minded officer that had handcuffed him following the fight. With his hands tied it was hard to use him effectively and get himself released. He'd only just been thwarted when a couple more bobbies arrived, and it was these other two that frogmarched them back to the station.

His only plan now was to hope that the Bobbie, who he'd hypnotised, would turn up in the cells where he might be able to use him to escape somehow. Other than that he hoped Elliot had an alternative idea on the cards just in case, or this would be a long night. He was about to ask him when there was a commotion from the front of the station. A crowd of police came through to the cells, and a plain clothes detective inquired why the two men were locked up. Elliot looked at Desangé expectantly. The custody sergeant explained, and the officer said he needed the cell to examine the bodies immediately. The detective argued that the brawl was nowhere near as high profile as the Ripper case and with two girls murdered in one night the sooner they could get evidence the better. The custody sergeant said he needed to check with his commanding officer and got another Bobbie to fetch him.

Desangé turned to Elliot, "Looks like we could be in luck, either way, I think we can use this to our advantage."

"Don't count on it Leonardo but it would be amusing if the Ripper gets us out."

The detective argued that these looked like two wealthy gentlemen judging by their attire, who could be trusted to report back to the station tomorrow. There was more commotion, and another plainclothes detective came in and spoke to his colleague.

"Damn it man there bringing the bodies in now, I need this cell." The custody sergeant gave in saying that given the lack of previous convictions he would allow it. He turned to another officer telling him to get their details, give them a warning and make sure they promise to return and get them out of here."

A few moments later they were both being led out the back of the station. They were passed by officers carrying the lifeless bodies of two murdered women on stretchers. The crude sheet covering the second body got trapped in the door, and Elliot tapped Desangé on the shoulder as he recognised the distinctive red bonnet. Once outside Desangé slapped Elliot on the back "that was the girl, I'm certain of it, I never forget a dead face" he said laughing. "We may have been given lucky double thanks to Ripper."

"Yes, not only did he get us out of this place he also finished half the job for us."

"I know you've gotta love a bit of irony and to top it all I would like to see the face on that detective when they find out she was the one involved in our arrest."

"Do you want to find the other gent while we're here and finish the job?" Elliot asked.

"I think not, I've had about enough of Victorian London for one day. It was bad enough the first time." Desangé also had other plans. "I want to get back and see what the aftermath will be." What he really meant was that he planned to find Aston North but he knew how Elliot would react. "Come on let's get out of here."

CHAPTER SEVENTEEN

Aston sucked in a large gasp of air and then grabbed at his chest, his heart felt like it was burning a hole in his body. It was not only burning and beating too fast as he rebooted back from the nightmare of losing his friend. 'If only it was a nightmare' he thought just as the pain pierced his whole body. He clutched his heart again, it was broken but again the reboot meant it was physically broken not just metaphorically! His desolation only compounded the heart arrhythmia and he knew he was slipping into cardiac arrest. There was nothing he could do, he knew when he started that there would be no friends standing watchfully over him when he returned. He gone to save them and hadn't thought about the consequence of rebooting back alone. His failure tore into him as did the pain in his chest and he realised he'd never see either of his friends again.

There was someone standing over Aston, it wasn't anyone he knew but the man who had abducted him from St Mary's Axe. The man had spent the last ten minutes watching the "sleeping" body of his captive twitch and jerk, his eyes moving rapidly behind his eyelids in a manner that made him look like he had been possessed. He had tried a number of times to raise him from this sleep. He needed to wake the boy so he could record his confession and get him to recount his ridiculous claims about reincarnation. Frustrated by the depth of his sleep he had started to shake him, he shook him with all his strength lifting him off the mattress but still he didn't wake. He dropped him back down and was horrified when the boy suddenly woke clutching his chest, his eyes wide open, gasping for air. He stepped back and watched as the boy grabbed his chest again, his face contorting with agony and as quickly as he woke he lost consciousness.

Aston wasn't unconscious he was dying, he knew from experience that without any medical assistance his heart would stop and there was a part of him that embraced it. To overcome the pain he searched for a true inner state in his mind, blocking all thoughts, all senses, just concentrating attention not on an individual area but on the twelve Meridien channels at once to encompass his whole being. A technique Grace had taught him to use as a child after she had found him cowering in his room during one of his parents fights. 'The mind can overcome all pain both physical and metaphysical' she had said. He needed both right now.

Aston found the relief he needed and as his heart stopped beating he experienced an unexpected and remarkable sensation. It was as if he relinquished the control of his own soul, just as he had when he rebooted into his previous souls, but now, he was looking down on his own body from an outside perspective. Aston watched as the bearded man who had captured him grabbed his arm and felt for a pulse. It was surreal as he physically felt the touch of the mans hand on his wrist whilst he also watched it second hand. The man couldn't find his pulse, Aston felt and watched the man shake him and then press his finger to his neck. He could sense the man's anxiety and literally recoiled as the man cried out load, "No!" Aston watched as his abductor started to lose his composure, he knelt next to Aston's body, looking upward seemingly directly at Aston's ethereal viewpoint, and began to pray.

"Forgive me father for I have sinned. I have brought this blasphemer into your place of worship, hoping he would recount his own sins. I should have not exposed your holy church to this sacrilege. I ask your forgiveness for my sins, for the sins of the blasphemer and with your guidance I hope you can steer my hand to ensure that none of this vile defacement of the beliefs we hold dear, will ever see the light of day." The man paused seemingly contemplating his predicament. Then after a while said, "Thank you Father you have shown me the true path of enlightenment. Amen."

He stood then looked to the air again as if staring straight at Astons our of body perspective. The man crossed himself and then picked up Aston's lifeless body and placed him over his shoulder, as he stepped out of the cold stone room Aston's vision of himself began to darken, his mind no longer seeing or feeling a thing, a mist like blackness overtook him and started to fill his being. There was no light, no tunnel and no longer any pain, there was nothing just black.

Ellie was so glad her sister had been willing to help. Even though they had only recently started talking again, she knew that they would always be there for each other when called upon in a crisis. 'Family is family' her mom had always said. The fact that nothing had happened for most of the day frustrated her, and probably more so her sister, who had been asking so many questions why Aston had been kidnapped. Ellie found it difficult to not tell her everything and had been sketchy about the exact details because of her sisters religious beliefs and the family bonds were getting a little strained. Ellie was happy to have someone though and it did mean that they had spent the time together and talking, which hadn't happened for a long time.

Ellie and her sister had walked around the seemingly deserted Church a number of times. The problem with old churches is a distinct lack of windows at eye level, and those that there were, were far too narrow and annoyingly stained so there was no chance of getting any idea of what was inside. Ellie knew Aston was there somewhere and she had knocked on, and shouted at, all the obvious doors, but they were all locked and no one answered. They traced the van she had followed to a lock up garage next to the vestry. There were tyre tracks in gravel leading up to it, Ellie recognised the graphics on the rear of the van, but still they couldn't find anyone. Their hopes had been raised after a man arrived to start digging a grave in the cemetery. He let them down though as it turned out he was just a contractor who received his instructions over the phone and didn't know much at all about anything.

It was starting to get dark when Ellie's mobile vibrated in her pocket, it was a message from Harrison.

"Finally he's here" she said to her sister who didn't appear at the least interested.

"Who?"

"Harrison! You know I told you earlier he's the one who shares the house with Aston in Oxford."

"Well at least it means someone else is actually here!"

"Aston is here Jess, I know it, like I said earlier, we just need some evidence that the nutter has him locked up so we can call the police."

"I just wish he'd hurry up and show himself, we've been here ages it seems and I've got to get home tonight."

"Come on let's go and get Harrison, he's bound to have some new techie way to help us locate Aston."

"Okay" Jess replied. Ellie thought her sister had reached her limit in regard to patience.

"Harrison!" Ellie yelled, happy to see her friend and hopeful he would bring some new idea, they hugged.

"Sorry, I'm so late Ellie, nightmare trying to get a car, eventually had to hack into Uber taxis and bump up my points. Then they took forever as it was long distance. The guy was a bit miffed about dropping me off here." Ellie rolled her eyes. He turned to greet Jess. "Hi, I'm Harrison, lovely to meet you."

"Likewise, I'm Jess." She said smiling. Ellie noticed a glint in her eye, a moment before she wasn't interested. Obviously, his charm appealed to her big sister.

"How's Celia?" Ellie said to highlight the fact Harrison did have another married affair on the go and she wasn't about to let her sister be the next. Harrison understood and quickly changed the subject.

"No sign of Aston!"

"Nothing? It been hours." Harrison pulled out his phone.

"I was hoping you had some news or some way of tracking him down."

"His phones not been activated since it was switched off at midday, just after he got here. I've been tracking that Schindler blokes gmail account, and he's not sent any other emails, but he logged on at this location about two hours ago. Look." He showed Ellie the screen but she wasn't sure what she was meant to be looking at and just nodded.

"We found the van earlier. It's in a garage up behind the vestry but it's locked. Do you think you could break in?"

"Probably, I've got my trusty tool set." Harrison waved his small set of precision screwdrivers.

"A crow bar would be better." Jess didn't sound impressed.

"You'd be amazed what these little things can do. Did you call the police?"

"No, we were hoping to get some evidence or at least a sighting so we knew he was definitely here." Ellie replied.

"He is here!" Jess screamed pointing at the church door adjacent to the cemetery. "And he's got Aston!"

Ellie reeled around to watch the bearded man, she now knew as Schindler Whit, coming out of the church and striding across the grounds toward the cemetery. It was dark but she could clearly see that the man had Aston on his shoulder carrying him like a rag doll. Ellie could not believe what she was watching as the man paused in the middle of the graveyard.

"Oh my god!" Ellie's sister screamed as the man lowered Aston from his shoulder and dropped him into the grave that they had seen being dug earlier. Harrison, Jess and Ellie started running towards the cemetery. Ellie watched in horror as Schindler Whit got off his knees from what she thought must have been some kind of prayer pick up the shovel and start to bury Aston.

As they sprinted forward Ellie noticed Harrison was recording the events on his iPhone. They were about one hundred metres away when Schindler looked up and saw them coming, he dropped the spade and bolted across the cemetery. By the time they reached the grave he was through the lych gate at the churchyard entrance. Ellie looked down into the open grave, the flashlight from Harrison's phone revealing the lifeless Aston covered in a scattering of dark earth which accentuated the shocking paleness of his skin.

Ellie jumped down into the grave, "Oh my god he's killed him!" "Aston, Aston!" She shook his body and felt his neck for a pulse. Nothing, "Jess where's Harrison and call an ambulance!"

"He's gone after that madman." She replied and pulled out her phone. "Is he alive?"

"Aston can you hear me, stay with us — please God stay with us!". Ellie shouted at Aston. "He hasn't got a pulse but I don't know how long he's been like this." Ellie knew that the one man who knew was currently being chased by Harrison but she also knew she couldn't wait to find out if he could catch him.

"Aston - stay with us" she shouted in a vain hope his subconscious would somehow hear.

"Ambulance please" Ellie heard Jess phoning emergency services."I need an ambulance — at Christs Church, Hampstead Heath. Quickly my sister's boyfriend is dying!"

Ellie didn't register her reference to Aston as a boyfriend, she was desperate to save him.

"How long?" She asked.

Jess asked the question and replied. "Eight minutes!"

"Too long, that's way too long" Ellie had to do something.

'What did my training say' she thought to herself. 'Check the body temperature.' She brushed away the earth and felt his skin. Although he was quite pale, the skin still felt relatively warm, that gave her the encouragement she needed.

"I need to get his heart started." Suddenly she remembered what was in her bag. "Jess throw me my handbag."

She rummaged around in her bag cursing

"Why didn't I think of this straight away!" She pulled out the adrenalin shot she'd been keeping in there since the first time Aston had rebooted and waved it at Jess. "Got it!"

Ellie measured the correct distance from the rib cage, paused for a second and then jammed the needle through his breastplate into his heart. "Aston don't you dare die on me."

A pinpoint of light penetrated the blackness, like a pinhole camera at first and then the lens became wider clearing away the black mist and filling Aston's mind with light. He could hear a muted voice calling his name, willing him to join them, to stay with them. As the voice became clearer, Aston recognised who it was calling his name. 'Am I dead now? That's Ellie's voice, and she wants me to stay with her. Then I must be?' His memory of seeing his body and the guy in church cellar came to him. 'I saw myself. I know I died? Ellie's voice begged him to stay once more and then went quiet. She was gone?

Suddenly Aston's senses were jolted again as his whole chest was pierced by a short, sharp stabbing pain. Then it felt as if his heart was being ripped apart, 'no not ripped apart, this was different to before, it was being restarted.' A powerful rush of energy filled his entire body giving him immediate focus and clarity, followed by a pounding in his heart, 'no it was in his chest.' His lungs filled with air breathing oxygen into his soul, his mouth tasted a mixture of dirt and a sweetness that touched his lips, Aston knew he was alive now.

Aston opened his eyes and the face he thought he'd never see again was staring back at him. There was hardly any light but her face was so clear to him, she looked shocked and concerned, her brow furrowed but as he started gasping for air, her beautiful eyes lit up and that smile he knew and loved, lit up her face.

"You're alive!" he said and hugged her. "I thought I'd lost you, Ellie."

"We thought we'd lost you — you were dead and buried for a while!" She kissed him. He held the kiss for a moment, embracing her, embracing life and the reality that her soul hadn't been altered and she was still his Ellie. He broke away from the kiss.

"You were a prostitute!"

"That's not nice I just saved your life!" Ellie shoved him playfully.

"No, sorry, it was back in 1888, I had to save your past soul from Desangé! He was going to kill you and Harrison. You and H met in a past life. That's what I found out in his office."

"What? You're not making any sense."

"I'd heard him plotting it so I had to reboot back to stop him murdering your previous souls. It worked, I stopped him but your soul ran away and ended up being massacred by the Ripper."

"What?"

"I saw the body and thought I'd caused your death. I felt so helpless and thought that you and your life here now we're gone. Lost to follow another souls path so you wouldn't be you."

The sirens and blue lights signalled the pending arrival of the ambulance.

"So while you were being held by the lunatic, you rebooted to save me and Harrison. You're crazy Aston. We thought he'd killed you as some kind of religious sacrifice, he must have found you when you booted back. You know how dangerous this is."

"I know but I had to Ellie, I didn't know how long he'd lock me up for and Desangé had said he was doing it today or tonight so I had no choice."

The blue lights lit up their faces as they looked at one another. Aston heard the ambulance doors open and someone tell the paramedics where they were. He kissed her then said, " I'll tell you more later, but I'm so bloody glad you're here." She kissed him back just as the paramedics arrived.

"An unusual method of CPR miss but it looks effective enough."

Aston laughed but Ellie looked embarrassed. "Give me your hand miss and we'll get you out and see whether we can help your friend!"

Ellie told the paramedics about what she had witnessed, how they found him and the adrenalin shot. They asked Aston if he could stand, he tried but had to be helped out of the grave by the two paramedics. Once out, they strapped him to the gurney and wheeled him into the ambulance. The first paramedic checked him over and he heard the other one telling Ellie something. She climbed into the ambulance, smiled at him and said. "There taking you to the nearest emergency, Jess and I will follow once we've found Harrison and we'll meet you there."

Harrison stuck his head around the door of the ambulance.

"Hey! Aston looks like your back from the dead then." He said out of breath. "Schindler Whit gave me the slip I'm afraid, but he did drop this," he waved Aston phone in the air, "and I think I've got enough footage of the lunatic to post online and give to the cops."

"H, how you doing? Glad to see you again. You'll never guess where I've been."

The paramedic climbed in the ambulance " sorry guys you'll have to continue your conversation in the ER." He turned to Ellie "are you coming along miss."

"Do you mind?"

"Not at all, but there's only room for one."

"I'm more than happy to follow along with Jess." Harrison winked.

"Jess, are you okay with that?" Ellie shouted to her sister standing outside.

"It's okay with me Ellie, we'll see you there."

"Thanks, Jess."

The paramedic said they had to go now and closed the door. Aston felt Ellie grab his hand and he smiled, thankful that they were both alive. His smile disappeared as the realisation that Desangé was still out there struck him. As long as he was still at large, there would always be a dark shadow hanging over both his own and his friends lives.

Harrison would have liked to get to know Jess a little better now they were alone. But as Ellie had mentioned his girlfriend he didn't mind being a little rude and spending the journey time on his iPad. He knew timing was crucial if he wanted to find Schindler Whit. He felt responsible for the fact that this guy was even around, and really pissed off he couldn't catch him earlier, but he did know of a way to track him down and the person who would help - Professor Ferris.

As Jess drove to the hospital, he was able to edit and enhance the footage he'd shot of Schindler Whit dropping Aston's body into the empty grave. The video was quite dark but by adjusting the contrast and brightness levels it was usable. Harrison also spliced in the surveillance pictures he'd found in the professors email which added further evidence to the piece he was confident he could use as leverage to get him to reveal Whits whereabouts.

As the video uploaded onto YouTube Harrison realised Jess would be able to help.

"Can I borrow your phone?"

"Oh, of course, it's in my bag. It's on the back seat."

Harrison reached behind to get it, normally he would have rummaged around to find it but he thought it best to hand it to Jess so he placed the bag in her lap.

"Thanks" she got the phone out. "Here you go." She paused and passed it to him, Harrison could see a load of questions just waiting to come out.

"Once I've made this call, I'll tell you what's going on! Or at least what I know!"

She smiled and said, "Yeah that would be helpful."

Harrison started to dial the professors mobile. "It's been an eventful few weeks!" His attention switched to the end of the line as Ferris answered.

"Hello"

"Hello professor, I've got something you need to see."

"Is that..."

"Harrison" he cut the professor off knowing he needed to control the conversation. "You know who it is. Are you in your office?"

"Yes," Harrison pressed send. He heard the Professors instant messenger alert ping. "Open the link."

"This is really quite inappropriate Mr Ng, calling this late, I must..."

"No professor, I must insist. Insist you watch the man you gave our private information to drop my friend's body into a grave!"

"Oh my god" the professor was obviously watching the clip. Harrison could hear the sound of their footsteps as they ran to help Aston.

"Yes professor, that's your friend Schindler Whit and you may recognise Aston. He's the boy he's about to..." Harrison paused and let the video have the impact he knew it would.

"Heavens above. Oh no. What has he done!" The professors reaction was exactly as he'd hoped.

"I need to know where he is Professor. Your friend almost killed Aston."

"He's not dead?"

"Luckily we were there to save him but your Mr Schit got away," Harrison smiled to himself realising the combination. "So unless you help me turn him in that clip goes public. In fact, I'm going to need you to send this to the police for me." He pressed send on his iPad.

"I took the liberty of preparing this for you." Harrison heard the email arrive. He had used the Professor own email account he'd accessed back at Oxford the day before.

"This was sent from my own account — how did you?"

"You taught me well Professor. I'm going to need you to find out, and fill in the whereabouts of your lunatic friend and forward it on to the Police."

"But why?"

"No buts Professor, I've seen your Gmail inbox you're an accessory to attempted murder and don't think about trying to talk your way out of this because there's a second email if you don't help. This one outlines your part in this crime including the passing on of confidential student records and I'm sure your esteemed contacts and colleagues in academia and the business world would love to read it to."

"You can't expect me to agree to incriminate myself."

"Oh I think it would be in your interests to come forward yourself rather than have me expose what you, and your friend, have done."

Harrison waited for the professor to work out that he was right.

"Okay, Mr Ng you're quite right. Clearly Schindler has taken this a lot further than he originally intended. I'll track him down and send your email to the authorities."

"Thank you professor" he could tell that Ferris was now thinking about damage control and could now ask him for his final request.

"There's one other thing I'm going to need. You know the remote systems administrator login and password for the Oxford computer suite right. Well, I'm planning a little experiment and the processor power will come in handy."

"I can't possibly. I could be..."

"Now professor, if this email gets sent then you wouldn't be able to get a job teaching Kindles to kindergarten.

The professor sighed and told Harrison the details after which Harrison told him he'd be monitoring the email account and expect something within the hour.

Jess looked over once he hung up the phone. "Wow, I guess that covers one side of the story, I can't wait to hear the rest! And I think you'll be paying for my next top up! When you asked to use my phone, I thought you were calling your mom to say you'd be late for tea!!"

They both laughed.

"I can show you how to never pay a mobile bill again if you like!" Harrison said.

"You're on," Jess replied. "First, you can tell me exactly what my sister has got herself into."

CHAPTER EIGHTEEN

"How are you feeling?"

Aston thought for a while, he was once again lying in a hospital bed. The morning sun shining through the window of his private room. The monitoring equipment in the corner pinging out his heart rhythm, a drip attached to his hand providing his body additional fluids and the two people whose souls he'd tried to save sat by his side. Ellie was holding his other hand.

"I'm feeling okay H but I'm bloody worried it won't last."

"It won't last or you won't last. You had us worried there, I can't believe you rebooted on your own and with no technology."

"Hah, well the risk was worth it" he squeezed Ellie's hand "and I would have used the app if that maniac hadn't taken it off me."

"Well, he's taken care of. Ferris came through last night like I said it was just a matter of leverage, and I expect the police will be picking him up as we speak."

"That's a relief," Ellie said. "I'm not going anywhere close to a church for a while."

"Well, if your past life's anything to go by, your not likely to become a nun!" Harrison ducked just in time to miss Ellie's playful swipe.

"Well Mister, it was your previous soul who was paying for it. So watch out!" Ellie jabbed him in the ribs and laughed.

Aston smiled enjoying their banter, he'd told his friends how he had saved their former souls and the connection they had when they got to the hospital last night. He'd been surprised how well they had taken the news and maybe their joking was a way of suppressing the thought of almost being erased from their own existence. He had woken in the early hours of the morning thinking about when Desangé might try again and hadn't stopped thinking about it.

"Like I said guys, I'm worried. Desangé is still out there, he's tried it once and I'm convinced he'll try it again."

"I thought you said the Police had arrested him?" Ellie said.

"I just know he would have got out or shifted back, I'm pretty sure if we phoned his office and asked for him he'd be there."

"I for one think this guy needs payback, we sorted out Schwit face we can do it again."

"That was pure luck H if I hadn't been there and seen the van. Aston would be dead and buried. I say let the authorities deal with him."

"Did you manage to get back in touch with Agent Baker Ellie?" Aston asked. " He saw Ellie's startled reaction.

"Oh my god I completely forgot. It was really weird. I called his mobile and got transferred a couple of times and then some guy asked me if I knew where Agent Baker was."

"What?" Aston and Harrison said together.

"I know weird, right? And the man knew my name! I panicked and hung up!"

"Jesus Ellie, why would they ask if you knew where he was?" Harrison asked.

"I reckon Desangé has a hand in it." Aston was convinced. "There's too much coincidence that he goes missing shortly after you told him about Desangé!"

His two friends looked at each other, then back to him.

"And we're next. Unless we do something about it. Now!"

"Fuck! He's right Ellie."

"Surely it's safer going public — getting the police involved. With the evidence re Baker, we have something, Aston. Right?" She lacked conviction.

"I know where you're coming from Ellie, I really do, but this guy can pick a date in time, slip back and bang, we're gone. And I don't think the cops can help, even if they lock him up, he's got money and power and I'm sure his offsider or one of his groupies would be able to do it."

"It's dangerous Aston. I'm not prepared to lose you again."

Aston smiled, he didn't want to leave her and the thought of rebooting didn't exactly thrill him either. But he knew it was the only way.

"So when and where?" Harrison said breaking up the tension.

"Well, I'm convinced there's some significance to the Battle of Trafalgar" the fact Harrison had found out that he and Desangé were once brothers, blown apart on the Belleisle, which may have started this journey was playing increasingly on his mind.

"I think if we stop him there, we stop it all at the source!"

"Hang on Aston, if you stop him there, then you don't die, and your souls are changed, then you don't get to be you." Ellie had a point. "That's how it works right? You would essentially be committing suicide!"

"True, I wasn't thinking rationally enough. So when then, we keep it recent?"

"We need to get him and get his business, he may play at being a hypnotist but he's just a glorified banker, hit him where the money is and he's ruined."

"A glorified stockbroker to be exact, which is worse! You might be on to something H, if we can find a way to take out him and his group then there's no come back on us."

"But when, we hardly know much about him, let alone when he started his company. What was it called Trafalgar investors?"

"Trafalgar Investments, and that's as good a place to start as any, Ellie. We know about the link to Trafalgar, he must too. Desangé has made a mistake naming his company and I reckon we could trace things back and see what opportunities come up. What do you reckon H?"

Harrison reached for his backpack and pulled out his MacBook and beamed. "I have a free pass into Oxford's computer suite thanks to Professor Ferris."

Aston sat upright squeezed Ellie's hand. "Hand me the iPad." He said rubbing his hands together with anticipation. "With that kind of processing power and access, we'll find something in no time."

Leonardo Desangé walked into his office, Giselle was waiting to greet him. "Coffee?" she asked and handed him his regular double espresso. "All went well I'm guessing?" She brushed his shoulder affectionately and kissed his cheek.

"Well enough, despite a few hiccups." He didn't want to tell her the whole story, not yet. He had an inkling that there may still be some twist in the story. The boy still bothered him but he knew he was starting to become obsessive.

"Tell me later. We are still on for dinner tonight. I have a surprise planned that I know you'll like." She winked and walked out smiling.

"I definitely need some of that!"

He drained his coffee, sat down at his desk and opened his laptop. He had just started checking the overnight market positions when his door opened.

"Elliot. Got back okay then I see!"

"Did you see the Hang Seng?"

"I was just checking."

"Dropped almost 15% overnight, unprecedented. Our Chinese friends will be pleased."

"They will indeed, just as well, it went how we predicted. Aren't you glad I let you convince me it was a good idea to play them again! I think we should look to set them up for an even larger amount next time."

"Let's take this short, and keep them wanting more Leonardo."

"Speaking of more..." Desangé wasn't able to finish as his secretary came in followed by a woman he didn't recognise.

"Sorry Mr Desangé but this lady insisted on seeing you."

"Mr Desangé" the woman introduced herself. Desangé could tell she was MI6, her manner was similar to Agent Bakers and she had a similar air of authority. A trait and misapprehension that found Agent Baker at the bottom of the Thames. "I need a moment of your time."

"It's okay," Desangé said trying not to show his annoyance. "The officer is more than welcome." Both he and the agent knew this couldn't be further from the truth. What the smiling Agent didn't know was that she had unwittingly just delivered a very upsetting realisation that Lee's recent endeavours back to 1888 had failed. Elliot wore a look that told Desangé that he too knew that whatever they thought they'd achieved, they hadn't.

"Excuse me gentlemen but I'll get right to the point. I'm following up a line of enquiry that was being pursued by an agent Baker, who listed you, Mr Desangé as a person he was planning to interview in relation to a current investigation."

"I assure you, I'm sorry I didn't catch your name?" Desangé debated in his head whether he could quickly hypnotise her, he decided it was a little too risky.

"The names Hammond, Megan Hammond."

"Agent Hammond, I'm very sure that my personal assistant or I would be able to remember speaking to your agent or whether we had been contacted about any investigation. Can you tell me the details it's rather disconcerting to learn that I may have been a line of enquiry within an ongoing MI6 investigation."

"I'm not, I'm afraid, but don't be alarmed, as I said it's merely routine that we follow up all leads." The agent looked directly into Leonardo's eyes with definite intent. "Especially when one of our men goes missing without contact."

"Your agent is missing, that's very troubling. I'm more than happy to help out, but as I said, I have never heard of, let alone met your other colleague. When was he due to speak to me? Maybe my assistant can check back through my appointments."

"I don't think that will be necessary at this point Mr Desangé. I was merely here to confirm if he had or hadn't contacted you. Thanks for your time." The agent turned to walk out the door. As she opened the door she looked back and said: " We will be in touch with you should we need to."

"That's good to know Agent Hammond and do let me know if you find your missing agent." He replied, hoping the agent got the hint of sarcasm as she left.

Desangé slammed his balled fists on the desk. "Damn it, Elliot, I fucking knew that we failed. It had to be something to do Aston North like I said in the cells I'm sure he was that cabbie."

"I'm more concerned about this investigation and any fallout to the business. Your obsession with this kid is what got us into this situation."

"Look Elliot" Leonardo's temper had reached its tipping point. "This is my business, I created it, I built it, I know how important it is. As you well know I can shut it down and start up again anywhere without any traces. So I don't need you to lecture me on my obsession with this kid."

That damn kid he thought, he knew he needed a solution and quickly, maybe subtlety wasn't the way to go.

"Well, Leonardo just remember on whose advice you were able to build this company and don't forget who told you to get out of certain ventures when the going was good. I'm telling you now the kid is not the issue, we need a calm, clear and calculated approach to what we do next. I for one am not going to jeopardise what I've helped build."

Desangé knew he'd relied on Elliot's advice at times, probably too often as far as the markets were concerned, but he also knew that he needed to be kept in check. Elliot had major influence and held close relationships with a number of key investors, the Chinese being just one. Maybe now would be a good time to pull the plug on this version of Trafalgar Investments.

"Boss?" Nigel poked his head around the door.

"Yes, Nigel? This better be worthwhile to warrant another intrusion uninvited."

"I think you really need to see this!" Nigel walked in holding a laptop. "The security team were reviewing the alarm systems following the evacuation the other day and came across this."

Desangé was intrigued although could have done without the interruption. "This involves you to Elliot. Take a look" he pressed play on the video file on the screen.

Desangé watched as Aston North walked into the reception area wandered around peaking into brochures.

"The cheeky bastard what on earth is he doing here?"

"That's not the half of it Mr Desangé! Watch this!"

They watch on and see him dive into one of the meeting rooms as Elliot and Desangé come into shot.

"That's how he knew" Elliot looked at Desangé "that was when I told you about 1888 and how we could get at the two kids souls in one go."

"I fucking told you he was there!" Vindicated somewhat Desangé held his emotions in check as he watched the events unfold and Elliot and himself re-enter the shot and exit out the front of the office.

"That's all until a little while later, watch" Nigel fast forwarded the video of the empty reception until people started to appear and exit. "There! He just joins the rest of the group as they leave" Nigel pointed the kid out as he came into shot and looked straight at the camera before walking out with the other employees evacuating the floor.

"We think the kid must have raised the alarm. Building security traced the call to the meeting room four which is where he went into during the tape."

"Cheeky little bastard. Forget what I said Leonardo. I want to go and pick the prick up now and sort him out once and for all." Elliot said changing his stance.

"Nigel, thanks for this and do me another favour."

"Yes, boss?"

"Tomorrow morning make sure you and a few of the boys are ready for another little trip to Oxford. This time Elliot and I are coming."

"Okay, will do. It'll be good to finally get this kid and teach him some manners." Desangé smiled as Nigel rubbed his hands together, picked up the laptop and left the office.

"You don't want to slip back in time again and do this?"

"Fuck it, Elliot, I say we finalise today's trades and then call time on Trafalgar Investments. Then we start a new venture possibly in the Hong Kong or the States, but first we pay our last respects to our little Mr North and his friends."

Aston checked the time on his iPad and saw they had been searching for just over an hour which was a little longer than he thought. The nurse would be back soon and knew time wasn't on their side.

"So what have we got that we can work with?"

Ellie spoke first "They are bigger than we thought. I've found links to subsidiaries of Trafalgar Investments in New York, Hong Kong, Moscow, Sydney and Tokyo. They seem to have a seat or representative in every major market worldwide."

"That's good the bigger they are the harder they fall. Right?"

"Or more places for them to hide" Ellie didn't sound so confident.

"H, what have you got?"

"Just a second, I think I might be on to something."

"Okay, interesting. Well, I've got something. Ellie you know you said Agent Baker mentioned Desangé was suspected of insider trading.

"Yeah, that and money laundering I couldn't find much on that one."

"I think I may have uncovered a link between the major stock market crashes and their profits. I figured out that on each of the years when crashes occurred, Trafalgar not only recorded a profit but outperformed any broking house in London."

"Me too," said Harrison. "But I took it a little deeper."

"Ready to tell us now then," Aston said smiling.

"Sorry just waiting for the search at Companies House to come back with something. I can now pinpoint to the exact day when Trafalgar investments largest trading profit was!"

His best friends hacking prowess always seemed to trump his own but this time, Aston didn't mind.

"It was on a Wednesday."

"Wednesday! How does that help us?" Ellie added.

"It was Black Wednesday that's how. They were one of a handful of brokers that came out the other side still trading. That day wiped out a significant number of investment firms and stockbrokers but Desangé and his Trafalgar Investments hedge fund came out of it with a shit load of money."

"How? I thought the British pound crumbled along with the markets." Aston said reading the headline after he had quickly googled Black Wednesday on his iPad.

"It did, but they bet against it, they short sold the shit out of the Sterling currency market and made almost a billion. It says in this report that it was an early example of how brokers used short selling to benefit from a stock market crash. Unfortunately, the Companies House report was never made public."

"So how did you find it?" Ellie asked.

"You know me, Ellie, I can get almost anywhere, you just need the right access. Companies House has an admin account for their content management system, once I got into there I could access their internal network user id's and what can I say, it becomes relatively straightforward after that!"

"So you can see where the Trafalgar Investments office was on Black Wednesday?" Aston had an idea.

"Easy, I probably don't need a back door to find that out." Harrison chuckled at something.

"What's funny?" Ellie asked.

"Backdoor, office address? Oh never mind. Here it is - Canada Square, in Canary Wharf. Does this guy like new London buildings or what?"

"It's not that new."

"It was in 1992 Ellie and that's where I'm going."

"What?"

"That's the perfect opportunity to create some serious damage to their reputation and maybe also take on Desangé."

"Yeah you could throw him off the top!" Harrison said laughing. Ellie's stare curtailed his amusement.

"Not funny H!"

"Why not Ellie, it's not that ludicrous. I could set up an accident and no one would be any the wiser." Aston quite liked the idea. "Maybe we could kill two birds with one stone."

"I'm not sure Aston but it does sound like our best chance," Harrison said.

"No, it's too dangerous. Why don't we just leak the document H has found and get MI6 involved?"

"That still doesn't overcome the distinct possibility he's after us now and could shift back and bingo were all dead and there's no leak."

"You could go back and leak the document just after the trade."

"Yes H that's a better idea, then they'd be ruined and it might change whatever happens after that. The less danger, the better."

"Maybe but that's still leaving too much to chance. If I can reverse the trade order and switch Trafalgar's position, it would lead to a massive negative position that would be unrecoverable and ruin them. If I can also stop Desangé with a staged accident, suicide perhaps, then it all goes away."

"Aston you can't take this man on, it's too dangerous. You know what he's capable of." Ellie stood up and turned away from the bed. Aston could see she wasn't going to come around that easy.

"That's exactly why I need to take him on Ellie. He's too dangerous if we leave anything to chance or don't act now he could wipe all of us out in a number of ways. I for one don't want to keep looking over my shoulder or thinking that when I next see you and H you might not know me. He can shift back anytime and change all our futures. I'm going to reboot, Ellie and make sure we have a future. I love you and I'm not letting chance or Desangé take that away."

Ellie turned back to him, her eyes starting to weep.

"I love you too Aston but I can't believe you're thinking of killing him. It can't be the answer. We should call the police, MI6, anyone who'll listen and use the correct authorities. I don't want you risking everything and resorting to murder, it's not who you are."

"Elle, I do not intend to take him on face to face, I'm going to ruin his business first off, and then, if needs be, stage some accident, overdose or something as a last resort. I need to stop this man when he's least expecting it and this is our best chance."

He reached for her hand "I'm going to need you, need your help and support. I'm not entirely happy having to do this but I'm doing it knowing it's saving you, me and H."

"I was starting to feel a little left out for a second," Harrison said lightening the moment.

"Okay, okay, I get it. Let's do this." Ellie smiled, took his hand, squeezed it gently, then checked the drip in his arm.

"Right now?" Aston was a little shocked by her sudden change of mind, but it did kind of make sense.

"Why not, if you're going to reboot a hospital bed is perfect cover, a controlled environment, once the nurse has been we have most of the day if we tell her you're tired and want to skip lunch. The sooner we get this over with, the better."

CHAPTER NINETEEN

Within minutes of the nurse leaving Aston was ready. Harrison had attached the TDCS headset and connected the display to the rooms TV monitor. Ellie, who had earlier procured a saline bag, and after making sure the nurse didn't remove the cannula from his wrist, had connected the fluids to his IV drip.

"Do you think you need the headphones to help you?" Harrison asked.

"I'm pretty certain I'm okay H. Getting used to this now my friend." He held out his hand to shake Harrison's. "Thanks, H, and keep Ellie safe, try not to let anyone in eh!" He winked and his friend returned the same.

"See you on the other side!"

"You too, speaking about that I've saved a file in your Dropbox account, it's a note, you'll need to open it if I succeed because you may not remember any of this if he's removed from time."

"Okay," Harrison didn't seem to grasp what he meant.

"And speaking of time remember it's Tuesday the fifteenth, we need the day before to make sure I can get this done for the Wednesday!"

"Aston, this was my idea remember," Harrison said cheekily, checking the app settings.

"I'm still not a hundred percent about this," Ellie said as he turned towards her. "Be bloody careful, any sign of danger, come on back and we'll find an alternative."

"Elle, I am not going to let this man ruin any more of my life, but I'm hoping to make damn sure I seriously mess up his."

"Just be careful. It might be nice to see you again."

"Might!" He laughed and she smiled at him. It reminded him of the smile that had attracted him to her, her face lit up for a second, but the worried expression returned and betrayed how she really felt.

He knew he needed to go. "Right let's do it. H are you set?"

"All good."

Aston grabbed Ellie's hand, squeezed it tight and closed his eyes. "Set."

It was becoming all too familiar now as he cleared his mind, concentrated his inner focus and embraced the blackness. Again Aston North rebooted his soul, although this time he knew he had everyone's destiny riding on his success.

Aston opened his eyes, the reboot process left him a little disoriented and his immediate reaction was that the it hadn't worked. He was lying in a hospital bed, an IV drip in his arm, staring at the roof in a private room similar to the one was just in. He shook his head, half expecting Ellie and H to appear, but once his eyes became accustomed to the light, he realised he was again looking through the eyes of Warwick Scott. Although this time his former soul was a 60-year-old man in the Nineties. The fact he was in the hospital was unexpected. Aston took over his soul and glanced around the room, hoping to pick up a few ideas as to exactly which hospital this was. He sat up and went to swing his legs off the bed, he noticed he wasn't in a gown which was odd. It was hard to shift his body weight, there was a sickness in Warwick's body, the plan hadn't figured on this, then Aston remembered what it was. 'Chemotherapy, Warwick died of cancer' he had seen the obituary. He checked the wristband on his left hand. Warwick was in the Royal Marsden hospital as a day patient, Aston looked at the IV in his wrist, then the bag of fluid.

"Damn," he said aloud. The actors voice sounding a little more rasping than before.

A nurse burst through the door just as a small beeping alarm sounded.

"Are your all right Mr Scott?" She was as old as his mum with a shock of blonde hair. She checked the monitor connected to the IV and turned off the alarm. "See first time in chemo's never that bad." She checked the amount of fluid left, it looked half empty so she expertly removed the drip from his wrist and applied a small dressing to cover where the cannula had been." That will need to stay in for a while." She wrapped the bandage around his wrist. "Not so talkative now are you? Lost your charm with all that in you." She checked his temperature, popping the thermometer under his tongue." You should be okay to leave in a while. Just when you feel up to it."

"I feel fine nurse" Aston felt compelled to say something albeit with the thermometer under his tongue.

"Like I said before, the oncologist has put you on a mild cocktail of Chemo that's quite aggressive. It's designed to target the cells that are growing and dividing which is how the tumour increases. This is why patients suffer hair loss, stomach complaints and sickness." She took out the thermometer.

"How long until the symptom's start?" All Aston needed, was for Warwick to be incapacitated.

"Soon but they will peak in a day or so. Remember you're stage two so you shouldn't go out dancing all night like you asked me before." Aston noticed the glint of affection in her eyes.

'Had Warwick been flirting with the older nurse' he thought. Maybe he could use that to his advantage.

"But there's every chance the therapy will reduce the tumours so I may hold you to your offer after we're done."

"Can I ask a favour of you?" He checked her name badge. "Karen, I really need to make a call, is there any way I can get a phone in here or are you able to take me to one."

She put her hand on his knee. "I think I can manage that as you've been such a good patient." She squeezed his knee and left the room. Maybe Warwick's charms would come in handy. Aston stood up and walked into to the toilet. He was a little taken aback at the dramatic change in Warwick's features since the last time he'd rebooted into his soul. The face in the mirror looked familiar but it wore the burden of the additional years and the strain of Warwick's excessive lifestyle. 'He obviously didn't slow down in his later years' thought Aston as he studied his reflection, wondering if the cancer had played a significant part in Warwick's haggard features.

Aston suddenly realised a potential way for tackling Desangé and darted out of the bathroom. The bag had been left by the nurse, he looked around for something Warwick was very familiar with handling, he knew there's must be some, especially given the nature of the room he was in. Aston contemplated taking the remaining bag but knew it would be a risk and it would raise alarms, all he needed was a decent sized hypodermic syringe. The yellow hazard label caught his eye of the disposal container and there immediately below on the next shelf were the packs he needed. Aston grabbed two just to be safe, stashed one and ripped open the other. It took him a few moments to get what he wanted, carefully withdrawing some of the chemicals through the connecting leads. The clear plastic chemo container bag was now about a third full and Aston hoped the nurse wouldn't notice. He hoped he could rely on Warwick's charm when the nurse got back to sidetrack her attention from what he'd done.

He didn't have to wait long as the nurse came back. He had flicked on the TV to check he was back on the right day. The weather report confirmed the date and time just as she appeared.

"I'm sorry Mr Scott."

"Call me Warwick" Aston started the charm offensive.

"I'm sorry Warwick but I couldn't bring a phone to you."

"That's a shame."

"But you can use the phone in the nurses lounge if you'd like?"

"I'll just get my things and you can see me out too." Aston was relieved as she failed to look at the IV stand.

"So who do you need to call?" The nurse made small talk as the walked through the ward.

"My broker!"

"Really?" Aston's tongue in cheek truth missed the mark so he told a lie.

"Actually, I need to arrange a lift back home."

"Well, that's a little more understandable." They reached the nurses room. "The phone is underneath the wall clock. If anyone comes in, just say that Karen let you in here."

"Thanks, Karen, I'm in your debt."

"Just make sure you're back tomorrow for your afternoon appointment."

"I wouldn't miss it for the world." Aston was surprised that his own reactions were like Warwick's, the smooth patter seemed to come to easily. It was as if he didn't have to think what to say, or his soul was talking through him rather than the other way. Aston shook off the existential thought and got back to the plan.

He picked up the phone dialled the office number he had memorised before rebooting.

As he waited for the number to connect, Aston thought he'd utilise Warwick's acting talents and pretend to be an American. He needed some leverage to ensure he got the desired result, and a visiting American journalist seemed more plausible.

The receptionist picked up "Trafalgar Investments how may I direct your call?"

"Can you confirm if Leonardo Desangé is a partner there?"

"Yes sir, he's our senior managing partner."

"Could you put me through to his office, I need to confirm an appointment with him."

"Can I ask your name?"

"Yes, it's Phillips, Sam Phillips." Aston pulled the name from nowhere.

"Putting you through now Mr Phillips."

"Hallo, how may I help you" the French accent sounded familiar, it sounded a little like his assistant from the show thought Aston.

"I would like to book an appointment with Mr Desangé."

"Are you an existing client?"

"No, miss I'm not."

"Unfortunately, Mr Desangé doesn't take new business calls, I can connect you with a junior partner."

"I'm a journalist over from the States and I didn't want to speak to Mr Desangé about his business but about his interest in hypnotherapy." Aston hoped this would maybe peak her interest and play on Desangé's ego. "My editor is keen on doing a feature article on his unique mixture between business and hypnotism."

"And what newspaper are you representing."

"I'm a freelance writer working for a magazine called Vanity Fair."

"I can schedule an appointment for lunch on Friday."

"I was hoping to be able to catch him today if possible. I'm only in London for two days and have to be back in New York by Thursday. The article can be kept discreet, a little mystery can add intrigue don't you think." Aston was conscious not to push and was aware of Desangé wanting to keep his anonymity. He just hoped the lure of Vanity Fair would tempt him at least to arrange a meeting.

"Hold on Mr Phillips." The assistant put him on hold. Which at least told him Desangé was in the building if this didn't work out. Plan B might be called for.

"Are you there? Yes, Mr Phillips can you be here by twelve?"

"Of course, I can."

"Good, we look forward to seeing you then."

Aston had never contemplated or even imagined what it would feel like to be really ill. Let alone experience a life threatening sickness that required a toxic chemical, that inhibits cell growth, to be taken as a cure. He also hadn't really thought about the effects of his soul's old age and how it would have an impact on how the body felt. He remembered the nurse had warned him of the side effects of chemotherapy but she had said it might be a while before it kicked in. 'Well, it was kicking and screaming right now' though Aston. He had struggled out of the hospital, learning to cope with aches and pains in his bodies muscles and joints. He'd figured it was just the fact his soul was over sixty now and he hoped he would become used to it. Going from twenty something to sixty was an eye opener but the nauseating pain he was in right now, had him screwing his eyes shut and bending over double in the back of a London taxi. The driver pulled over, obviously concerned the man he'd picked up from the hospital might need taking back.

"Are you okay?"

"Sorry, chemo obviously doesn't..." Aston grabbed at the door handle, pushed open the door and just managed to lean out to be sick in the gutter.

"Oh my God." The driver shocked, probably more concerned about any potential damage or the clean up needed for his cab. "Seriously mate do you need me to take you back?"

Aston pulled a handkerchief out of his jacket pocket and wiped his face. It seemed the nausea had a detoxifying effect on his whole body. "I'm fine, I think. Is it alright if we carry on to the wharf?"

"You're paying Mister. But please don't spew in the cab. We're about to hit the bypass and I ain't got a hard shoulder for you to be sick on. So speak now or spew again before I set off." The cabbies play on words was lost on Aston who had a mission in mind and he needed to focus. The sickness did give him an idea though and as he watched his destination seemingly grow in size as the cab drew closer, the idea grew into a plan, one he knew his friends would be proud of, and one, given his state of health might help out considerably.

The cab pulled up into Canada Square just out front of the three massive towers. Aston realised he'd never been to Canary Wharf before, he'd had no call to, no one he knew had lived or worked there, or had parents who had, so why would he. The recently restored wharf was a very impressive landscape and a hive of activity. London's newest landmark had all manner of projects starting up around it as well as all the new businesses.

Aston paid the driver, who was still concerned about his fares health.

"You feeling better Mister?"

"Yes, thanks."

"You don't look it old fella. You should be back in bed mate, not out here."

"Unfinished business I'm afraid." Aston stood looking up at the Tower. "Hoping to sort it out today though," he said more to himself. "Well good luck, it's full of lawyers and bankers looking for prestige and status. Fancy offices for fancy Dans if you ask me. You take care of yourself." Aston pondered his sentiment as the cabbie took off.

He looked back up at the imposing glass face of London's newest skyscraper. It seemed that Desangé was drawn to having his offices in the new buildings in London, maybe the prestige filled a need somewhere or maybe it was a good way of hiding assets or illegal practice. Before getting too deep into the why's and wherefore's of his opponent choice of office real estate. Aston's immediate need was to locate him. He knew Trafalgar Investments had offices on the forty-fifth floor from the research they had done but double checked on the named list of companies as he entered the imposing foyer. It took him a while to find which bank of elevators would take him all the way and luckily there was no security to restrict access as there had been in St Mary's Axe.

As he rode the elevator, he could feel his pulse racing, he stymied a wave of nausea, not sure if it was nerves or symptoms from the drugs, he closed his eyes and tried to control his breathing. The last person exited on level forty, Aston watched the doors slide shut and pushed the already lit button again, he was just five floors away from finally confronting the man who had changed his own life so dramatically back at the Oxford only a few weeks ago. It seemed like a hell of a lot longer, and a hell of a long journey to get here.

"You can do this." He said to himself looking a Warwick's reflection in the elevators mirrored wall. He just hoped his soul's physical state wouldn't let him down as he wasn't looking particularly well. He wiped the sweat from his brow and realised from the warm, clammy touch his temperature was running high. The elevator pinged and Aston stepped out through the opening doors into Trafalgar Investments. He wobbled slightly as he made his way to the reception desk, he stopped once the girl at the desk looked up, took a step towards her, then collapsed in a heap on the marble floor.

Aston opened his eyes as soon as the receptionist left him alone. His plan seemed to have worked, his staged collapse had taken the receptionist by surprise. She had been quick to help the old man as Aston expected, considering he looked a little worse for wear, and had taken him to the company's rest room. He had apologised acting up the sickness and explained he was due to meet Desangé but asked her if he could snatch a few minutes rest. She had offered to call an ambulance but agreed not to once he told her about the cancer therapy. She said she would check back in ten minutes as Aston had pretended to sleep.

He was up on his feet once he was sure she wasn't going to come straight back. Ten minutes should give him enough time to do what he needed. The rest room was also a make shift store room, which was obviously well organised? The boxes of brochures and promotional flyers neatly packed and listed making his search for an internal phone directory pretty simple. Harrison and Ellie had found out from the information they recovered from the Trafalgar Investments records that, before Black Wednesday, they used a specific broker to place any currency trades and positions. What they couldn't find out was the name of the contact at the broking firm. With the directory in hand and access to an internal line through the phone placed by the door, Aston set about with phase two of their plan. He cracked the door open to check if anyone was close by, it was all clear as far as he could tell. The finance directors secretary was Sheila Warren according to the directory. Aston had tried out his impersonation of the Desangé on his two friends, he was close, but now he hoped that Warwick acting skills would get him over this hurdle.

"Sheila, it's Lee, there's a complication with a Constantine's trade, I need to check. Can you confirm who issued the latest trade from them. I think they're in trouble." It sounded good to Aston, the slight accent was right there and he hoped the stern tone was convincing. This was a moment of truth if she didn't buy the voice his backup plan would be far more difficult.

"What date did you need Mr Desangé?" She bought it. Aston fist pumped the air.

"Just the last trade will be sufficient. I just need to check it's not changed from our trusted source." This elaboration was a guess but it seemed plausible.

"Just a second while I check the files."

Aston had imagined this would be an easy search on her desktop computer, a few mouse clicks and it would be there. He'd forgotten that in the early nineties some filing was still paper based. He heard her footsteps step away from the desk and the clang of filing cabinets. Too much of a delay might result in the receptionist checking in on him and he'd be found out. He thought about looking through the door but then heard footsteps that seemed to be heading in his direction.

"Hello" he called into the receiver, hoping the secretary would answer. He was certain the door would open any second.

There was no reply, he could hear the sound of filing cabinets opening and closing down the end of the phone. The footsteps stopped outside the door and the handle turned. Aston put his foot by the door, it was the only thing he could think of. He felt the weight push against his shoe, but before he had to stop anyone coming into the room he heard a telephone bell go off, someone calling reception saved him as the girl went back to answer it.

At the exact same moment the receiver sprang to life, "It was signed by our usual contact Mr Kennedy, sir, dated Friday but filed in the wrong place. I need to speak to our clerk, obviously living in another time to the rest of us!"

Aston might have made more of her unwitting pun but needed one more piece of information "That's great Sheila, can you confirm his direct number. I'm away from my desk?"

"01,564,777 extension 182. Can I help you with anything else Mr Desangé?"

It was very strange being called the name of the man he was looking to destroy, but it did mean that his soul's voice talents were better than he'd ever hoped.

"No thank you." He was keen to get off the phone and Aston hung up and hopped back on the rest room doctors couch just as the receptionist came back in.

"How are you feeling Mr Phillips?" she enquired. "Rested?"

"Yes, thanks." He replied even though Aston could feel his heart racing and felt, physically sick.

"Mr Desangé will be delayed about 20 minutes and if you're better, would you like to wait in his office?"

Aston couldn't believe what she had just asked, this was a massive stroke of luck, he had hoped to stall her and try to stay in the rest room. That way he thought he would be able to the call to the brokers, but it would be so much more convincing coming from Desangé's office! It took some self control to not show her how eager he was to accept the offer.

" I'm feeling a lot better thank you" Aston had to correct himself mid-sentence, as he realised in his excitement he had forgotten to put on the American accent from before. He managed his composure "waiting in the office would be perfect. It would be good to get a feel for the man before the interview."

Ellie checked the monitors and then her watch. It had been a few hours, but it seemed a hell of a lot longer. Aston's vital signs were tracking all okay, and his heart rate monitor beeped steadily away. Was it only yesterday she was pounding on his chest hoping for his heart to restart. It all seemed perfect, and he looked at peace, serene just as if he was sleeping soundly. She felt his pulse just as she'd learned, the machines may be super efficient but physically feeling the blood pounding through his veins was a tangible indicator that her man was alive and well. Well, at least his physical body was well, his mind she had no idea about, apart from the activity displayed on Harrison's iPad, it was currently elsewhere fighting an enemy in another time.

Ellie questioned his, and all of their sanity, most of all her own. She couldn't believe that she had allowed him to do this one more time, especially after what they had just come through. She put her hand up to brush his face. 'I shouldn't have let him under my skin,' she thought. His charm disguised behind friendship had undoubtedly broken down her guard. Finally admitting how they felt for each other had been a breakthrough, for both of them. Where might they be now if she had known how he felt sooner or if he'd had the courage to ask her? 'What was it about men and their feelings?' Ellie couldn't understand why Aston had been content with just being friends and for so long. She was, however, glad that they finally come to realise just how much they meant to each other, which made what she had decided to do next all the more difficult. She looked over at Harrison, who had fallen asleep about an hour ago. Now would be a good time, he wouldn't hear especially above his snoring and definitely, wouldn't notice her step out for a few minutes. Ellie opened the door and was confronted with the incoming nurse.

"Just doing my evening rounds, how is the patient doing?" She breezed past thinking Ellie had just opened the door for her.

"He's been out for a few hours, exhaustion I'd say."

"His levels are okay, plus his vitals which are important. How's his hydration?" The nurse, who didn't look much older than her, was obviously not concerned about the IV fluids that Ellie had attached, probably on a rotation from a med school. Ellie had removed the TCDS headset once he'd been under for a while, as she was certain that would draw attention. The nurse signed the monitoring schedule and looked at Ellie and Harrison in turn. We are closing to visitors in a few minutes if you want to wake your friend.

"About that" Ellie started. "Is there any way we can hang around, maybe stay overnight?" Ellie knew that in some cases, next of kin were offered rooms or pull out beds. "It's just that we're concerned about him being alone when he wakes. What with the trauma of being found in an open grave." She held Aston's hand for effect. "I'd really like to be here when he wakes."

"I'm awake!" Harrison said waking up.

"Not you, I was talking about Aston. I just asked if we could stay late just so we're here when he wakes up."

The nurse was no doubt busy and keen to get on. "I don't see it being an issue, I'll check with Staff and bring in a pullout." With that, she left Aston room with an efficient haste.

"Score, well played Ellie. I was wondering how we'd wrangle that one. How's he doing?"

"Looks okay, his signs are fine. No significant REM movement that I noticed. You were worse. Had a good sleep? And don't start me on the snoring. If we are staying overnight you're on the first shift." She laughed, Harrison looked sheepishly wounded.

"Let me make it up to you. I'll go get us some coffee and a bite to eat. Good?"

"Sounds good H, I'll have a skinny Cap'."

Ellie didn't feel like food as she had other things weighing on her mind. She knew what she had to do but didn't feel like sharing.

Either Harrison noticed a look of concern on her face, or he must have known what had been worrying her earlier.

"He'll be ok, you know. It's a sound plan."

"I know, but I just wish I could do more to help."

"Elle you saved his life remember. I think you're holding your own." He opened the door. "You'll feel better after coffee." With that, he went off down the corridor.

Ellie wasn't so sure but was certain she knew a way to protect Aston and all of them should he fail. With Harrison out of the way for a while, she had the opportunity she needed.

She took her phone out her pocket, found the number she needed and made a call she knew the boys wouldn't approve of.

Aston couldn't believe his luck, here he was literally inside the dragons den, Leonardo Desangé's actual office. He stood for a while absorbing what the eyes of Warwick Scott were seeing.

The office was a little sparse but the view was amazing looking out over the whole of London, the Thames weaving its way through the city's landmarks. He was tempted to try and get out on to the balcony but his attention was drawn to the display cabinet along the side wall of the office which contained interesting artefacts and antiques that Desangé had collected around him. Unless you knew the truth about his prolonged life, anyone visiting the office would just think he was interested in particular points in history but Aston instantly knew the significance of some of them. The old brown bottle of bourbon with the makeshift label, date stamped 1931 was an obvious draw, Aston remembered Peter Latchford's run-in with the Boston mob vividly, it seems Desangé also had a memento. Next to that was an intricately detailed, Ivory pipe which Aston noticed due to its seemingly Chinese origin, it looked much older but Aston figured Desangé picked this up during his Navy commission Antoine Claudet had mentioned. On the opposite wall was a large gilt frame picture of the battle of Trafalgar, the artist had captured the gun fight between two of the ships. Aston walked over to read the small inscription in the frame. What it said shook him somewhat and confirmed that Desangé must have known more about their connection. The ship was the Belleisle, the very same one both their souls died on. Aston studied the detail, remembering where this journey had started for him and the battle he'd seen during his first encounter with the hypnotist. Did Desangé know more about what happened or was he just paying homage to the fact his soul had died at Trafalgar. Maybe he would ask him he thought, although his moments contemplation was interrupted.

"Your drink sir?" The receptionist stood at the office doorway holding the tea he'd requested.

"Mr Desangé will be about ten minutes. We have a celebratory event shortly after so he may cut your meeting short." She placed the tea on the small table and then opened the side cabinet and pulled out a crystal decanter. It looked antique, and the glass with it added to its grandeur.

"So Mr Desangé isn't having tea then." Aston felt the need to comment.

"No, this is how he celebrates a big deal or celebration. It's the companies first anniversary so I expect he'll be wanting this."

"Very grand I must say."

"It's his favourite, an exquisite Napoleon Brandy." She walked past him and placed the glass and the brandy on the shelving overlooking the view of London. Obviously, Desangé liked to admire this position of power while sipping his fine wine.

"I'll stick to my tea thanks." Aston needed her out of the room and was glad when she headed back to reception.

Aston walked over to the table and took a sip, 'Ten minutes to set about the downfall of this arsehole and his whole company' he thought. 'Hopefully it may only take five.' Aston walked over to the excessively grand and somewhat tacky desk, sat in Desangé's leather executive chair and started executing their plan.

The research Harrison had done pinpointed the trade being placed just prior to the Wednesday market run on Sterling, Black Wednesday was tomorrow, and his meeting was at 3.00pm, so he had just enough time to reverse the trade position so long as the broker believed the voice on the end of the line. His fingers shook dialling the number, so many variables, he wished that this was ten years later, and Harrison could have hacked into the trading back end and wiped them out electronically. Those systems were a few years off so this was one of the better options. The call connected, Aston crossed his and Warwick's fingers and said: "Kennedy, what's our position on Sterling?" He thought being direct with a question may put him off guard and confirm whether the position had been placed.

"Is that you Mr Desangé, no pleasantries this afternoon?" The voice had worked again! "The orders have been placed as you requested Leonardo. We're shorting Sterling and going in with around $20 million. I've channelled it through various markets just as you requested. Why do you ask?" Kennedy sounded intrigued.

"I've just come from a meeting with my contact and he's got wind that the Government have something up their sleeve."

"Go on."

"So I want to reverse our position and go long, start buying now and continue first thing. Use whatever you can get liquidity on and double the amount to $40 million."

"That's a ballsy move Mr Desangé no wonder you sound a little nervous." Kennedy sounded concerned. Aston took a risk and hoped an aggressive response would help persuade him to take the bait. He raised his voice, confronting Kennedy head on.

"I can spread this trade around if you're not up to the task Mr Kennedy." Aston's hand was shaking, he needed both hands to steady the receiver. For a moment there was a worrying pause but, much to Aston's relief, his ploy worked.

"I'll get on it if you're in the know Leonardo, trust me. I'll use the same accounts as last time."

Aston had a view that brokers were money grabbers to the core and was certain the guy would profit either way. He heard Kennedy start the trade call to his junior at the end of the line.

"Oh and Kennedy I'll be out of the city until tomorrow so keep buying until I call — you'll hear good news tomorrow about 11 am so don't be concerned if it starts to go south for a while! Got it?"

"Okay I'm your man, I'll speak to you tomorrow."

He hung up the phone to avoid any further dialogue and to allow him time to set up for the next part of the plan. Aston fell back in Desangé's chair. The chemo was affecting Warwick, and he could sense the tiredness. His heart was racing and Aston wasn't sure if it was his head spinning or Warwick's, he tried to clear his mind as he still needed to finish the plan but he couldn't focus, he tried to stand but there was nothing he could do as the body of Warwick Scott feinted and passed out.

CHAPTER TWENTY

Aston woke, hunched over the desk. He sat upright not knowing how long he'd been unconscious, it was a weird sensation, the body and mind of his former soul having blacked out whilst he was supposedly in control. However, his own mind was racing now as he checked to see how long he'd been out. It was only two minutes since he'd hung up on Kennedy according to the clock on Desangé's desk.

He still had time to instigate part two of the plan, he padded his jackets pockets. 'Still there' he thought to himself. He took out the hypodermic syringe he'd lifted from his hospital room, it was still intact, the chemo fluid levels were still at 250 ml. He pulled off the protective outer covering the needle and placed the syringe on the desk. Aston knew he needed an edge for the confrontation with Desangé, he reached into his opposite jacket pocket and found the medication Warwick had been given earlier. He swallowed four of the pseudo-ephedrine tablets to keep him alert, he reckoned Warwick could cope knowing his drug history from the sixties.

He hoped the ephedrine would boost Warwick's metabolism but not affect his ability to control his actions.

Aston took a few deep breaths then felt the speed kick in and as he hoped he still had focus, very sharp focus he thought so he set about the final piece in his plan. He retrieved the sleeping tablets he'd also been given, popped them out of the packet on to the blotting pad on Desangé's desk and started to crush them with the underside of an ink bottle. It didn't take long to break down the tablets, he folded the blotting paper and carefully funnelled the powdered sedative into the elaborate brandy decanter. He had just replaced the stopper when he heard the door close.

"Admiring my brandy or the view?" Leonardo Desangé spared the pleasantries and offered his hand.

"The view. It is amazing" Aston went to shake his hand when he noticed the hypodermic still on the desk.

Behind them, Desangé's secretary opened the door "I'm heading out to

213

join the others Mr Desangé but wanted to check if you needed anything further?"

Aston used the distraction to sweep the syringe off the desk, into his hand, and his jacket pocket.

"No, that's fine Melissa I'll be joining you guys in a short while." Aston got the less than subtle indication that he was only planning a short interview.

"It's so good of you to see me at short notice" they shook, and Aston felt his body tense at the touch of his nemesis. His grip was firm, and his stare seemed to be looking right through Warwick's soul and deep into his own. "I'm keen to hear your thoughts on hypnosis. I've been advised you are becoming somewhat of a thought leader in the field, and the research will actually help my dissertation."

"Aren't you a little old for a student? I thought you were a journalist?" His stare was unrelenting.

Flustered at his mistake Aston countered "Yes I am, but as well as the story I'm hoping to use this as research for my postgrad psychology degree. Academia was something I missed out on in my youth."

"I've always believed you can tell a lot about someone's true psychological self when they are under hypnosis." Desangé relaxed his stare, probably thinking he might have a new soul to interrogate. "Would you like a drink? The firm is one-year-old today and between you and me we are about to have a huge day in the markets. So it's somewhat of a double celebration!"

"I do fancy a drink, but as you may have heard I'm not that well, and the medication I'm taking means I cannot, but I will raise a toast to you with my semi cold tea!" Aston retrieved his cup from the small table and watched as the hypnotist poured a healthy glass of brandy from the decanter.

"Cheers!" They clinked glass against China.

"Here's to Trafalgar," Desangé said then winked as he drank.

Aston felt the hair on his neck spring to life with the thought that Desangé may be playing him.

"The view is outstanding" Aston's mind was buzzing, his defensive nature turning the conversation and he turned to look out over London.

"Yes, you can get out through the windows, they should be sealed but couldn't resist once we moved in. It's the best balcony in London!"

He was standing next to Aston now and starting to pour another brandy. He obviously hadn't noticed the powdered sleeping tablets.

"Are you sure I can't tempt you, it's the finest, I have it on good authority that Napoleon himself used to drink this."

"No thanks. Like I said it's not wise to mix alcohol and medication."

Aston watched as the man who had threatened to turn the life of his friends inside out swirled the crystal snifter glass to circulate the liquor, a sly smile fixed on his face as he basked in his self-importance. The same smile he'd seen from Desangé through time during his reboots and when he kidnapped him only a week ago. Aston decided that he really didn't want to drag this out any longer.

"We should probably crack on."

"Yes, it's been a busy day, I have guests waiting and I can feel my eyes getting a little tired." Desangé took a last mouthful of the brandy and Aston seized his chance.

He swung around, pulling the hypodermic syringe out from his jacket pocket, and in a swift motion stabbed it into Desangé's neck right under the Adam's apple, he managed to deliver most if not all the contents into the oesophagus in the split second this chance gave him.

Aston had timed it perfectly, the brandy helped deliver the chemotherapy drug into the stomach, but he wasn't ready for the violence of Desangé's reaction. He grabbed Aston's arm and pulled down with massive force, the motion causing Aston to spin off balance, lifting him off his feet and straight into the glass windows. Desangé grabbed at the syringe still stuck in his throat, pulling it out. His bemused glance at the empty barrel had an air of hope, expecting to reveal the contents instead of the capacity measures. He threw it at Aston, who for a second thought it wasn't going to work.

"What the fuck was in there?"

Aston didn't have to answer as the poison designed to kill the reproducing cells in cancer incited a massive stomach trauma, just as Aston had hoped for. Leonardo Desangé bent double, he tried to vomit but his digestive system was in toxic shock. Aston got to his feet, dropping the accent he let him know the truth.

"This is a message from Aston North, your shifting days are over Desangé. Think of me as an echo coming back from your future to teach you..." He didn't finish, Desangé lashed out viciously striking Aston who had underestimated his adversaries will to survive and his fighting instinct. Desangé then hurled himself at Aston, the tackle took them both through the glass doors and out onto the balcony, forty-five floors up from the Thames.

Harrison was awoken by the vibration of his phone. He had hooked up Aston's monitors to it so he would get notified if they passed a specific threshold. Aston's heart rate had gone passed 160 beats per minute. Groggy from his sleep, Harrison called for Ellie.

"Ellie wake up there's something wrong. Ellie!"

His phone was indicating the heart rate monitors had increased to 195. Ellie wasn't in the room, he called out again just in case she was in the bathroom but she still didn't answer. Now he had two problems. The first more pressing but without solving the second there wasn't much he could do if the first got complicated.

Aston's vitals were maxing out, and the monitors were going crazy. Harrison turned the volume down on the heart rate monitor just in case it brought in a nurse. He tried to remember what Ellie would do. Blood pressure first he thought, Aston's blood pressure was stable, his heart rate was 220 and climbing, 'not good' and didn't seem to be slowing down. He checked his brain activity, and that was off the charts. 'Holy shit, I need help.' He looked at his friend lying on the bed. Aston's rapid eye movement was just that, very rapid and erratic and to add to that his arms and legs were twitching and flicking. 'Where on earth was Ellie? Why did she have to leave me alone?'

He considered pressing the call button for the nursing staff but erred on the side of caution and tapped the call button on Ellie's contact. He waited for the call to connect "Engaged!" The dull, repetitive tone was the last thing he wanted. 'She better not be calling her sister' He pushed the message icon and recorded a voice message for her "Ellie where are you, Astons vitals are going crazy and there's nothing I can do. Where are you? Call me when you get this." He pressed send and then thought about her sister, he had asked for her number in the car earlier and it was worth checking. If they were both engaged it might explain things.

He dialled, she wasn't engaged and Jess picked up.

"Hey! I was hoping you might call."

"Jess I'm sorry, I was after Ellie. Is she with you?"

"Story of my life," she said and snorted a little laugh. "No, I've not seen her since I dropped you at the hospital. Is everything okay?" Harrison figured she sensed the urgency in his voice.

"She should be here but she's not. I can't get in touch with her because her phones engaged and I kinda hoped she was talking to you. If she does call can you tell her to call me ASAP."

"Of course but are you alright, is Aston okay?"

"I don't know, he's here but his..." Harrison didn't want to explain the details. "Look I can't explain but I will call you back, I just need to sort this out. See you." He hung up.

"Ellie where are you?" He said it out loud it of frustration. He was used to being able to find a solution but it usually involved computers. Then it dawned on him that he had a source of information at his fingertips. With one eye on Aston and his monitors he managed to absorb about fifty websites covering a plethora of topics about heart rate, arrhythmia, sleep patterns, brain activity and associated conditions. All of which led him to a

ASTON NORTH AND THE WINDOW TO THE SOUL

similar conclusion. That without administering beta blockers to bring down the heart rate which he didn't have, or trying to defibrillate his friends heart into a regular rhythm which again he didn't have, he couldn't do anything but watch the monitors.

He was torn, he knew this had happened previously but never this bad and for a sustained amount of time. If he got help, then they would surely bring Aston back from his reboot. That had too many repercussions, not just questions from doctors and god knows who else but Harrison had no way of knowing what Aston was doing or where he was. They had a plan and Harrison had hoped it would be done by now.

All he could do was sit and wait, keep a check on temperature, blood pressure and Astons vitals. They were still sky high but his heart rate had come down and stabilised at 235 bpm which he knew was way over the maximum. It was a gamble waiting for either Aston's heart to give out or for him to reboot back. Ellie would probably have said the same had she been here, but he didn't know where she was either.

He stood up realising that was something he could find out. She had her phone on her which meant he could locate her. He pulled out his laptop, he'd need to hack the Android GPS locator app but when did that ever stop him.

Aston willed the body of the sixty-year-old cancer patient Warwick Scott off the balcony floor. He figured Desangé would put up some resistance but had originally hoped the toxic chemicals would have done more damage. He knew Warwick would be no match for a man like Desangé on a normal day, but he had only this one chance. He had to fight, the quick thinking mind of a twenty-year-old in Warwick's body could stand up to a man who'd been handicapped with of a cocktail of chemo drugs and sleeping tablets.

Aston took his opportunity and punched his adversary with all his might, although Warwick's body didn't react as he'd liked as his opponent managed to block him and came back at him. Desangé connected, and Warwick was clipped with a stinging punch to the side of the head, Aston thought he'd anticipated it, but again he wasn't quick enough as Warwick took another blow. Aston's anticipation meant the force wasn't what it could have been so he used the momentum and made his counter work harder, it was aimed at Desangé's weak point, his midriff and he followed up with his knee sending his opponent reeling.

"You need to be stopped." Aston yelled.

"Stopped! I can't be killed fool, do you think I haven't encountered your sort before." Desangé span from his crouched position, sweeping his leg and knocking Warwick crashing down on his back. Desangé stood, looked down at him and said "take that back to your friend Aston, old man." I could shift back now and you wouldn't have that chance to drug me." Aston willed his souls body off the floor but Desangé landed another blow to the side of his head, one that couldn't be ducked in time, the blow crashed through his thoughts.

Aston shook it off, spat out a mouthful of blood and played his trump card. "Shifting is something out of your control now Desangé. Those drugs I stabbed into you should put paid to that — your cells will have a hard time regenerating when exposed to chemotherapy chemicals."

Desangé's expression twisted slightly, "Bullshit!" He took a step back, closed his eyes, and it looked like he tried to shift. This gave Aston one last chance. He channelled as much energy as he could summon and exploded straight towards Desangé tackling him, lifting him off his feet and smashed him onto the balcony rail. The force was enough to leave his opponent off balance, who tried desperately not to topple over the rail. Aston too felt off balance, in danger of going over the balcony along side Desangé, so he threw himself back in an arc and brought the top of his head into contact with Desangé's chin. The final blow helped shift Aston's balance away from the balcony edge and increased the Desangé's momentum over the railing. As his nemesis started to fall backward, Aston felt a hand grab his own arm as Leonardo Desangé frantically grasped for a last hold on life.

Aston span to face the man who had haunted and hunted him over the last few weeks. The look on his face was now of a man who was terrified, desperately clinging to life. It brought reactionary feelings of remorse and compassion into Aston's mind, he remembered the connection between them, a long time ago their souls were once brothers and had they survived the accident in the ship their destiny may well have followed another path. Aston couldn't let Desangé die, it defied his own upbringing and compassionate nature. He began to pull, to try to lift him up, then just as he gained a little upward momentum Desangé pulled down on his arm and tried to grab his throat, his fingers touched him ever so slightly before Aston instinctively snapped back from his grasp and in doing so let him go. Desangé glared at him defiantly for an instant before his eyes closed hard and then he dropped. Aston watched him all the way down, somewhat surprised he didn't make a sound but also taken aback at the speed he fell, it took only a few seconds and it was over. Aston had to turn away as the body of his nemesis seemed to explode on impact with the street below. Leonardo Desangé was well and truly dead.

Aston sucked in the air, standing on the balcony on top of Canada One,

218

buffeted by the chill wind. He was not only trying to come to terms with what had just happened but also needed to breathe some life back into the tired lungs of Warwick Scott's soul. The adrenaline rush was starting to wear off, and he knew he had to get out of the Trafalgar Investments office and pretty damn quickly.

He couldn't just reboot out and leave Warwick exposed to the consequences and interrogation of being found at the scene, with no idea of why he was in the office of the man splattered all over Canary Wharf below. Getting to safety and fast, would ensure that Warwick had the best chance of seeing out his remaining lifetime. Aston realised that the physical trauma of the fight might have increased Warwick's chances of dying sooner and that wasn't in his own best interest. He also figured that if the authorities ever managed to work out what happened and were able to trace the sickly reporter who was the last one to see Desangé alive. They would hopefully be more lenient once they discovered he had stage two lung cancer that was about to spread to his liver and take him within the year.

It made sense to Aston that getting Warwick back in hospital care would be the best place for him to be. It would also be a safe place for Aston to bid farewell to rebooting and get back to living his own life. It was becoming increasingly obvious that rebooting his soul was definitely not good for his health and the health of others.

With his breath back, his head clear and a sound plan in mind Aston stepped back through the balcony doors. Surprisingly it didn't look like there had been much of a fight, once he'd picked up the broken glass, the office looked completely undisturbed once he closed the doors and this gave Aston an idea.

He'd noticed during his clean up that Desangé had an old style Dictaphone on his desk and this prompted the idea. One more of Warwick Scott's voice deceptions may introduce an added element of doubt into the investigation into the death of Desangé. He sat in Desangé's chair and started to record a suicide message using his impression of him which had already convinced two people who had known him. Aston cleared his throat."

My name is Leonardo Desangé, and this is the last time you will hear my voice. I've just found out about that there's no way back from the positions we have put on Sterling. It seems the governments position will now lead to a stock market collapse, resulting in my personal bankruptcy and the ruin of this company. This is entirely down to my own actions and naivety. I'm sorry, I cannot face myself, my friends or my colleagues. Adieu."

Aston wound the tape back and replayed it, it sounded passable, almost spookily real, Aston thought it might work. He wiped the Dictaphone so as not to leave any fingerprints and left it upright on the desk.

Aston quickly made his way out of the office and half expected being caught as he walked through the main reception, he'd taken far more time than he wanted and there would be quite a gathering outside by now. He remembered seeing a service elevator next to the room he had been taken to earlier. Aston knew this was the quickest and best way down. It should be quiet at this time of day, and it would get him directly into the car park, avoiding the lobby, and the massed ranks speculating about who, how and why a jumper would dive out of the Canary Wharf tower. The lift took an age, or so it seemed, but Aston made it down to the underground car park where he calmly walked passed the rows of company cars and out through the rear entrance. The wailing sirens of an ambulance approaching down the North Colonnade hurried him along, he flagged down a passing taxi and got in. He started coughing and the driver spoke on to him with a concerned look on his face." Are you okay Mister?"

"Not really, I need to go the Royal Marsden Hospital in Westminster."

"Are you sure you don't need an ambulance."

"I think they might be needed elsewhere."Aston commented on the ambulance sirens and flashing lights responding to Desangé's demise.

"Don't see what good they can do. Apparently it's a right mess."

"Really?" Aston feigned interest.

"Dead as a dodo mate, some jumper from the tower. Probably some blackhearted yuppie stockbroker upset about missing out on his next big bonus."

"You're probably not far off the mark my friend."

"Royal Marsden it is then, be there in no time."

"Thank you." Aston sat back in the seat of the cab, the cough and subsequent pain in his chest made him realise the Warwick was in a bad way. He stared out of the window as the cab pulled out of the wharf and made a right turn on to Trafalgar Way. The signposts irony wasn't lost on him, and he allowed himself a smile, he was starting to believe that the end was in sight, the plan had worked so far, but he needed to get Warwick to safety.

Warwick's cough seemed to be getting worse as he made his way into the Royal Marsden hospital. After a fit that lasted a few minutes Aston stopped by the lift, the pain in his chest leaving him breathless, all he could do was stand still and wait for it to subside. A few people coming out of the lifts asked him if he needed help and Aston himself was now really concerned about the physical state of his former soul. The battle with Desangé had affected Warwick Scott's health far worse than he had planned. Aston could feel how constricted Warwick's breathing had become, and now the adrenaline had worn off, he started to feel the resulting pain from the strikes Desangé had landed during the fight.

The lift opened onto the cancer ward which he had left only that morning. The nurse who had helped him was still there, the horrified look on her face added to his concern and made him realise that Warwick actually looked as bad as he felt.

"Mr Scott when you left this morning you looked fine, I had you a certain candidate for remission. What on earth has happened? You look like you've been in a car crash."

"I feel like I have been." He coughed and grimaced as the pain seared his lungs. "Is there any chance you able to admit me to the ward?"

"Oh my god, of course we can." She called towards the staff nurse "Annabel can we get Mr Scott into a bed, maybe a room given the state he's in, and call the doctor so he can have a look at him ASAP." She turned her attention back to her patient "Mr Scott what on earth have you been doing?"

Aston was at a loss what to say as the nurse inspected him.

"Your face is starting to bruise quite badly. These contusions are somewhat profound" she touched his eye socket causing him to shy away. "There is a significant abrasion on your chin and that lip looks very sore." She ran her finger over his lip, which judging by the pain and the taste of blood had been badly split.

"Have you been in a fight Mr Scott?" She inspected his hands, the knuckles swollen on both.

"You should see the other guy!" Aston said trying to lighten the moment, coughing at the same time.

"It's not funny Mr Scott. You're in a bad way. Seriously I'm worried about you. That cough cannot be good for your lungs particularly since you started your first round this morning."

The staff nurse returned to say that they had a room free and took nurse Karen to one side. Aston, although happy for the interruption was becoming a bit paranoid that he might have jeopardised Warwick's already short life expectancy. He knew the best way to check, and with Warwick now in safe hands of the nurses, he thought that this would be an ideal time to head back to his present and find out. In addition he would avoid any further interrogation questions from the nursing staff. He looked around to see who was watching and was just about to reboot when his attention was grabbed by a TV in the patients lounge opposite the nurses station. The news was running a breaking story about the potential suicide at the newly completed Canary Wharf tower.

Aston went into the lounge. The announcer was speaking to camera about the dramatic events and the vision cut to a reporter at the actual scene. There was a crowd gathered, and Aston recognised the secretary crying on the shoulder of another distraught girl. Next to them Aston noticed the man who had been with Desangé in the bar in Whitechapel, his right-hand man was looking at the camera and speaking to another man Aston thought he recognised. 'That's odd' he thought then, the on-screen caption flashed up "Canary Wharf Suicide." That means, at least the media believed that Desangé had killed himself, Aston was transfixed by the footage and didn't notice the nurse now standing behind him.

"Mr Scott are you okay?" She had to pull on his arm to get his attention. "Mr Scott?"

"Yes, yes, so sorry I thought I recognised someone, terrible news don't you think?"

"You've got your own health to worry about Mr Scott. Now if you sign this form, I'll get you to your bed. The doctor wants to examine you."

Aston scanned the admission form and noticed the time was not filled out on the form. He entered 3.00pm just to give Warwick an additional alibi should anyone come around investigating, although from the news headline it appeared they probably wouldn't.

He handed back the form to the nurse, hoping she wouldn't check the time he'd added. She signed it and placed it on the desk which was a result, but his primary concern was whether Warwick would see out his remaining days. There was only one surefire way to be certain as he followed the nurse to his hospital bed, he knew now was the time he had to leave Warwick in the hands of the cancer ward nurses. Aston closed his eyes and took a final nervous step back to discover his future.

Aston rebooted back bracing himself, not only for whatever faced him in terms of his own future, but also the anticipation of having to be resuscitated once again, remembering that his heart usually tripped into an arrhythmia when he returned. He opened his eyes and took a huge breath, mildly comforted there was no pain as the air filled his lungs, unlike the cancer-stricken body of Warwick Scott. Aston knew he was back, another deep breath and another couple of seconds ticked by but there were no alarms to indicate the anticipated cardiac arrhythmia. He was back and his heart wasn't going to arrest. The heart monitor beep at his bedside was stable, Aston stared at the display, encouraged that his heart rate was 114 bpm. The regular pulsing beep was welcoming, although not quite the sound he had expected to greet his return.

Aston looked around the room, it was the only noise being made, his friends were no where to be seen. There was no sign of Harrison or Ellie and for an awful moment he thought his fears about Warwick were right and he was now in some other soul or paradigm in time. The monitor beep signalled his heart rate starting to increase and then Aston realised, how could he not be in the same soul, his memory was in tact, this is the same hospital room, and that was his iPhone still connected to the monitor.

He grabbed the phone to double check, 'I must have succeeded' he thought. But he just wished that someone was here with him to share the occasion. Where was Ellie, where was Harrison, another moment of doubt ran through his head so he flicked through the contacts on the phone. They were both still there, he checked his photos just to be doubly sure that it wasn't a bad coincidence. No, his friends were right as rain, the moments captured were still the same as before, although because of what happened, Aston knew he never would be. The thought about what and where he'd come back from made him wish his friends were here, so he could tell them both what had happened while it was still so fresh in his head.

Then it struck him, would he be the only person who would remember? If Leonardo Desangé had died, then there was a chance that from everyone else's perspective that this never happened. The last few weeks after the show at the student union, would be some alternative course of events. His friends wouldn't have been involved and wouldn't remember anything.

He unhooked the leads and diodes connected to the monitors and got out of the bed. It felt great to stand on his own two feet. He carefully extracted the IV drip attached to his arm so he could walk around.

He picked up the phone and dialled Ellie, there was no answer, the phone just rang out. He called Harrison next, no answer again. He was tempted to push on the hospital bed comms button to find out why he was in here, maybe that would give some indication as to who knew what. He messaged Harrison and Ellie. "I'm stuck in hospital and where are my two best friends when I need them?" He thought it might get some response.

He waited a few minutes staring out of the window considering what to do next and hoping for a reply. He decided he needed to find out from the hospital why he was here and was about to push the nurses call button, when he heard a commotion outside the door. The noise grew louder, someone was coming, from the voices he knew it was his two friends. The door opened and Ellie rushed in followed by Harrison.

"Thank god you left a note!" Ellie proclaimed.

"You could have mentioned which hospital you were in. It's taken an age to find you."

Aston smiled he'd forgotten his backup plan.

"When did you read it? I've only just rebooted back."

Ellie looked shocked "I still can't believe it. Harrison had to save me. I found myself at the offices at MI6. They were about to caution me for wasting police resources! I had absolutely no memory of why I was there or what I had asked them. They were talking about Agent Baker, Trafalgar Investments and Leonardo Desangé and I just blanked."

"It must have coincided with when he died. History changed at the exact moment you were there." Aston smiled at her "You thought I might not make it."

"I must have been covering your back, we'll all of ours I guess, but if you hadn't sent the Dropbox file to Harrison, then neither of us would have known what had happened."

"It's true, Ellie called me to help her out, I googled Desangé and the search found the account of his suicide and the collapse of his investment group in 1992. But also, it found an encrypted Dropbox note from you explaining everything. Bloody smart move and I'm kinda jealous I didn't think of it."

"So once Harrison told me what had happened, I made my excuses to Agent Baker who wasn't very pleased and threatened not to let me go but Harrison was on his way, so he met me and backed my story up."

"It was kinda lame. Even I could have come up with a better idea than a dare."

"Don't" Ellie swiped at Harrison

"But then we realised that we had no idea where you were. Ellie phoned around a number of hospitals before I remembered Find my Phone and that led us here. It's great to see you're okay."

"You too, both of you."You had me worried for a minute. I booted back and nothing, no one for a moment I thought I'd really fucked up."

"You've just changed the course of time Aston. How do you feel about that?"

"I'll tell you something, I've had enough of hospitals for a lifetime. Let's get out of here and I'll tell you everything over a stiff drink. I could murder a brandy!"

"Sounds like a plan." Harrison said, "Oh and you might want to think how you explain this." He showed him the last line on his Dropbox note that read. 'Tell Ellie that I love her.'

Aston smiled wryly at his friend "Does she know?"

"Of course" Harrison slapped him on the shoulder.

"In that case, make mine a double!"

THE END

ABOUT THE AUTHOR

Anthony Green was born in the late sixties, the youngest of four boys he grew up a child of the seventies on a close-knit council estate in Solihull, England. Like most kids of the time, he played all hours with friends from next door and a few doors down, making the most of the freedom and the green fields, open spaces and safe streets without the distraction of today's technology. His childhood education at Greswold infant, then junior school was supplemented by Disney's Wonderful World of Knowledge encyclopaedia, his Mothers early attempt to give her boys a little deeper knowledge of the world with the help of Mickey and his friends. Walt's well-worn editions gave way to a comprehensive education at Malvern Hall competing with teenage distractions of eighties music, BMX bikes, break dancing, football and girls. Sixth form beckoned after O levels, but higher ed wasn't agreeable, so Anthony took an option and the lure of a weekly wage on a Youth Training Scheme.

The apprenticeship at the head office of a menswear retailers exposed him to all sections of the business and eventually led to his first full-time employment in the state of the art computer centre. The technology industry became the basis for Anthony's career over the next ten years, and working shifts allowed him the indulgence of downtime to enjoy his twenties to the full, especially when a switch to a finance company bought with it new experiences, colleagues and some life long friends. Completing the three peaks challenge a highlight of the summer of 94, although a knee injury in 95 meant missing out on a starring role in a Cup final plus the chance to walk the four peaks. After assisting the marketing team, an opportunity for a nine to five position was taken and a chance to advance down a more creative path. This opportunity brought new challenges, new experiences plus exposure to creative agencies and avenues which would set up a later move to a startup agency based in Northampton. A let down then a holiday alone which became a holiday for two as Anthony met the love of his life, Anita and sparked a catalyst for him leaving middle England for the beaches and bays of Jersey in the Channel Islands. Married exactly a year later they enjoyed the expat lifestyle Anthony working in the offshore finance industry before the two made plans to continue the expat journey and move to Perth, Western Australia.

With better beaches and sunnier climbs, Anthony chose to follow his passion for sport as marketing manager for WA's football association. The dream job lasted over three years until he stepped back into the corporate sector and the finance industry. Still, the lure of sports was there, and an offer from a stockbroking firm to manage a million dollar sponsorship of a stadium couldn't be refused. The experience was a roller coaster ride and provided eye-opening insight into the cut-throat world of trading. When the market turned sour the investment in marketing was cut, the role deemed redundant, and Anthony was cast adrift. Thus followed jobs at an agency, the start-up of a sideline t-shirt business and to keep the bank happy a contract at Perth's largest university. The industry was new ground, exciting and the vibrancy of the campus and working in a University, although ironic for someone who shunned higher ed 30 years before, was a breath of fresh air and provided stability and opportunities to explore other creative outlets. Picking up a 'How to Write a Novel' book bought years before Anthony started another journey and during his commute to work began penning the Aston North story. Two years on and twenty chapters later the story was finished, and another chapter in Anthony Green's own story may have begun.

ACKNOWLEDGEMENTS

Thank you to my lovely wife Anita for her support, encouragement and unending enthusiasm during my foray into the world of writing. Having her as a sounding board for storylines, dialogue and general sense checking of my wild ideas not only kept me moving forward but also on the right side of sanity.

Thanks also to my colleagues and friends who have been kind enough to offer advice, feedback and encouragement while I've been on working on Aston's story.

From a content perspective, I have to acknowledge the masses of contributions made to the wonderful reference library known as Wikipedia and a massive thanks to Google for making it all the more easier to find. Tim Berners Lee may have created the internet, but Larry Page and the folks at Google made it all the more findable, and I do hope he doesn't mind his mention in the story.

They helped me use true events to add realism to the moments in history entwined into the story of Aston North's former souls. The characters were my own imagination plus a few names of people that inspired me or I admired, thanks to you all. Also thanks to the National Archives 'Nelson, Trafalgar and those who served' exhibition that provided research material and background behind The Belleisle which was severely damaged at the Battle of Trafalgar and one of the ships involved where there were a number of brothers serving on that historic day. The horrible death of Elizabeth Stride and her last visit to the Bricklayers Arms are sadly true, dates, places were again referenced on Wikipedia, but my elaborations as to the coach passengers involvement were speculation echoing some reports and theories from that dark time in Whitechapel's history. Photographer Antoine Claudet was a pioneer in early photography specialising in daguerreotype portraits and is credited with the invention of the dark room using red light. A storyline again researched using Wikipedia when an alternative plot didn't work with the dates. Another was the Jimi

Hendrix gig, lauded by many as one of his best and I only wish I could have been there at the Marquee Club with some of the glitterati of the day. I'm glad I wasn't around when Boston's crime boss Charles Solomon met his end at the Cotton Club, I took licence with the story and dates but used Solomon's demise at the hands of rival gunmen as inspiration.

I should also mention some of the modern day technical elements that have been included. Researching Harrison's tech solutions took me down some odd paths and although I've exercised some creative licence with his app development and hacking skills the advances in Transcranial Direct Current Simulation was very real and thanks to the foc.us website for the inspiration.

Thanks also the many sources for background info that helped develop the hypnosis and regression storyline, having thought of the what if someone could reboot their soul premise, my eyes were opened by the myriad of opinions, theories, therapies and actual real world experiences around the subject. By chance, I had the pleasure to meet John Petricevic, and our discussions about his documentary Life after Life was enlightening, fascinating and very helpful.

Printed in Great Britain
by Amazon